off
the
TRACKS

Diane Foley

Prominence Publishing

www.prominencepublishing.com

Cover artwork by Mark Garbett.

Off the Tracks/Diane Foley. -- 1st ed.

ISBN: 978-1-988925-72-1

Cannery Row is the gathered and scattered, tin and iron and rust and splintered wood, chipped pavement and weedy lots and junk heaps, sardine canneries of corrugated iron, honky tonks, restaurants and whore houses, and little crowded groceries, and laboratories and flophouses. Its inhabitant are, as the man once said, "whores, pimps, gambler and sons of bitches," by which he meant Everybody. Had the man looked through another peephole he might have said, "Saints and angels and martyrs and holymen" and he would have meant the same thing.
— John Steinbeck, Cannery Row

When you can stop you don't want to, and when you want to stop, you can't...
— Luke Davies, Candy

But where do you live mostly now?
With the lost boys.
— J.M. Barrie, Peter Pan

Acknowledgements

This book has had quite a journey. A lot of starts and stops and detours. I have many people to thank for the encouragement and support that I have received along the way.

Firstly, I would like to thank my legendary, brilliant editor, Betty Keller, who waved her magic wand over my manuscript. Betty long ago earned her angel wings for all the invaluable work and help she has given to the writers in my hometown on the Sunshine Coast, B.C. Secondly, a huge thank you to my creative nephew, Mark Garbett, for his wonderful book cover.

There were many people who encouraged me over the years. I want to extend a special thank-you to Liz Lee, Andrew Woodley, Bud Fisher, Diane Fleming, Louise Lefebvre, Kathleen Hunter, Janet Clarke, Sandy and John Stanton, Sharyl Forster, Anne Luna, Connie McComb, Emmett Wade, Diane and Peter Mohan, Jan DeGrass, August Vermassen, Buncy Gill, Joyce and Eric Trygg, and Marilyn Helgason. A special hug to Silas White for the generous help he gave.

I am truly indebted to the wonderful people I met during my time living in the South End of Nanaimo who made me feel welcome and part of the neighbourhood. And the most heartfelt thanks of all to the colourful personalities who passed through Big Sab who shared their stories and taught me so much about life.

As a single mother my children are my life blood and are responsible for the very way I look out and view the world. They have been my emotional support and my rock through the hard times and the good. They are my reason for struggling to do the best I can. They encouraged me to finish Off the TRACKS and send it off into the world. Thank you, to my daughter, Kelly, and to my sons, David Paul and Guy - and to my son-in-law, Andrew, and my daughter-in-law, Arlene.

For Kelly, David Paul, and Guy.

Table of Contents

1
Tracks

Nanaimo, March 1994

Doors opening and closing. You never know when you pull one open what you will find on the other side. And you never know what might disappear forever when you bang one closed.

I certainly didn't know what I was opening the door to the day Lewis grabbed our brass door knocker—the knocker I loved because it was shaped like a lion's head. Well, after all, I am a Leo. I was too busy that morning making beef stew whilst stewing over Larry to recognize the opening scene of a life-changing event.

Lewis was dressed in... how I can describe it? An eye-opening, turquoise Hawaiian shirt flagrant with pink flamingoes, the brilliance of the shirt taking away from his personal appearance for a moment. His unwashed blond hair had been slicked back neatly with water, the marks of the comb still streaked through it. He immediately made eye contact. Hazel eyes. Warm. Gold-flecked. Around thirty years old, 5 feet 10 inches, pleasantly muscled, tanned arms and a smile that could have fast-tracked him into the movies.

"I hear you have rooms for rent to non-drinkers. The ad said it's a drug-free house?" His voice, a husky-throated one, faded away. He stuck out his hand. "Lewis Nordrum."

"That's right. We have rooms for rent." I had zoned out for a moment in those gold-flecked eyes. I shook his offered hand. His palm felt dry, hot, like your hands feel over a winter fire when you've come in from the cold. As you have probably already gathered, I have an over-the-top romantic notion about life.

Maybe this Lewis would become our second client. (We were supposed to call our renters clients.) Larry would be pleased.

"Come on in. I can show you what rooms we have available. Actually, there are quite a few to choose from. We just opened up, you know."

I walked down the hall into the kitchen, Lewis following. The sunshine streamed in, bathing that worn old room in a butter yellow light, thankfully giving it a welcoming, cheerful aura. The huge window in the kitchen was pretty amazing. It went from the floor to the ceiling, taking up the whole wall, and it overlooked our rambling woodsy-looking garden.

I poured two cups of coffee and gestured for Lewis to sit down at the wooden table pushed against the wall.

"How did you hear about us?" I asked, giving the simmering stew a quick stir and throwing in the pile of potatoes and carrots I had chopped. "By the way," I grinned over my shoulder at him, "I forgot to introduce myself. My name is Diane."

He flashed a smile back. "Pleased to meet you, Diane. I saw your ad on the Sally Ann bulletin board. About you being a safehouse. I can't tell you how much I need a safehouse right now."

I wasn't yet used to the terminology, but safehouse meant no drugs or alcohol consumption allowed while you were a tenant, or you were thrown out.

"I'll try and explain my situation to you," he said, cleared his throat and then continued, "I guess you would call it a desperate situation." He bowed his head for a moment in concentration and thrust his hands through his hair. "I woke up this morning lying on the railway tracks."

I gripped the arms of my chair momentarily, staring at him like he was completely bonkers.

Lewis nodded his head in appreciation of my reaction. "Yeah, the railway tracks downtown, the ones that cut across Prior Street. I woke up still clasping a six-pack to my chest. I was wet through to the bone. I guess I had passed out cold." His eyes clouded momentarily. "Comatose, the guy said who found me. Even the rain hadn't woken me up. Jesus... I could have been killed by a train in the night except they don't run to Victoria until 8:00 in the morning. Thank God for that. Anyways, the way things have been going... it's time. If you know what I mean?"

I didn't know what he meant, but I nodded because I guessed it was expected of me. The look he was giving me—guilt-ridden or was it embarrassed?—was so straight from the heart, and he seemed on the brink of what? Tears? Confession? I swallowed a big mouthful of my coffee. I didn't know what would come next, but I waited, curious as hell.

"I have to straighten my life out, Diane. Have to. This has scared me—that I could be so liquored up that I actually passed out on the *railway tracks...*"

Lewis leaned back in his chair and gulped down the hot coffee. He looked dazed and still in shock. Which he probably was. On the other hand, it could be the look of man with a massive hangover. Now he was saying, "And the thing is, I never let go of that lousy six-pack. All night long I held onto that sucker like it was the only important thing in my life. That's pretty sick, eh?"

I stared back at him. Honestly, I was a little speechless at his story. Well, have you ever met anyone who has passed out on the railway tracks?

Larry and I had just made an arrangement with the John Howard Society to rent rooms to men coming out of jail with a history of drug problems. The idea was to give them a starting-off place where they would have a chance to regroup and assimilate back into society. It was the most unlikely business I could have ever imagined getting involved in, seeing as I like to have a drink now and then myself. Well, actually quite often. And liquor being filed under the category of drugs, if you get my take.

Believe you me, Larry and I had no notion of doing this when I first came to Nanaimo from Vancouver. But this was 1994 and I had searched for work and found nothing. Zilch. Vancouver Island was a depressed area at that time except for Victoria where the provincial government offices are housed and the accompanying government jobs were available.

I had, in fact, left a secure government job on the Mainland, a job with benefits and pension, and had been facing a picture of bleak un-employment after I moved to Nanaimo. So why had I put myself into this compromising position? It gets a little complicated. You see, Larry, my boyfriend, had been going to leave his wife for the past five years. Actually, he had left her but still lived in the basement suite of their house because his wife said she needed him there to help her with their two teenaged boys. I am guessing you have heard this story many times before. *Because so have I.* And I hate talking about this because obviously I come across as some idiotic naïve fool. Believe me, I agonized.

Being forty-nine didn't help. You feel you have run out of all your options when you are forty-nine. That huge ominous fifty is looming, half a bloody century, and when someone turns up who is totally tailor-made for you, it is hard, that's all. Very hard to turn away. We had been involved for five years, and the reason I left Vancouver for Nanaimo was to be with him. I was once and for all determined to demand, beg and insist that he finish with "his sergeant-major bossy English wife"—as he called her—and move completely out and live with me, or I would finish with him. So far he was still successfully sitting on the fence—staying with me while he was in Nanaimo and still living in the Base-ment Suite.

I swear he was afraid of his wife or more likely of her tongue that could, apparently, lash better than a cat-o'-nine-tails. The man was only 6-feet 1-inch, 260 pounds and a prospector to boot who had been air-lifted into wilderness areas full of bears, wolves and other man-eating wildlife plus ice and snow, conditions that could kill a normal city slicker in less than twenty-four hours. He'd once worked in the jungles of Ecuador where random bandits were killing people for their boots. Scared of a tongue... you get my point?

I wasn't a fool, but I was sure won over by him. Totally spell-bound in love, and nobody else but me could understand why I loved him in such a crazy way. And on many a lonely night lying in my bed alone maybe I didn't understand why either. Or maybe I wished I didn't. *Love him, that is.* It was Shirley Bassey singing "What I Did for Love" all over again.

I always thought I had gone to school with Shirley Bassey. That's not a long shot because I grew up in Cardiff, Wales, and this skinny little black kid with huge eyes and a voice that shook the whole building when she sang had arrived in our class one day. Her voice was so incredible that her talent stood apart from the rest of us, and that is saying something in a Welsh school where singing talent is a way of life and all children sing like angels. My whole class could have auditioned for *Oliver Twist* and driven Andrew Lloyd Webber instantly insane with the difficulty of trying to choose the best voices.

Anyway, this little black kid was transported into our upscale neighbourhood, if you can call working class poor upscale, which you can if you are being transported from the slums of the notorious Tiger Bay dock area. She became the only black person in our hundred percent white school. We all fought over who could play with her, a black kid being a huge novelty, the first one we had ever seen in the flesh. She looked so black. I mean black, and we all looked so horrifically anemically white beside her. But it was lucky me who became her best friend. Her name was Shirley and she disappeared two school terms later as easily as she had arrived. When Shirley Bassey emerged years later singing the title song for the James Bond movie *Goldfinger,* putting Tiger Bay on the map, I always wondered, was she my Shirley? I was always going to write her a letter to find out. But for starters, I had not an idea in hell where she lived. Shirley Bassey, I mean. And my family had long ago emigrated to Canada.

But getting back to why I came to Nanaimo—sorry, I have a bad habit of getting off subject—Larry was renovating old houses in Nanaimo and selling them. Some of them were over one hundred years old, full of character and with magnificent views of the ocean and the Gulf Islands, definitely one of the most beautiful places in the world. It was a huge reward and a thrill restoring these neglected houses to their former charm and dignity. This was a recent project for Larry because mining, which had always been his bread and butter, had gone—as they say in BC—"tits up."

The real estate market, however, was soft at the moment, and Big Sab, one of the old houses Larry had renovated, was so big he was having problems selling it. It had been the home of the mining manager in the bygone glory days of the late 1800s when Nanaimo was a big successful coal-mining town. The house had nine bedrooms, all told, albeit five of the bedrooms were small. A difficult house to sell because who wants a nine-bedroom house these days? Most couples plan on only having two children and many opt for nought.

Plus, the South End of the city had quite a reputation. The first day I arrived I had taken a taxi from the ferry. The cab driver and I chatted about life, about how excited I was to be starting a new one here in Nanaimo. He sized me up from the vantage point of the rear-view mirror of his cab as he drove. "We've nicknamed the house Big Sab," I told him excitedly as we pulled up to the curb, "because it's the biggest house on Sabiston Street." As I searched for change for a tip, he cleared his throat and let me have it.

"Why would a decent sort like you want to live in this neighbourhood?" he asked. Then looking at my startled face, he added, "You know this is the South End? This is a bad neighbourhood, lady. Wrong side of the tracks. You're new here, right? From the Mainland, right? *I know.* None of my business, but lady, I wouldn't want my family living here. Break-ins, nothing but a bunch of thieves and drug addicts live here. Bad stuff... *and* the Indian Reserve is right there." He nodded toward the far side of the road. He was the fatherly type, I thought, staring at his wrinkled, friendly face and tired smile.

"Thanks for the warning," I said, not knowing what else to say. For some reason the old saying, "Lie down with dogs and you'll get up with fleas," popped into my head.

I had already surveyed the area with the eyes of a stranger in town, having heard it had once been Nanaimo's upper-class neighbourhood. The first doctor had lived in one of Larry's recently bought houses, and as I mentioned, Big Sab with its nine bedrooms had belonged to the prestigious coal mine manager. Another large house had been the first modest operating hospital. Around the corner a now shabby mansion had been the home of a sea captain who had brought specimen trees from around the world, and though he had been planted six feet under long ago, those tall, magnificent trees now screened the old home's fall from grace from curious eyes. The glamour of past days.

I had to admit the area was now more than a bit seedy-looking. I had even heard people call it Nanaimo's Skid Row. Some of the yards held abandoned, rusting, tire-less vehicles. Like more than one or two of them. Neglected gardens, broken fences. Dogs running unheeded. People walking the twenty-five blocks or so from town carrying their groceries and beer. Actually, it looked more like mega beer. Mothers pushing shabby prams full of kids and shopping. Like they didn't have a car. Many of the men had ponytails and beards and looked like throw-backs to the 1960s except they didn't quite have the hippy look. Worn-out jeans and cowboy boots seemed the norm. No love beads, no slave sandals. And I'm guessing no granola.

Big Sab stuck out like a sore thumb because she sat on an extra-large, unfenced corner lot. And she was freshly painted. Pale lemon with white doors and window frames. The wrap-around veranda was also white. Queen of the Block, I thought, looking fondly at her. The spin-off from living here was that you could see the sea sparkling and dancing only two blocks away in the big, rounded bay that gave Nanaimo its famous harbour with Protection Island and Newcastle Island sitting out there in the lacey blue water pretty as a picture postcard. A million-dollar view, reminding me of the pricey neighbourhoods of Kitsilano and Point Grey in Vancouver, which was the whole point of coming over here. That these charming old character houses with their massive Hudson Bay lots and their fabulous views would appeal to first time buyers or retirees. That people would overlook the fact this was the South End, the roughest neighbourhood in Nanaimo, and love the value they were getting for their money. Larry had already bought and renovated four modest little cottages in the South End and had rented them out while he waited for the neighbourhood to catch on. So far, the only renters had been Welfare recipients and Indigenous people. The cottages with their fresh lemon and white coats—Larry's favourite and only colour scheme for all his houses—shone out like little jewels in the shabby South End neighbourhood. His defence for the uni-formity was "I got a hell of a deal buying the paint in bulk. Hey... what's wrong with lemon and white?"

Larry had already told me that Big Sab was across the road from the Reserve, so the taxi driver hadn't told me anything I didn't know al-ready, and the Reserve interested me. I could just see the rooftops be-cause the land sloped downhill to a big stretch of beach and the sea.

But I knew nothing of their lifestyle. I had worked with a variety of ethnic cultures in Vancouver because that's what Vancouver is all about, being a multi-cultural society. I could write a song like that truck driver's song Johnny Cash used to sing—"I've been everywhere, man. I've been everywhere..." And then really fast he named all the places where he'd been. Mine would go something like this:

I've worked with every nationality, man, worked with every race,

Fijians, Chinese, Japanese, Portuguese and one from Bangladesh,

Singapore, Somalia, even Sri Lanka, and Patagonia fair

You name the country; I've worked with someone from there.

But I had never worked with Indigenous people. In Vancouver they were an invisible minority unless you went to Skid Row and then, sadly, you would see them from other parts of rural BC, people who had lost their way and ended up in that hell.

I remember thinking on that first day in Nanaimo that I would have to walk over and explore the Reserve. And I remember how I turned to walk up the stairs to Big Sab, music playing in my heart. Shirley Bassey was once again singing "What I did for love" as I turned the key and opened the front door.

I was a woman in love all right. My friends and family regarded me as besotted. They were right. I had left them behind on the Mainland along with my well-paying job and everything familiar and dear. It wasn't going to be easy, but regardless of obstacles I was going to make my new life here work.

2
Gordie Ryder

Just as Larry had been despairing about having an unsaleable nine-bedroom house on his hands, I had seen the ad in the paper: the John Howard Society was looking for rooms to accommodate men coming out of jail. *Jailbirds.* I wasn't keen. In fact, I said, "Bloody hell, Larry, you've got to be kidding me!" But he said, "At least we should find out more about it."

So we had made an appointment to find out if we qualified. That's when we met Ray Findlay and Gord Ryder.

Ray was a tall, thin man dressed immaculately in a pinstriped suit. He was gaunt with pale, watered-down blue eyes. You would have thought he was a regular run-of-the-mill business executive type except that he was hooked up to a breathing contraption that fed plastic tubes from his nose into a small portable machine. He wheezed when he spoke.

Gord, however, was an intimidating bulldog of a man. Around 5 feet 10 inches, 190 pounds, receding hairline. He looked a little like Ed Harris, you know, the guy who played the ground control manager in *Apollo 13*? You know the type. Tough but charming. He hunched over his desk as if he was getting ready to swing a punch. Brilliant blue eyes and a husky voice that bellowed speech. Larry, of course, immediately loved him.

Gord took over the meeting with Ray huffing and puffing in the background. First he reeled off some information about the John Howard Society, told us how Howard had been the sheriff of Bedfordshire in the late 1770s and had embarked on a much-needed prison reform platform for England and Wales. The living conditions in the prisons in those days were so appalling that people generally died of disease and malnutrition before their sentences were served. But Howard had developed empathy for prisoners, having been imprisoned by the French after he was captured during the Seven Years War. When he died, he left behind a sizeable fortune to be used to humanize the prison system, and so the John Howard Society lives on today, making valuable contributions to prison reform and assisting the men who have been incarcerated.

The first question Larry asked Gord was "Can we make any money out of this?"

A shuffling of the chair. "Well, not really, Larry." Gord hesitated, all twinkling eyes and perfect timing. "But if you take this on, you sure as hell will get yourself a ticket into heaven."

Larry leaned back in his chair and laughed out loud. "I get my ticket, eh?"

Gord then told us he used to be a member of the Hell's Angels. Had also been a drug addict and had gone to jail at age nineteen. He had quite a history behind him. I bet you do, I thought, looking at him through my sheltered Welsh childhood spectacles as if he was a strange animal in a zoo.

"And now I'm on the Other Side," he said. "I'm in the business of saving drug addicts, working with them, fighting for them."

"How many do you save?" Larry asked.

"Around 11 percent. The rest are either in jail or they die. Those are the options for an addict. Jail or death—either one is all you're ever going to get. So I'm the guy who tries to intervene."

He took me aback by this brusque speech, but I thought I'd ask an intelligent question. "If I take these convicts in, will I be in danger? I mean, could they get violent?"

Gord gave me a bemused smile. "Not at all, Diane. I really mean it. These guys will look on you as a surrogate parent. None of them have grown up, for Chrisake! They've been on drugs most of their juvenile lives, in and out of jail. Missed the teenage scene, the girlfriends and dating. Missed the grad and the prom. They've been in limbo for years. They have no sense of what real life is all about. They are all lost kids. Treat them like that. Remember, the guys you will be getting as boarders have only been in jail for two years. Their problem is drugs, drugs and drugs again. That's what they've been in for, *meaning* no violent crimes committed, otherwise they would have spent time in a federal prison. They're coming out of a provincial prison for mainly petty crimes like breaking and entering, done to support their habit. Big difference."

He leaned back in his chair, all on fire. "These men will lie and cheat. Some come from really lousy family situations, abused as kids. Some are from respectable homes. Addiction has no boundaries."

Then he had lowered his voice to a seductive level, and I felt myself leaning toward him to hear his words more clearly.

"Addiction is not selective. But once an addict—look out! You have never met a more charming, lying son-of-a-bitch than a drug addict. They can charm the birds out of the trees. Professional manipulators. And a drug addict's girlfriends..." Gord shrugged in a gesture of despair. "Well, I'll tell you, they usually are the most conniving pieces of human shit. Why? Don't ask me. These men need stability and support and encouragement, but you are going to see the most co-dependent behaviour. These are weak women who will not put their feet down. They support the men's weaknesses in a totally negative way. Like they *love* looking after these guys, and if the guys get better, then they will be out of the care-taking job that they need."

"That's so sick," I said. "How can they consider that love?"

Gord stopped swiveling in his chair, the blue eyes radar-like, searching my eyes, my face, for what? There was a silence. A peculiar silence. I realized a long time later it was probably because he was thinking, "Jesus Christ, save me! This woman is so naïve!" I learned later that when Gord had done his first jail time at nineteen years old, he had been put into a cell with a 400-pound Hell's Angel to keep the guy "entertained." This brutish cellmate, an influential captain of an Angel's chapter, had taken Gord under his wing, and when Gord was finally released from jail, this guy had advanced his career like a shooting star in the Hell's Angel's organization. Gord Ryder had explored and digested the word "love" in all its multi-faceted forms a long time ago.

3
The Boozer and the Druggie

I noticed that Lewis was limping badly as I accompanied him up the wide staircase leading to the top floor.

"What's up with your leg?"

"I guess I twisted my ankle when I fell on the tracks. Don't ask me how. To tell you the truth I can't remember." He laughed ruefully. "It hurts like hell, though."

Big Sab was a beautiful old house. Three large bedrooms upstairs all with spectacular ocean views. A large bathroom and a unique alcove in the upstairs hall that had a sink with running water, cupboards and a counter that housed a small bar fridge underneath. Perfect to set up a coffee station if you didn't want to use the main downstairs kitchen. The ground floor had three small bedrooms running off one side of the main hall and a big living room off the other side. The basement was at ground level and had another three large bedrooms that Larry hadn't yet renovated. They were huge rooms, all of them with their own sinks and kitchen cupboards, a hangover from the days when Big Sab had been a run-down rooming house. The place had been a shambles when Larry had bought it. Neglected and filthy. But underneath the squalor lay a hidden charm. Gracious bay windows. A large sweeping staircase. Fabulous views of the Gulf Islands.

I had taken care to co-ordinate all the curtains and quilts in each room. Larry had thought I had gone a little overboard on being *artsy-fartsy,* but I had managed to give each room a distinctive look with a dresser, a bedside table with a lamp, a small table and chair and framed pictures on the walls. All the rooms were carpeted with second-hand carpet, but as we had been told that all recovering addicts smoke like crazy, I had put an extra-large ashtray in each room.

The phone in the hall rang. It was Larry.

"I'm showing a prospective client around," I told him.

"Oh really. Does he look like he's got money?"

"Larry..."

"Make sure you get his money. I'm coming over on the 3 o'clock ferry. I'll be there for three or four days."

As I hung up the phone, I heard a door open and close. Luke had come out of his bedroom. I guess he had heard voices and was curious.

Luke was our first client. What can I tell you? He'd been brought to us by Narcotics Anonymous (NA) two weeks earlier. Well, let's say he'd been more half-carried into the house. He was a tall, well-built young man, twenty-six years old, but when he arrived, he had been so pale, actually white as sheet, that it was shocking. And he was trembling all over. Shivering like he had a tremendous fever. The story unfolded that he had been off drugs for two years, but his girlfriend, Joanne, was trouble. He loved her, but she was a bitch. Then he'd found out she was going to the Hell's Angels' clubhouse and was fooling around on him, and the Hell's Angels were supplying her with drugs. He'd gone on a two-month drug binge, and so here he was in Big Sab, wanting to dry out again. Body and soul, you might say.

I treated him like an invalid. What did I know of drug addicts? Cooked the best food and took it up on a tray. He had brought his own TV with him and a big blue stuffed chair, which he sat in by the hour watching the tube. I listened patiently over and over again to his Joanne stories. But his shaking had stopped, and his normal colour was coming back. As I had no previous experience with addicts, I used a common-sense approach. I loaded him up with fruit juice, gave him vitamin pills. He was crazy over my cooking. "I've never eaten so good! Man!" His plate was always scraped clean.

Luke had these piercing blue eyes, and he drilled us with them as he told us his story. He was so tense it was as if an electric current gripped every muscle in his body. His jaw was clenched, his fists coiled. He had been a foster kid and had been bounced from home to home, but he had a chip on his shoulder, a sort of *poor me, I never had a chance* that could be quite wearing. Like, wake up kid! Have you seen the children in Africa who have been born with AIDS? Now *that's* never having a chance. In other words, Luke was quite the piece of work, and I had already decided I didn't really like him.

"Hi Luke," I called out. "Come and meet Lewis. He might be our next client." Lewis limped out into the hall and shook Luke's hand, the two men eyeballing each other. The boozer and the druggie.

Luke surprised me by being sociable and saying, "Oh great, man. Pleased to meet you, Lewis. Been a little lonely here rattling around by myself."

Lewis decided he would take the Willow Room, so-called because the branches of the giant willow tree in the garden brushed against the window, and at night delicate shadow patterns of willows danced on the walls. It was a pretty room with a brand new chocolate brown quilt and a lamp with an apricot-coloured lampshade. I had been so thrilled when I had found a huge glass ashtray that was the same apricot colour. (I know. I go overboard on this sort of stuff, but what the heck—it's fun.)

Lewis had opened the window and was leaning out to look at the large wooden fire escape outside. "This is great. Be good to sit out here when it gets too hot."

"Okay, so I should tell you our rates. We charge $350 for the room, and if you want meals, it will be $500 a month."

Silence.

"Is there a problem?"

"Uhm... well, Diane..." There was a stretch of awkward silence. "I'm not working. Haven't been for a while... been on the booze real hard."

His head was down and he was looking at his runners. The left one had a hole in the toe.

I waited. Surely there was more to come.

"I was thinking for the first couple of weeks would you consider me working the rent off? And then I can try and catch up. You know... I can go to Welfare and when they realize I am in a safehouse and, um... confronting my addiction, I'm sure I'll get help. They'll pay my rent."

"But what work could you do here, Lewis? I mean... what?" To say I was taken aback by his proposal is understating it. He had some nerve.

"I was looking at your yard. A lot needs to be done out there."

I stared out the window at the woodsy look in the garden that I loved, at the bluebells growing randomly under the trees. Well, maybe it was a bit too natural-looking, and the grass desperately needed cutting. And the back end was still full of junk. While the house had been empty, the neighbourhood had been using the yard as a dumping ground. Larry never had time to do anything about it, not with commuting between the Mainland and me. That is, me and his bossy sergeant-major wife.

"I'm real good at yard work," Lewis said. "I could have this place looking like a show place. I'm a pretty good handyman. Diane, please? I just need a break."

There was a long awkward silence. He was begging, but I resented being put on the spot like this. Was I a pushover? I stared at the gold flecks in the hazel eyes. The sincere from-the-heart smile. I thought fleetingly of Larry, of our empty bank account. I said to myself, "Is this crazy or what?" But what I said to Lewis was something else.

"Okay, Lewis. But I really will have to see results if this is going to work."

Back downstairs I stirred the beef stew furiously, throwing in the parsley and a bay leaf. I hated myself. For a fleeting moment I felt alarmed like I had just been conned by the best, then I poured more coffee, gulped it down and started to relax. Lewis had the most genuine, grateful look in his eyes when I had agreed. Relief even. I felt good. After all, we were here to help addicts, weren't we?

4
First Nights

I had just glanced at my watch thinking I would have to leave shortly to pick Larry up from the ferry when the phone rang.

"I'm not going to make it after all," Larry said.

"Larry!"

"I know."

"You mean you're not making it *at all?*"

"I'll be on the 7 p.m. tomorrow. God's honour."

I was silent for a moment. Disappointed and raging.

"Okay?"

"Okay."

He hung up. I understood he couldn't embellish. His English wife was probably hanging around in the background, and of course, he was more paranoid than any mental patient locked up in a rubber room at Riverview. He hadn't told her about our relationship because he said it would complicate the divorce proceedings. That Phyllis was a very vindictive woman, and if she thought he would find happiness with someone else, she would find every way known to man to suck all the money she could out of him.

I wondered again what I was doing with my life. Why did I love Larry so? When I look back on those days, I have to say that he wasn't handsome. But then good-looking men had never been my bag. It had always been a man's mind that captured me. I guess most women would agree with that. And please let him have the power to make me laugh. I had found my bra seemed to mysteriously unhook itself and sail through the air, my knickers flying right after it, when a man had the ability to make me laugh. And Larry sure knew how to make me laugh. He was a soldier-of-fortune kind of guy, a gambler, an establishment misfit, but he couldn't have cared less. He was a tall, overweight guy with thick blond hair that was always in disarray. In town when he was wearing The Suit, his tie was somehow always half inside out and flying uncontrollably like a kite over his shoulder. But he was the most generous hugger you have ever met. It was a trip just to be hugged by Larry, the arms like a tree and the softness of the embrace, like coming home when you're a little kid and being hugged. He knew how to do it, and both men and women hurried to be hugged by him. Also he had that Peter Falk "Columbo" slightly out-of-focus eye. The previous year at age forty-four—*yes, I was almost five years older than him*—he had an eye operation to fix the problem, but the operation was a dismal failure. As he said ruefully but with good humour, "The doctor was a damned alcoholic. I should have known. I guess it wasn't one of his good days."

I told him, "You should be so lucky. It makes you look vulnerable. What woman can resist a vulnerable man?" Ain't that the truth?

After all that, sometimes when the sun made his tangled mess of blond hair glint and a beer had made him, as he would say, all lovey-dovey, there was a lazy, sexual charm in his vulnerable blue Colombo eyes that made him beyond good-looking, and I, with love-filled eyes, would say he was more than handsome. He was a prince.

I was getting ready for bed. It was only 10 o'clock, but it had been a full day and I was tired. I was missing my kids, David and Kelly. I had meant to phone them earlier. Where had the day gone? David was married; Kelly had her own apartment and a high-profile job with an engineering company. But I hadn't seen them in two months, and I wasn't used to living apart from them like this. Guy, my oldest son, had moved to Nanaimo two weeks after me and lived in a cute cabin ten minutes away. But his is a very different story.

That night I just wanted to curl up with my book and switch off the world of Diane Foley. I turned on the bedside table lamp and pulled down the covers on the lovely old-fashioned, iron-rung bed that Larry had found in a second-hand store. Browsing in second hand stores was Larry's way of relaxing. He loved finding discarded antiques and "treasures" as he called them, and he'd been exhilarated by this find. We had spray-painted it pale yellow, and now with my Mennonite patchwork quilt that had red, pale lemon and white as its main colour scheme, the whole room had taken on a Mexican south-of-the-border look. The quilt had been handmade by a friend's mother who lived in Steinbach, Manitoba, which is the real orthodox Mennonite country. The Mennonites there don't read novels, own TVs or watch movies. They don't even have pictures or photographs on their walls. They just cook and pray a lot. I know because I've been there and found that, with everything cut out of their world that related to mine, I was stuck to find anything to converse with them about. I mean from O.J. Simpson to *Alice in Wonderland*, they didn't know what the hell I was talking about. But they created the most magnificent quilts and for that I was grateful.

I loved our bedroom. It had a large window overlooking the bay and white, freshly painted walls, and I had put up light white curtains. A long, dark red dresser complete with brass handles and an oval mirror ran along the wall facing the bed. A print of Ken Danby's *Pancho* with his bright yellow oilskin hung on one wall. An ex-boyfriend, a Sikh, had bought it for me when I told him I thought he was a dead ringer for Pancho. What man could resist such a compliment? He really was a fabulous looking man—the Sikh, I mean—a fact I hadn't shared yet with Larry. I didn't think he'd appreciate a dead ringer of an ex-boyfriend looking down on us as we made love.

I opened up the dresser drawer to look for a big sloppy T-shirt. I love sleeping in loose comfortable clothes rather than lacy nighties.

That is when Larry is away. I had no sooner pulled the T-shirt over my head when a knock came on the bedroom door. I jumped, startled, and threw on my robe.

"Who's there?"

"Lewis."

I opened up the door and peered into the hall. Lewis was standing there looking apologetic. A sight to behold. Bare-chested, just wearing jeans and a smile.

"Sorry... I was wondering if you had something I could read. I'm feeling a bit restless."

"Oh, for sure."

Well, what do you know? This was something good. He liked to read.

"What do you usually read? Mysteries? Non-fiction? We have a bit of everything here. Larry and I are both big readers."

"A mystery would be great... or whatever. I'm not fussy."

"Let's see." I went over to the bookcase and pulled out William Deverell's *Needles*. "You might like this; it's set in Vancouver. It's fun reading about the local scene for a change instead of New York or San Francisco or some other alien city."

"It's not about drugs, is it?" he said and laughed.

"Not in the sense it's a lecture or moralizing. It's a detective story. It's a really good read. Fast-paced and full of twists and surprises. Believe me, you'll enjoy it."

Later when I went down the hall to the bathroom, it startled me to see him in his bed. He had left his bedroom door open, and I could see he had moved the furniture completely around so that, when he was in bed, he could look out of his bedroom door into the hall. Larry and I had positioned it behind the door and facing the window and the view of the garden to provide the bed occupant with more privacy.

"You changed your bed around."

"I hope you don't mind. I like looking out of a room. I felt claustro-phobic the other way." He didn't wait for me to answer. "And you're right." He waved the book at me. "This is a good read. I'm hooked already." He suddenly grinned. "No, I'm not trying to make a pun. Hooked?" We both laughed.

As I came back down the hall from the bathroom, I glanced into the open door of his room again. His door was directly across the hall from mine. His had the No. 5 in brass figures on it and mine had No. 3, the numbers being a leftover from Big Sab's former rooming house days.

Lewis was propped up on his pillows reading. He had showered, and his hair was still damp. His bare chest glowed brown against the white sheets. He was a handsome devil. The dark blond-streaked hair. The mischievous grin. Those lazy golden eyes. I bet he'd broken some hearts in his day.

"Goodnight, Diane. Sleep well." He wiggled his fingers at me in a half-wave. He acted like I had known him for years, snuggled in his bed like he had slept there all the years he was growing up. And like I was his long-lost aunt or something. But I felt more like Wendy with her hands full looking after the lost boys of Never Never Land. A Wendy without Peter Pan. *Larry.* I felt a pang of loneliness gripping me. I just plain missed him.

I went back into my room and picked up my book. Truman Capote's *Music for Chameleons.* I felt a little disoriented. I was here alone sleep-ing across the hall from a half-naked stranger who had slept on the rail-way tracks the night before and that mealy-mouthed Luke down the hall who had more track marks on his arms than the entire CPR railway line. Tracks coming and going. It was a little disconcerting. I mean, was I even safe? I thought about that, mulling over it, got up, tippy-toed over and slid the small bolt on the door. It wasn't a very substantial latch. Serial killers are my worst fear. Who knows? Luke or Lewis could be one. Look at the Boston Strangler. "Who would have known?" dear old Albert DeSalvo's neighbours must have muttered, watching out their windows as the police hauled him away.

I heard faint music wafting from across the road. It sounded like gypsy music, and I looked out the bedroom window. It was a magnificent night. A black velvet star-studded sky overhead. Bobbing pinpoints of light marking the leisure boats anchored in the harbour, and Jack, our neighbour across the road, out in his garden stoking a massive bonfire, its sparks spluttering, sailing high into that black night sky. A Coleman lamp was lit on the nearby picnic table, and an oversize jug of wine sat next to it.

Jack and his wife Yvonne were middle class people from Victoria who for whatever reason had just dropped out. They were both in their fifties with four grown-up, respectable, college-educated children, all married now, all professionals, yet Jack and Yvonne with their middle-aged freedom had chosen to live in the South End right next door to the Reserve. Jack loved drinking with the Native guys, getting rip-roaring drunk, yahooing and dancing in the moonlight with the best of them. He insisted on traipsing around barefoot like he thought he was another Huckleberry Finn, his shirt always unbuttoned, an Australian digger hat perched on his balding head, and his little pot beer belly hanging out. He really was a riot. He was an articulate man, well versed in politics and poetry and generous to a fault. Just totally nutty in an irresistible, lovable way. He and Yvonne would set up camp in their back yard and put on music—rock and roll, opera, it didn't seem to matter—and create another world for themselves. He loved to sleep there on warm nights under the stars, and Yvonne slept right there with him, both snuggled in their sleeping bags. In a way I felt wistfully envious of them, at their closeness, at the way they created fun out of nothing. As I watched the huge fire Jack was stoking, I thought it was a good job they had moved into the South End. Neighbours in other parts of town would have reported them to City Council long ago for disturbing the peace and trying to set fire to the neighbourhood.

I opened the window and hung out, yelling over to them. "Hey guys, I love your music. Can you turn it up?" Jack waved a charred, smoking stick happily at me, and the sound of the Gypsy Kings filled the night air.

That was stupid of me, I thought. If I screamed for help through the window now, they wouldn't be able to hear me. What the hell. I climbed back into bed. I had once lived in a Mexican village, Yelapa, down south of Puerto Vallarta, for two months. No electricity, no police, and the palapa I slept in every night had no doors or windows. Anybody could have walked in and bumped me off on any Mexican night. For the first four or five nights I had hardly slept a wink, then a feeling of fatalism had rescued me. So now I told myself that if I was to die a violent death in the South End, it was already written up in the book. I decided it would be a good idea to stop reading Truman Capote's macabre story, *Coffins*, and just go to sleep. But now Jack was playing Sinatra singing *Strangers in the Night*, and I was back to my serial killer paranoia again. Hell's bells. I turned off the light and went to sleep.

5
Crack

The next morning the sun woke me up by streaming through the window. I stretched and looked out over the bay where gentle, foamy white wavelets danced on a navy-blue sea. What a beautiful day! By the time I had showered and gone downstairs, Lewis was already in the garden and had started cleaning up the overgrown lawn.

"I'm getting all the crap out of the grass before I start to mow," he yelled. I watched him for a moment limping here and there then went to put the coffee on.

Luke came down for breakfast, and as I scrambled up eggs, I already knew I would ask Lewis to come in for breakfast. What had I let myself in for? Here he was getting free room *and* board. Larry was going to have a bird.

A while later I was listening while Luke filled Lewis in on his story of Joanne, drugs and betrayal.

"I couldn't stand it no more. What's the use? I give up drugs for her, get my life on track *for her* and she fucks around on me... man." Luke gulped for air. "Anyways, that's why I went back on the drugs 'cos I just didn't give a shit anymore. I didn't care..." He stared off into space then shook his head. "I thought if I got back on, she would party with me again, we would be having fun together again... like old times. But all she does is hang around at that fucking Hell's Angels clubhouse doing God knows what."

But we all knew what God knew—that dear ole Joanne was fucking her brains out with the Hell's Angels in exchange for drugs.

Straight after breakfast Lewis lit a cigarette borrowed from Luke and was back out and working on the yard again. I watched him through the day and couldn't help but be impressed by the results. In spite of his sore ankle he was soldiering on. I was frankly relieved big time that he wasn't lazy, and he was actually being sincere about working for his rent. The lawn was mowed, the grass raked into a neat pile. He had loaded half of the rubbish that had been heaped at the far end of the yard into Larry's old blue Ford truck with its mismatched-coloured doors—one pale pink and one white—and taken it to the dump. Now he was working on a second load. A miraculous change in the garden was already taking place. He limped and worked and limped some more. It was obvious he was in pain, but he didn't complain. In fact, he was whistling and humming as he worked. Stripped to the waist, he was glistening with sweat under the hot sun. I took him a glass of iced tea and we sat under the willow tree.

"I've got so many good ideas for this place. How about a fire pit over there? And I thought a horseshoe ring pitch would fit here." He waved toward the side of the house. "This is a huge yard. I even thought chickens against that far wall."

"Chickens? They wouldn't allow chickens in a residential area." But I couldn't help but grin at his enthusiasm.

"Who said anything about being allowed?" He smiled. "This is the South End. Listen." He held up his hand to shush me.

Sure enough, I could hear a faint cock-a-doodle-doo. Why hadn't I heard that before?

"That must be coming from the Reserve," I said. "They have a different set of rules over there."

"Naw." He waved over the road. "It's over there at the back of that house. White folks. Her name is Deb and she'll sell you a dozen eggs for a dollar. I went over this morning and checked it out. She has a neat operation over there, about fifteen chickens."

"Well, I'll be damned. Chickens would be fun. We'll have to ask Larry."

"Larry is your boyfriend, right?"

"Yep, he's coming in on the 7 p.m. ferry."

"Hmm. It will be interesting to see what kind a man you selected for a mate."

His eyes assessed me for a moment. Why was I blushing? I collected up the glasses and turned, hiding my confusion, to walk back to the house. I felt his amusement at my discomfort travelling with me. I suddenly felt old and matronly. Me. Or was I just wishing I was fifteen years younger?

I was almost at the kitchen door when I heard a shout from across the road. I peeked around the corner of the house. Shane was running like a bat out of hell towards Big Sab. His feet were hardly touching the ground, his mane of blond hair streaming out behind him.

Then the door to the house across the road—the one we called Little Sab—burst open and Dennis came racing out. He was stripped to the waist, exposing a thicket of startlingly black hair on his chest and upper arms. Willfully barefoot, oblivious to the sharp gravel on the road, he raced after Shane like he was possessed, swinging a two-by-four and screaming, "I'll get you, you fuckin' bastard!"

I was mesmerized. The scene was so unbelievable. Only a month earlier Larry had rented Little Sab to Shane and Dennis, two guys who had lived very briefly at Big Sab. While Dennis was kind of a weirdo, introverted and a hermit, Shane was full of fun, a happy-go-lucky kind of guy.

But now Shane had entered Big Sab through our front door, and I could hear his footsteps thudding down the hall towards the kitchen. He emerged through the open kitchen door, leapt off the porch, ran past me like a blurred streak and managed to shout over his shoulder as he raced past Lewis, "Phone 911! He's going to kill me." Then he was off down the garden and out onto the side road in a cloud of dust like some crazed road runner. Dennis, anticipating his move, was already running down the side of the house, almost but not quite, cutting him off, still shouting bloodthirsty cries as he swung his two-by-four around his head.

Lewis leaned back on his shovel, watching them with a bemused grin on his face. Then Luke came out onto the back porch and the three of us watched the chase, hypnotized as Shane turned into the parking lot of the Patricia Pub on the next corner and disappeared. No one had yet called 911.

"What the hell was that all about?" I said as Dennis disappeared around the same corner in hot pursuit.

"Crack," said Lewis and Luke in unison.

"*Crack?* What the hell do you mean by that?"

"They're both on something, Diane," said Luke, smirking as he leaned over the rail. "I always thought that Dennis was using. The way he holed up in his bedroom for hours on end, never coming out, I figured as much. But not Shane." He laughed. "I guess Dennis has turned him on. Boy, were they both wired."

"My God," I said, shaken. "Is the whole world on drugs?"

"Maybe not the whole world, but remember this is the South End." Lewis was wearing that bemused smile again. Why would he think this was so damn funny?

"I thought Dennis wanted to be alone because he had a broken heart—that's why he holed up in his bedroom," I said, looking first at Lewis and then at Luke. "He told me his wife left him back in Ontario, and he came out to the West Coast to get over it."

Luke laughed so hard he almost fell over the rail. "Boy, did he suck you in! Broken heart, my ass. He has a worn-out nostril, more like it." He went back into the house still shaking with laughter after saying casually, "I'll call 911."

I glared at his retreating back as I felt my hackles rising. He sure knew how to hit my buttons. Then I thought out loud. "Larry is going to be so pissed off. We're going to have to evict them."

"It's not your fault they're both coke heads," said Lewis.

"But right under my nose. I mean how come I didn't see it? I thought they were both nice guys."

"Most drug addicts are," said Lewis. "Or they start out that way."

I stared at him.

"They're just normal people with a habit, Di. Everyday Joes who screw up. Until they get to this stage, chasing someone down the street swinging a two-by-four, you probably wouldn't pick up on it. You probably would think they were just happy."

Another alarming thought entered my head. "I just remembered. This Vietnamese guy came around asking about Dennis, and Dennis told me the guy was a friend, that he'd bought his car off him. Said the guy was looking for car payments. Now I wonder."

Lewis shook his head. "Vietnamese. That should have been your first clue. The Vietnamese run the drug trade in Nanaimo. The Hell's Angels used to, and you know what happened?"

"No."

"The Hell's Angels captain's decapitated head was found on a spike down by the ferry terminal, and from then on the Vietnamese ran the show over here."

"Are you kidding me? My God... what a horror story! They don't fool around, do they?" I felt a little taken aback. I had sat talking to a drug dealer on the veranda of my house and hadn't even realized it.

Lewis patted me gently on the back. "I'll help Larry evict these guys. I'll be his back-up. When you're on crack, you think you're invincible. Think you can rule the world. Don't worry," he said smiling into my troubled eyes. "You're on a learning curve here. You'll be fine, Di. You'll be okay."

That familiarity again. *Di.* But I found myself smiling back.

When Larry came through the ferry terminal door, I ran to greet him.

"How are you? How's it going, love?" He was so big I always disappeared into his arms. It was a good feeling, especially when you are a little chunky like me. Nymph-like I'm not, but we won't go there. He had a beaming smile as he kissed me on the cheek. Kisses on the mouth were for when we were in bed or when he was drunk. Don't ask me why. I don't know, he wasn't shy. His blond hair was as usual in disarray, blowing in his eyes. He was wearing a bulky blue sweater and jeans. He hurled his carry-on like it was a paper bag into the back of the old Ford truck and off we went.

How to tell him about Lewis and my deal for free room and board? I started with Dennis and Shane instead. He listened intently as he drove, glancing over at me rapidly as the story reached the punch line.

"Those fucking pricks. Their rent is due tomorrow. I bet they don't have the money."

"You have to evict them anyway, Larry. We can't have them staying there—they've both gone fucking nuts."

"If I evict them, I'll get stuck with an empty house for a month. Be out a month's rent. Shit."

We pulled up in front of Big Sab, and Larry stopped dead looking at the garden.

"Well, look at this! Who did all this work? Did you cut the grass?"

"I haven't told you that bit yet," I started lamely. "This guy called Lewis turned up. The one I told you about on the phone. He's going to work for us in exchange for a room... until his welfare kicks in." A gut survivor instinct made me leave out mentioning the free board. "I wanted it to be a surprise—how good the yard looks."

Larry turned his head slowly appraising me, giving me a Dirty Harry dead pan look. "For $350 a month he'd *better* make it look good," he said grimly. Although he was displeased with me, he had just arrived and I could see he didn't want to make waves already.

We were in the kitchen when Lewis came in.

"Hi Larry, Lewis here. Pleased to meet you." He offered his hand.

I could see Larry was appraising him. Their eyes locked, then their hands shook. I could see Larry relax. Whatever happens between guys when they first meet had happened. Larry instinctively liked him. Lewis had passed the male testosterone inspection test.

We sat around the kitchen table eating silently, a compliment I take for my cooking. I had grilled pork chops in a mushroom sauce and served them with scalloped potatoes. The scallops were just right. Brown and crispy on the outside and plenty of creamy sauce on the inside. A big bowl of Caesar salad and crusty rolls rounded off the meal.

"Are you a good cook!" said Lewis, wiping his mouth on a napkin. His manners were impeccable. "My step-mother, Sue, is a great cook but not on par with this." He kissed his fingers with a smacking noise and blew a kiss into the room like Tony Soprano.

I could't help but like him. He had a natural charismatic flair about him and, as I have said, was very handsome, but please, I am not that shallow, though it has been proven that people who are good-looking get all the breaks. Apparently having someone attractive to deal with sugar coats many a pill. I remembered when I owned an answering service In Vancouver that before our annual Christmas party, we would all be filled with curiosity about meeting the clients we had never seen but had spoken to daily. Our favourites, the clients who had joked and laughed with us, the ones who had shared their little personal ups and downs with us throughout the year and the ones whom we had grown to love, invariably turned out to be plump, short or balding, bespectacled, too thin or lumpy though undeniably the sweetest people in the world. The ones we thought had soul. The assholes, the rude obnoxious pricks who made my operators grind their teeth and sometimes brutally reduced them to tears, would turn up in their tailored $2,000 suits, immaculate, dashing, handsome James Bond types. Before our eyes these devils whom we had cursed all year would somehow make us forgive them for their year's sins and seduce us into changing our minds about them. Good looks are lethal.

Now Larry was pushing away from the table happy and content. Food does that to him.

"Why do you call this place Big Sab?" Lewis asked. "The ad says Sabiston Lodge."

"Well, we officially gave the house a dignified name for the John Howard Society's sake," Larry said. "Big Sab is its nickname. The house Dennis and Shane live in is called Little Sab because it's a little house and... well, both houses are on Sabiston Street."

"We spent a whole night trying to pick out the name," I added. "We tried Holly House because of the big holly trees in the garden, New Start, Harbour View. You name it, we had it. But I love the name Big Sab."

"It's like Big Sur, sort of a romantic name, eh?" Lewis smiled.

Luke excused himself from the table and put his dishes in the sink. He had no social skills, and I could tell he was miffed that Larry was getting along with Lewis so well. I felt a little sorry for him. It was exactly what Gordie Ryder had warned us about: Luke was like a kid who hadn't grown up.

"Lewis, you didn't bring your stuff over from your old place yet," I said. "Let's go and get your things tonight. Larry can help... right, Larry?"

"Sure. I don't mind. Where did you live before?"

There was a small silence. Lewis weighed his words. "Well, it's a bit awkward. I owe the landlord money. I really don't want to run into him just yet."

"But you need your clothes. You can't wear the same thing every day."

"I guess I could whip in and out real fast. There's a window off my bedroom that overlooks the alley. I'm on ground level. Maybe you can park in the alley, Larry, and I'll throw the stuff out the window? If I can get some big garbage bags from you, Diane, that would work."

"The alley?" Larry said, his eyes dancing. He loved a covert operation.

"Oh, let me come," I cried. "I love a moonlight flit."

"A moonlight flit?" Lewis looked at me questioningly.

"Oh, don't take any notice of her. She's speaking that funny Welsh lingo again, aren't you, love?"

"Yep... I guess... a moonlight flit means moving secretly so the land-lord doesn't nail you. I haven't done it in twenty-odd years. Come on then. Let's get cracking." I saw out of the corner of my eye that Luke was staring at us like we'd lost our senses, and I wondered uneasily if the John Howard Society would approve of moonlight flits.

When we arrived at Lewis's old apartment, I was the one designated to go through the front lobby and open the apartment door. Once inside, I was to open the window overlooking the alley and let Lewis in to organize his move. I felt a little nervous walking down the hall, and I fumbled the latch key, but finally the apartment door clicked and swung open. I stood there speechless. The place had been ransacked. Clothes were scattered all over the place, the floor was covered with stuff pulled out of the kitchen cupboards. All the cupboard doors were open, gaping with spilled cereal, and a ripped bag of sugar lay in its own white circle of sugary mess on the floor. Broken china littered the kitchen counter.

I stepped gingerly through the mess to the bedroom window and pulled the window open. It wasn't locked. Lewis immediately swung his legs over the window ledge.

"Either you're a terrible housekeeper or someone has broken in here, Lewis. Look."

He surveyed the scene not saying a word, but there was a tightening of his face and his body tensed. I heard a soft whistling at the intake of his breath. I'm not sure but I think he mouthed the word "*bastards.*"

"Let's hurry this" is all he said.

We shoved clothes indiscriminately into the garbage bags, then I went into the bathroom and piled towels, deodorant, his shaving gear and toothbrush into plastic bags. What else to take? I hurried, feeling nervous. There was something radically wrong with this scene.

"Let's go," Lewis was saying as he handed filled garbage bags out of the bedroom window to Larry.

"Are you sure you've got enough stuff?" We'd been there all of ten minutes. "There are still clothes hanging in the closet."

"Yep, let's get out of here." And he was out the window and gone.

I closed the window, locked it and left by the front door. The hall was deserted, and I was thankful I didn't meet anybody on my way out through the lobby.

We had been driving for at least fifteen minutes before I saw that Lewis had started to relax. "Phew," he said. "I'm glad I've got that over with."

"What about your furniture? Will you go back later for it?"

The furniture had been modest but there had been a comfortable Lazy Boy chair and a pine coffee table.

"To hell with it... I don't know. I'll see."

"What was that all about back there? Like, aren't you shocked someone broke into your place and made that mess?"

"You were broken into?" asked Larry, surprised.

"It could have been anybody. Street people. Who knows? I owe some people money. Maybe they were just being assholes. Got in through the window. Letting me know they're pissed off at me. That's why I couldn't live there anymore, Di. I never knew who was going to knock on the door. It was getting out of control... my life I mean."

He stared out the window, but I knew he wasn't telling us the whole story. Whatever was going on was more than just owing rent. Was it something more sinister? He sure was scared... But what the hell. He was safe with us. Making his jump at the brass ring, a brand-new start, a new life. And anyway, who in hell would think to come looking for him in the South End?

6
The Crew

Larry had quite a motley crew working on the reno work. If you didn't know them, you would probably be afraid of them. Davey, the team leader, was a jack-of-all-trades kind of guy from Saint John, New Brunswick. He had left school at fourteen so was street smart in a worldly sense and the best unqualified tradesman you could ever hope to meet. That sounds a bit odd, doesn't it? Unqualified tradesman. But that's what he was. He could literally do anything—roofing, carpet laying, carpentry and plumbing. He was a godsend. The hard life he had led showed in his rough, calloused hands and the wariness he carried in his eyes so that he looked older than his forty-five years. A long thin scar ran down his cheek, and his dark blond ponytail was already streaked with grey, but he had a winning smile that could melt your heart, and his grey eyes were always twinkling.

Steve, a plain-looking guy who stuttered, was the painter. He had a nose an airline carrier could land on, and he always wore ripped T-shirts and holey jeans. And then there was Donny who was simply crazy. He was a short wiry man who drank like a fish—well, to be fair, they all drank like hellions, but Donny was out of control. He was a Ginger with thinning hair, and he always wore shorts that showed off his skinny white legs covered in fine red hair. Dancing was his thing. Larry had told me he liked dancing on tables and doing swallow dives. They never ended well. When he showed up for work, he was a hard-working genius, but then there were the hangovers. But the one thing the entire crew had in common was they all loved Larry. He had given them employment. He paid them well. He had changed their lives.

Davey asked me one day if Larry and I would like to come over to his house one evening to meet his wife, Rita. *You know... have a few beers and some laughs.* I was excited. At that time I hadn't met anyone in the South End socially, and Larry casually told me Rita came from an Indigenous village in Clayoquot Sound on the west coast of Vancouver Island.

I fussed around, checking my wardrobe. What to wear? I wanted to make a good impression. I decided on my Carole Little jacket and black pants. Carole Little had made a big name for herself on the Vancouver fashion scene before being catapulted to the glamour of the New York fashion world. I loved my jacket—black with exotic pale yellow roses and red stitching. It had cost and arm and a leg in the days when I could afford to splurge to indulge myself. Then I thought, should I pick up some snacks to take along with my bottle of wine? Larry had already picked up beer.

"I'm going to pick up some appies," I shouted up the stairs.

Wrapped in a towel, Larry peered down over the stair railing. "In that case I'll meet you there." Davey only lived two small blocks away.

In the end I picked up a bucket of Kentucky Fried Chicken. What the hell, it was the South End after all. I couldn't see sushi or bruschetta going over well. As I parked I could hear the music blasting. It was ear-splittingly loud. I knocked on the scarred wooden door a few times to no avail, so I finally opened it and walked in. I found myself in a huge kitchen with a crowd of people sitting around a big kitchen table. Everyone seemed to be dragging on a cigarette, and the room was blue with smoke. Davey sprang to his feet to welcome me. "Come on in, Di. This is Di, everyone! She's the lady from Big Sab," he shouted against the music's throbbing beat.

I smiled around the room as he introduced me. I had never felt so out of place. Everyone was wearing worn jogging pants or jeans and T-shirts. Rita, who was already pretty drunk, was an attractive, plump lady of about thirty with almond eyes and shoulder-length jet black hair. She was much younger than Davey. Beside her sat her sister Linda who probably weighed 300 pounds. Linda scowled at me, totally uninterested in who I was, and chug-a-lugged down the rest of her beer. Beside her was a skinny white guy called Emil with untidy blond hair and bad teeth. Then there was Glen, the biggest man I had ever met or seen except for Sumo wrestlers on TV. He was in his early thirties and had to weigh almost 400 pounds. He was Rita's brother. He staggered to his feet and shook my hand. His dark eyes were kind and dancing. "Whoa," he said. "Finally get to meet you, Diane, my pleasure." Then came another of Rita's brothers, Paco, who wore a black Trilby hat but who was of normal weight. He smiled but never said a word.

A beer was put into my hand, a chair pulled out that I sat down on, and Larry waved to me from across the room where he was sitting next to Steve, the painter. I took a deep breath. *When in Rome,* I thought and chug-a-lugged down the beer. Nobody touched the bucket of chicken until I said, "Please dig in, everybody. I brought the chicken for you." Then everybody delicately took a piece and within minutes the bucket was empty. No other food was put out, but the beer flowed. Did it flow! I had never seen drinking like that. The fridge was constantly opened, and I noticed that beer was stacked on every shelf. I was feeling a little overwhelmed when Emil pulled up a chair beside me. He had just come back from living in Argentina for a year, he told me. Had gone with an old school chum whose family came from there. He was unemployed but was hoping to get a job in computers. It didn't take long for me to realize he was way above average intelligence, well-read, funny and a poignant storyteller. It's a lesson worth repeating: don't judge a book by its cover.

Linda kept scowling at me. What was that all about?

When Emil vacated his chair to get himself another beer, big Glen lumbered over and sat down. He beamed at me. "This is great! You've joined our Friday Get Wrecked Night. I only come down to visit Rita and Davey every two months or so."

"Hi, it's Glen, right? So where do you live?"

"Ucluelet. Do you know where that is? On the other side of the Island? I work in the sawmill there. Good union job. Only job I've ever had. Been there fifteen years. Do you want to dance?"

Was he kidding?

Oh no! But there we were, up and dancing to Meat Loaf's "Heaven Can Wait." For such a big man Glen was amazingly light on his feet, and surprisingly, he held me like a professional dancer, so we just glided around the kitchen like we were angels with wings.

Before the song ended, everybody was dancing. Next it was Willie Nelson and Neil Young, then Johnny Cash with "The Folsom Prison Blues."—"*I hear that train a-comin', It's rollin' 'round the bend...*" And everyone was singing at the top of their lungs. Larry and I were rocking pretty good together when Donny arrived. He was more than pretty well drunk. He kept jumping in the air and clicking his heels like some inebriated Fred Astaire. "Sorry I'm late," he yelled at me above the music, "but I was giving the big one to Mae at the Chinese Grocery Store." He was grinning like a Cheshire cat.

"You're kidding me," I said, slightly horrified. Had I misheard him? Mae was a skinny, bad-tempered, shrill-voiced Chinese woman who was openly rude to the people from the Reserve. Her corner store was dark and suspiciously dirty with dusty shelves, and the stuff she sold was overpriced. Everybody pretty well hated her. Plus, she was at least sixty.

"She's nuts about me," said Donny and jumped and clicked his heels again.

I sat down feeling I was in the *Star Wars* bar with a bunch of aliens surrounding me. Crash. Linda's chair broke and she landed with shrieks on the floor. It took two strong men to get her up. "You'll need another beer after that, Lindy," said Davey cheerfully, dusting her down and repositioning her in a big armchair.

On the way home I said to Larry, "Why didn't you warn me?"

"Warn you of what?"

"Don't give me that. You know—the whole scene."

"Don't get judgmental, Di. It's not going to work in the South End. It is what it is."

I was silent. I wanted to make my point. But how?

"Didn't you have fun?" he demanded at last.

"Sure, I had fun, but at least you could have told me not to wear my Carole Little jacket."

Larry looked over at me, scanning me as though he was looking at a woman for the first time since the creation of Eve. He had a quiet, bemused smile on his face. Then he leaned over and gave my cheek a smacking big kiss.

"They invited you back, didn't they?"

It was true. They had. Apparently Friday Get Wrecked Night was happening again. You guessed it. Next Friday.

7
Indian Chiefs

Jack, our neighbour, was turning out to be a man of many surprises. He had invited me over to show me how he made his hunting knives. Apparently he had developed an international reputation for producing hand-carved knives, and people from all around the world were contacting him for customized work.

I knocked on the door and Yvonne let me in. She was a natural blonde—I knew this because a few strands of telltale silver shone through—with her hair cut in a short cap around her face. With her faded blue eyes and her fine features she had an aristocratic look and a natural reserve. The house was spotless. Hardwood floors with scattered Peruvian rugs, big, black leather couches, glass cabinets showcasing Waterford wine glasses and a huge oak family dining room table and buffet. High end stuff not often seen in the South End. This couple might be practicing gypsy living in their back yard, but the remnants of a once-gracious lifestyle floated around these rooms like friendly ghosts.

"Feel like a beer?" Jack roared from the kitchen. He didn't wait for my answer but poured a Molson's Canadian into a frosted glass. I glanced at the clock on the wall. It was 11:15 a.m. Oh, what the hell.

Between gulps of beer Jack showed me his knife collection, and I was totally surprised and impressed by the knives of all sizes, and I fell instantly in love with an exquisite little pocketknife. The carved, polished wood handles of his knives were works of art. No wonder he had so many customers.

By the time I was on my second beer, I had told Jack and Yvonne how excited I was that my oldest son, Guy, had come over from the Mainland to live in Nanaimo. Larry had fixed up a little cabin for him two blocks away. I was about to explain that Guy had been diagnosed with schizophrenia when he was seventeen, a day that had probably been the worst of my life. I have a hard time telling people new to my life about Guy because I have found that many people are afraid of the mentally ill. I was trying to choose my words carefully to describe Guy when Yvonne broke in to ask about the ruckus in front of Big Sab a week or so earlier. So I explained in detail what had happened to a friend who had come over to visit.

"You mean," Jack said, wide-eyed with concern, "that a whole tribe of little Indian kids harassed your friend?"

"Jack, it was the strangest thing I've seen since I moved over here. These Native kids surrounded my friend, Derek, on their bikes. There were about fifteen of them of varying ages, some maybe fifteen or sixteen years old, and they kept whooping and circling and wouldn't let him walk along the sidewalk. And when I ran out, they wouldn't let me near him. Then after about a half an hour of this they all took off and left us alone."

"I'll be damned," said Jack, very excited. "And your friend hadn't done anything to provoke them?"

"No way. Derek is the sweetest little man. Fragile actually because he has a bad heart. I think they scared him half to death, and I don't think he'll be back here in a hurry. He was shaking like a leaf when he finally came into the house. He thought it was Custer's Last Stand all over again."

Jack sat back on his chair. "Did you hear this, Yvonne? This calls for action. Diane, I want you to come down to the chief's house right now and repeat this story to him. He'll straighten those little buggers out."

"To the chief's house? They have a chief?"

"Oh yes, but they call them band chiefs now. Come on, let's go. This is serious."

I followed him out of the house and down the road. I felt pumped. I had never been on a reserve before, but I suddenly realized we were walking on gravel. "Jack, why haven't they black-topped the road here?"

"My-my, my dear. You have a lot to learn, haven't you? The municipality only maintains the roads up to the city boundary. The Reserve is not under their jurisdiction, so no black top for the Indians." He laughed in his pleasantly crazy way, striding barefoot on the gravel as if he was wearing shoes. He carried a six-pack under his arm. I glanced curiously about. The houses were mostly ranchers, most of them in need of a paint job. The back yards with their sparse grass looked neglected. No flower beds. But it was quiet and peaceful. Three children playing on a tire swing in a back yard broke the stillness momentarily as they laughed companionably. A slim young man around thirty years old with black shoulder-length hair and a pretty woman holding hands approached us.

"Hi Jack. How you doing?"

"This is Sly and Linda. They live in that house just there." Jack pointed to the first house on the Reserve, the one next to the black top. Jack introduced me, "This is your new neighbour, Diane. She lives in the big corner house on Sabiston."

I shook hands with them both, but I couldn't take my eyes off Linda. She was really beautiful. Coal black hair and dimples, and a smile that lit up her dark eyes and made them dance, and those eyes, believe me, had fire and the very essence of life in them.

"We're going up to buy some beer," said Sly.

These people and their names. *Sly?* Maybe it was a form of Native humour that was going right over my head because he looked like an honest-to-goodness sort of a guy to me. Kind of cute really, with a puckish grin and a modern shag haircut, but he had a nasty scar on his cheek. Was that from a fight? I wondered. I realized I had seen him many times from my kitchen window walking up the road and always returning with a six-pack in his hand. Always a six-pack, never a dozen beer, but he went up two or three times a day. His idea of paced drinking or what? We waved them goodbye.

"Over here, Diane," said Jack, pointing to a house overlooking the water. He strode up the steps and knocked on the door.

A handsome man in his forties opened the door and immediately laughed. "Hi there, Jack. Come on in."

"My friend Diane here, Charlie, she has quite a story for you."

"Oh, I love stories. Come on in, Diane."

I followed him into a modestly furnished living room, but it seemed bare, and I realized there were no pictures on the wall, though I could see a huge purple and white dream catcher on the kitchen wall beyond. But it was what was outside that stopped me in my tracks. "Oh my God, look at that view!" As I moved to go outside onto the deck, Charlie quickly stopped me.

"The deck isn't safe. I have to fix it."

I saw now that the deck was a shambles, planks hanging loose and some missing. But what a shame not to be able to sit out there and enjoy the fabulous view of the Gulf Islands. The deck overlooked the beach, and the sea was so close you could have thrown pebbles into the water.

Jack snapped open three beers and I was encouraged to tell my story.

"That's bad news," said Charlie when I finished. He was a handsome man with a mess of wavy black hair and a moustache, and I remembered hearing stories about early Spanish explorers being shipwrecked along the coast and mingling their Spanish genes with Coast Salish ones, which accounted for the Coast Salish curly hair and Latino-looking eyes. And this chief had a roguish charm about him, something like Anthony Quinn in *Zorba the Greek*.

"Well, Charlie, what do you think?" Jack said.

"I'll look after it, Jack," the chief said. "I'll bring it up at the next band meeting. We can't have a bunch of little punks running the show around here." He laughed cheerfully and swallowed his beer. "Where are you from?" he asked me. His voice had the soft sing-song quality peculiar to the local Indigenous people.

"I came over from Vancouver. I'm running a halfway house on the corner of Sabiston over there."

"Helping people, eh? That's good."

"I'm originally from Wales though. A Celt—one of those wild ones."

"Really. My last name is McGregor. Scottish, I guess."

"Scottish? Hey—that means you must have some Celtic blood in your veins too." We smashed our cans of beer together in a brotherhood gesture. All this time I had been aware that something or somebody was moving around in the kitchen, and I kept expecting whoever it was to pop his head around the door and say "Hi."

Now a Native lady came storming into the room from the kitchen. She was wearing a muumuu and underneath it her flesh moved like a runaway locomotive. She was a big, handsome woman with a full head of silver-streaked dark hair pulled severely back from her face. She had deep furrows like forked lightning running down her forehead, stopping on the bridge of her nose that were caused, I guessed, from too much frowning. She was frowning now. Big time.

"What nonsense are you talking about?" she asked.

I haven't a clue who had been talking nonsense, so I stayed quiet as a mouse. Jack flashed me a warning look.

"I was just telling them my last name is McGregor. What's wrong with you?" The chief was not the happy part-Celt of two minutes earlier. "This is my wife, Polly." He waved his hand as an introduction.

"You should be ashamed that your last name is McGregor. Those damn Scots brought nothing but harm to us Coast Salish. Coming here, taking our language away and pushing their Christianity down our throats. Almost wiping us out with their damned smallpox."

Holy Smoke. This woman was boiling mad. It was disturbing and intimidating to witness this raging frenzy. Instantly sobering, too.

"Well, that was a long time ago," I ventured. "We all get along now." I gave her a bright smile.

"Do we?" she said, eyeballing me with contempt. "Well, I for one will never forget. Do you know what those first bastards did when they arrived? They cut the chief's head off and used it as a football." She banged her fist on the table, and the chief jumped even higher than Jack and me. "I will never forget, and I make sure the children here will never forget. Your name is McGregor," she said, now turning her fury onto the chief, "because some white bastard *raped* your great-grandmother and that's how you got your fucking Celtic blood. What's to be proud of in that?"

"Well, Diane," said Jack, rising to his feet. "I promised Yvonne I'd take her down to Harbourside Mall this afternoon, so we best be on our way. Thanks for your help, Charlie."

We made it down the stairs and Jack grabbed my hand. We tried not to run because it would look undignified, but our feet fairly flew across the gravel road to the safety of where the blacktop began and we were within reach of the sanctuary of Jack's house.

When we were securely out of earshot, I said, gasping, "What the hell was that all about?"

"Check my back for arrows," said Jack, brave enough now to laugh.

"Arrows? I thought she was going to fucking scalp us."

"I need another drink. Christ Almighty! Sorry, Diane, I didn't expect that hornet's nest."

"Don't be sorry for me. Be sorry for the poor old chief!" We both looked back at his house for a moment of sympathy then bent over laughing until we cried.

"Oh, my God," said Jack, tears streaming down his face. "I haven't laughed like this in years. It's doing me good."

"What's going on out there?" Yvonne called from the front door. "Why are you out there laughing and hiding behind that bush? Are you going to let me in on the joke?"

"Open us up a couple of beers, dear, and we'll come in and tell you."

We sat around Jack and Yvonne's dining room table laughing and talking most of the afternoon. It was good to be with companionable people. I had spent too much time on my own, and I realized how much I was missing my Vancouver friends, my kids, and the rich social life I had left behind on the Mainland. The beer flowed. Yvonne didn't get hysterically crazy with laughter like Jack and me as we recounted our story, but then she hadn't been there.

"Do you think there was an actual incident all those years ago when the British first arrived here, and they really did decapitate a chief?" I asked Jack.

"And played football with his head? I doubt it very much," said Jack, munching from the plate of crackers, cheese and pickles that Yvonne had set out. "But if it did happen, it wouldn't be in the history books, that's for sure."

"When did the British start playing soccer anyway? I mean did they play soccer that far back?"

"You have a point there, Di," Jack chortled gleefully. "We might catch the witch in a lie. She was right about the smallpox though. Almost wiped out the Native people here on the Island in the 1860s. I know that for a fact."

"Boy, she's filled with hate. Reverse prejudice in full swing."

"Why call it reverse? Prejudice is just plain prejudice."

"Sad, isn't it, the way she said she was making sure all the kids knew. It just fuels hate. Like it only happened yesterday instead of a hundred and more years ago. By the way, what's the time, Yvonne?"

"Five o'clock."

"Oh my God, I have to make supper for the guys at Big Sab."

"Let them make it themselves—they're grown men." Jack grinned foolishly at me.

"I haven't even taken anything out of the freezer. Hot damn! Where did the afternoon go?" I stood up and suddenly felt woozy. Oh boy, I'd had too much beer. "Oh, dear—I think I'm drunk." I giggled and sat back down with a wallop. "Do you think you could make me a coffee, Yvonne?"

"Sure," she said. "Are you going to be okay?"

"Those boys over there don't drink, so I feel a bit awkward going home tipsy. I guess I'll make something simple for their dinner and then hightail it to my room."

"To hell with them. Just because *they* have a drinking problem, why shouldn't you have some fun?" Jack was slurring his words and his blue eyes twinkled at me. "Stay here and have supper with us. To hell with *them*."

"How many do you have to feed?" asked Yvonne thoughtfully.

"Just two. Lewis and Luke. But Luke can be a real prick."

"Well, I was making hamburgers for dinner. Those store-bought patties are made up already. How about if I make some up and you take a platter of them home for them? Then you're off the hook. You don't look so good, dear." She bent over me and in a motherly move fastened two undone buttons on my shirt and patted my hair down. I always pull dramatically on my hair when I drink. Don't ask me why. It makes my hair look like ruffled eagle feathers. "There you are," she said. "That looks better."

"Oh no! I didn't realize my blouse was undone. Gee, and I was wondering why the chief was inspecting my boobs so intensely."

Jack laughed heartily, slapping his thigh, tears running down his face again. "Oh my God, Diane, you were flashing the chief."

While Yvonne was cooking up the hamburgers, Jack leaned back on his chair and tipped his head toward Yvonne. "She came from a high society family in Victoria, you know, and gave up her family fortune for me."

"What do you mean?"

"Well, her parents hated me and told her if she married me they would disinherit her. We got married three weeks later." He laughed uncontrollably at this.

"Why's that so funny? She must have really loved you."

"That's what so funny," he cried. "She gave up all that money *for me!*"

I looked at Jack with his little brown pot-belly sticking out of his unbuttoned shirt and his dirty bare feet and Aussie digger hat and started laughing with him.

"Yvonne, have you ever regretted your decision?"

"You bet. Of course, she has. A thousand times," cried Jack, slapping his thigh again.

Yvonne cooked calmly, methodically flipping hamburgers. She rolled her eyes once or twice toward the ceiling, but she was smiling.

With a platter of hamburgers and dish of pickles in hand I wobbled across the road. The kitchen was empty. I saw Lewis's head bobbing by the hedge outside.

"Your dinner is on the kitchen table," I yelled, waving through the door.

Where was Luke?

I poured myself a glass of cold milk and carried it up the stairs. Just as I was opening my bedroom door, Luke came out of his bedroom.

"Hi, where've you been?"

"I was across the road at Jack and Yvonne's. We visited the Indian chief." I giggled then hastily pulled myself together. "Your supper is downstairs. It's hamburgers." I felt woozy again and hung onto the doorknob. "Hamburgers with pickles." I smiled at him fondly. Dear old Luke, he wasn't such a bad sort really. I closed my bedroom door and made my way over to the bed. "Home, home at last," I sang the words out loud. I gulped down the milk, feeling the icy cold liquid soothing my hot throat. My head was throbbing. The walls around me throbbed. Home at last. I think I heard myself sing the words out loud again. I lay down on the bed. The pillow felt cool against my hot cheeks. I kicked off my sandals and passed out.

The next day Ray Findlay phoned. Could he come over for a small visit? Would this afternoon be convenient? Now here he was knocking on my door.

"Hi Ray. Come on in."

"I need to talk to you in private." He looked over my shoulder and down the hall. "Maybe we should do this outside."

"Okay."

We walked around to the back garden. Lewis was working on the fire pit. He was a marvel at getting free stuff. He had gone down to the brick manufacturing plant a few blocks away and talked them into giving him damaged and chipped bricks. He had hauled them back to Big Sab in a borrowed wheelbarrow, the property of Sammy, a neighbour across the road, and the fire pit was growing in front of my eyes. A master of invention. A never-say-never sort of guy.

"Who is that?" asked Ray, wheezing.

"Lewis Norstrum. He's a recovering alcoholic."

"He didn't come here through our program?"

"No. But he's a great character. He's really trying."

"We have to get him to AA meetings, Diane. If he doesn't plug into the help available, he won't make it." He looked nervously around. "I really do want our conversation to be private. Maybe we should go over there by that boat."

Jack had parked his small boat at the far end of the yard up against the hedge. I looked at Ray. What the hell was this all about? Was he going to ask if I was working for the CIA? We walked to the back of the lot, and I leaned against Jack's boat.

Ray went straight for the bull's eye. No tippy-toeing around for this guy. "Diane, do you have a drinking problem?"

"A drinking problem? No." I stood up a little straighter. "I drink, though. Why?" I stared aghast at him. *What an impertinent question.* It was a little like asking me how often I had sex. None of his business, and it certainly was not what I had expected. I had thought he might tell me that Luke, that pain-in-the-butt, was a serial killer and they were transporting him out of my house.

"We've had a complaint. How much do you drink? Would you classify yourself as a social drinker?" He leaned against the hull of the boat, wheezing.

"A social drinker, yes. I like a beer with the football game. Rum and coke. Vodka." Actually I drink everything except gin, but at that particular moment I thought it was best if I kept the rest of that list to myself. "I go to pubs. What is this all about? Like who has been complaining?"

"I don't think you realize that these men can have absolutely no alcohol around them. None."

"I realize that. I haven't had alcohol in the house. I only drink away from the house, and that has only been a couple of times."

"Well, we were told that you were breathing alcohol fumes in one of the client's faces, and it really upset him. Like you were right in his face with it. He felt that maybe he shouldn't stay here anymore if you have no respect for his fight against his addiction."

It had to be Luke. The little creep. He must have smelt my breath in the hall last night. Breathing alcohol fumes in his face! My ass. Well... I guess I had been drunk... but he had only seen me in the hall for less than a New York minute.

"We are going to overlook it this time, Diane. We want you to succeed here. I just want you to be aware that, if you drink, you should have no interaction whatsoever with the men."

He was looking me up and down, sizing me up like a Catholic priest trying to figure out whether an extroverted nun was still a virgin. I decided I didn't like him. Who the hell did he think he was? Gordie Ryder had told me that Ray had spent fifteen years in jail and that a heavy-duty drug habit had damaged his lungs permanently. Thus, the inhalator. And now he was coming onto me holier than thou. Me? And I had never been arrested for anything in my life.

We went back into the house. Luke wouldn't meet my eyes, but I fancy he had a little Judas smirk on his face.

Three days later Larry arrived from the Mainland. As I told him the story, he surveyed my face carefully. "How drunk were you?" he asked brusquely.

"Tipsy. I admit I was tipsy, but geez, who the bloody hell does Ray think he is? He is questioning my private life."

"Diane, you are running a halfway house, for God's sake! Don't you think a little discretion would be a good idea?"

"Yeah, sure–from now on I'll keep mouthwash in my purse." I was mad at him for not taking my side. "Look, Larry, you get away from here. You can vent, let off steam. I'm here twenty-four seven! Give me a break. I am not going to give up my social drinking to satisfy that asshole."

"Maybe it was a mistake for you to get involved with this... Maybe running a halfway house is not a good idea if drinking is so important to you."

I stared at him with ice in my eyes. "Drinking is not so important, but my freedom to do what I want is. For Chrisake, I am not being bossed around like some juvenile delinquent kid by that damn ex-con."

I stormed out of the house and went down the road at a fast click. Damned men always want control. Seriously. Think about it. I didn't know where I was going until I saw the Patricia, the local pub, sprawled comfortably on the corner lot. It was dark in there. I blinked my eyes, trying to accustom myself to the dim light. Then I saw Linda, the lady that Jack had introduced me to. She waved for me to come over. She was sitting with some other Native ladies, and I recognized Shifty's wife, Theresa. A compact woman, sturdily built, with ample breasts and sad, dark eyes. She and Shifty had recently rented one of Larry's houses just down the road.

"Hi, Diane. What's up?" Linda was smiling, all dimples and welcome.

I sat down on the proffered chair and, don't ask me why, I found myself blurting everything out. Men. Control. Love. Loneliness. The women were so sweet and sympathetic. A beer was pushed my way, and before I knew it, I was listening to all their troubles with men as well. For some reason we laughed until we cried when Linda told us how she beat Sly up the first time she caught him cheating. He'd been true ever since... she thought. This very pretty, feminine lady had rolled up her sleeves and creamed her guy? Tossed him over the veranda rail? This was a different world where women were tough enough physically to be the boss.

An hour later the front door of the Pat opened, and Larry stood blinking like a mole in a shaft of daylight.

He finally saw me and came over.

"Hi, Linda, Theresa. How you doing, ladies? Hi, Diane."

They all smiled fondly at him, slurring a chorus of "Hi, Lar." Obviously, they all knew him well. He had spent time here before. He sat down and beckoned for the waiter.

"What does everybody want? It's my round. A double rum and coke for Diane, I bet." He winked at me and smiled sweetly at the women around the table. "That's my girl's favorite drink."

The women screamed with laughter as, with a conspiratorial wink, Larry slid a bottle of Listerine mouthwash across the scarred wooden tabletop to me.

I stared at him contemplatively across the table. One thing for certain, I'd never be able to pick up that 260-pound mass of bone and muscle and throw it over any veranda rail.

That night in bed we talked it out. I admitted I had overreacted to his remarks. I knew it. I wanted to be fair to our guys, and I would make sure I didn't breathe alcoholic fumes over them again. "But, Larry, the problem is I am on my own too much. I'm here by myself holding the fort. I know you have to leave town when you work in the bush, but when in the hell are you going to leave Phyllis?" I stared at his face pressed against the pillow and half-hidden by blankets.

His muffled answer, coated in sleep, came back surprisingly serene. "Soon, kid. I really mean it. Hang in there. I have some money issues to settle... then I'll be freed up. Try and be happy, Di. Please try." His encircling arm gave me an extra squeeze.

I stared at the ceiling and tried to figure out how wide and how comfortable the fence was that he was sitting on.

8
The Three Stooges

Our big stab at renting rooms had arrived. It was Welfare Day, also known in Nanaimo as Moving Day, and Larry and I were braced and ready. We had put an ad in the *Nanaimo Times* and a notice on the bulletin board at the Sally Ann's Nicol Street shelter. Big Sab was looking her best and all the rooms were gleaming and ready to show to prospective clients.

Lewis had already been up to the Welfare office with his application forms and had been told he could come back at 2 p.m. to pick up his first cheque. Now he was back, jubilant with the money, and had promptly paid me the $350 for his rent, his eyes fairly dancing with pleasure as he counted the money into my hands. I felt ashamed that I had experienced a fleeting moment of doubt that, with money in his jeans, he would take off, hightailing it to some pub, and leave us high and dry.

Then, all within five minutes of each other, three men had showed up looking for rooms. Now Larry was in the front bedroom interviewing the man named Scott, while I was in the kitchen interviewing the other two men. I couldn't decide which of the two was the weirder. The younger one, around twenty, short yet plump like a Christmas roasting turkey, was nervous and kept twisting his Welfare forms in his pudgy hands. He was wearing a well-worn pair of blue jeans and a XXLarge size white T-shirt. His name was Larry and he even had a "Colombo eye" like my Larry. Geez.

I turned to the second man who was around fifty years old and looked like he had escaped from the set of The Grapes of Wrath. He was wearing a dirty, stained navy suit with a matching waistcoat, and rivulets of sweat ran down his brow. Seeing it was 80 degrees outside, was he overdressed or what? A pair of broken-down dress shoes were on his feet, no socks. His name was Richard and he looked like a skid row bum, but most peculiarly he was in possession of the polished speech of an educated man. They had both walked separately the twenty-five blocks from downtown Nanaimo to arrive within minutes of each other on our doorstep.

"I have the cash right here, lady," Richard was saying with deep respect for womanhood and apple pie and God-knows-what-else resounding in his speech. "And here's my deposit." He handed me a creased Welfare form and a pile of bills. His hands were seamed with dirt and his fingers were stained yellow from nicotine. "I have one problem, though, I guess I have to tell you about." He cleared his throat, then coughed. "It's best to be up front." He looked far away and distant through the kitchen window at the ocean view as if in search of India.

"What kind of a problem, Richard?" I asked. I thought here it comes—*I used to be a serial killer.*

"Well," he said, grinning with nervousness and showing a mouth full of broken, dirty teeth. "I have a chemical imbalance problem. I have to take pills."

Totally comprehending, I stared at him. With my son Guy being a schizophrenic, I knew all about chemical imbalances.

Now Larry the kid was speaking. "I'm not an addict, but I want a safe place to stay. I've been living with my Dad, but he has a girlfriend now, and I kinda feel in the way... if you know what I mean." He smiled in a shy, boyish way, but because his eye was all over the place, I wasn't sure if he was looking at Richard or me. Or maybe out there at India. "I'm not from here," he continued. "I'm from Thunder Bay, and I just need a safe place..." His voice tapered off. He had stated his case.

I'd better get my Larry in on this, I decided. How would these two fit in? A kid who was a nervous, non-drug addict and an older guy with mental problems? I excused myself, went down the hall, knocked on the first bedroom door and went in.

A wild-looking man was sitting on the bed with Larry towering over him. The man was saying, "Yes, I had to do time for it... two years. I cut the bastard up into a million pieces with a knife. What do you think? Of course I did time."

Larry swung around in my direction.

"Can I see you a moment?" I asked, sending smoke signals with my eyes. "It won't take a minute."

When we were out in the hall, I whispered, "Geez, I thought I had two weirdos in the kitchen! What the hell have you got in there?" I pointed to the bedroom. "Did he say he'd cut a guy to pieces?"

Larry dismissed my question with an airy wave of the hand. "The guy lived," he said. "What do you want me for?"

"The two guys I have don't fit the bill. One's a schizophrenic and the young kid is just leaving home and wants a cheap, safe place to live."

Larry strode down the hall to the kitchen. "Hi, guys, my name is Larry." He put his hands on his hips. "So you want to come and live at Big Sab." He held out his hand and shook their hands vigorously. "Have all your Welfare forms? Got your deposits and first month's rent?"

They waved their money and forms at him, both of them dwarfed by his size and weight. He the father figure reducing them to sheepish little boys.

"Okay, guys, welcome aboard." With a flourish he stuffed the money in the back pocket of his jeans. "Diane will help you choose your rooms and give you your receipts." Then he smiled a conspiratorial friendly smile. "But, Larry, seeing my name's Larry, we have to call you something else to stop us from getting all confused around here."

A small silence.

"How about calling me Little Larry and you can be Big Larry," said the kid. *Little Larry?* The kid weighed 200 pounds and he was only 5 feet 4 inches tall!

"Yes! That will do 'er." Big Larry beamed down on Little Larry who was looking up at him like he had just met God.

I chased my Larry down the hall. "What are you doing?" I choked. "That old man is so dirty he smells—well, stinks!—and that kid is just a normal kid, except he's weird. They don't belong here."

"We have to get this house filled up, Diane." He was stern and silent for a moment, eyeballing me like I was a new Foreign Legion recruit that he'd just realized might not survive in the desert heat. "It will work out. Don't worry. Come on, help me interview this guy. He's a little uptight. Just got out of the can, but he seems all right."

"Larry," I whispered outside the bedroom door, "I just heard him say he had attacked someone with a knife. We agreed we wouldn't take violent men."

"Come in and talk to him. You'll see. You'll like him." And with that he pushed me into the room. And that's how I met Scott.

Scott was also streaming with perspiration. It was stinging his eyes, and he was using a clean white handkerchief to mop it up. His face was flushed red, and he looked hot and miserable. He had a shock of black hair oiled back and eyes like a raven's—black, bright and inquisitive. He was dressed in khaki shorts and a black T-shirt, spotlessly clean. He had a large haversack sitting by his sandaled feet on the floor, and I noticed that his toenails were neatly manicured.

He stood as I entered the room and offered his hand. All manners. An officer and a gentleman. "Scott Anderson. Pleased to meet you, Diane."

I cut straight to the chase.

"So, Scott, Larry tells me you're just out of jail and that you were in for attacking a man."

"That's right. I was in for two years."

"I have to say that worries me, Scott. I mean, do you have an anger management problem? A drug problem? Can you explain why this happened?" I hoped I was sounding like a professional in-charge kind of dame. I actually felt afraid of the man.

"It's a long story but I appreciate you have to ask. The guy I attacked actually came into my bedroom in the dark at night, and I thought he was going to attack *me*. He was one son of a bitch, a real asshole. Sorry, excuse my French, Diane." He smiled apologetically at me. "Anyway, this guy was trouble and had beaten up other tenants in the house, stealing off them, the whole works, and I had decided I wasn't going to be one of his victims. So I always made sure I took a knife to bed with me in case he tried anything on me. When he did try it, I was ready. I was drinking heavily in those days. An accumulation of personal problems and what with this bastard on my case..." This whole confession had started the perspiration rolling down his face again, and he began energetically mopping it up with his handkerchief. He looked like he was testifying in a witness box in court and desperately trying to convey his perspective on the truth.

Larry came to his rescue. In a soothing tone he said, "Well, Scott, thanks for being so honest. We just have to know who we're accepting under our roof. I hope you feel comfortable here and make it as much a home as you can. Now if you have your Welfare forms and your first month's rent and your deposit, we can sign you in." Scott handed over the money and the forms, a shuddering sigh emitting from his lips. His ordeal over. Acceptance and a room of his own. He looked weak with relief.

When Larry and I were out of earshot, I stared at him accusingly. I was feeling slightly dizzy and a little surreal. All of this was too far out in left field for me.

But Larry was all smiles. "Our best day ever." Chortling with glee, he happily counted out the money, deftly putting the bills in order. My stony looks unnoticed, flying right over his head. Instead, he reached out and lifted me into a bear hug, his arms squeezing the breath out of me.

"We have some money and we are going to celebrate! I am taking you to the Jolly Miner Pub for lunch." And with that, he grabbed the keys off the desk and headed outside for the truck.

The Jolly Miner was one of the oldest pubs in Nanaimo. It had a list on the wall of the first passengers coming from Britain to Nanaimo to work in the coal-mines. According to that list, in 1851 an Indigenous man dubbed Chief Tyee or the Coal Chief told a Hudson Bay clerk, one Joseph McKay, about the presence of coal in Nanaimo, and the first twenty-four miners and their families set sail for Vancouver Island three years later. The ship, the Patricia Royal, had taken six months to sail around the Horn, enduring horrific storms, and not all the passengers had survived. Travelling by sea was certainly a life or death proposition in those days.

As we left the house, I saw my son Guy coming up the dusty road. It was taking him a long time as he was lost in thought, concentrating on circling each tree he came to on the road allowance six times in a strange compelling ritual. Unfortunately, he had no insight that he was schizophrenic, and we fought constantly over his refusal to take his meds.

"Hurry up, Guy," Larry shouted. "I'm treating you and your mum to fish and chips at the Jolly Miner."

Guy waved and speeded up. Only two more trees left, thank the Lord. He looked unkempt and his shirt was inside out. Larry threw a casual arm around him and thumped his back affectionately.

"How are you doing, Guy old man?"

Larry was great with Guy. His own brother had schizophrenia, and so he was comfortable around him and accepting of an illness that many other people skirt with fear. Of course, seeing that Guy looked a lot like Rasputin with his long unkempt hair and neglected beard, you really couldn't blame them—society, that is—for standing back. You had to look deep underneath to see the gentleness of the man, appreciate the mischievous humour that had somehow survived his illness and register that the brown eyes were beautiful and kind.

We piled into the old Ford truck and hurtled towards the pub. As we bumped along, Guy fingered the compass that always hung around his neck. (He thought he was in charge of the weather and took his job seriously.) I grinned at Larry as the broken springs jiggled us up and down, and he waved gaily and honked the horn at a group of men from the Reserve as we passed them on the road. One of them, Shifty, was staggering from one side of the road to the other. (Why he deserved such an incriminating name I never discovered.) But why, I asked myself, was he so drunk this early in the day? He almost landed in the ditch as he shouted at Larry and waved his arms for us to slow down.

As we passed, I heard him shouting, "Rats! Rats!"

"What the hell is he saying?" I asked Larry.

"Oh, they have mice. I keep forgetting to go and over and check it out."

"Then why is he shouting 'Rats'?"

"Who knows?" said Larry, winking at me. "Maybe the more he drinks the bigger the mice get. Ho, ho, ho." Larry loved laughing at his own jokes.

But we all broke up with laughter. Geez, Larry could be so funny.

I thought of the fish and chips that would be waiting for us. The fish would be in thick, deeply battered, golden brown pieces, the chips just right, and Guy started chanting in anticipation, "Fish and chips, fish and chips!" Larry and I joined in, "Fish and chips, fish and chips!" The three of us bounced in unison over the rough, pot-holed road, but we were happy as three skylarks when we pulled up outside the Jolly Miner pub's door.

Maybe it was a good day after all. The fact three rooms had just been rented was good. The uneasiness I was feeling that they had been rented to three weirdos was something that for the moment I chose to ignore.

There is always a bigger picture. Why ruin a great lunch?

9
Lewis Meets Louise

I was waiting up for Lewis and Luke. They had gone to an NA picnic in Ladysmith, and I had told them they could stay out until 12:30 a.m. Now where the hell were they? The house was quiet. I prowled from the kitchen to the living room drinking coffee. It seemed absurd in a way, these grown-up men having a teenager's curfew, but those were the John Howard rules. Eleven p.m. and you were in for the night. I heard a car in the driveway and Lewis came bounding up the steps. He swung me off my feet.

"You should have come. You would have loved it. It was a great time. We played a lot of music, and I've met the girl I'm going to marry."

He put me down on my feet.

"What do you mean—marry?"

"So help me God, Diane, she's the one. That's why we're late. We gave her a ride home."

"Goodnight, Diane," Luke was trudging up the stairs as if he was going to his execution.

"What's up with him?" I asked

"Oh, he's blue. He's missing Joanne, and his nose is out of joint because I've found a girl. *The perfect girl.*"

Lewis strode into the kitchen and poured a coffee. I followed behind. He was on a roll. We both plunked down on chairs at the kitchen table.

"She's beautiful, part Native, part Mexican, long hair, beautiful eyes, but that's not it. We went down by the water and talked all evening long. Diane, she's my soul mate. I feel I've known her all my life. Wait until you meet her. You'll fall in love with her, too."

"Well," I said, thinking out loud, "what can I say? I've done it myself. Fallen in love at first sight." I gulped down my coffee and stared at him over the rim of my cup—nodding in response to the question in his eyes. "Yeah, Larry. Who else? In Murphy's, the neighbourhood bar next to my office. It was like *Cheers* in there. You know, where everybody knows your name. Except I had never seen him before, even though we had both been going in there for years. So it was sort of like fate. These friends I worked with insisted I go in for one beer after work. I wanted to go home because I was tired, but they dragged me into the pub—and there he was. Sitting one table over. Zing! Lightning struck."

"Like right away, the lightning?" Lewis eyes crinkled, inviting the story.

"Almost. He stood up and unsolicited... Can you believe this? He recited to the whole bar Robert Service's 'The Spell of the Yukon.' You know the one? 'I wanted the gold, and I sought it, I scrabbled and mucked like a slave...' That one. Then after that, or I guess during it, I felt the lightning. I felt like you do now, I guess. I've found him! The 'one.'" I felt a rush of the old emotion at the memory. "Oh, Lewis, I hope she's your 'one.'" I pushed back my chair and, reaching over, impulsively hugged him. He smelt of Old Spice and cigarette smoke. "I'm going to keep my fingers crossed."

He talked into my hair as we hugged. "I'm going to court her like crazy. I'm going to woo this girl, this lady. And I'm going to ask her to marry me. And I'll keep asking her until she says yes."

We pulled away, both a little moist-eyed, smiling at each other. I raised both my hands, showing my fingers crossed on both hands. We sat up talking until late that night, swapping stories and laughing together. For the first time I could see hope and more in his eyes. And for the first time I felt real hope *for* him. Maybe Lewis had found something powerful to fight for and powerful enough to hold onto him.

10
Inmates

Luke decided to go back to live in Vancouver, and I must admit I was relieved to see him go, but within three weeks Gordie Ryder had placed another two young men with us. Tom and Rick had come from the Wilkinson Jail, and they were to complete their sentences under house arrest, which meant they could only go as far as the veranda on the front of the house and the fire pit in the garden at the back without causing an alarm from their ankle bracelets to emit a signal. I felt sorry for them. They were so confined. I felt they would be almost better off in prison with the large grounds to move around in.

They were two very different men. Tom was a good-looking, quiet Indigenous man, while Rick was a tall, thin, nervous youth with long blond hair and a twitching, jack rabbit personality. Like at any moment he would bolt.

The following week Ray Findlay placed one of his old chums from years back with us. They had, in fact, gone to school then prison together. His name was Wayne, but he was nicknamed the "Little Professor." Apparently his gig was stealing rare and antique books, hence the name.

In the meantime, our three weirdos, our very own three stooges, had somehow become three of the most popular clients at Big Sab. Richard turned out to be a sweetheart. He had been only twenty-three years of age, a professional engineer and happily married, when schizophrenia had claimed him. He had lost his marriage and his career but was still in touch with his wonderful mother who was now in her seventies. She visited him faithfully every month from Victoria, bringing him care packages of food and little gifts of socks and underwear.

Little Larry with his calm and steady approach to life was a gem. Nothing ever ruffled his feathers. And as he was so good-natured and generous, the drug addicts loved having him around, and he often ran out for McDonald's burgers, KFC chicken or cigarettes for our ankle bracelet prisoners. He worked part-time at his dad's property management business doing janitorial work, and in a constant losing battle to take off weight, he walked everywhere, but always with his head down as he walked so that he would pass you on the road without realizing you were there. Why he wasn't brained by a tree or didn't smack into a Hydro pole was a mystery. The other guys loved to tease him because he always found things on his travels and would come home with his pockets stuffed with the most unusual treasures—a little beaded moccasin purse, a glass figurine, items people had either discarded or lost. When he walked in the door, we all loved discovering what he had found that day.

But as it turned out, Scott was our Main Event Walking Contradiction, one of our best clients though our most unpredictable. He was almost forty but looked younger, maybe because he was so full of energy. Though taut and nervous his first week at Big Sab, as most of the guys were when coming off a two-year stretch, he quickly adjusted to civilian life. I would find him all showered and oiled for sunbathing and looking like a sleek cat stretched out on a towel on the back lawn. He had a way of pushing up his sunglasses and smiling lazily at me, those black eyes of his with their impenetrable depths, and his thick black hair slicked back reminding me of Rudolph Valentino. "Just like an old-time movie," I would hum, staring at him out the kitchen window as I washed dishes. His white prison skin had quickly turned to a golden brown. His crisp white shorts, his manicured hands, his attitude, and his sunbathing pose suggested he was on holiday on the French Riviera instead of a halfway house for junkies. Luxuriating in his surroundings, turning Big Sab into a holiday resort in his mind, effortlessly creating his own world, his own cocoon.

He was always the first one up, cheerfully making the first coffee of the day, the rich smell pleasantly waking us all up. He was one of the few men who volunteered daily to help with the housework. His own room looked like a monk's cell, immaculate with an almost Spartan sense of order. Fastidiously clean. Clothes laundered and folded with precision. Books on philosophy piled on his bedside table within easy reach for late night reading. But he was like an actor portraying a man who possessed an inner sense of peace and love for mankind, the secrets of the universe lurking behind his smile, yet I knew there was another Scott. The real one was far more complex and troubled. He was an intellectual and one of the best-read people to cross my path, the answer to every question spilling so easily from his lips that some of the guys viewed him as an arrogant know-it-all bastard. And it was true he could be quite patronizing to the poor diminished savages at his feet, but to me he was a delightful walking encyclopedia.

"Do you know when the Brits started to play soccer, Scott?"

"Eton established the first official rules in the early 1800s... I think around 1815. Then the Cambridge rules were adopted. Before that, the game had been outlawed because so many people were hurt. I guess they were playing a barbaric form of the game without rules—almost like war games."

Wow—he knew!

How do you make marmalade? Who is the president of Chile? Is Mickey Mantle dead? Where is Timbuktu? He knew! He knew, he knew, *he knew!*

Yet notwithstanding all of this intelligence, he had a self-destructive streak within him so savage that when it surfaced even he didn't expect it. And he harboured a rage that was disguised from us all, sheathed as it was in a subtle caustic humour. Yet he could be so generous and so gracious. When he received his first welfare cheque, he arrived back at Big Sab with two massive packages of chicken legs. He marinated them in a secret herbal coating then wrapped them with strips of bacon secured with toothpicks and cooked them until the house was groaning with the appetizing smells. Then he arranged them on a platter complete with scattered parsley sprigs, set the whole works on the kitchen counter with a neat pile of white paper napkins and a note saying, "Free chicken snacks. Please enjoy." The others were completely taken aback. Usually food was hoarded, so this was a gesture that had the guys at Big Sab baffled.

From the beginning he and I shared a rapport. He had an off-the-wall personality, an unfettered spirit, and I loved hanging out with him and especially loved laughing with him as his humour was absolutely wicked. He was genuine when he told me he wanted to settle down and would love to have a family. "It's still not too late, Di." He wanted to love someone almost desperately, but where would this lonely heart hunter find a worthy place to bestow his stored passion? He had a gifted, accomplished mind that had taken too many wrong turns. Sometimes, catching him lying in the grass, staring intently at the night sky, I sensed the stars alone might be the only compass left that could guide him back to earth. He seemed so isolated as if stranded by a Milky Way fiasco, a possessor of a lost-in-space traveller's status. Relationships capsized, relatives gone, he had long ago severed ties with his wealthy Shaughnessy family.

This exile now in my home was gradually endearing himself to me with a genuine, conscious effort. Like a peacock spreading the glory of its feathers for attention, Scott displayed his flair, his style and his genius. He was out to gain my confidence, but more than that, he wanted my approval, my friendship. He had fully recognized before I was even aware that I, too, was a lost traveller, one of his stargazing clan, one of his tribe.

11
The Five-Year Cake

Everybody at Big Sab, except the guys with ankle bracelets, was going to the NA meeting for the presentation of Gord Ryder's five-year cake. Gord was a real favourite at Big Sab. He called in almost every day, had time for everybody and always brought an upbeat positive attitude and a cool way of communicating with the guys.

Now they were trying to persuade me to go with them.

"I feel I would be trespassing," I said, "like I was spying on addicts on their hallowed ground."

"Don't be silly, Diane. Anyone can go," said Scott. "Anyway, you should go and introduce yourself to the NA crowd so the recovering community know who you are."

That made sense, so I hurried and threw on some lipstick and my coat.

The NA used the Fireman's Hall for their meetings, and it was packed on this night. For such a small town, Nanaimo sure had its share of addicts, I thought, but then, I guessed, maybe every town does. Gordie was surrounded by people, but he waved across the room just before the meeting started.

Gordie made a heartwarming, funny speech before his cake was presented to him to thunderous applause, and it suddenly came to me with a bit of a shock that he had only been clean for five years. *Only five years!* Just then a weird, hollow voice from somewhere behind me started talking. I couldn't see the person, but it was obviously a woman, and she sounded like the Phantom of the Opera, a disembodied voice droning on and on.

"Who the hell is that?" I asked Jim, a friend of Luke's, sitting beside me.

"That's Gordie's wife, Joan."

Immediately I was full of curiosity. I strained my head and finally saw a thin, hard-faced, middle-aged woman sitting at the back of the hall. She was dressed in the black outfit of a motorcycle gang, leather pants and jacket, but it was her voice that was disturbing. She sounded soulless, like the living dead. What was she saying?

"It's hard and sometimes you want to give in," she said, "but I know I will die if I go back... and I have to keep on trying..." No inflection or emotion in her voice. Why wasn't she sitting with Gord on his special night? That's when I noticed a young girl who looked a dead ringer for Gordie sitting by his side, leaning into him and occasionally whispering into his ear.

I nudged Jim. "Who's that?"

"Gord's daughter. She's a recovering addict as well."

"What! She looks like she's no more than sixteen."

"She is."

After the meeting was over, I went up and congratulated Gordie. "Hey, that was quite a speech, and you are quite the comedian," I said, laughing. "Congratulations."

He was stiff and polite. "Thanks, Diane. Nice of you to come out." Other people came up, and he turned away from me. I felt confused. Why was he being so unfriendly? I turned around and almost bumped into his wife. She had been standing right behind me.

"Oh sorry... Hi... I'm Diane Foley from Sabiston Lodge. Your husband has been a great help to us."

She took my proffered hand, said a curt, "Pleased to meet you," turned and strode out the door, a motorcycle helmet swinging in sync with her stride. She was certainly not the kind of woman I would have expected Gordie to have as a mate. Well, I thought, what sort of woman did you expect him to have married? And I baffled myself because I realized I had absolutely no idea.

12
Listen to the Music

One afternoon Lewis arrived with a friend to ask if he could rent a room. Ken didn't have a drinking or drug problem but needed a place to stay. Of course, Larry immediately said "yes" accompanied by his usual "show-me-the-money" line.

Ken was a sunny, good-natured young man who loved to laugh and joke. He had a guitar, and I always knew when he was home because his cowboy boots would be sticking out of his upstairs bedroom window, and country and western music would be drifting out onto the street. Often he would be singing along to his favorite songs, and boy, did he have a great voice.

Ken's problem was that until recently he'd been a big, overweight guy weighing almost 350 lbs. *A really fat man.* He had lost the weight over a year earlier and would be considered by many to be just a regular big guy now, but he didn't see it that way. When he looked in the mirror, he didn't see the sparkling Irish blue eyes and black wavy hair, the devil-may-care cleft chin or the manly frame. He still saw a fat man. Consequently he was shy and insecure and blushed if an attractive woman paid him attention. Or even if an unattractive woman did. And sometimes when he was nervous, he would stutter.

Ken was obviously into aircraft as he had a large model of one on his table and a framed picture of a Spitfire on his bedroom wall, and one day when we were chatting, he mentioned that his father had been quite a hero in the RCAF. He had been written up in the history books and was one of the pilots assigned to fly the Queen when she visited Canada.

"Where are your parents now?"

"Here in Nanaimo. We were raised in Ottawa and my brother and sister still live back there. Mum's great, but none of us kids got along well with Dad. I mean, I love him but he's quite the disciplinarian." He laughed. "Very disapproving of my lifestyle. He thinks I'm a loser."

"Why a loser?"

"Oh, he wanted me to go to university. Make something of myself. I can't explain it. It's hard to have a famous father, you know. I'm happy working cleaning carpets. I pay my own way, but, of course, my living here in a halfway house just kills him." Ken laughed again. One of his big hearty laughs.

"Maybe you're doing it to bug him."

"Maybe." He grinned at me.

One day Ken came into the kitchen where I was having a quiet coffee. He was all flushed and pumped up. "They're having a talent contest at the Pat. I'm thinking of giving it a go..."

"Oh my God, that's great, Ken! Can I come and watch? When is it?"

"Tomorrow night. What song should I sing? I was thinking of that Vince Gill hit, 'The Girl with the Faraway Eyes.'"

"If you sing that song, you'll win for sure!"

"Now listen, Di, don't tell anyone here at Big Sab. I'll be nervous... you know me. You can come but no one else!"

"How about Little Larry? Just to keep me company?"

Little Larry adored Ken. Actually waited on him. Would happily run to the store to get cigarettes for him or make him coffee or do anything else he thought Ken needed. A simple case of hero-worship. And when Ken had swung a job for Little Larry at the same carpet cleaning business where he was employed, the hero worship had increased tenfold.

"Okay... but just Little Larry!"

The next day dragged. I was so excited waiting for 8 o'clock to arrive.

"I don't know what to wear. Like I don't have anything fancy." It was 7:00 p.m. and Ken was already white-faced and sweaty-palmed.

"I have just the shirt for you. Now make sure your jeans are clean." I raced upstairs and brought down one of Larry's shirts, white cotton with an open collar and slightly flowing sleeves that ended in tight cuffs around the wrist. It was a little Mexican- or Spanish-looking, you might say, but definitely a Big Man's glamour shirt. I had bought it for Larry years ago, but he had only worn it a couple of times. Ken looked at himself in the mirror, relief on his face, and he glowed.

Finally we took off down the street to the Pat. Its real name was the Patricia Hotel, and it was one of the first pubs built in Nanaimo, making it around 120 years old. Across the street and on the corner of the block, the other neighbourhood pub, the Jolly Miner, catered to the classier drinkers in the neighbourhood. They served steak and stuffed mushrooms and seafood fettuccini, while the Pat served fried chicken, hamburgers, chips and two kinds of pizza. And a pint of beer cost a dollar less at the Pat. A designer had created a collage of historical items from Nanaimo's coal mining history for the walls of the Jolly Miner, while the Pat had a frantic party atmosphere.

As the politically correct term "Indigenous" hadn't yet reached the reserve in Nanaimo where most of them lived at that time, the Indigenous people in Nanaimo still called themselves Indians as did everybody else in the South End. And they all drank at the Pat, but I rarely saw an Indigenous person *or* an Indian at the Jolly Miner. Not that they weren't welcome. I'm sure it was just that the Pat felt more like home.

The Pat had booths on a raised platform on the right-hand side as well as booths at floor level, and there were clusters of tables and chairs around the dance floor in front of the stage. The busy bar and kitchen were situated at the other end of the room. The Friday and Saturday night dances brought people from everywhere to dance up a storm. The music was great—rock and roll and country and western music reigned—and it was loud, the pace feverish. People threw themselves onto the dance floor. No modesty here as everybody shook everything they were born with and more. Native people and whites all danced together while blue tobacco smoke circled in clouds above their heads. Everyone shouted, drinks were spilt, and laughter cascaded like out of a boom box, and it was entertainment beyond to just sit there sipping on a drink and watching everybody in action. Sure, people got a little too drunk. Sure, sometimes there were fights, but it was Saturday Night Fever South End-style.

Little Larry and I parked ourselves at a table up front near the stage and sipped on our glasses of beer. Ken looked terrible. A bundle of nerves. I was starting to realize what this planned exposure to the public was costing him. Probably years off his life. His face was strained, his hair already damp with sweat.

A group of Indigenous women sitting at a side booth called me over. I recognized Theresa and Linda.

"Diane, sit here." Linda pointed to the empty spot by her side. "Guess what we're celebrating?"

"It must be something pretty good," I said, grinning at the crowded pints of beer lined up on the table. It was the habit of patrons at the Pat to order two beers at a time because your waiter might take forever to make the rounds again. It was that packed on a busy night.

"We all graduated today, our grade 12. We all did it together!" She started weeping with happiness and opened her arms to hug me. These women were completely open to their feelings and cried as easily as they laughed when the spirit moved them.

"Tell me all about it." I sat down and took the beer pushed in my direction.

"Well, they had a special course up there at that Tillicum College for us Indian women to get caught up on our grade 12... so we could get started on getting jobs. And we all passed it!" The four women around the table beamed shyly at me. "It's a *big* celebration here to-night, Diane."

"What kind of jobs will you try for?"

"We don't know," said Theresa, "but I was thinking of being a cook or something."

I wondered how, in a depressed area such as Nanaimo, a promise of jobs could become a reality. For these women with pre-school children and in all probability husbands who thought their schooling was a waste of time, it had taken tremendous sacrifice and determination to pass grade 12. I hoped they weren't going to be disappointed. I hoped the jobs would materialize for them.

"Well, here's to you all! Congratulations, ladies!" I raised my pint. Just then the MC walked onto the stage and announced the start of the contest. "Oh, I'd better go! See Ken over there? That big white guy in the fancy white shirt waving at us? He's in the talent contest tonight, and he's scared shitless. It will be his first time up singing in front of a crowd here, so make sure you cheer for him."

The talent contest started. The first contestants were two big-breasted girls in red and white slinky outfits singing, "Will You Love Me Tomorrow." They weren't bad. Then a balding man in a stained T-shirt sang, "I Walk the Line." But he was pretty drunk and wobbled on his feet, which caused everyone to scream with laughter. I kept saying after every act, "That's no competition for you," and Ken would give me a terrified look. I was just worrying that he was going to bolt for the door when the MC announced his name. Little Larry and I grabbed each other's hand under the table and hung onto each other for dear mercy. We were just as nervous and scared as Ken was.

Ken took the mike and the music began. He missed his cue. Oh agony! He had to start all over again. Then out came his voice in a croak. I hung my head and died. Then looking up at him, I locked into his stage-frightened eyes and cupped my hand around one ear to indicate that I couldn't hear.

Suddenly out it belted—"The Girl with the Faraway Eyes." His voice sweet and strong carried over the crowd. When it was over, he brought the house down. Everyone was clapping and stomping, "More, more." I could hear Linda's table thumping, the four dear hearts whistling and stomping their feet like mad. I would definitely buy them a round.

Ken looked so confused up there. Dazed. He hadn't thought to practice another song. I shouted over the crowd's madness, "'Ruby!" for the song "Raven Hair and Ruby Lips" by the Eagles. I had heard him singing it a hundred times, and off he went. What a hit! When he sat down, Little Larry and I pounced on him, hugging him and laughing all at once. He was trembling like a leaf, still shaking, pulsating with nerves, downing half a pint as quickly as his throat could swallow. But there was a shine in his eyes I had never seen before. It was Show Business grabbing him by the vocal cords. He had heard applause and it had been for him, and that sound was more gratifying than flying any Queen around Canada.

He won the talent contest. They gave him a T-shirt with "The Pat Pub" written on it, but it was his confusion at all the female attention he received that night that I loved the most. From then on, Little Larry and I had a new hobby—following Ken around to local karaoke nights and talent contests. We became groupies.

13
Movie Star Hairdos

It was Welfare Day. Everybody at Big Sab was happy and smiling, with money in their jeans. Scott had announced the night before that he would cut and style anybody's hair for the sum of $5. Now it was 1 p.m., the time he had said he would start, and already there was quite a lineup in the kitchen. I reflected for a moment if it was wise to be around him with scissors in his hand. This being a man who had served time for cutting someone up? But when I saw the array of professional tools lined up on the kitchen table complete with a big green hairdresser's bib, I relaxed. Apparently in another life and before prison Scott had held a job as a stylist in a high-profile beauty salon in Vancouver.

"Who's first?" He waved his scissors.

Grinning, Lewis waved his hand and climbed into the chair.

"Now," said Scott seriously, devilment dancing in his eyes, "you can choose who you want to look like. What or who will it be, Lewis?"

"Make him look like the Sundance Kid, you know, Robert Redford," I cried, getting right into the mood.

"Yeah, sure, go for it, Scott." Lewis was laughing. "Robert Redford would be fine."

Snip, snip, the blond hair fell rapidly. Scott standing back, looking, snip, snip. It took ten minutes. We all stared in amazement. There was the Sundance Kid!

"Gee, me next!" I yelled and jumped into the chair, anxious as all hell for the make-over.

"Yes, Diane?" he said, arching his eyebrows with the question.

"Sigourney Weaver, the way she looked in Alien." Scott stood back, examining my face.

"Well, can you do it? Too much of a challenge?"

"Diane!" he mocked. "Ye of little faith."

Off he went, snip, snip. Everyone crowded around, grinning and watching. When he was finished, I ran to the mirror. It was startling. Now all I had to do was lose some weight and find a spaceship. The gang were wolf whistling at me.

"Gee," said Larry, "can I ask you for a date? Before any of these other guys start booking you up."

"It will depend on how you look when Master Scott finishes with you," I said, enjoying all the nonsense.

My son Guy pushed himself awkwardly forward without being asked and solemnly climbed into the chair. "Keith Richards," he said. Larry and I grinned at each other. Guy had every record the Rolling Stones had ever made.

"Good choice, Guy," said Scott seriously and went to work. We all gasped at the transformation. Guy's messy shoulder-length hair had vanished, and here he was, ten minutes later, Keith Richards, even with the one unruly lock of hair falling over his eye. Fascinated with himself, he couldn't stay away from the hall mirror, twisting and gesturing. Then grinning like a Cheshire cat, he plunked his $5 on the table. "Thanks, Scott. Okay, I'm off." I watched him through the window loping down the road.

"I think he's gone to buy a guitar!" I said, and we all laughed.

Now Larry. We argued over whether it would be Drew Carey or Brian Dennehy. Brian won out. "Okay," I said, inspecting the finished work. "I'm definitely on for that date. You look adorable!"

Larry almost blushed. "Oh shucks, Sweetie Pie," he drawled.

Then Richard shuffled up. Amazingly, he arrived in a pair of gaudy purple walking shorts with a mismatched floral shirt blazing with orange and pink daisies. Where had this outfit come from? Maybe he had gone shopping at the Goodwill store for summer togs. His legs were hairless and chalk white. The guys whistled at him and he grinned self-consciously, showing his missing teeth.

"I know exactly what I should do for you, Richard," cooed Scott, and whistling softly through his teeth, he went to work. He was doing a thorough job, I noticed, watching from behind Richard's head, even tidying up Richard's ragged moustache.

When he was finished, I was aghast. I shook my fist at Scott behind our new look-a-like Hitler's back. But Richard, full of trust and unsuspecting, was delighted. He paid his $5, wobbled off the chair and was off to seek new adventures with his new look and bare bony knees. I worried how large and pro-active the Zionist Society in Nanaimo was.

"Don't worry," Scott hooted. "I'll fix his look tomorrow." He bent over laughing. "*I promise*, I promise! I will fix it tomorrow."

"You're a perverse bastard, Scott!" I said through clenched teeth, but now that Richard had vacated the kitchen, I realized that Larry and Lewis were holding up the wall in stitches, Larry with tears running down his cheeks. Even our new client, Ron, who was usually so serious, was holding his sides and going, "Oh, oh, my God. That is the funniest thing I've seen since..." He couldn't even finish his sentence.

"You're *all* bastards," I said with my hands on my hips. "It's not funny! It's not..." But it was too late. I could feel the laugh bubbling up from deep within, and before long I collapsed on the floor laughing as Larry—or was it Brian Dennehy—choked, "As though it wasn't bad enough for you to do his hair, you had to do his moustache as well!"

14
The Sundance Kid

Lewis was outside on the back porch, smoking. Since the fun hair-cutting day he seemed to look more and more like the Sundance Kid. Maybe he was cultivating the look. His dark blond hair, short and wavy, was brushed back off his face. He had gone to the Goodwill store and bought himself blue jeans and a white denim cowboy shirt. Tonight, his family—his dad and step-mum and sister, Nairie—were coming to visit for the first time. We had been forewarned they would be bringing guitars and it would be a night of music and song. From Lewis's stories they seemed like a regular loving family. They were originally from New Zealand, and his Dad had remarried when his children were young to a part-Maori woman who Lewis adored and considered his "real" mother.

I joined him leaning on the rail. "You never wear that flamingo shirt anymore."

"What shirt is that?"

"You know... that shirt you wore the first time I saw you. Turquoise with pink flamingoes. I thought you were gay, so help me."

"Gay? Like hell you did." We both immediately laughed. We had that, Lewis and me. An easy, intimate, fun-loving rapport between us. "That shirt happened to be my cleanest dirty shirt that day. I was trying to impress you."

"With pink flamingoes? Give me a break. You even batted your eyelashes at me."

"That's because you were batting your eyelashes at me." We laughed harder.

"Seriously, what's up? Why the glum face?"

He turned towards me squinting, the sunlight in his eyes making the golden flecks of his irises glitter.

"Oh, I just wish I had my boots." He scuffed his shoes in the dirt. "I don't feel dressed right without them."

I studied his face. I'd heard a lot about these boots. They were in a pawnshop in Parksville, up the highway north of Nanaimo where he used to live with his family.

"How much would it cost to get them out?" I knew this conversation was leading down a one-way street. Straight to my pocketbook.

"Twenty-five dollars, but they're worth two hundred bucks. They're real leather. I was a fool to pawn them."

I had discovered that in Nanaimo's South End everything gets pawned the week before payday, Welfare day. You would see multitudes of people on the street carrying TVs, stereo systems and everything but the kitchen sink up to the pawnshops for cash. When I first arrived in Nanaimo, I said, "What is this? There's a pawn shop on every corner here," but everybody mistook my accent and thought I had said, "*a porn shop on every corner,*" which caused a big hoot. The pawnshops were a new weird way for desperate people to borrow money, a twentieth-century twist on the Shylocks of old.

But I had never heard of anyone pawning their boots before.

I looked over at Lewis again. He was staring off into space, being careful not to give me any pleading looks that could possibly have hardened me.

"Okay, let's go and get them, but you have to pay me back when you get your cheque. I really will have to have the money back."

Lewis raced over and hugged me. I always had misgivings about being worked over by him, but he had an irresistible boyish charm, and I enjoyed his good-natured fun. Compared to some of the other guys in the house, he was easy to be around, always laughing or humming a tune. I hated to see him down.

When he came out of the pawnshop, he immediately pulled his boots on, tossing his old runners into the back of the truck. The boots didn't look so special or so hot to me. Just worn-looking, plain brown leather cowboy boots. But he sang and laughed all the way back to Nanaimo. Mainly Tom Jones songs like "Delilah."

"Are you singing Tom Jones songs because I'm Welsh?"

"No, darling Diane, I'm singing Tom Jones because you paid for my boots... and well, yes, because you're Welsh."

He sure knew how to get around me. I wanted to say to him, "Please don't tell Larry about me lending you the money," but I felt it would be compromising myself if he thought I would keep secrets from Larry. At the time it didn't dawn on me he would never tell our secret in a million years, that he knew all about conspiracy and how not to reveal a source.

When his parents arrived, I was taken aback. They were so sweet and dear, such genuine people, and his stepmother was a riot.

"Oh, us Maoris used to keep you white men on the hoof, you know?"

No, I didn't. What the hell did that mean? Hoof?

"We used to be nomads. We captured you white guys and herded you like cattle. Take you around with us, fence you in cages during the night, so when we killed you for food, you'd be nice fresh meat." Her brown eyes were dancing and sparkling when she said this. Obviously she wanted to get a rise from us and have some fun with her horror story. So I asked, "Do you have any white man recipes? You know, old family favourites that you would trade with me for some Welsh ones? Or I'm really good with Mexican food as well." Of course, she loved that and immediately fell in love with my sense of humour.

I don't really know what I was expecting from Lewis's parents. As I said, I was surprised by how normal they were and how they obviously loved him so much. Lots of warm hugs and his Dad's eyes lighting up every time Lewis entered the room. How did a favoured son with such loving family support fall so far? His father, a tall, pleasant man, a small-time businessman with a worried face, cornered me in the kitchen. "Thank you for trying to help my son," he said. "I can't figure out why he gets himself in such dire straits. He's an intelligent fellow. Has a great personality, everybody likes him. Seriously, everybody. He was top salesman at the car dealership almost every month he worked there. It doesn't make sense. He was always such a good kid."

Scott appeared in the kitchen and broke up our conversation, so Mr. Nordstrum patted my arm and went back to the living room.

But it was Lewis's sister, Nairie, who commanded all the attention. She was stunningly pretty. A knock-out. Her hair was thick, rich auburn and fell to her shoulders. Her green eyes were almost too large, dominating her face. She was tall, almost as tall as Lewis, she had a generous figure, and her white blouse was cut low enough to show tanned cleavage. She was mesmerizing. I couldn't take my eyes off her. She had a way of throwing back her hair and laughing a husky belly laugh that made you want to laugh with her. I could see the guys buzzing around her. She was the jar of sticky honey.

All of the Nordstrom family played instruments and immediately got down to business. We crowded into the living room, some of the guys sitting on the floor. I was expecting an amateur performance night, but instead Big Sab rocked. We were all stamping and hollering and joining in the singing of well-known songs—"Good morning, America, how are you" and Neil Diamond's "Cracklin' Rosie." I kept catching Larry's eye across the room, and we would grin at each other. It was one of those wonderful nights when Big Sab felt like a real home, and all of our guys there were happy and content. It was late when our guests left.

"What a wonderful family you have," I told Lewis. "Your dad is great. And your stepmother, Sue, is such a warm, loving person. Maybe a little crazy, you know. Her cannibal stories! But she was so much fun. And can she ever play that guitar! Your whole family is so musical. They think the world of you, Lewis." I realized I was doing all the talking so I shut up.

There was a silence as he dragged on his cigarette, blowing out the smoke in a swirl around his head. We were standing on the back porch overlooking the little fire-pit it had taken him all those hours to build. We had lit a fire there earlier that evening, and the embers were still glowing. A little white, twisty smoke still drifted up.

"I know... Mum loves to freak out people with her Maori stories." There was a long silence then he said, "I haven't told you this yet, Diane, but my older brother was killed in a truck accident three year ago up on the Island Highway outside of Courtenay. It broke their hearts. Well, broke all our hearts. Nothing has been the same since. It's like we're all living like robots now. We can't seem to get plugged back in. It was after that... Brad getting killed... that I went from heavy drinking to cocaine." He gave a short bitter laugh. "Boy, he'd love that. Brad, I mean... me blaming my drugs on him."

"You were on drugs? You never told me that. I thought it was just the booze with you."

"Yeah. Booze. But drugs as well. Cocaine mainly... until I ran out of money. Then I downgraded back to booze. I had a good job at a car-dealership, top salesman of the month, all that sort of thing, and then I got into cocaine and lost it all. The job, the house, the marriage... the kids."

"You've been married?" I was thrown off balance. Marriage? Drugs? And I had thought I knew this guy.

"Yeah. I have two little kids, they'd be four and six now. I don't have visiting rights. My wife has custody. She's living with a guy right now. Apparently, a decent sort, good job, etcetera."

"Lewis, I can't believe you were on drugs. You're too smart for that shit."

He laughed a short hard laugh, "Diane, what has smart got to do with it? I had a load of money, met up with a fast crowd, and believe you me, cocaine is very fashionable in the higher echelons of society. They're snorting it up their noses, going at it like bitches in heat."

"How come you lost visiting rights? That's pretty harsh." I mean, really, what could he have done to deserve that?

"Maybe I deserved to lose my kids. Before my wife and I broke up, I was into cocaine pretty bad. I was totally paranoid, freaked out. I thought everybody was out to get me. I wouldn't leave the house. I ended up packing a gun, and there I would be running up and down the stairs, hiding behind curtains. If anyone came to the door, I was ready to shoot their heads off. I scared the kids and my wife to death." He dragged on his cigarette, "I don't blame Lisa for not wanting me near the kids, for divorcing me. She hung in there with me longer than I ever deserved. She's a good lady, real pretty on top of that."

"But if she realized you were clean now; wouldn't she give you a break?"

"I don't think so... I've promised to clean up before. She doesn't believe me anymore. I'm a fuck-up, Diane. You don't really know me. I wish with all my heart I could be a better person for the people who care for me. I think the world of my mum and dad, but I'm hurting them more than Brad dying with all this shit I lay on them. The drinking, the drugs." He tapered off. "I keep trying and I keep right on going back to it... to the shit."

"But you're getting better," I said. "You all had fun tonight, and there will be other nights and weeks and years. You will have more wonderful times together, Lewis. You will make it all up to them and more."

I instinctively reached over and hugged him to me. He felt taut and uncomfortable, and he pulled away from me after a moment.

"You're right. What the hell am I doing spoiling a great night anyways?" There was a note of something in his voice that I couldn't quite identify. Sorrow? Bitterness? What was it? A long time afterwards I realized it was probably hopelessness I was hearing. It was the sound of him telling me that I would never understand. I had never been high on drugs. Never felt the ecstasy or the rush. I didn't have a clue what he was struggling with... or missing.

He turned away, the half-light shining off the porch catching the gold gleam of his hair. "It was a great night. Thanks for everything, Di."

I watched him walking back into the house, shoulders hunched, the light from the kitchen window catching him before he closed the door. His new blue jeans and denim shirt, a natural frontier swagger in his walk. A cowboy in the new Wild West fighting for what? His life, I guess. It was a staggering thought.

I stared off into the night. Jesus. Lewis of all people had been running around with a loaded gun?

A light gust off the ocean swirled the willow tree gently and made me shiver in the dark. I felt disturbed and uneasy, my good mood shedding off me as if I had been pushed and held under cold water. It was true what Gordie Ryder had said. Death was out there waiting and stalking these guys. Stalking them while they were down in the dirt struggling to get back on their feet and recover from their ruined lives. A vulnerable moment, a slip, a slackness in their resolve, and death was waiting to spring on them and take them down. These drugs and the power of them, the pain from them that spilled over into innocent lives. I was glad I'd sprung the $25 for his boots even if I'd never see the cash again. It had made him so happy for a while.

As I turned to go into the house, I saw the twinkling lights of the Pat beckoning from the corner, and I thought I'd kill for a dry vodka martini right then. A double. Straight up with two honking big olives. Or a rum and coke. Dark black rum. I abruptly turned my back and went back into the house. Disturbing, wasn't it, how much I felt like I needed a fix?

15
The Old Codger

"Diane," Larry called as I walked in the door. He was just hanging up the phone, and his bags were at his feet, packed ready to go. "I just had a call from a social worker at Nanaimo General Hospital. They have an elderly man who is looking for a place to stay."

"So?"

"They called the Salvation Army, hoping they had a vacancy, but they don't. But the girl in the office there remembered us. This old fella can't live on his own because he's too feeble or something."

"Larry, I don't want to look after sick old men!"

"Well, it's $700 a month. You just have to cook for the old guy, maybe do his laundry."

"Bloody hell! Have you said 'yes' already?" I put my hands on my hips. "Larry?"

"I did... but what the hell, Diane. We need the money. At least go and visit him, okay? If you still figure it wouldn't work out, then don't do it." He picked up his duffel coat and heaved his bags down the hall. I followed him to the truck. He was flying out to Anyox, an old mining town a hundred miles from the Alaskan border. It had been legendary for its gold, silver and copper finds in the early 1900s when Larry's grandfather had worked there, but it was a ghost town now.

I hated fighting with Larry when he was leaving on a trip. British Columbia leads Canada in flying disasters with an annual 24 to 32 percent of the nation's plane crashes. The rough terrain and steep mountains combined with weather that's big on heavy rain and mist creates poor visibility, and the standard joke describes old BC bush pilots as an oxymoron. So I couldn't help worrying when I saw Larry off on a prospecting trip that the words we exchanged would be our last.

"Okay... I'll call the hospital and arrange a visit," I said, leaning into the truck window and kissing him goodbye. He was a good kisser, my Larry. His lips had a tendency to make me space travel. But as I watched the truck bumping down the road, a cold empty feeling came over me. I used to tell him, "You take the sun when you leave," and he would laugh, thinking I was sweet-talking him, but that's how it felt. The day would immediately feel grey and tired and lifeless.

I called Nanaimo General Hospital and arranged to go and see this elderly man, John Hammond, the next day. I was hoping he would turn out to be one of those lovely, weather-beaten old men like Spencer Tracey in *The Old Man and the Sea,* but this one looked like an awkward, stubborn cuss as he sat there on his bed, fully dressed, with a ramrod back and a surly expression on his plain face. His navy-blue suit jacket hung on him like he had lost a lot of weight. He was a tall, large-framed man with massive, bony hands and a pale face, gaunt and thin, and as we went through the formality of shaking hands and introducing ourselves, I stared into the unfriendly, watered-down blue eyes that seemed to dominate the landscape of his face. His smile was stiff. There was no warmth to the man.

"I am hoping you will be able to rent me a room. I am used to looking after myself. Just need a bit of help until I get back on my feet. Had a heart attack. It's set me back." His strong English accent had a well-educated tone, and I noticed his teeth were crooked like a lot of English people's teeth. Why haven't they discovered braces yet in that country? But some teeth on the left side of his mouth were missing. Odd for a person of his class. He coughed throughout his speech, raising a Kleenex to his lips each time.

I really didn't want this stranger in my house. I stared at him, silently wishing I hadn't agreed to the interview. But how sad no one else would look after him. Where was his family? So instead of wriggling out of the commitment, I found myself saying, "I should be able to look after you for a few months, John, until you get better, but I should explain to you what kind of a house we have. We take in men just out of jail who are recovering drug addicts and alcoholics. Would that bother you?"

Please, I thought, be shocked and horrified and say, "You expect me to room with addicts? No bloody way!"

But instead he said, "Not at all. I keep to myself. Couldn't care less what others do."

"Okay." I offered my hand. "It's a deal then—I'll pick you up tomorrow morning."

I went back to Big Sab with a heavy heart, chiding myself. Why couldn't I have just said "no" to the man? Was it pity? I needed to take self-assertion courses or something. I have no nursing instincts whatsoever. I hate cleaning up after sick people unless they are my own family. Maybe he would be well enough to leave us and live on his own in a few months. Then I told myself, "Bite the bullet, Diane. Get his room ready."

I decided to give the old man a large sunny room in the basement—the only one of the three down there that Larry had renovated as yet—as the basement was at ground level and had its own entrance to the street so it would be easier for him to get outside. The only other rooms available were on the top floor, and it would be too awkward for an invalid to navigate the winding stairs to the main floor. I made the bed up and picked some yellow and white daisies from the garden and set them in a vase on the dresser. This room had its own sink and kitchen cupboards, and I set up a coffee machine on the little counter so he would be able to make his own coffee or tea. I stocked the kitchen cupboards with the usual sugar, tea and coffee and added every Brit's delight—English Cadbury chocolate biscuits and Jacobs' cream crackers. As an afterthought I threw in a carton of Ensure.

The next day I needed help to get him out of the car. Gee, I thought, I didn't realize how weak he was. Lewis helped me to put him on the bed where he just collapsed on the pillows, breathing heavily. I covered him with a light blanket and left him to sleep.

Later I took him his dinner on a tray, a traditional British dish, shepherd's pie with broccoli and carrots. The smell of the onions and the rich gravy created, I thought, an appetizing meal. He was propped up on his pillows looking white and wan.

"Here you go, John. I hope you enjoy this. And I've made you a pot of tea." He waved for me to set it down on the arborite kitchen table placed against the wall.

Hmmm, I thought, quite the chatty, ungrateful piece of work. When I went down to collect his tray, I found to my dismay the dinner was sitting untouched on the table, the gravy now greasy and congealed.

Larry phoned later that night. I was sitting up in bed reading Anne Rice's Interview with the Vampire and craving lace and velvet and bites on the neck.

"So, did you go and see the Old Codger?" Larry asked.

"He's here already, sleeping in the basement."

"Good for you, Diane! How is he?"

"Well, Larry darling," I said in a matter-of-fact, somewhat sarcastic voice, "the Old Codger is in bad shape. He didn't even eat his dinner. I feel worried about him as he has a bad heart. Do you think they've sent him here to die?"

"Jesus Christ, Diane, you've got one hell of an imagination!" Silence. "Well, who knows? Maybe they have."

"I'll freak out if he dies here. So help me, Larry, I will! I'm not cut out for corpses!"

I could hear him laughing far away on the other end of the phone. It sounded like he was in a bar with the noises of people laughing and partying behind him. I strained my ears—was that an Alaskan husky I could hear barking?

"I'll be home in a week, kid. Hang in there."

A nurse from the hospital called in daily, but the Old Codger seemed worse each day, barely eating. Most of the time he slept, the noise of his erratic breathing filling up the room. I hovered over him helplessly, waiting for him to wake up and even trying, to no avail, to rouse him. Was he in a coma? As soon as I heard a movement in his room, I dashed in. I insisted on him drinking fluids because even with my lack of medical knowledge, I knew that fluids were vital. I forced him to drink at least one can of Ensure each day, and he grumpily complied. On the fifth morning when I entered his room, he asked, "Would you have bacon and eggs in the house?"

I flew up the stairs and made a big fried egg and bacon breakfast even down to baked beans and fried bread, an English breakfast tradition, then watched him eat the whole darn shooting match, mopping up the egg yolks with his bread.

"Well, John, you've finally found your appetite!"

He smiled weakly, but I knew we had turned a corner.

"What day is it?"

"Friday."

He was shocked. Where had the time gone? "I must have been out of it for a few days." He seemed afraid.

When the nurse came, I went out to her car and asked her point blank, "How sick is he?"

"I thought you knew," she said, studying my face. "To be honest with you, I am totally surprised he made it through this last week. It's a miracle really. Every day I thought, this is it. He won't make it through to another day."

I looked at her, shocked. "He could die?"

"Well, he has emphysema and a very bad heart. They can't operate on the heart because of the emphysema, and they can't operate on the lungs because of the heart. He's in a no-win situation. He knows that. It's just a question of time."

"If he dies," I asked, looking at her terrified, "what do I do? Whom do I call?"

"Call me," she said matter-of-factly, choosing to overlook my distress. "Don't do a thing, just call me." And she handed me her card.

Now that John was a little better, I had a chance to talk to him over morning tea. He was a reluctant conversationalist, but I garnered bits of information. He had been living in his camper trailer on a beach outside of Tofino on the West Coast but had spent the last four winters in Mexico. Loved fishing. Loved living away from the crowded places and, I suspected, from people in general. Was a loner. He had lost his teeth when he found some Mexican youths burglarizing his camper. He had gone down fighting, hitting them with his heavy iron frying pan. They had eventually fled, but it had rattled him as he had been badly beaten up. However, he had still returned the following winter. He hadn't been scared off, so he had guts.

But he had a superior way of talking about people that I didn't like: "Welfare bums. Scum. Feeding off the system." He had disgust for people who were weak and "couldn't cut it." He was proud that he had been a sergeant major in the army. I could imagine him bellowing on the parade ground. Strutting his stuff. God help the men who had served under him. Frankly, he was a horse's ass, but I still couldn't help feeling sorry for him. He spent hours playing solitaire, a lonely figure sitting at his little kitchen table. He never got dressed, just wore pajamas, a robe and worn slippers.

But there was a lot he wasn't telling, and maybe I would have never found out the rest if a stocky, muscular little man hadn't knocked on the door one day. "May I see John Hammond, please?" he asked. "I hope you don't mind me dropping by. The hospital gave me your address."

His name was Doug, an Englishman with a thick Yorkshire accent who had been a boxer years ago, which I guessed accounted for his broken nose. He still kept in touch with the boxing world he loved and with his son ran a boxing club in Ladysmith for youth. He had worked for John when he first immigrated to Canada, and I discovered immediately that he loved to gossip. After his visit with the Old Codger, the two of us sat outside drinking coffee, and he filled in some of the missing pieces.

"It's a sad story. John had money, a big factory, a thriving business. He used to live in the British Properties, you know. Oh yes, he had it all. A wife... two kids. But he was always travelling, put the business before the family. He was an arrogant bastard with his employees and his family alike. Bit of a power monger. Made enemies. Anyway, he lost it all in a bad business deal, and his wife stuck the knife in by leaving him when he was down in the dust. The kids won't talk to him. They know he's dying, but they won't give him the time of day. That's why he became a hermit, lived over there on the West Coast, nobody for miles around. He's bitter and angry. Disillusioned."

"How bad could he have been? I mean, are they really going to let him die alone?"

"I've phoned his wife. I've told her how bad it is. That John is at the end of the end. You know what she said? Call me and let me know when he's dead."

I felt goosebumps on my skin. "Was he really that much of a monster? Does he really deserve this?"

"He *was* a bastard... but you know he sent those kids to the best schools. The girl had a pony, riding lessons. The wife travelled everywhere—she was a regular clotheshorse. They sure knew how to spend his money. *Loved* to spend his money. They had everything money could buy during the good years." He rose to leave." Well, I'm glad he's here with you, Diane. You seem like a kind-hearted soul. I know you'll make him comfortable." He stopped on the veranda stairs, pointed back at John's room and shook his head. "He used to be a great big man—250 pounds or more—had a big appetite. Would eat up a big thick steak and a mound of food like this." He cupped his hand in the air. "Loved to wash it all down with a few pints, but he's a shadow of himself now. Please keep in touch. Here's my phone number, you know, just in case."

In case what? John croaked?

"I'll be stopping by from time to time to see how he's doing. You know I was down and out once, and that's when John offered me a job. I owe him for that alone."

I was bringing in a dinner tray one evening when I heard voices in John's room. Pushing open the door, I saw a most unusual sight. Scott and Lewis were sitting with John at the little kitchen table playing cards. Coffee cups and Cadbury chocolate biscuits were on the table. Laughter careened in the air.

"Guess what, Di?" said Scott. "You'll never believe this small world story. Remember I was telling you how I took Julie to this deserted beach outside of Tofino, and we met this old guy who gave us tips on where to fish? That old guy was John!"

"You must be kidding," I said putting down the tray. I love small world stories. "That must have been over two years ago, Scott, before you went to Wilkinson!" Julie had been Scott's girlfriend before he went to prison.

"Yup. I can't believe it either and now we meet again here at Big Sab." He was smiling. "Who would have known that our paths would cross again, eh John?"

John looked a little uneasy. I knew it was because Scott had also told me that John had been rude that day, a true hermit who had resented his space being invaded. Scott had described John as an enigma, a man living alone on an isolated beach, and he had been curious as hell as to what would make a man choose such a life. Small world was right!

Lying in bed that night, I thought about life's ironies. John, the classic snob, an arrogant, patronizing bastard, a victim of his own sense of superiority, dying alone, abandoned by the world, dependent on the whim of strangers and the camaraderie offered by ex-cons and drug addicts. Spending his last days beneath the unlikely roof of a halfway house. Makes you think, doesn't it?

16
The Flirt

The lazy warm days of late summer had arrived. I was happy and content. I felt settled in my role looking after the guys at Big Sab. I felt Larry and I were *doing good.*

Earlier that day we had bought some big red Coho salmon off Sly on the Reserve. The aboriginal people were not supposed to sell their catch, but that was the biggest joke in the South End. Every white man's freezer was full of salmon. We white guys just felt good that they would let us in on their deal, and at $7 a salmon, it was the best deal in town. We had just barbecued a 10-pound beauty that I had stuffed with thin slices of onion and lemon and sprinkled with chopped garlic. With baked potatoes and corn, it had been a feast. Now we sat around with our stomachs full, content with that salmon-satisfied feeling Nanaimo's Indigenous people had been experiencing for thousands of years. Most of the men sat out in the garden contentedly smoking cigarettes, but Lewis and I sat together at the top of the big wooden stairs that served as a fire exit for the second floor where we could catch a bit of the breeze off the bay but be shaded by the willow tree's sheltering branches. Even though it was 8:00 p.m., it was still like a summer's afternoon, and we were enjoying the warm evening air.

Lewis had told us that very afternoon that he and Louise were planning to get married. I was thrilled but a little worried. Lewis, true to his word, had seen Louise almost every day since they met but really, they hadn't known each other that long. Don't get me wrong. I really liked Louise, she was not only beautiful, gentle and kind, but she was fun and intelligent with her soul shining out of her dark Latin American eyes.

She had a hidden passion radiating from her, spilling out. She looked sad until she smiled and then her whole face lit up like a hundred candles, her eyes flashing fireworks. She had told us how her grandfather had walked with others from Mexico all the way north to Canada. The most remarkable part of the story was that they had brought a church bell with them from their old village, something old and dear for their new church wherever they settled. Her grandfather, being one of the stronger men, had carried the bell for many of those miles. I hoped she had her grandfather's stamina and mental endurance. She was going to need it taking Lewis on, but I could see she was a woman in love and her eyes followed him everywhere.

Nairie had been visiting and now she waved goodbye as she walked to her car.

"Your sister is attractive, but I have a feeling she's a real man-eater," I observed.

"She's pretty all right," Lewis said, "but she's also pretty screwed up, like she never grew up. Acts like a naughty little girl. I love her, but she sure can piss me off."

"Like how?"

"She's always flirting, getting in trouble with guys. Man-eater isn't quite the right description." He shook his head. "I hate to say it but she's promiscuous. She needs counselling or help of some kind. Now me, I have never cheated in my life. Totally a one-woman man."

"Really? I don't think there's a man alive that's totally a one-woman man."

"Diane! You of all people to be so cynical." He pretended to be shocked, and we grinned at each other. "I guess if a Meg Ryan type hit on me when I was in a relationship, I could be tempted... but I would honestly hope not. How *could* you be tempted if you were in love? But I guess I'm a true romantic... or I like to think I am anyway." And Lewis did look like a romantic figure dressed in blue jeans, a blue jean vest opened to expose his tanned bare chest, a battered straw hat perched jauntily on his head.

"I always loved that quote in Caldwell's *God's Little Acre*... something about God making a terrible mistake when he put the soul of man in the body of an animal."

"That's a damn good quote," said Lewis, chuckling and shaking his head.

"Joking aside though, I wonder why Nairie is like that?" I said. "Promiscuous, I mean. She seems so confident, so together, though she did tell me she's on Prozac. I never would have taken her for someone with depression." I looked over at him to get his input.

"Well..." Lewis paused to light a cigarette before he returned my gaze. "It's a long story and I kinda of feel troubled because it's a story that I've never told anyone. And I know I should have." There was silence as he blew the cigarette smoke out. I stayed quiet until he continued. "I think it all started when she was a kid in New Zealand. She was the prettiest little girl, as you can imagine, with those big green eyes of hers and her friendly personality. My mother took off. Left us. We were quite little but after a while Sue and Dad started dating."

"Your stepmother?"

"Yep. Sue's brother was this big Maori guy and he used to baby-sit us. Well, this asshole used to sexually molest Nairie. She would have been about six at the time, which would have made me around four. I slept in the next room and I walked in on them a couple of times, but I was a little kid... I didn't understand what was going on. Too young to get it. Years later I realized what I'd seen. I've talked it over with Nairie, but she would never say anything to Sue, wouldn't hurt her for the world. I always thought if I ever went back to New Zealand, I would kill that bastard." Lewis dragged on his cigarette. "But... I went back five years ago and I never said a word to him. We kind of avoided each other like he knew I knew. I don't know if I'm a coward for that. It was like it was so sick I hesitated to open that door. Balked at opening up that can of worms. But... Nairie is screwed up over it. Like she's hitting on Ken right now." Lewis flashed a look at me. "Have you noticed? Even though she's getting married in a couple of months to a decent guy who worships the ground she walks on. Meanwhile, poor old Ken is being teased and twisted and generally all stirred up. She'd love nothing better than to have them fighting over her. That's her style. She truly is a bitch. I've warned Ken, but he's too far gone."

"Too far gone. What do you mean?" I felt alarmed. "Are you saying she's been to bed with Ken?"

Lewis turned to me and grinned mischievously, dragging deeply on the cigarette and the smoke drifting into his eyes. "That, my dearest Lady Di, is a question you'll have to ask him."

17
The Move to Haliburton Street

It seemed that everybody found out about Big Sab at the same time. AA and NA now had confidence in Larry and me and had put up notices on their bulletin boards advertising rooms for rent in our safehouse, and Gordie Ryder referred men to us from Wilkinson Prison and Nanaimo Correctional Centre. Big Sab filled up with astonishing speed.

Larry had renovated two more rooms in the basement, big pleasant rooms with windows overlooking the garden, and they became the most sought-after rooms in the house because they were away from the hubbub of the main floor. Larry wanted to put two men in each room, but I told him to get real. He was turning into such a moneybag. We scrambled desperately to find furniture and linens. I bought old dressers from the Goodwill store and sanded them down, repainting them with bright crisp colours that would complement the second-hand quilts and curtains I found there. I was amazed at what people discarded. Perfectly good items with little wear and tear. Maybe they were just rich and wasteful or maybe they were starting a new life in Borneo and didn't need warm quilts. I was just glad to get my hands on their throwaways.

"I should go into the antique business here," Larry said, eyeing some of the furniture. "Look at this. You can tell by the way the wood is joined in this drawer that this dresser is at least fifty years old. I bet the antique hunters have overlooked Nanaimo and just concentrated on Victoria. My God, I could make a fortune here."

"Larry," I said one day after we had to turn two guys away, "why don't we move into the Haliburton Street house that Eric, the bartender, has just vacated? We would have more privacy, and we could rent out another bedroom in Big Sab."

"By Jove, you're a genius! That's an excellent idea." Larry was beaming. So was I. Living with all the men in Big Sab was not easy. We had no privacy, and it always felt strangely odd when Larry and I went to bed at night, the only two people in Big Sab that had partners. Like we making the rest feel lonely. Or hornier. Or something. It just didn't feel right. And this probably being totally my Welsh imagination, I didn't like the way they scrutinized me in the morning. Like did I have a happy I've-been-laid look?

"The only problem is John, the Old Codger," said Larry. "You can't run back and forth to look after him. Maybe we should take him with us. Haliburton has three bedrooms—well four, if you count the one in the basement."

My heart sank. I didn't want to take the Old Codger with us. I had been thinking Larry and I would finally live on our own. Finally have some intimacy—like watch TV in our underwear and screw on the living room floor. Plus, I didn't like the old man, the coldness about him, the aloofness I hadn't even tried to overcome.

"Just think," Larry said, "John's money will almost pay the mortgage on Haliburton Street, and we can rent out his room in Big Sab. This is such a great idea!" He was almost jumping in the air.

So we moved around the corner to Haliburton Street with the Old Codger in tow, and I consoled myself that one bedridden old man was better than nine frisky young men running all over the house. And the house on Haliburton Street with its huge garden overlooking the ocean and the glamourous Gulf Islands was truly beautiful. It was a character home with a fireplace in the living room. The three bedrooms ran off a long, dignified, high-ceilinged hall that led from the front door. This hall had a Casablanca fan overhead and it begged for mirrors and plants, an aura of mystery. I couldn't wait to get started on the transformation. I figured I could be happy there.

18
Freaky Deaky Clothes

It was a hot sunny day, a day for the beach, I was thinking, when Larry hung up the phone. "Guess what?" he said. "Ahmed is coming over with his girlfriend today."

Ahmed was Larry's stockbroker in Vancouver. A middle-aged Iranian with a gentle, fun-loving disposition. His wife had left him a year earlier, and he nearly had a nervous breakdown. He couldn't quite believe it. They had been married for twenty years, and he had thought she was happy. But unknown to him she had grown tired of his workaholic hours long ago and had thrown in the towel. Now he had met this new lady, and Larry and I were curious about her, worried whether she was right for him because we both loved Ahmed.

"Oh geez, what will I cook for dinner?" I threw open the freezer door. "Oh good. I've got a beaut of a roast sitting here, so let's have that for dinner, but Larry, for fun why don't we take them to the Dinghy Dock for lunch?" It was settled.

We didn't get many visitors, so we were both excited. In those days the Dinghy Dock advertised itself as the only floating pub/restaurant in Canada. As it sits off the shore of Protection Island, you travel there via a little ferry shuttle, and when you sit on the restaurant deck, you look back at the Nanaimo harbourfront, which is such an incredibly picturesque view, and all the while you sling back drinks and eat fabulous seafood.

Ahmed's girlfriend, Fara, was lovely. Well educated, a pharmacist. Around forty years, gracious and soft-spoken. I warmed to her immediately. It was obvious she and Ahmed were very much in love. And they seemed so sophisticated. I mused wistfully that I had been spending too much time around ex-cons. Fara was wearing a dress that must have cost at least three hundred dollars, gold earrings and a couple of rings with precious stones that would have weighted her to the bottom of the sea if she had fallen off the ferry. When had I stopped wearing my Carole Little outfits? And where was my one and only Ports skirt? Why hadn't I dug that out instead of wearing my tank top and jeans? I felt shabby and suddenly insecure. How would this glamourous couple view sitting around our dining room table with our schizos and ex-cons?

"They wouldn't care less," said Larry, viewing me with a bemused smile.

Don't you find that it's the people who have grown up with money who don't care about outward appearances? It's those of us who haven't who worry about image. Larry had grown up in moneyed West Vancouver. Me? A small Welsh mining town where women worried so much about public opinion that they went down on their knees and scrubbed the pavement clean in front of their terraced houses each day.

"I can't help caring, Larry. How about if we set up the dining room table outside under the cherry tree here and dine away from the gang? We can make it an enchanting garden affair."

Larry didn't really care. He was too busy enjoying himself catching up on the Howe Street gossip and swapping stock trading stories. Ahmed explained that the stock market had hit him hard this year. Mining stocks were way down. A bad year all around. Larry was lucky he had got out of it when he did, he said. Fara told me she was worried about Ahmed's health as his blood pressure was outrageously high. The pressure of being a stockbroker should be left to younger men.

After lunch I left Larry to drive them around sightseeing and went home. When I reached Haliburton, I called over to Big Sab. "S-O-S," I cried into the phone. "Who's there who can help me set up a dinner party in the back yard here? Send whoever over *fast.*"

Most of the guys walked down the road to help. Jostling and laughing, they carried the dining table and chairs out and set them up under the cherry tree. I found a good white tablecloth buried in the linen closet. Ron blew up balloons and we tied them to branches of trees. I set up a small serving table for the casserole dishes. "Candles!" said Lewis and ran to the corner Chinese store. Scott laid the table. He had picked a beautiful bouquet of wildflowers for the centrepiece. It was coming together.

When Larry and our visitors returned, even Larry was impressed and stood outside the garden gate whistling approval. We sat under the shade of the cherry trees drinking wine and laughing. As I was serving up the roast beef dinner complete with Yorkshire pudding and roast potatoes, I had another great idea.

I called over to Big Sab again. "Lewis," I whispered into the phone, "do you want to sing for your supper? Roast beef, Yorkshire pudding?"

"Be right over," he said. And faster than a New York minute he came loping down the street from Big Sab, his guitar slung over his shoulder, cowboy hat perched on his head, ready to play the part. And boy, did he know how to work a crowd—smiling, shaking hands, getting a stool and sitting a little apart from us. "Any requests?"

Ahmed and Fara looked a little startled. This was an ex-con? They tensed just a little in their chairs, and then Lewis's voice took over. The lovely ballad "Stand by Me" flowed smoothly from his throat. Then the beautiful, "Wind Beneath My Wings." "Spanish Eyes" followed. On it went.

"Do you need a break?" I called out as I served up the cheesecake.

"No, no... I'm having fun." Lewis looked quite the picture lazily leaning back with his cowboy hat tilted back on his dark blond hair. His shirt was unbuttoned just enough to expose the soft curly hair on his chest. His tan, the white even teeth, the beguiling smile. He was the South End's answer to Hollywood all right.

"Could you sing "Memories" from *Cats*?" Fara asked shyly.

"No... Sorry, don't know the words... but how about this one?" Lewis's husky voice singing, "You don't have to say you love me, just be close at hand..." rose over the candle-lit scene and went soaring into the night air.

The guys at Big Sab leaned over the fence clapping approval but behaving. Kind of a back-end audience. Craig shouted from across the street, "Hey, Lewis, sing "I Walk the Line." The little mongrel dog. Asking for a song... and of course, it was a song about something he had not yet learned to do.

When Lewis sang my request, "Desperado," I noticed Fara had tears in her eyes. Then he did Eric Clapton's lovely hit, "Wonderful Tonight," and when he sang the words, "You look wonderful tonight," he made a point of nodding and smiling right at Fara and me. We were both butter in his hands. *Butter.*

At the end of the evening I piled up a royal plate of food for our singing hero and slid a $10 bill quietly into his hand. "Sshh. Don't say anything. This is between you and me. You were terrific, darling. They loved you."

Ahmed and Fara stayed talking in the warm night air, asking questions about the kind of guys we had at Big Sab and wanting to know their stories. Larry spun yarns about our guys, making our guests laugh, and told them about the Old Codger.

"That Lewis seems like such a lovely young man," Fara said, pressing one hand to her breast. "I hope he makes it. Oh, I hope he does." Lewis had sure made an impression.

"I hope they *all* make it," said Ahmed, taking Fara's hand, making sure she knew he was still there sitting beside her. "I had the wrong idea about all of this, thinking hopelessness, hardened criminals, that kind of thing. You guys are doing a good thing here trying to help these guys."

Fara's gentle brown eyes smiled at me. "I hope you don't mind, Diane, I slipped Lewis $20. He was truly wonderful playing for us like that."

I gritted my teeth. That scheming little rat taking my $10 on top of Fara's $20. And a roast beef dinner as well. Then I grinned... I had been conned by a con. What did I expect? He had sung for hours like a nightingale.

A month later a huge box arrived addressed to "The Guys at Big Sab." Ahmed had gone around to his broker friends, and they had donated their old suits, sports jackets, sweaters and pants—you name it. It was like Christmas. All the guys duded up. They looked like freaky-deaky stockbrokers going around town in $1,000 suits. Ron was the one that astonished me by looking the most glamorous. The suits fit him like a glove, as if they had been tailor-made for him. Did he have the body of a stockbroker? I kept looking at him, riveted by the change. He had always reminded me of someone. But who? I had never quite put my finger it, the image always evading me. Now here he was—a handsome young Harrison Ford. It was uncanny. *Doth clothes the man make?*

Four months later the phone rang. Ahmed had died of a heart attack. Larry and I were devastated.

"The stock market finally hit our friend too hard," said Larry, brushing his hand across his eyes. "Thank God I'm out of it."

19
The Wedding

Lewis and Louise were married in the living room at Big Sab.

It was quite the wedding. We all chipped in for the food and refreshments. I cooked a beef roast, baked a ham and made scalloped potatoes and salads. Lewis's family surprised me by only bringing snacks, but maybe second marriages weren't big for them. Somebody threw in a 15-pound salmon; one of Louise's friends baked the wedding cake. A host of the NA crowd showed up. We strung lights in the backyard. The minister was the funniest, strangest looking little man of God I had ever met.

"Where the hell did you get him from?" I asked Lewis.

"He was the only one we could get. The only one who would come here to Big Sab to get the job done."

"Jesus, Lewis, he looks like Mel Brooks in *Blazing Saddles*."

Lewis looked upset with me. "Di, please don't start."

But every time I looked at the guy, I had to suppress a grin. I could understand why this minister had a lot of free time on his hands.

Yvonne, Jack's wife, in her quiet organized way had decorated the room with pink Japanese dogwoods and late-blooming lilacs from her garden, and lilac and white crepe paper garlands hung from the ceiling. The result was so beautiful it was astounding, the room transformed into a bridal bower. The living room was packed. The children were lined up sitting on the floor talking in loud whispers, and I kept telling them to shush! Lewis was resplendently glamorous. Blond hair slicked back, face smooth shaven. He had gone to the Goodwill and bought a white dress jacket and black slacks. He still wore the same retrieved-from-the pawnshop worn cowboy boots, but they were polished. He couldn't stand still, fidgeting, tense and nervous. I knew he wanted more than anything for the occasion to have dignity and was starting to wonder if we were going to pull it off.

I wondered myself, looking around the room, scanning the faces of Little Larry, Richard and Scott. Everybody was dressed in their best, perspiring, uncomfortable and excited. Little Larry looked choked by his unaccustomed tie, I grinned at Ken across the room but realized he was fully occupied with flirting with Nairie's cleavage, which was a vista of treacherous hills and valleys. Then the "Bridal Chorus" played by Lewis's dad floated on the air. We all jumped, tension rippling through the room.

A moment later Louise came down the stairs on the arm of a beaming Larry. There wasn't a dry eye in the house. She was dressed in a high-necked, ankle-length, white lace dress that had been her grandmother's. A garland of small white roses was pinned like a halo in her long dark hair. She was pale and trembling when she reached Lewis's side, and her soft dark eyes shone with a look of rapture that was frightening. Lewis immediately gripped her arm as though his life depended upon it. And maybe it did. Intense doesn't quite describe the scene. Two people in love committing to a future. They were so in love I felt a lurch of fear for them or was it the heady scent of the blossoms decorating the room that was making me feel so dizzy?

The Mel Brooks-look-alike minister was surprisingly good. He waved his arms a lot, his speech was stirring, and except for the fact that one of the smaller children crawled between his legs to grab a loosened balloon that had come to rest by his feet, the ceremony went off without a hitch. (If the kid had grabbed the balloon, the ceremony would have finished with a bang!)

Almost on cue, the sunlight from the high living room window shafted down and caught the faces of the groom and bride, capturing

Lewis just as he bent over and kissed the upturned dark-faced beauty of the bride. As their lips touched, it felt like a holy moment right there in the living room of Big Sab. Then the moment dissolved as we all clapped and cheered and crowded around to hug and kiss the bride and groom. Except for Little Larry who was already in the kitchen stuffing his mouth with my sausage rolls. We all ate too much and laughed too much. Larry dashed around taking photographs like he was Antony Armstrong-Jones at a society wedding. Ken flirted with Nairie too much, never leaving her side, and she flirted right back. But she was marrying her real estate agent boyfriend within the month, so why was Ken bothering? Or maybe I should have asked myself why was she?

Years later I remembered the wedding for its simplicity and sweetness and not for the nightmare that was to come. It was Big Sab's finest hour and after that nothing ever quite topped the moment.

Lewis unexpectedly asked us if Larry and I would join them at the Dinghy Dock for a small celebration. "I want to dance on my wedding night," he said. "Come on, I love you guys, and I want you to share the moment with us."

"Please come," Louise said. "It will make it more special if you come."

I hesitated, "Will you be drinking?" *Why did I know the answer?*

"Just a glass of wine," Lewis said. "Jesus, it's our wedding day. Larry, what do you say?"

Larry was silent for a moment, weighing it up. "Okay, we'll come. We'll be honoured to come."

I was uncomfortable with it. On the little shuttle ferry going over to Protection Island I held onto Larry's arm. It was such a beautiful night. The stars were out, a peach of a moon was hanging in the blue-black sky, but there was an underlying discordant note. Larry bent over and kissed my cheek. "A penny for your thoughts."

"I'm worrying about Lewis drinking there. I feel guilty... like we are collaborating in a crime or something. I just don't want a perfect day spoilt."

"Loosen up, honey-bun!" He had been into calling me "honey-bun" or "sweetie-pie" ever since we had seen the movie *Pulp Fiction*. "Lewis is on his own now. Living with Louise from this moment on. We have done everything we can for him. It's his decision if he wants a glass of wine on his wedding day."

At the Dingy Dock the music played, and we all danced. Louise was still wearing her wedding dress, and when people realized the reason for the celebration, drinks were sent to the table. All of us watched as the bride and groom—glued together—slow danced, a smile of old rekindled memories on our own faces. Lewis's glass of wine became two and three, then there was a rum and coke, and his face became flushed with the liquor. He started laughing and talking too loudly. Bigger than life, blowing up like an inflatable doll. An exaggerated version of his true self. I felt a churning in my stomach. A sickness inside. I feigned a headache and we all trooped home before midnight.

Larry and I lay in the dark. I was propped up on my pillows watching the lights of passing boats gliding across the waters of the bay. We didn't talk, just fell asleep holding hands. We didn't say a word, didn't say what we both thought. *They're not going to make it.*

20
The Little Professor

Ray Findlay was mad at me. Furious was more like it. "How could you be so careless as to leave Tylenol 3 around? I don't understand it. For Chrisake, Diane, you are working with addicts! Addicts! Not kindergarten kids!"

I had slipped in the bathtub and hurt my back, and the doctor had prescribed painkillers. They had gone missing from Haliburton Street, and the next day I received the call from Big Sab saying Wayne, the Little Professor as he was nicknamed, was passed out cold on the living room floor with Little Larry's bucket of Kentucky Fried Chicken, apparently stolen from the fridge, scattered around him. A half-eaten drumstick and a chicken wing were still clutched tightly in his fists, his lips and hair glistening with chicken grease. His arms were positioned across his chest as if he had been laid out in a funeral parlour. Only the lilies were missing.

I stared at Ray anxiously. He was turning blue and breathing so hard that his inhalator wasn't doing the job. Geez, if he passed out, would I be committed to giving CPR to those narrow, frothing lips?

"Ray," I said. "Look, I'm sorry, but it didn't even enter my mind that our guys would be remotely interested in Tylenol 3. I thought heroin, cocaine, crack, booze, whatever, but never in my wildest dreams Tylenol."

"That's my whole point!" He gasped for air. "You and Larry haven't the slightest fucking idea what you're doing here. You think you can give them shelter and cook nutritional meals and everybody is going to get better. Tylenol 3 can get you high, and you," he stabbed his finger at me, "didn't even know that. If anybody dies at Big Sab, I'll blame your ignorance. You are a liability. How can you help these men when you are so ignorant of their problem? When you don't have a fucking clue what addiction is about? I'll... I'll..." He checked himself as if realizing he had gone too far. "I'm not a happy man about this. Wayne is from my old crowd. I grew up with him, I've done time with him. I love the guy, for Chrisake. He's been out of Wilkinson for one lousy month and here he is high as a kite!" He slammed his hand down on the table. "I'm supposed to report this, and if I do, they'll throw him right back in the can..." He looked like he was going to cry.

"Couldn't we give him a second chance? Just tell him he's on probation now?" I was grasping at straws. "Get everybody at Big Sab to vote on whether to give him a second chance... or something?"

"We could, but it's not the usual procedure. It could get us into... or me anyway... into trouble with the John Howard Society. Let me think about it." With that, he abruptly swooped up his inhalator kit from the kitchen floor and marched out without a backward glance. The front door slammed.

I sat at the kitchen table, feeling tired and used up.

The Little Professor was a petite man with a halo of wild, gingery, curly hair, thick-rimmed glasses and crooked teeth, giving him an impish, puckish look. He had acquired his nickname not only because he was so well-read—he was like a walking encyclopedia—but also because his specialized crime was stealing rare books from antique bookstores in Victoria and selling them on the black market. One stolen book could bring enough money to support his drug habit for months, and he was so intelligent and well-educated that he knew which books were coveted the most. Even legitimate book dealers and respectable businessmen would turn a blind eye to his obvious crime by purchasing the books they craved.

He loved to come over to Haliburton Street, drink endless cups of coffee and bullshit with me. In fact, he hung around too much. Not that I didn't like him, but he was a compulsive talker and he wore me out. I knew he was lonely and loved to talk to me about all the intellectual subjects he couldn't share with the other guys because they would tease him, but he even wanted to go grocery shopping with me, for God's sake. There was no escape.

Now I was furious with him for stealing my pills. When had he done it? When I was in the bathroom? Had he seen them on my bedroom dresser? The little bastard. I wondered how many Tylenol 3s made you high? I know when I took my prescribed two pills, they made me sleepy. And then to have Ray shouting and giving me hell like that. Did he have a clue how much hard work went into every day here? How sometimes I felt like I was bled white emotionally supporting so many anxiety-ridden, tense and hurting men. And Larry was in Nevada on a mining job and hadn't been home in three weeks. I felt lonely and abandoned. What the hell was I doing here? Ray was right. I didn't know anything about addiction, about drugs, and I was probably a liability. I gave in to my feelings of inadequacy and bowed my head as I felt the tears trickle down my cheeks.

That's when I heard the doorbell ring. That damn asshole, Ray, had probably forgotten something. I hastily grabbed the first thing at hand, a tea towel, and wiped my eyes as I went down the hall. But it was Gordie Ryder standing on the step.

"Gordie, come on in." I made my voice cheerful. "For what do I owe the honour of this morning visit?"

"Oh, I was driving by and thought I'd drop in and see if the coffee is on."

I avoided looking at his face and busied myself with pouring coffee. I hoped my eyes weren't red. "Did you hear about the Little Professor and the Tylenol 3 caper?" I asked, figuring it was probably the real reason he was dropping in.

"No. What caper?"

"The little jerk stole my pain killers... Tylenol 3... and was found passed out on the living room floor at Big Sab. Ray was just over here reading me the Riot Act, saying I'm a liability and someone is going to end up dead..." I felt the tears stinging my eyes, and I swallowed hard. Like hell I was going to cry in front of Gord. "Ray said I don't know how to help the guys because I don't understand addiction. It was sort of funny, though, the Little Professor on the floor surrounded by stolen Kentucky Fried Chicken and clasping a chicken leg to his breast..." I laughed and then choked as the tears came. I felt hot with embarrassment and gripped the tea towel in readiness again, swallowing hard and then swallowing again. I felt an arm around me, patting my back.

"Go on, let it out. It's all right, Di. Cry it out."

I sobbed and sobbed. "I really care for them, but maybe I am useless. I can't believe he stole the Tylenol right under my nose. I trusted him..."

I still hadn't recovered from trusting Tom, the Indigenous man who had been our first client from Wilkinson. He had been a likeable, courteous, dignified man whose family came and visited him a few times a week. He had sat outside many evenings enjoying their company, laughing and talking with his two older brothers. I used to watch them through the kitchen window, thinking what a close, loving family they were and only found out weeks later when Tom slurred his words and nodded off at the dinner table that the brothers had been providing him with heroin. Can you believe it? I had been stunned. It had been a wake-up call for me. But now this.

Gord kept patting and stroking my back gently. I turned, and he held me against his hard, muscular chest, not like Larry's soft cuddly one, and I was suddenly very conscious again of my attraction to this man. It felt comfortable there in his arms, and I pulled away and we stared at one another. His eyes were sapphire blue and gentle.

"Kentucky Fried Chicken, m-m-m-m yum..." he said. We both burst out laughing, huge belly laughs.

"Circled by dead chicken like a berserk witch's curse." That started the laughter again.

"Don't take Ray too much to heart, Diane. He's lost some really good friends this year. That old, tired Death by Drugs. He's frustrated and angry. I think he took his frustration out on you."

"He was totally pissed off at me!"

"We can't all be perfect like him, can we?" Gord gave me a sly grin.

I thought about skinny, emaciated Ray, still living with his mother. An ex-con, an ex-addict whose lungs were so damaged by drugs that he was sentenced to breathe through an inhalator for the rest of his life, and I found myself gratefully grinning back.

As I walked Gord to the door, I said genuinely, "Thanks, Gord. You sure dropped in at the right moment. I was thinking of leaving town on the next ferry."

He turned around in the dim hallway and faced me. "What? Don't ever walk out on me, Diane. I need you here!" he said jocularly in his usual booming voice. Then in a softer tone, "I know Larry's not around much. I know you're running this place by yourself most of the time. I know it's tough, but I mean it, we need you. Please don't run out on us."

"Larry has no choice but to go out of town a lot on his mining business." I guess I was defending him. "It's what he does."

Gord's eyes appraised me for a moment, then he said gently, "Larry's explained that he's married?"

I was shocked. I felt stunned and humiliated. How could Larry undermine me like this? I was reduced to feeling like a cheap, dumb broad. Never in a million years did I want Gord, the John Howard

Society or anyone else to know. Know what? That I was a fool in love and that maybe Larry wasn't being straight with me?

"Di, really... you're doing a great job." He bent over, brushed his lips on my cheek, then left.

I stood in the darkness of the hallway for a long time, the feel of his lips staying like an imprint on my face. *This was insane. How could I possibly be attracted to an ex-Hell's Angel biker?* The hall was hushed, the giant, fronded leaves of my prized palm tree reflected dimly in the mirror on the far wall, my own silhouette framed, mysterious and motionless. I could hear the sound of the rain outside. Grey relentless weather. Where the hell was Larry? I felt very alone, a woman in need. In need of what? Love, a hug? To be taken out dancing? To have someone to laugh with, confide in? Someone to kiss me silly? The house felt dark and empty. Then a rasping cough from the Old Codger's bedroom reminded me that I had to start cooking dinner soon. A meal for a hungry tenant. I had no heart for it. I wished I could order in Chinese food and a bottle of rum. And now that I thought of it, Larry was probably throwing dice in some Nevada desert casino, laughing and swigging down cold beer, basking in a temperature of around 80 degrees.

Ray Findlay set up the meeting for two days later. All the guys crowded into Big Sab's living room. Ray made a short speech explaining how the Little Professor had broken the rules and it was up to the clients living in the house what the outcome would be. He then passed the floor over to me. The Little Professor looked even smaller than he usually looked, his face pale and miserable, his hair looking even more gingery. He kept his eyes downcast, his hands nervously twitching in his lap.

I addressed the men. "Wayne has screwed up. So I am going to ask you to vote on whether you want him living here or not. He stole from you Little Larry, and he's broken one of the primary rules here. He got high. You all know if he leaves here, he will be going back to jail. Wayne, have you anything to say before the guys vote?"

Wayne croaked, "I'm sorry. Truly sorry. I will replace your KFC, Little Larry. Truly sorry." He looked up briefly, his eyes behind the glasses shimmering with tears.

"Put your hands up if you want Wayne to go."

The guys standing around looked uncomfortable. No one looked at the Little Professor. Some cleared their throats. Not one hand was raised.

I saw Ray Findlay limp down the hall and exit the front door.

"I guess that's it then. I guess the Little Professor stays."

I saw the Little Professor take out a Kleenex and blow his nose. Little Larry went over and gently patted his back as the rest of the guys dispersed.

That was Little Larry for you. The sweetness in him.

21
Shiner

It was a brisk end-of-summer day in the South End, and I was collecting rents for Larry. I knocked on the big wooden door, and when the tenant, a young musician named Rob, answered, a grey ball of fur came hurtling down the hall, barking and skidding towards me. He looked like a baby wolf. "Where did you get such a gorgeous pup?" I asked, picking him up and cuddling him.

"A friend of mine on Bowen Road. His bitch had twelve puppies. She's lovely, isn't she? I've called her Sesame."

I could feel myself falling in love. "Would you like to sell her? I'm only kidding! Do you think there are any puppies left in the litter?"

"I'll phone and find out."

Rob returned saying," Only four left. They've been selling like crazy. The father is a pedigree husky and the mother a cross shepherd and wolf. You know Nanaimo— everybody here loves that wolf look."

"I'm going to see if Larry will go for it. How much are they?"

"Fifty bucks but I'd hurry. Twist Larry's arm."

I raced the truck back to the house. Larry wasn't there. Maybe he had gone over to Big Sab. I phoned over and to my relief he answered.

"I have a big surprise for you. I'm picking you up in three minutes."

I knew the word *surprise* would get him. Larry was like a kid when it came to surprises. I screeched to a stop in front of Big Sab and picked him up. The address on Bowen Road was only ten minutes away. When I pulled up in front of the house, Larry looked puzzled. "I thought you were taking me to lunch," he said, disappointment in his voice.

"Come on... hurry, you old slow poke." I raced up the drive. Rob had told me the puppies and their mother were housed in the carport. Larry begrudgingly trailed behind me as a young woman in jeans and a T-shirt came out of the house.

"Can we have a look?" I asked, pointing to the carport. She nodded and opened the gate.

They were a sight for sore eyes. All those little bundles of fur and the mother patiently licking while being assaulted from all sides.

"Puppies?" said Larry in disbelief. "I don't believe you, Diane." But he was the first to lean over and pick one up.

"Most of these have been taken," the woman said. "I'll show you the ones left." I was holding my breath because unbelievably these puppies looked so different from one another. There were even two that had red coats. Two more looked like Labs. Such a mix. The lady held up two that looked like shepherds and then there was one she held up that was a mirror image of Sesame.

"Oh, Larry, that's the one."

He looked at me in shock. "You want to buy one?" What did he think we were there for? A petting zoo?

"Larry, you *know* you're away a lot. He'll be company for me."

He caved immediately. "How much? *Fifty bucks?*" Of course, he had to play the shocked-beyond-belief look, but he peeled off the bills grumpily to the grinning lady. She winked at me behind his back.

"I hope you know how much work a dog is, Diane." He was all stern and master-of-the-house as we drove away in the truck. I nestled my face against the ball of fur and using my little girl voice said, "Yes, Larry." I was thinking happily, *Kiss my ass, big guy.*

There was a huge debate once we were home. Davey, from Larry's crew, stopped by and some of the guys from Big Sab drifted over. What to call the puppy?

"Rajah," said Davey.

"Shadow," said I, thinking of another dog I had loved.

"Big Foot," said Ken. The puppy did have big feet.

"I've got it," said Larry. "Shiner. Look under his eyes. He has black markings that look like black eyes." We all cheered in unison. I especially loved the name. It meant he would be a champion, a fighter, a spirit that would not surrender. A happy disposition. And sunshine too.

"Diane," Richard said quietly, his grin showing his broken teeth, "your puppy... Shiner. He just peed on the rug."

22
Lazy Eyes

As Big Sab filled, a funny pattern emerged. Humorous actually. So many guys had the same name. Ken, Richard and Scott for starters, but then the names John, Guy and Jason became really big. Craig was another popular name. So after a while we already knew by his name when a guy arrived whether or not he would take one of our rooms. Not all prospective tenants appreciated the twenty-five-block walk from town, but if they had one of our names, we knew they were a shoo-in. The other identifying factor was bizarre as hell. So many of the men had a Columbo "lazy eye." (Peter Falk, the actor who played the detective Columbo in the TV series, actually had a glass eye, but it always looked out of focus.) We couldn't understand it. I had never seen so many lazy eyes in my life! A phenomenon. If someone showed up with a lazy eye, Larry immediately started writing out the rent receipt.

One of the new boys had both qualifications—a lazy eye and his name was Craig. He drove me crazy. He was a tall, lanky kid who couldn't stop grinning like he thought life was the funniest thing that had ever happened to him. He didn't walk, he loped. Awkwardly. Never looking where he was going. Almost walking into walls. He called me "ma'am" very politely but didn't listen to a word I said. Incorrigible. He played a guitar and would sit under the willow tree singing his heart out. His voice wasn't bad but not that great, so I couldn't help smiling when I overheard him telling the other guys he was going to be a rock and roll star one day.

I was over at Big Sab one morning talking to the Little Professor when I realized that everybody was acting a little odd. Not their normal selves. I smelled a rat.

"Where's Craig?" I asked matter-of-factly as I looked around. It was 11:30. He should have been up. There was some mumbling but no answers from anyone. The Little Professor left the kitchen so quickly he spilt coffee on the floor. I heard snickers. Craig's bedroom was on the ground floor. I banged on his door. "Craig, can I see you for a moment?" Sounds of muffled speech. Who was he talking to?

"Craig, I'm coming in," I called out as I pushed open the door. And there he was. Sitting up in bed grinning at me. That grin. A large suspicious lump lying under his quilt by his side. "Do you have someone in here, Craig?"

"No ma'am." Grinning.

"Then why do you have two lit cigarettes in your hand?" I could hear the guys guffawing behind me in the living room. I went over to the bed and prodded the lump. "Come... On... Out!" A plump, blonde, feathered-haired creature with a tattoo of a flying unicorn spread across her back and a pair of breasts that would have made Dolly Parton gasp emerged from the sheets. Buck-naked. Unbelievably, she was grinning in a daft sort of way just like Craig.

"Craig, get dressed. I want to talk to you. Now!"

The guys sitting in the living room wiped the smiles off their faces when they saw how mad I was.

"Don't be too hard on him. He's just a kid," Scott said softly behind me. "You know, raging hormones."

"It's just that he never listens to a word I say. He's hopeless. I told him last week no girls when I found that other piece of work in his bed. What was her name? Something weird... Esmeralda? That time he said I had never explained no girls in the bedroom, and maybe I hadn't then..." My voice trailed off. "It's like I have to explain everything to him—like don't eat the daisies—you know what I mean."

"I know. But don't be too mad at him. I'll help you keep him in line. Give him one more chance, Di."

I stared at Scott helplessly. Why did all the guys love this dumb kid so much? Always sticking up for him. Protecting him. Only last week Craig had been stumbling around more than usual. When I had asked him pointblank if he had been drinking, Scott had quickly answered for him. "He's OD'd on cough syrup with codeine. Taken too much. I've told him to get back to bed and sleep it off." Craig had obediently headed away from me, staggering back to his room. *Codeine? Cough syrup? Please.* But then maybe I had it in for the kid. Did I?

Craig finally came out of the bedroom, a small feather from his pillow sticking ridiculously in his hair. "Yes ma'am?"

"Craig, I have told you no girls in the bedroom. You've broken the rule. Again." My voice was like ice.

"Yes, ma'am. But ma'am, this one here, Antoinette. Well, Antoinette and I got engaged. She's my fiancée."

Antoinette? Esmeralda? Where did these girls get these names?

"Engaged?" I was stumped. "To be married?"

Antoinette came out of the bedroom. She had dressed and stood beside him proudly, two enormous hickeys on her neck. "We got engaged last night, Miss—otherwise I wouldn't have slept with him."

"Where's the ring?"

Craig beamed from ear to ear. "I'm buying her the biggest diamond you've ever seen, ma'am, when I become a rock and roll star. She believes in me. Don't you, sweetheart?" Putting his arm around her, he squeezed her plump shoulders. "She knows I'm going to the top. I even wrote a song for her. She's just glad she's met me now before I become a star. You know—before I'm rich and famous—because she wouldn't have a chance to get near me then."

Maybe this dumb kid Craig wasn't so dumb after all. Engaged? What a line! I was beaten and I knew it. Once more I croaked pathetically, "Craig, the rules at Big Sab are no girls in the bedrooms. Next time you break the rules, you'll have to leave."

I made as gracious an exit as possible. Behind me the guys were no doubt gleefully making notes on "How to Get Laid in a New York Minute." As I hurried down the stairs, I could hear them shouting and laughing, "Congratulations on your engagement, dude." No doubt half of them were blind with tears at the audacity of the kid.

Know when to fold them, know when to walk away, and know when to run. I ran.

23
Ron's Agony

It was about 8 o'clock, the supper dishes were washed, and I was thinking about what to watch on TV when the doorbell rang. Ron stood hesitantly on the doorstep, his tall, spare frame silhouetted in the half-light.

"I was wondering if it's too late for a cup of coffee?" he asked.

"No, come on in." I liked Ron. Sort of a loner who hated dropping in if the other guys were around. I was still trying to figure him out. I poured us some coffee and sat down at the kitchen table. He was looking at the fire crackling in the living room fireplace, but his eyes wandered over to the stove where the remains of a pot of pea soup with a meaty ham bone and onions, rosemary and thyme was throwing off a pungent smell. Without him saying a word, I knew he was enjoying the homey warm feeling, the ambiance of the house.

"So, what's up, Ron? Anything interesting happening?"

He toyed with a folder in his hands. "I wonder if you'd take a look at this. It's for my writing course up at Malaspina."

Three of our guys at Big Sab were taking special courses to finish grade 12 at Malaspina College. It was called Rapid Education, a course for older students who had dropped out and a real bonus for our guys at the halfway house who had spent the last two years of their lives in jail. I was thrilled at this opportunity for them and would drive them up to the college every morning and pick them up in the afternoon because the college was at the top of a steep hill overlooking Nanaimo, too far for them to walk.

"I have to write a piece describing someone I know so I wrote about this girl I see every day at the Sally Ann." Ron worked as a volunteer in the kitchen there. For this labour he received his dinner each night for free, not that the Salvation Army charged much. Quite a few of the guys went there for dinner and at $2.50 a meal it was the best deal in town.

"I was wondering if you would take a look. Kind of check the spelling and stuff."

"Sure, I'd love to." I took the folder and scanned the neat writing on the lined note pad. I raised my eyes when I was finished and viewed him in a different light. The writing was exquisite, emotionally moving, yet written with a deft, light touch.

"Ron, this is beautiful. This is incredible writing. Have you ever written before?" The story had captured the essence of Ron's subject, the girl at the Sally Ann. She was apparently somewhat intellectually disabled but was a pretty straw-coloured blonde, blue-eyed and shy, so that men hit on her in spite of her handicap. Her confusion and innocent delight at their attention was the focal point of Ron's story. He was concerned about her welfare. I poured us more coffee.

"I used to write when I was a kid," he said. "It was my favourite subject at school... but then I dropped out at eighth grade."

"How come, Ron?" I had never really talked to him about his background. I just knew he was an alcoholic and had been out control with his drinking for years before arriving at Big Sab two months earlier. He had been referred by the Salvation Army.

"My family didn't have much money. I was expected to go out and work. A lot of kids quit school early in those days. My old man was in and out of work a lot."

"What did he do?" I asked.

Ron's face tightened. A short laugh. "What did he do? He drank a lot. He went to the war, and when he came back he became the town drunk. And the town bully. You could say most people were afraid of him. We lived in a little town in Novia Scotia, so everybody knew us. It was real hard for my mother. He had an evil temper when he drank and used to beat the shit out of us. My mum and my brother and me. I remember one time he pulled me out of bed to play a game of checkers with him. Woke me up out of a dead sleep. I beat him for the first time. He looked at me quiet and deadly for a moment and then without a word took his fist and blind-sided me. I went down like an axed tree. He made my mother leave me there unconscious on the floor."

I shifted in my chair as I watched him tell his story, the blue smoke of his cigarette swirling above our heads. His words were heavy, reaching out like the tendrils of the smoke invading my lungs, my blood, my mind. Emotional and thought-provoking words. A good storyteller. He was a good-looking man with wavy brown hair and a neat moustache, but it was the marks of deep hurt in his eyes that caught my attention. They were light brown, expressive eyes that looked wary like those of a dog that had been beaten too much. He had once told me that he never wanted me to see him drunk. He had lived like a skid row bum when he was on the booze, filthy and unkempt, sleeping under bridges and begging outside of liquor stores for booze money. He used to laugh and say, "You'd pass me on the street and not recognize me—that's how bad I look when I'm on the booze. I hate to tell you, but sometimes I would throw up and lie there in my own mess."

I would shake my head in disbelief at his stories and say, "I can't believe that, Ron! I find that hard to believe, Ron." And it seemed to give him a strange sense of contentment that I thought he was above such a lifestyle. And I truly did.

Sober, he had a natural dignity about him. He kept his room at Big Sab spotless, his bed made up hospital-style with the blankets and sheets tucked under tightly. He was articulate, well-read, and always dressed neatly, but like the girl in his story, self-conscious and shy. The words "a gentleman and a man of honour" would have easily fallen from my lips if I had been asked to describe him. Now, looking at the man sitting before me, I wondered if he was a new twist on the classic Dr. Jekyll and Mr. Hyde. Scholarly gentleman and skid row bum?

"My dad died when I was around sixteen. Crashed his car driving drunk one night. A one-car accident, so no one else was hurt, thank goodness. I guess we were all relieved that it was finally over. The violence. My brother had already escaped. He left home and went to university. He made something of himself. Unbelievable really... my brother... he became a microbiologist. Married with kids. Lives in the States... happy... successful."

"How old were you when you started to drink" I asked. I guessed he would be about forty-five now.

"Thirteen." He smiled at the memory. "This kid, Jimmy Fulbright was his name, got hold of a mickey of rum. We went up behind the house on this little hill and started swigging. I will never forget that first swallow as long as I live. I felt myself relax, like all the worries of the world were melting away. I took hold of that bottle and stared at it. I thought this stuff has to have magic in it."

I looked him over now. Thinking how he was always so tense and uptight. How he didn't laugh easily so that I felt rewarded when I finally got him guffawing. The magic stuff in the bottle. No wonder he craved it so. And his father, a victim of the war, with no psychiatric consulting or help for the men coming home in those days. A returned soldier playing war-games with his own family. And now the soldier's son, Ron, sitting here before me, the invisible scars hiding behind the pain in his eyes.

"I sure enjoy dropping in and chatting with you," Ron was saying. "Big Sab is real good, great for me right now, but I get a bit lonely at times. I just go to my little job at the Sally Ann and then home to my room. There's school, of course, but really I have no one to talk to... the guys at the house... I somehow don't click with them. Of course, when I was drunk I could talk to anyone... not fussy then." He laughed, his eyes shining.

I had the beginning of a nasty, suspicious thought. He sure was talking and laughing a lot. Not like the quiet Ron I was used to. Surely, it couldn't be that he had been drinking tonight. Dear God, please let it not be so. I scrutinized him critically. He was almost flirting with me. Holding my eyes locked in his while he shared his stories. He was saying, "Well, how long have you and Larry been an item?"

"Five years," I said.

He hesitated, mulling his question over. "Some of the guys at Big Sab say Larry is still married. Is that so?"

Jesus. God Almighty. I decided to kill Larry next time I picked him up from the ferry. Just push him off the dock into the salt chuck. Surely, he hadn't told the guys at Big Sab. I felt helpless rage.

"I shouldn't have asked that," said Ron hurriedly, looking at my face. "I'm out of line. Sorry."

"Oh, it's okay," I said pleasantly, clenching my teeth. "Yes, he's still married, but he is getting a divorce. It's been over for a long time. Between him and his wife."

Ron jumped awkwardly to his feet, avoiding my eyes, gathering his file folder from the table. "Thanks for the encouragement on the writing, Diane. And thanks for hearing me out."

"Oh... hold on, Ron, I'll get you some pea soup to take home." I hurriedly ladled soup into a Tupperware bowl, making sure there were some good chunky pieces of ham in it, then threw the container along with a crusty roll into a plastic bag.

We walked down the hall and then, unexpectedly as I was opening the front door, he gave me a brief clumsy hug of goodbye. I watched him walking down the road, a lone figure in the mist and fine rain, finally disappearing into the night. I had smelt liquor on his breath when he hugged me. Now what to do?

I went over to Big Sab the next day, my lines well rehearsed. He opened the door quickly when I knocked, surprised to see me there. The small black and white TV that he had scored from the Salvation Army was sitting on his dresser tuned in to a Blue Jays baseball game. The room was immaculate, the little sink scrubbed and shining, the tea towels clean and crisply folded over the rail. His schoolbooks were stacked neatly on his table, the notebook and pen lined up in readiness beside them.

"Ron," I started, "I have something to say to you, and it is not going to be easy, so please hear me out. Were you drinking yesterday? After you left, I thought it over real good and figured you had been drinking."

He looked stricken. "No way, Diane. What would make you think that?"

"Just the way you were. You were different. I thought I smelt liquor on your breath." I searched his eyes.

"I wouldn't do that, Diane. Scout's honour." *So much for the Boy Scouts.*

"You know, of course, that—for the sake of all the other guys here who are trying so hard—I would have to throw you out if I found you are drinking. You know that. Even though I would hate to do it, I would have to throw you out... and... shit, Ron... you've been doing so well, Malaspina College, your writing? You're one of the best guys we've got here." I tapered off, looking at him helplessly.

"Diane, I swear I wouldn't let you down. I swear."

Well, one thing was for sure—he was a brilliant liar. Convincing.

"I'm going to give you one more chance. This conversation will be kept just between you and me. I'm going to trust you. Trust you won't be drinking while you're here. Please don't screw up. I'll end up blaming myself if you screw up." I was surprised to feel tears well up in my eyes, my voice a little croaky. This right after the Little Professor plus I hate confronting people, nailing them down.

Swiftly he crossed the room like a man possessed and pulled me against him. I put my arms around him and patted his back. He felt so thin, almost frail. I could feel his heart thudding against my chest. His body was trembling, his shirt rough against my cheek.

"I promise. Don't cry. Jesus, Diane, I'm not worth it, believe you me. You have my word while I'm here I won't drink. I give you my word. If I start, I'll clear out."

We pulled apart. He looked so miserable, so distraught, his face white and strained. I turned and left him standing there.

I sat in the truck for a moment feeling wretched. A part of me had surprised myself by wanting to stay. To hold him and make him feel better and good about himself. I had totally confused myself by feeling that. Does someone else's hunger, someone else needing you, make for a powerful seduction tool? The power of being able to comfort someone so easily if I had chosen, was that my confusion? I didn't know. Maybe it was my maternal instinct. *Yeah sure.* Maybe I wished there was another Diane I could have left behind without compromising the Diane that drove away. Anyway, I had walked out of Big Sab and left him. Left him to what? I thought, as I started the truck and drove off. I guess I had left him to his demons and to his struggle. Left him to the perfect, sterile neatness of his room and to the echoing loneliness and emptiness filling it.

24

9-1-1

In my mind schizophrenia is the worst illness anyone can have. If you have diabetes, you know you need a shot of insulin a day, but when your mind is ill, you are unable to perceive what's needed.

My son Guy was getting worse. He was filthy, he wouldn't bathe, and as soon as he entered a room, you could smell him. His breath stank. He was becoming aggressive. Even the way he walked stated, "Don't touch me!" He was the proverbial orangutan.

For whatever reason I was always his target. The one he loved the most.

I would phone the Mental Health Division for help, but according to the Canadian Bill of Rights, unless a mentally ill patient is a danger to himself or to another, he cannot be hospitalized against his will or forced to take medicine. So I had to wait helplessly until Guy became so deranged that he would attack me or someone else. No mother should be made to watch her son become an animal.

Now Guy had decided he didn't want to sleep in his own place anymore and insisted on crashing on our living room chesterfield every night. Part of this was due to his paranoia. He thought he was being watched by the CIA. If a plane flew overhead, he would rush to hide behind a bush or, if indoors, behind a curtain. He felt safer in our house at night, but by the time we had endured two weeks of this, Larry's patience was wearing thin.

If only Guy would just go to sleep, who would care? But no, he would have the TV on until three in the morning, and the worst of it was that his body odour would come wafting like rotting garbage into our bedroom. Sometimes we would jolt awake to the sounds of banging pots as he cooked up leftovers or to the sound of his laughter. Loud manic incessant laughter. To say it was wearing and disturbing doesn't quite conjure it up. It was the laughter of a madman, and we lay awake night after night, nervous and afraid, waiting for something insane to happen. Insane being the key word.

I kept asking him to go home. He lived just three short minutes away in the cabin that Larry had renovated for him. It boasted the usual bachelor setup with a kitchen, living room and bedroom all in one open room with a beautiful, walk-in, glassed-in shower—unused as it was. It was perfect for a single guy.

But Larry was spitting nails now. Angry because Guy had turned everything on its side. His bed was tilted with bricks underneath; all the pictures on the walls were askew. When you walked in, the sight stopped you dead in your tracks. Van Gogh came to mind! Maybe I should have bought him an oil painting kit.

Davey wanted to take pictures of the room to enter in a photo competition.

"It's a work of art in a weird way," he said. "I kinda like it. It looks so different. It's *artsy-fartsy*, Diane." His laughter made him choke on his cigarette. He thought he was being cute, stealing *artsy-fartsy*, one of my favourite expressions.

But Larry was not so forgiving, seeing the fridge was also in a horizontal position and consequently ruined. "How the hell did he get it over like that?" he puzzled, hands on hips, looking at the fridge positioned sideways on bricks. "Your son must be as strong as an ox!"

Now here was Guy again, belligerent, yelling at me in our living room, "I don't want the Pope visiting here... do you understand?"

"Guy, the Pope's visiting Vancouver. He's not coming over to the Island, I swear to you."

"You're lying!" Spittle on his lips, his eyes wild. "Religion is evil. The Pope is evil. Don't you get it?" He slammed his fist on the coffee table, making us jump in unison like a pair of circus acrobats.

Larry stood up. "Okay, Guy, I want you to go home now. Just go home and calm down."

In one fast movement Guy had jumped over the coffee table and had Larry thumped up against the wall, his hand on his throat. "Don't you talk to me like that, you asshole. This is my mother's house. I'm not going anywhere." He pushed away from Larry and smashed his fist into the wall leaving a hole. "I don't want the fucking Pope here and that's that." His face was purple.

I stood trembling by the door. Larry was white as a sheet. I tiptoed down the hall and called 9-1-1.

"My son has schizophrenia. He's not on meds, and he is getting violent. Please hurry."

It took the police fifteen minutes to get there. *Fifteen minutes!* We could have all been dead.

RCMP detachments have a special police car for psychiatric incidents that they designate Car 87. It's manned by special crews trained to handle unpredictable psychotic behaviour teamed up with mental health nurses. Unfortunately, tragedy can still happen, and mentally ill people often become the victims of police shootings. Larry and I were questioned. Guy always keeps silent in front of police personnel, some kind of internal radar system warning him to keep quiet. But finally the police took him away to the hospital. They explained Guy would have to be examined by a doctor to make *sure* that he was a danger to someone or himself or the hospital wouldn't accept him.

After they left, we were joined by Ken from Big Sab, and we all sat around troubled and unhappy. I could barely look at Larry. He had always been so patient with Guy, and I hoped he understood that Guy was really fond of him. Difficult to explain that to a man who has just been attacked. Ken patted him on the back. "Come on, Big Man, let's take you over to the Pat for a beer."

I went over to him. "Thanks for not hitting him back." I kissed him on the forehead. Though it would have been an involuntary reaction, Larry with his size and strength could have downed Guy with one punch. "Go on. Go and have a beer. I'm ready for bed anyway. I've had enough of today."

I lay in bed in a half-twilight sleep, then suddenly wakened fully, thinking I'd heard the front door open. Were the guys back from the pub already? I peered through the dim light. A figure was standing at the foot of the bed watching me intently, motionlessly. I felt the hairs stiffen on the back of my neck.

"You bitch," said a voice. "I'm going to off you, you bitch! You shouldn't have taken his side."

I froze in the dark. It was Guy. Why was he here?

"What happened at the hospital, Guy? Why are you here?" I kept my voice as normal as possible. I didn't want to trigger anything.

"They said I was okay. I am okay, you bitch!" He screamed the words so loudly, so viciously that my body jackknifed with fear, momentarily lifting me off the bed. There was a glint of something in his hand. A knife.

Please, dear God, let the guys come home soon, fast. Larry, hurry! Then inexplicably, Guy walked out of the room saying, "I'm going to take a bath."

Taking a bath was something he wasn't allowed to do in this house, but maybe, I thought, on some sub-conscious level he knew his lack of hygiene was tied in to demonstrating the existence of his illness. Only when I heard the water stop running and heard faint splashing in the tub did I tiptoe out of the bedroom and into the hall. I strained in the dark to see the telephone dial and hit 9-1-1. It seemed forever before someone answered, but when I tried to talk, I found my voice had left me. When I am on emotional overload, that can happen. My throat was frozen in fear.

"Help," I tried.

Surely they could pick up my address on their computer. Didn't an incoming call pull up an address?

"Please speak up."

"Attack," I said. "Hurry." I strained to hear if water was still splashing in the bathroom.

"Your address?"

Dear God, didn't the police have computers in Nanaimo?

"55 Haliburton. Hurry, please." My voice was the tiniest croak.

Last time the police had taken fifteen minutes to arrive. Oh God! I was so afraid. Maybe they wouldn't get here in time. I hung up and called the Pat and asked the bartender who answered to get a message to Larry or Ken—Ken being well-known there because of his singing on talent nights. My voice was still whispery, but the man seemed to understand.

"I've got it. An emergency. Tell them get home fast."

I could see through the kitchen that the bathroom door was ajar.

"Mum, what are you doing?" I froze. Act normal. Don't show any fear. Guy was out of the bath with a towel wrapped around him dripping water onto the kitchen floor. He was holding a large carving knife casually by his side. "Get back to bed, you stupid bitch." He was literally snarling, baring his teeth in a feral-like grimace.

I heard the front door open, footsteps running down the hall, Larry's arms coming out of nowhere to grab me, the police coming in right after him, their bulk and their uniforms filling the kitchen.

They took Guy away handcuffed with just a towel around him. As they pushed him into the police car, I heard him saying, "I just didn't want the Pope to come here! What's all this fuss about?"

The phone was ringing. It was Guy's mental health nurse, Karen, calling to explain why the hospital had not admitted him the first time. "He holds it all together so well at the hospital. He told them that he'd argued with Larry, and it was just a family dispute. The admitting doctor bought into it. They are so strict about admitting someone unless they're violent, and Guy talked to them like a choirboy. He'd had time to calm down while he was waiting there and well... he pulled it off, Diane. It's so frustrating. At least now they will admit him."

"The whole system stinks," I said. "He needs help and they worry whether he is *really dangerous?* It makes you wonder what their definition of dangerous is."

"I know. It's very upsetting."

I said goodnight, thanked her and hung up the phone. One day, I thought, recalling the sinister figure standing at the foot of my bed, the police are going to be too late and schizophrenia disguised as my son is going to kill me.

25
Elvis

"We have too many schitzos at Big Sab," said Larry, munching on his toast.

He was right. The other guys didn't relate to them, and I felt uneasy about the mix.

However, I also felt protective of my schizophrenics, and Gordie Ryder cinched what I had worked out as a plan for that problem when he asked me if I would take in Elvis. This was Gordie, of all people, who had once told me that in the joint they called mentally ill people "bugs" and how everybody hated them and ostracized them. And I am pretty sure that he, Gordie Ryder, had belonged to that particular ostracizing group. Now here he was pleading for me to take one in. A bug.

"Elvis is different," Gord said, smiling. "He's a mentally retarded aborginal kid who has Coke-bottle glasses and a smile that would melt butter." He kept nodding and smiling at me. "Wait until you meet him... you'll love him."

Love him I did. We all did. He was certainly the sweetest, the most lovable and without a doubt the ugliest prospective tenant to come our way, but after a very short time, we all thought he was also the cutest, proving again that love is blind. He had black, coarse, ragged hair that wouldn't lie down and a lisp, and he talked about himself in the third person.

"Elvis is going up the street to have coffee, Diane."

"Okay, Elvis. See you later."

Or he would stand smiling at the door. "Elvis is going to the bowling alley to find friends, Diane. Elvis will like that. Elvis likes friends." And off he would trot, a chubby little boy on a mission, coming back with hilarious stories of people he had picked up along the way. Soon everybody in the neighbourhood loved him. He was an irresistible lovable puppy. But why and how in the twentieth century this mentally retarded Native boy could have ended up in jail, mixed in with the adult population, remains a mystery to me.

Elvis was born outside of Williams Lake and placed as a foster child with a Norwegian couple who ran a small cattle ranch. Besides Elvis, they raised eight more foster children there. When he came to us, he still called these foster parents Mummy and Daddy even though he was now twenty-two years old. And boy, did he love them. "This much!" he would say, spreading his arms as wide as he could.

Unfortunately, after this couple had been raising these nine children for over twelve years, Social Services, citing the couple's advancing age—they were now in their fifties—decided to break the family up and disperse the children to other foster homes. This after providing twelve years of dedicated, loving childcare. We found out later the real reason behind the government's decision was a new policy that white people shouldn't have Indigenous foster children.

The foster parents fought back but to no avail. Elvis was devastated and kept running away from his new home, and although he had the mentality of a six-year-old, he had the homing instinct of a pigeon and would always end up back at "Mummy and Daddy's." Social Services put him into homes farther and farther away from Williams Lake and finally into a special needs boarding school. Elvis broke out and hitchhiked over 100 miles to get home. Social Services finally gave up, but by then many harsh words had been exchanged between the foster parents and the department, and their relationship was never repaired. Elvis loved telling the story about how "Daddy picked this bad social worker up and heaved him in the garbage can because he was mean." Elvis's eyes blinked owlishly and he nodded very seriously when relating this tale. "Yes. *Right in the garbage can!*" God, how I wished I had been there!

Naturally, after being taken repeatedly from the home he loved, Elvis had become fearful and angry in his attitude towards his social worker. Then one day she promised Elvis a bike if he drummed up some of the money himself. Apparently Social Services wanted to encourage him to get around independently, but this could also have been a step in trying to heal the breach in their relationship. Elvis looked forward to that bicycle as any six-year-old kid would have done, but when he went to collect the prize, his worker informed him there would be a delay. He would have to wait until after the Williams Lake Stampede was finished, three weeks away. Elvis was distraught. He begged, he pleaded, he cried. He reminded his social worker she had promised, *had promised him!* Finally she told him to get out, told him she was tired of arguing with him. He leapt across the desk and threw her off her chair onto the floor. He was charged with assault and went to jail for two years. Yes, two years. Some story, eh?

After Elvis came to us, we placed all our clients with mental problems into a little four-bedroom house around the corner from us at Haliburton Street. We called it Harmony House. Each man had his own bedroom but shared the single bathroom and kitchen. The Harmony House gang came over to our house for meals, and I helped them keep the place clean, though really they did a good job of it themselves.

Elvis, however, soon ended up living with us because Gordie called and said, "I have another client for Harmony House. Robert, a schizophrenic, is finishing a two-year stint and needs a place to live, so Di... would you be a pal and let Elvis live with you? I'd feel happier if he was with you."

It has always baffled me how mentally ill people committing petty crimes while they were off their meds have been tossed into ordinary jails with the rest of the "real criminal" populace. Doesn't it seem crazy to you that they would do that to crazy people?

26
The Paper Chase Kid

We had been running the halfway house for almost six months and felt we were getting the hang of it. Things were settling into a pattern. Guys would come and stay at Big Sab for an average of three to four months then would launch off into the real world. Some would keep in touch for the first month or so and then, like diving off a high board, would plunge into the cold reality of real life and swim to a distant shore. Sometimes we would receive letters and postcards from faraway places like Montreal, Regina, Moose Jaw and once even from Come-By-Chance, Newfoundland. Scribbled messages. "I'm doing real good." "I've found a girl." "I've found a job. "I'm doing fine." Then like the string of a balloon that the wind pulls from your hand, our guys would tug free and disappear over an unseen horizon. Gone.

Some of the men were sad and broken, and I feared for them when they left us. Some went back to drugs and died. More than a few ended back in jail as though life was more comfortable there than in the straight world faced with the fearful act of trying to succeed. One sweet, innocent-faced kid with a mass of blond Shirley Temple curls came out of jail and broke down crying unabashedly as we sat in the car in front of the house before we went into Big Sab.

"I'm so scared," he said, squeezing my hand so tightly it hurt. "I want to do good... I really want to. I learned to cook in jail, and I want to buy my own restaurant one day. That's my long-term plan." The words "long-term plan" seemed strange coming from his earnest twenty-year-old lips. I didn't get it then. His fear. He was dead three weeks later when an especially strong batch of heroin hit the streets. The police had gone on TV to warn addicts how lethal and dangerous this particular heroin was. Addicts were overdosing every day on the stuff.

But I couldn't quite grasp that this baby-faced kid was dead. He had seemed so alive. Did I feel in any way responsible? No, not really. The boy had left Big Sab after two weeks of residence to live with a friend. So what did I feel? Baffled and perplexed. Angry that the kid had taken to drugs so soon after his release. But why had he done it just as his dreams of a new life seemed possible? A strong hint was coming through that his anxiety might have driven him to the numbing comfort of drugs. So many of these guys had high, seemingly uncontrollable, painful anxiety running through them. And Gordie Ryder's long-ago words began to have a special meaning. Death or prison. These, he had said, were an addict's only options.

But their stories weren't always sad. Some of the guys were funnier than hell, and on quiet boring days they would cause me to laugh with the memories they left behind. One fellow especially comes to mind. He was a long, gawky youth with an exceptionally long face and long nose, long arms and legs. In fact, he was just long all over. From underneath a big, curly, untidy bush of hair his deep-set eyes peered out at life with a puzzled and confused air. Comprehension of the deeper meaning of life, the so-called rules of the game, seemingly evaded him. It was as if he didn't quite get what life was supposed to be all about. His skin was alabaster white, and he loved to wear biker spandex shorts that made his long, skinny, white legs look even more stork-like.

I would be kind if I just stopped there, but he was a farm boy from the prairies and his name was Clarence Funk so that even his name caused us to smile. He told me on his first day at Big Sab that he was a victim of anxiety attacks, and would it be all right if he came over and sat with me if an attack came on? "Sure," I said, "that's fine with me." I was getting ready for bed one night shortly after this conversation when a loud knock on the front door startled me. I was hesitant about opening up. It was 11 p.m. and this was, after all, the South End.

"Who is it?" I shouted, standing two feet inside the door.

"Clarence."

He stood on the stoop, eyes blinking, so tall the porch light shrouded his head like a halo. His chest was heaving. "Anxiety" was all he said.

I led him to a chair and watched helplessly as he fought for breath. What was I supposed to do? The gasping slowly subsided and then disappeared. I poured him a cup of tea. "What can I do to help you, Clarence, when this happens?"

"Just being with someone I trust calms me down. A paper bag helps. I blow into it and it helps to stop me hyperventilating."

"Okay, I'll remember that for next time." I viewed him uneasily, watching his gaunt, pale face out of the corner of my eye. I didn't really know him yet and felt somewhat nervous being alone with him at this hour, dressed in my nightie and a terry robe no less! (Why do we feel more vulnerable in nightclothes?)

These nocturnal visits formed a pattern, happening three and sometimes four times a week. At first I let Clarence in reluctantly. He was such a weird-looking young man, such an odd duck, and when he stood, he towered over me. I was always waiting for something unexpected to happen. *What?* My old favourite fear occurred to me on more than one late night occasion that, Jesus Murphy, he could be a serial killer for all I knew! What did I really know about him? These anxiety attacks could be a cover-up for murder. A cover-up for getting access into homes late at night. With my imagination after seeing movies such as *Psycho,* I was capable of even thinking that Larry sometimes looked murderous. Thoughts of the warnings of my family, the perils of my job, running a halfway house for jailbirds, flitted through my mind. No kidding. Clarence looked that strange and weird in the flickering light from the TV screen, his deep-set eyes like the eyes of a killer. Just like Norman Bates!

But Clarence would always sit quietly until the attack passed and then would immediately leave so my uneasiness at being alone with him at such odd hours slowly passed. Sometimes when the anxiety attack was really bad, he would breathe into a paper bag to slow his agitated, agonized gasping. He would never leave without turning on the path to wave a long arm and saying, "Thank you, Diane. I'm grateful for your time."

Then in no time at all his weird, strange looks faded before our eyes, and instead we saw an overgrown puppy dog eager to please. A simple, good-natured country boy. Sometimes when he came over, we would talk a little while sharing a cup of tea. He had been brought up on a farm, he said. His mum and dad had been killed in a car crash when he was ten. He and his older brother had been put into a chain of foster homes. One night after a mild anxiety attack had subsided, I asked, "Do you have any idea what causes these attacks, Clarence? Have you ever figured it out?"

"I get scared at night. I lie in bed and start to get scared."

"But why? Was there an incident in your life, a burglar maybe, or anything that happened at night one time to scare you? When you were a kid?"

"It was no fun in foster homes. Some were bad."

I looked over at him curiously. His face was grim. "You mean they were unfair or cruel?"

"Aaah... Aaah..."

I looked at him alarmed. He was stuttering and suddenly the gasping and shuddering kicked in like I had never witnessed it before.

I flew to the kitchen, my feet hovercrafting over the floor, and grabbed a brown paper lunch bag out of the cupboard. Clarence was covered in sweat, hyperventilating like mad. His eyes looked desperate.

It was horrifying to watch. I wondered whether you could die from such an attack. Should I call 9-1-1? When it was finally over, the fighting for air, the wrenching, gasping sounds at last silent, he said one clear word like it had accumulated on his tongue during the attack and now was slingshot out of his mouth.

"Abuse," he said clearly. "I cccccan't talk about it, Diane." He looked away. I briefly saw shame in his eyes.

I shushed him quickly, my finger to my lips. Dear God, I didn't want to see him go through that again. He was anxious to go. I walked him to the door.

"Take care, Clarence. Try and get a good night's sleep."

He looked exhausted. Drained.

I closed the door and made it to the bathroom. I felt nauseated. Sick. My head, my stomach, just sick through and through. What had those bastards done to him to have made him so afraid? Whoever had hurt him must have come into his room at night because that's when all of his anxiety attacks occurred.

I heaved, gripping the edge of the wash basin until my knuckles were white. It had to have been sexual abuse, I thought... or extreme physical and mental cruelty. Poor, poor little sod. Poor sad, abandoned, unloved Clarence. I splashed cold water on my face and looked at myself in the mirror.

"And you? You were the one," I accused myself, staring at my distraught face in the mirror, "who wondered why Clarence couldn't figure out what life was all about." I needed a friend. "Come on, Shiner boy. Where are you?" A furry little ball staggered from his box and wobbled towards me. I picked him up, broke the rule and took him to bed.

One day Clarence surprised us all by saying he was taking on a paper route. He had seen an ad, had applied and was given the job of delivering the newspapers in our very own neighbourhood. We had never had the newspaper delivered to the house before, but as he would receive a bonus for new clients, we signed up to encourage him. I have never seen a more conscientious paperboy. A neatly rolled newspaper arrived on our doorstep every morning like clockwork at 6 a.m. Collections were made efficiently with receipts neatly written out. Who would have thought Clarence had it in him? Within weeks he had a second morning route assigned to him.

I said, "Clarence, I'm thinking you're another Jimmy Pattison in the making. Humble beginnings, big cash endings."

Two months went by and Clarence bought a shiny, new red bicycle with his wages. He was like a kid with a brand-new toy, but now he stunned us by announcing he was off to ride his bike back home to Alberta. Why Alberta? The family farm was long gone.

"Just want to do it. Maybe try and find my brother."

"Are you crazy, Clarence? You can't ride your bike all that way. It's over 700 miles through rough terrain."

"Oh yes, I've studied the map. I've picked out my route and I'm riding through the Rockies."

Larry had a try. "Clarence, do you realize there are hundreds of miles of wilderness? No shops to buy food. No telephones to ask for help. What would you do in an emergency? Where would you sleep at night?"

"I have a pup tent and I'm loading up with food." He proudly showed us a sleeping bag and a small pup tent that folded into a compact roll. Packages of Mr. Noodles, dried pea soup and a small saucepan. That was it. Oh sure, I thought. Mr. Noodles will sustain you biking through some of the highest mountain elevations in BC.

We despaired of trying to talk reason into him, but I held back on mentioning anxiety attacks in the wilderness. Finally Larry said, "Diane, he'll throw the towel in before he gets to Hope. There's no way he'll be stranded in the Rockies because he won't get near them, believe you me."

That made sense... so no more fruitless arguing.

Before he left, Clarence asked me to keep a photograph of sentimental value in safekeeping for him. He would write with an address when he arrived at his destination. I would forward it on. It was a photograph in a cheap frame of two little boys with sweet wistful smiles and masses of fair curly hair positioned in front of a dilapidated old barn. The bigger boy had one arm protectively around the smaller one. Their clothes were threadbare, their faces grubby. Their smiles were the only thing of hope in the yellowed picture. A feeling of the crushing poverty, such as in *The Grapes of Wrath,* pervaded the scene. Clarence and his older brother taken over twenty years earlier on the family farm. I had seen the picture before and had appropriately "oohed" and "aahed" over it, saying the expected words about nostalgia, sentimental value and family treasures. It was the only item Clarence seemed to have retained from his past. The rest of his belongings he could fit into a small carrying case. Old Goodwill clothes and a worn, navy-blue toque.

It was a bright sunny day when we all turned out on the street to wave him goodbye. Then the gallant, brick-red bike loaded to the hilt and staggering under the pup tent's weight wobbled down the road. A Canadian flag attached to the upright handlebars fluttered bravely in the breeze. The proud look of a modern-day explorer and adventurer was on Clarence's plain face as we hollered our goodbyes down the road after him. He stopped dramatically at the end of the street and his free long arm waved a last dignified goodbye. Larry shouted, "Go for broke, Clarence. All the way." Whatever that meant. After we had tried to dissuade him from doing that very thing. Some of the guys shouted, "Yo," as he disappeared around the corner. All that day and evening and on into the following day we would crack up when somebody said, "I wonder how far away Clarence is right now?" We imagined him sitting beside a lonely campfire at the side of the highway eating beans out of a can. An owl hooting in the night air. A solitary brave figure plotting his route for the next day.

Then a week later the phone rang. It was a lady from the *Nanaimo Times*. "Could we speak to Clarence Funk, please?"

"Oh, he's left town," I replied, adding the information for no apparent reason except for the fact it sounded thrilling, "He's riding his bike through the Rockies to Alberta."

"What?" said the voice. "You have to be kidding me."

"Why?" I asked. "Didn't he tell you he wouldn't be delivering the papers anymore?" Clarence was so goofy he had probably forgotten to hand in his notice.

"No. He didn't tell us anything. Not only that... he hasn't handed in his collection money. He owes us $650."

I sat down on the kitchen chair. "But I saw him collecting in the neighbourhood here. I paid him myself. He didn't give you the money?"

"A whole $50 the first month. He kept saying people told him they would pay double this month or they were out or they were on holidays. We bought into it like fools."

I was thunderstruck. Clarence had hoodwinked us all. Dear old goofy Clarence? So who felt goofy now?

Nanaimo, like most Vancouver Island towns, is a small and friendly community. People know and trust each other, not like in a big city where suspicion rules the day. Clarence would never have gotten away with this in Vancouver. Not two months' worth of newspaper money collections.

After I put the phone down, we sat around talking this one over. Had he really intended to ride to Alberta? Had he spent the newspaper money to buy the bike? I had wondered how he could afford such a lovely machine so soon after taking on the job with the *Times*.

Three weeks later our riddle was answered. Scott called in for a visit. He had been in Vancouver for a few days and guess who he had seen in the big city riding on a red bike? Clarence. He had been thrilled to see Scott and sent us his regards. "Tell them the first leg of my journey was fine, and I should be leaving in a week or so for the Rockies." *First leg of his journey!* Vancouver was a ferry ride away. How much cycling was that?

Scott laughed until he cried when I explained the scam.

"Maybe he's delivering the *Vancouver Sun* for a month over there. Maybe he'll deliver papers in every little town all across BC and Alberta. Maybe he'll be delivering papers for the rest of his life and keeping the cash. What a great little crook he turned out to be. We should call him the Paper Chase Kid."

"As usual, you're mentally warped, Scott! And to think I've been worried about Clarence. That's what gets me. I thought he'd be eaten by grizzly bears or he'd starve in the wilderness. I should get my head read. What was I thinking? And why am I so surprised by all of this? He'd done time in jail for theft!"

And then I told him the rest of the story. "Then to add insult to injury, the *Nanaimo Times* lady had said, 'Oh, now we have a real emergency. Who can deliver the paper for us this week? Would you do it until we get someone else?' Like a softie and thinking in some scrambled way that I was responsible for Clarence's criminal activities, I said, 'Well... maybe for a day or two.'

Thank the Lord, Larry was listening. He snatched the phone faster than a speeding bullet right out of my hand and said, 'Listen... Whoa! I said listen up! She's a middle-aged woman with nine men in a halfway house to feed every day plus a house full of schizophrenics to run and a dying old man to look after to boot. She isn't *delivering* any papers!' And with that mouthful said, he hung up. Can you imagine that poor woman getting such an earful? And that description of me! 'She's a middle-aged woman with nine men et cetera in a halfway house.' I mean, is that *me* now? That's what I'm reduced to? My resentment over-flowed, and I jumped up off my chair and smacked Larry hard across the head with a rolled-up copy of the *Nanaimo Times*!"

I looked up from the apple pie I was slicing to see Scott's reaction and was duly rewarded. He was shaking with of laughter. He loved a good story.

I still have that picture Clarence gave me for safekeeping. The little boy in his worn bib overalls holding his big brother's hand, both of them staring innocently out at the world, unwittingly expecting a differ-ent future. The jails. The transient life. The drugs and his terrible secret of abuse hidden, unseen, but always waiting for him just over the hori-zon. He never sent an address for me to forward the picture. I have often wondered if he had a final twinge of guilt at his little caper deceiv-ing us all so well and had given me the picture because he didn't have anything else to give. And in his own way he didn't want me to think badly of him.

"See?" he would be thinking. "I gave you my family treasure, didn't I? I'm not such a bad sort after all, am I?"

I hope one day he'll phone me. I'll ask him, "Hey, Clarence Funk. How's the newspaper business doing? You have a new name around here. We've dubbed you the Paper Chase Kid."

27
Awakenings

I pushed the buzzer on the door of the Psychiatric Ward at Nanaimo General Hospital and peered through the door's glass window. A parade of blue pajama-clad, zombied patients slowly circled the reception desk, paced down the hall and around past the reception desk again. The receptionist buzzed the door open. I could see Guy down at the far end. He waved to me—a good sign. Last time I had visited he had refused to see me. Now he approached me with a sheepish grin. "Hello Mum." He gave me a hug and bent down for a kiss on his cheek.

"You're looking good, Guy." He was. Bathed for the first time in weeks, though his hair was still a little matted.

He ignored my compliment. "Mum, why am I here? This is crazy, Mum. You have to get me out. Everyone in here is nuts." *Hello. Like I didn't know that already.*

"Let's go somewhere where we can talk," I said. "Do you have a visitor's lounge here?" I looked around. It was a very small ward with bedrooms leading off a main hall.

"I don't want to talk. *I want to get out!*" He had raised his voice and was now looking self-consciously down the hall to the reception area to see if any of the Powers-That-Be had heard him. When he got no re-action, he said, "Okay, there's a place where we can have a coffee. Come on, it's down here."

He led me into a small bright room painted in lemon and white. I thought Larry could feel happy here. There were tables and chairs and a worn brown leather sofa against the far wall. One side of the room was lined with kitchen cabinets and a sink. A coffee machine and a stack of mugs sat on the kitchen counter. Crayon drawings created by the patients were stuck on the bulletin board. Like in kindergarten.

When we sat down at the table with our coffee, Guy started talking. "I'm not staying here, Mum. I don't care what you say! I want out *now!*"

Where to start. "Guy, you don't realize how sick you've been. You need medicine—that's why you're here."

"Don't be ridiculous. I'm not sick!"

"You've been sick for years, Guy. Please listen. You have a chemical imbalance, and your brain doesn't work properly without medication. Like a diabetic needs insulin."

"Okay, that's it! I don't have to listen to this. It's pathetic, Mum. It's garbage and you know it. I'm locked up here and you won't help me. I'm ashamed you're my mother." He had tears in his eyes, and he stood up, trying to contain them. Then without a backward glance he walked straight down the hall back to his room.

I sat for a moment filled with frustration and despair, staring at his closed door. I could sympathize with Guy wanting out of this place. I felt claustrophobic already and I had only been there ten minutes, but I walked over to the reception desk to ask how Guy was doing. The team of hospital staff around the reception desk looked worn out. There was an unrelenting tension in the air as patients came up to the desk to argue about not having cigarettes or wanting to use the phone. A male patient with wild hair was railing, "If you had been followed by the police for twenty years—*twenty years!*—you'd be pissed off, too!"

A woman with a kind smile introduced herself to me as Jean and said she was Guy's nurse. "He's doing as well as can be expected. Don't be discouraged. Try visiting again in a few days—the meds will have kicked in even more by then, and we'll be moving him to another ward. He'll be able to smoke there and wear his own clothes. The patients there can even get day passes. It makes a big difference to their morale."

When I returned on Friday bringing clothes and some treats, I couldn't believe my eyes. A handsome, smiling man stood waiting for me at the reception desk. "Hi, Mum. How are you? Did you remember cigarettes? Oh good." He smiled fondly at me as I took them from my purse. "Come on down to the smoking lounge. I'll get us coffee."

I couldn't believe the change. It was like magic. I couldn't take my eyes off him. He was clean-shaven. Immaculately squeaky clean from top to toe, his hair neatly combed and shining. When he changed from his hospital pajamas into the clean clothes I had brought, it was as though my old Guy had come back from the dead. He chatted away like a social magpie. "The nurses are great—really decent." One of Guy's favourite words—decent. "Fun actually. See that little nurse with red hair over there? She loves the Blue Jays. She's neat. And you won't believe this—I met this guy who was in grade 7 with me at Beaconsfield Elementary. Small world story, eh Mum? So, when do I get out of here?"

"I don't know. Honestly, Guy, I don't. I'll have to ask your nurse. You look so great. I can't tell you how thrilled I am to see you so well... See what a little bit of medicine can do?"

"Don't get into that... I'm taking medicine because I *have* to in here. There's nothing wrong with me, Mum, so don't get started." He stared at me, old anger glaring from his eyes. I changed the subject.

As I was leaving the hospital, I saw Richard entering the parking lot. Trudging along, stooped over, walking like a Neanderthal man. "Richard, what's up? Why are you here?"

"I want them to check my medicine, Diane. I keep seeing things. I don't know if they're real or not. It's hell, Diane... I can't sleep... I see the devil outside in the night waiting for me." He shook his head in a lament and shuffled away. I stared after him fondly. Poor Richard, trying so hard to mend his broken mind, while my son Guy adamantly resisted the offered fix.

Guy was in hospital for three weeks, and after many hours spent in the smoking lounge with him, I became acquainted with all the other patients. Learned their names, handed out cigarettes to the ones who had no family visiting them, and realized how lucky Guy was to have someone like me active in his life. So many mental patients seemed to have been abandoned or have lost touch with their families. Some of this is the result of the fact that schizophrenics love to travel. Nobody really understands why. Maybe they're trying to outrun the disturbing, frightening delusions of their sickness and flee the cities, farms and rural villages of their past lives. Like bats out of hell, they catch planes and trains and buses that will get them away, frantically and hopelessly trying to arrive at a utopian, peaceful mental state someplace else. And this is why their families often lose them; they simply do not know where they are. When schizophrenia takes hold, its victims simply forget who they are or where they've come from. They also forget vital information about sources of help, whether they can collect welfare or, better still, a disability cheque.

I had seen enough homeless schizophrenic men and women living in Stanley Park in Vancouver to realize the truth of this fact. I had seen them emerge from the bushes and inner regions of the park during daytime hours to hunt for food in the West End's garbage cans. Filthy, incoherent, ragged people laughing with glee if they came across a big find like containers of leftover Chinese food, and I'd seen them eat this contaminated slop with their fingers. People reduced to animals. And this is in the twenty-first century! I'd seen enough of these horror scenes to frighten me about losing track of Guy. It is a real, justified fear.

When Guy finally came home, I was reminded of the movie *Awakenings*. I hadn't been able to talk to him seriously about anything for years... in fact, since he was seventeen years old. Now we laughed and joked, reminisced about his childhood, his favourite stories of Gran and Gramps and beloved holiday memories of the family cottage on

Otter Lake in Ontario's Muskoka country. I thought it was akin to a miracle. I couldn't get enough. All the family came over from Vancouver to visit and stared at him in disbelief. It was like Rip Van Winkle waking up or Lazarus rising from the dead rolled into one. We couldn't stop hugging him and laughing with him.

Sometimes he seemed a bit bewildered, staring at us with narrowed eyes as if trying to place a remark or comment. He had, after all, been mentally missing for fifteen years and many things were cloudy. I thought of all the times I had almost given up. Of all the years I had held on to hope—a hope that had been diminishing year by year—that somehow we would get Guy back. And here he was. No more the ragged Rasputin but a handsome man dressed in the stylish clothes that had been hanging unused in his wardrobe for years. Birthday shirts, Christmas sweaters never worn because he would be fixated on only certain clothes that he would wear for weeks at a time. Now resplendent before us, gorgeous in his sanity and full of fun.

I took him everywhere. Restaurants, movies, to Newcastle Island for picnics on the beach, everywhere the old Guy hadn't been interested in going because taking charge of the weather had been too time-consuming. I made the most of it. Every day, every minute. Obvious things like getting him booked into the dentist, a long overdue check up with our GP. But most of all we talked our brains out.

One subject, and the most important one I wanted to talk about, was schizophrenia. At last I could explain to Guy the gargantuan problems of his mental illness and all the miraculous modern-day medicines that were available to help keep it at bay. But he balked at these discussions and would become angry and upset. He was in total denial that he had a mental illness.

He was supposed to receive a shot once a month to keep him on track. To keep him sane. Now the month was almost up, and I brought up the subject with great trepidation.

"Karen, your nurse, will be dropping by at 11 o'clock tomorrow to give you your shot, Guy."

"What are you talking about?"

"You know. Your medication. You have to get a shot once a month so she's coming tomorrow."

"Mum, I don't want to argue with you, but you have to drop this. I don't need medicine. I'm fine. That's final." And when Karen came the next day he told her, "No, no medicine." She was a pretty young woman with unlimited confidence and a no-nonsense approach, but although she tried every argument in her bag of tricks, Guy refused to have the shot.

"I'm so sorry, Diane. He will get sick again. That's the bottom line. How long it will take I don't know—but he will go downhill from here on. It's too bad. He was doing so well. We can't force him to take it. He has his civil rights—well, you know." As she looked at the tears welling in my eyes, she gave me a quick sympathetic hug. "I won't give up. I promise to keep trying. I'll call in again next week."

I was heartbroken. The more I argued, the more stubborn Guy became. Until medication was such a taboo subject he would leave the house if I brought it up. I was stumped. Then slowly the subtle and insidious changes started taking place. And then the not-so-subtle. His hygiene started slipping. The body odour came back. The inappropriate remarks. His theory about a Point System where all men on the planet would be measured in points and Caucasians would start with a bonus 100 points at birth. The laughing brown eyes grew distrustful and morose. He was slipping back to a place where we couldn't reach him.

The day I watched through the kitchen window as he circled trees and chanted as he came up the road, I knew the Weatherman was back.

28
The Girl with the Far Away Eyes

We were having a smooth week when an unexpected curveball slammed into us. A bombshell. Ken went missing. We were all alarmed. Ken was so reliable, so conscientious and really was always just *there*. Never strayed from the fold except for his singing nights at the Pat, and then I was usually in the audience watching him. I phoned his parents. They hadn't heard from him in a week. We were contemplating registering a missing person's report when the phone rang. It was Ken calling collect from Ottawa. He had eloped with Nairie. *Could I believe this?* I wanted to say, *"Why?"* and then I had to say, "But she's getting married to Jerry tomorrow!"

"That's why we had to elope," he said. "She didn't want to go through with the wedding. She's in love with me."

"Ken, phone your mum and dad right away. They're worried sick about you. We've all been worried about you."

"Don't worry, we're fine. We're staying at my brother's place."

I was shell-shocked.

Lewis, who had dropped in for coffee, was quietly smoking a cigarette amidst the havoc. Now he ventured, "I told you she was screwed up."

"I wonder if she's told Jerry?"

"I guess he'll find out tomorrow when she's a no show at the church!"

And we were all suddenly laughing. Was it a release because we had found Ken? Nerves? I think because we were just plain sick. If this was *noir humour,* we were good at it!

We were still chattering like magpies over this love triangle—our very own—when two days later another collect call came in from Ottawa. Ken again. "She's changed her mind. She's flying back to Nanaimo today. Jerry is paying for her ticket. I'm broke, just have enough money for a ticket on the Greyhound bus."

It was a forlorn and broken Ken who returned to our fold. Larry suggested that he move into our front bedroom on Haliburton to escape the raw humiliation he was feeling over his foiled lover's plan. He was far too vulnerable to deal with teasing from the guys at Big Sab.

He holed up in his new room playing his guitar and singing sad love songs. The plaintive strains of "Far Away Eyes" drifted out of his door and floated down the hall along with Patsy Cline's "Sweet Dreams." But when he didn't want to eat, we realized the extent of his pain.

Nairie was married to Jerry in a small wedding service two months later. Ken brooded and slowly picked up the pieces of his life. Then one day I heard him on the phone arranging to meet someone for coffee. He jumped guiltily when I entered the room.

"What's up?"

Ken and I had developed a close relationship, so my radar was humming. There wasn't much we could hide from each other.

"That was Nairie. She wants to meet me for a chat." His Irish blue eyes looked troubled.

"H-m-m-m... Are you ready for this? I don't know, Ken. I think you're still in love with her. Why set yourself up for getting hurt again?"

"It's just coffee... She says she's happy with Jerry—just wants to talk. Maybe she wants to say sorry."

I remembered Nairie's mesmerizing green eyes, that heady laugh, and I thought of the lure of the Sirens of old calling out and enticing sailors, only to shipwreck them on the rocks, and I watched Ken go to his doom.

The trouble with Ken was he was still so insecure and shy. He still didn't realize he was no longer *that fat guy.* He had put Nairie on an impossible pedestal and was overwhelmed by any attention she might give him. He felt unworthy of such a queen's affection. Ate up the crumbs. This after all the emotional abuse she had given him. The next few weeks I saw Ken become moody and distracted. He was seeing Nairie two or three times a week. For coffee. *Yeah.*

"Her marriage isn't what she thought it would be," he told me one day.

I said sweetly but bristling with fury, "I wonder... what did she expect?"

"I know you dislike her," said Ken picking up on my tone, "but figure this. Jerry took her back and promised to forgive and forget, but he's totally paranoid now. She's like a prisoner almost... he won't let her out of his sight. It's a very frustrating situation for her. Would be for anyone. Right? And his temper—he blows up over nothing. Doesn't treat her the same way anymore."

"He has no respect for her? How strange. And she's a prisoner? Huh! But she still manages to meet with you often enough... I don't blame him for being suspicious. Come on, Ken!"

"He thinks she's at her mum's when she has coffee with me. She is sort of on the way there when I meet her."

"Ken, Nairie is *trouble.* I will say no more!"

And trouble she was. One night a car kept circling our house. Around and around the block. A BMW. How many BMWs do you see of a night in the South End? Larry finally went out and checked. It was Jerry and he was frantic. He stopped the car and leaned out of the window. "Would Nairie be visiting you guys?"

"No, we haven't seen Nairie in months." Larry, feeling sympathy for the guy, waved him off. "That man has dementia in his eyes," he said when he returned to the house. "He's close to cracking up, Di. No really. I feel concerned."

Ken came in later. And we *talked*!

"What the hell is going on?" I demanded. "Were you with Nairie tonight? Jerry is out looking for her and believe you me I wouldn't put it past to him to have a loaded gun in the car." The statement about the gun was, of course, just a figment of my imagination.

Ken looked pitiful. "What am I do? Yes, I was with her. But she's so unhappy, Di, and... Oh hell! I can't seem to stay away."

"Ken, if you had married her and she was running around with Jerry, how would you feel?"

"I know, I know... I'd feel like shit." The dark-fringed eyelashes looked suspiciously damp.

"Wake up and smell the coffee. She is *trouble*. She has no morals and she is dragging you down to a nasty, dangerous level. Something is going to blow here." I slammed my hand on the table. "Ken, you're more than a door mat! And," I continued, "if you are having sex with her, you're a despicable rat."

With that I headed down the hall toward our bedroom.

"Quite the little drama queen, aren't we tonight?" Larry's voice came sleepily from the depths of the bed. "It's kind of funny hearing you give someone hell for adultery when you do that act yourself."

"*I* don't have an adultery problem, Larry," I said coldly. "*You do. You're the one that's married.*"

Silence from under the sheets.

Then. "I'm sorry. My remark was uncalled for. I feel it, too... with Ken. Trouble ahead."

I could only think of saying in a dispirited mumble, "We ain't seen nothing yet."

And it was true. We hadn't seen *nothing* yet.

Jerry threw Nairie out. She went running to Ken, and elated, he made the plans of his wildest dreams. They rented a small apartment and set up house.

I didn't say a word.

A month rolled by, then two. On the third month sounds of trouble in paradise started to leak out. Nairie was uptight living in such a small apartment. She was restless. Why didn't Ken have a more prestigious career? How could he be satisfied cleaning carpets for a living? And then it was Ken wondering where Nairie was disappearing to in the evenings.

He called in at Haliburton Street for coffee and regurgitated all his fears, poured out his heart to us as we sat at the kitchen table. He thought Nairie was missing all the finer things in life that Jerry's money had previously provided. Jerry had the big house and the yacht and he was more sophisticated than Ken. That he knew. But he loved her and he knew she loved him. It should work out. He was thinking of taking a computer course at Malaspina College. Getting a better job. But she was a handful when she was mad. Threw things, walked out of the apartment, and he didn't know where she was for hours on end. "I don't blame her," he said. "It's very stressful not having enough money."

I stayed away from saying, "I told you so," and instead joked, "All I can say, Ken, is that you're getting grey hair."

He tried not to rush to the hall mirror, but he did. "Shit," he said, grinning ruefully as he looked. "Geez! Oh no... look at this," he said, fingering the grey. "Thanks a lot, Di!"

Just before Christmas Nairie left him a note. "I can't take it anymore. Goodbye." He didn't hear any news for weeks, and then, there she was back with Jerry.

Even for me it was mind-boggling. Why would Jerry take her back?

Ken moved back into his old front bedroom with us on Haliburton and made a miraculous recovery. As if a huge burden had rolled off him, he started humming again and singing around the house. Laughing easily, back to making his long-winded funny jokes. It was a relief to see him on track again.

But I have to tell you something funny. One evening Ken finally brought home a girl he had met at Talent Night at the Pat. She was a shy, mousy-haired, young thing who obviously thought Ken was a rock star. But the thing that made us all smile behind their backs was that she had a lazy eye. Seriously. Where did they all come from?

29
The Lamb of God

Gord Ryder often dropped in to have coffee with me, and I enjoyed and welcomed his visits. He had a presence about him that was calming. He wasn't really a big guy—actually when he stood next to Larry, he looked small—but somehow he was larger than life. I had the feeling he could take any problem on and lick it with both hands tied behind his back. He had such insight into the way the guys at Big Sab thought and felt. I had learned a lot from him on how to approach their problems. Now I needed his advice.

"Gord, I just interviewed a woman who wants to rent a room. Her boyfriend is here doing rehab at Surfside. She wants to be near him when he has his weekend passes so she will be able to visit with him. At present she lives in Victoria... and her name is Victoria as well... cute, eh? So she's moving to Nanaimo to be close to him. Sort of young love in middle-age."

"You want to know what I think?"

"Well, yes, but her boyfriend will stay with her at Big Sab when he gets his weekend passes, and when he finishes rehab, he will live at Big Sab until he gets a job—the usual routine. As if anything about this place is ever usual."

"So I'll tell you," said Gord, "you're looking at trouble. In my experience women always cause trouble. It doesn't mix—the guys and a woman."

"But this one isn't a vamp," I said. "She's a little, plump, motherly sort, really. About forty-five—nothing glamorous or wicked. I don't think the guys will be vying for her attention."

Gord was grinning. "Go ahead and try it. Nothing to lose, everything to gain. See if motherly works instead of vamp."

We walked down the hall onto the front veranda. "How long have you been married, Gord?"

"Twenty years. Why?" His eyes locked onto mine. Serious.

"Well... I guess... when you were in the Hell's Angels all those years, I was just wondering where Joan fit in?"

"We went through most of the hell-raising years together. Huh! I made a pun! Hell's Angels, hell raising—get it?" He grinned. "She was in the same shit as I was. We were married young." His eyes stared off into the distance. "She's changed these past few years. Our daughter Sherry got into drugs when she was fifteen, moved away to the Mainland. Got into heavy shit over there. She's a recovering addict now—you saw her at the NA meeting. But it did something to Joan. I saw her grow old, get burnt out. It just broke her heart. Broke her, withered her. Like it's changed her forever."

His voice was gruff.

This was unusual. Gordie Ryder with his guard down. I reached over and touched his arm. "I'm sorry, Gord. It must have been hard on both of you. Your only child."

He cleared his throat. We stayed there—hung in a dizzying frozen limbo, I thought for one crazy moment he was going to kiss me until the phone in the hall started ringing and broke the spell. It was the Psychiatric Ward at Nanaimo General Hospital. They had a schizophrenic patient named Tony. Did we have a room?

As I waved Gord goodbye, I wondered what his lips would have felt like. What was this all about? When I was honest with myself, I would have to admit I was attracted to him. Why? A *Dangerous Liaisons* theme? But it was ridiculous. I loved Larry. Maybe it was Gord's pheromones confusing me. Reg, my ex-husband, always swore that pheromones caused the state of love. Just a cunning trick of nature. I shook my body like a wet dog to shrug them off.

Larry and I picked Tony up the next day. He was an extraordinary 6-foot-3- inches tall with a good-natured grin. He looked a little like Jim, the nutty but loveable mental case in the TV series *Taxi*.

It was obvious he was a favourite with the nurses. "Now, Tony, you behave!" they said. "Be a good boy for these nice people."

When we were driving home, all three of us were scrunched in the front seat of the truck, Tony sitting in the middle. I said, "Tony, I want you to feel at home with us. You'll be eating your meals with us but will be staying in a little house around the corner. Any problems and Larry and I will be right there to help you."

"That's right, son," Larry chipped in. "Diane and I want you to feel at home."

"Home?" he echoed. Then he asked quickly in a tense voice, "Can I call you Mum and Dad?"

Larry and I glanced quickly at each other. "Sure, son," said Larry. "That's okay."

Tony burst into tremulous sobs and covered his face with his hands. "I haven't had anyone to be my mum and dad for so long," he sobbed. "Boo-hoo... boo-hoo... I haven't had a real home for so-o-o long. You guys, you guys..."

Larry and I exchanged a look, fighting for composure. I wanted to laugh myself silly, the floodgates straining to hold, but Larry patted Tony's back. "It's okay, Tony. It's okay."

Tony looked up, tears streaming from his cheeks and planted us both in turn with a big smacker of a kiss on the cheek. "Mum and Dad," he cried and boo-hooed all over again. It was quite the trip home!

When I showed him around the house, he shrank from meeting Richard and Robert.

"I want to come back to Dad's and your house."

"Okay, Tony, but this is where you will live."

He whispered, "Mum, I don't like the look of these guys."

I looked at him, amazed, forgetting my own first impression of Richard.

At dinnertime as we were sitting around the table, the group busily passing platters of vegetables and chicken, John, the Old Codger, asked Tony how old he was. Tony had been sitting with a stiff back, looking around uneasily, and I think for once John was trying to be kind, trying to make him feel at home. Tony kept his head down but raised his hand and wiggled it back and forth. Larry immediately recognized this as a clue.

"Twenty-three?" he guessed. Tony shook his head and raised his hand higher. "Twenty-nine," Larry shot back. Now everybody's eyes were glued on the scene, heads swivelling back and forth like tennis game spectators, the dinner all but forgotten. Tony's hand went down a tad.

"Twenty-four?" I ventured. The hand raised slightly.

"Twenty-five?" John was right in the game and yeah—he was right!

Tony nodded, a quiet, satisfied smile on his face. There was a bit of an odd silence then as we all resumed eating.

That night Larry and I were coasting in that lovely twilight moment before you finally drift off into sleep. I was curled up behind Larry's warm back, my arm tucked around the comfortable curve of his stomach when we heard a loud thump, thump, banging on the porch.

"What the hell was that?" Larry murmured. I could hear Ken stirring in the front bedroom.

I went nervously to the front door, Larry padding behind me. "Who's there?" I called.

"The Lamb of God," boomed a voice.

Larry flung the door open, and there stood Tony in his pajamas. His hair was sticking up on end, yet he held his posture erect, managing to look godly, while thumping a large piece of wood as tall as himself up and down on the porch.

We were speechless. He pushed us aside.

"The Lamb of God wants to talk to you." He strode regally down the hall, thumping the staff as he went. Somewhere dear old Mum and Dad had lost their status and were now reduced to mere flock.

We followed him into the kitchen.

"Tony, what's up?" Larry was curt.

"The Lamb of God doesn't want to sleep in that house. The Lamb of God wants to sleep here."

"Tony, there's no room here. We explained that to you. Come on, I'll take you back to your own house and bed."

We hadn't been back in bed for five minutes when the Lamb of God was back again, this time banging his staff against the door like a battering ram and shouting thunderously, "Open the door to the Lamb of God!"

Jesus Murphy. Bloody hell. We stared at each other helplessly. I could hear John moving restlessly in his room. It was 12:15 a.m.

"I'll try one more time," said Larry. "I'll stay over there until he gets to sleep."

In less than five minutes Larry was huffing and puffing into the house. "Quick! Call an ambulance—he's cut his wrist!" And he ran out again carrying our first aid kit. Thank God Larry had his first aid ticket from years of working in the bush. After the ambulance had come and gone, we sat around analyzing the whole scenario. Tony had obviously not been ready to leave the hospital, and his final act of cutting his wrist had dictated his return to where he felt safe. Fortunately, his cut, though nasty, was not life-threatening.

Because Nanaimo is a small town, during the next year we would sometimes see Tony around town, in a shopping mall or walking along the waterfront. Larry would love to make me chuckle by exclaiming in a loud voice, "Oh look—there's the Lamb of God." Innocent people walking by would stop in their tracks and scan the crowd, searching in bewilderment. They hadn't recognized the Second Coming of Christ, but we sure had. Of course, the guys at Harmony House would always refer to Tony by saying, "Remember the time that religious nut was here?

How the hell could we ever forget?

30
Boners

Vicky moved in and—as Gord had predicted—there was trouble, though not in the way we had thought. Just different trouble.

She was a card all right. She crammed her bedroom so full of her own furniture and knick-knacks that it looked like a swap meet that should have been held in a football field. There was hardly enough room for her. She was plump and short with tiny feet and a dimpled smile. A sense of humour that was dynamite. She loved to show her cleavage though not so much that she could be accused of being a tease, and I'm sure she thought of her exposed mounds as alluring. She had beautiful, long, thick, wavy hair cascading to her waist, and she always wore it down, which was a little bit much maybe for a forty-five-year-old. But what the hell—it was always brushed to a silken sheen.

She had black and white ideas on life that she loved to voice in a husky, gravelly tone that reminded me a little of Mae West, but it was so loud I'm sure it could be heard down on the Reserve. She had her own ideas on how the house should be run and scolded the guys for dishes left unwashed or bad language. "Now, boys. Boys! Have you forgotten a lady is present!" Body odour was a big issue. "Richard, did you bathe today?" In a very short time most of the guys detested her, thought her a nagging bitch. But after all of that was said, I found her warm-hearted and amusing.

She confided in me how head-over-heels-in-love she was, so it was her choice of boyfriends that astonished us when her boyfriend Rick finally had his first weekend pass from Surfside Rehab. We stared in amazement as this twenty-five-year-old brash kid with his arm around

Vicky's waist-less middle kept kissing her neck and cheek. He was like a kissing machine. Slobbering all over her as she showed him off to Larry and me in the middle of our kitchen.

"Well, here he is. Gorgeous, isn't he?" The throaty voice. Her face alight.

He was good-looking but such a child, and such an airhead. Like a Craig with good looks.

"She spoils me! She bought me this leather jacket for my birthday. She's the gorgeous one, aren't you, my sweetheart?" Kissing her neck again. God, it was sickening.

"Bloody hell," I said to Larry after they left. "What do you make of that?"

"Maybe he needs a mother... who knows? Vicky is enjoying herself."

"Larry, you always think shit like this is amusing. Why, I do not know. I think that kid is probably a big taker, and Vicky is going to get her heart broken. He's fucking her to take advantage of her. My God! She came all the way from Victoria for that!"

"Diane, you know your language is getting pretty raunchy these days. You never used to say fuck."

"Fuck off." Then I grinned at him. "You're right... it comes with the territory, hearing everybody swear around here a hundred times a day. A little fuck here and there in the conversation seems normal."

"Well, it's not you. Don't get South End on me. You used to have more class."

"Drop it. Class has nothing whatsoever to do with swearing."

Larry apparently wasn't in a combative mood so he changed the subject. "Anyway," he said, grimacing at me, "Vicky's a big girl—no pun intended. She can take care of herself. She should know the bottom line by now."

I wish I did, I thought.

A few days later Vicky dropped in for a visit.

"What did you think of my little honey?" she asked demurely. "You probably think I'm a cradle robber. Go on, say it." Her hazel eyes were dancing with fun.

"How did you guys meet?" I asked, dodging the question.

"I used to raise goats," she said as a starter to her story. *Goats!* That was pure Vicky. Always with the unexpected. Larry and I started laughing before she could say another word.

"What's so funny about goats? This friend of mine, whom I met because she also raised goats, introduced me to Rick. I took him in as a boarder. He was drinking like a fish in those days and was always in trouble. Fighting in bars. Money problems. He was a mess. I don't drink because my first husband was an alcoholic. That was enough for me! So, after we got involved, I said, 'Rick, it's either the bottle or me,' and that was that. I phoned around and found out about Surfside Rehab. I think he had people after him for money so he was glad to get out of town. You know, out of Victoria."

People after him for money. That started a bell ringing in my head. Why? Reminding me of something. What?

"So how did you two get involved?" asked Larry, leaning back in his chair, his blue eyes giving her that lazy, sizing-up look.

"Oh, it's such a funny story," Vicky said, giggling. "I was brushing my hair one night, you know, while I was watching TV, and Rick says can I do that? So he started brushing my hair standing behind me, and I feel this boner against my back." Her throaty voice paused as she raised an eyebrow. "I thought, hmmm, what in the John Henry is this? I mean I was taken by surprise."

"*A boner?*" roared Larry. He almost fell off his chair. "I haven't heard that expression since the fifties in high school." He was laughing with tears in his eyes.

"We *still* say boner in Victoria," said Vicky, seductively but a shade defensively in her gravelly Mae West tone. But she joined Larry in laughing now, the exposed mounds of her breasts shaking like Jell-O.

"God, what a seduction scene," I gasped.

"I have to tell you," her voice now lowered to a conspiratorial whisper. "The sex was *great.* The best I'd had in years... if not my entire life! Like *The Call of the Wild.* You know what I mean, guys?" Still laughing, Vicky's shoulders hunched tightly together with remembered rapture.

We all laughed uncontrollably. For a small moment I wished that Vicky drank. I would have poured us all a big one, and of course, you guessed it, we would have raised our glasses and toasted to "boners."

31
Mr. D

Larry's nephew Dave had just arrived. I had been looking forward to meeting him. Ken and I helped him in with his bags, taking in this tall, handsome young man's good looks and blond hair. He was huge, like a modern-day Viking. There was a faint resemblance to Larry, maybe the mouth and the hair, except Dave's hair had a sophisticated cut. He had just split up with his wife after a ten-year marriage, was also out of work and feeling pretty depressed. Larry had extended the invitation to spend time with us on the island to give him a chance to regroup and figure out what he wanted to do with his life.

The phone was ringing in the hall, and as I went to answer it, Dave's cell phone started ringing almost at the same time. I could hear him saying, "Hi, Mum," as I lifted the receiver to my phone and said, "Hello."

"Diane, get over here as fast as you can." It was Ron and his voice was tense.

"What's happening?"

"Richard is chasing that jerk Rick, Vicky's boyfriend, around the house with an axe."

"I'm on my way. Ron, call 911!"

I grabbed my purse and ran down the hall shouting at Dave and Ken, "Come on, hurry! Richard is chasing someone with an axe."

As we took off in the car, Dave was arguing with his mother. "Mum, I'm sorry, it's an emergency. I can't talk now. A guy is attacking someone with an axe... Bye, Mum."

When we arrived at Big Sab, the police were already there. There was a commotion going on, everybody trying to talk at once.

Vicky was crying into a balled-up Kleenex. "It couldn't have been your coat, Richard. Rick is no thief."

"What happened?" I asked.

It was Ron who answered. "That asshole showed up at the door wearing Richard's stolen raincoat."

Richard had lost his raincoat two weeks earlier. Ron had also lost a really good sweater and his radio just last week. As they both lived in Big Sab's basement, the theory was, barring it being an inside job, someone had come into the basement off the street when everybody was out and stolen the items. The only way that could have happened was for someone to have left the basement door unlocked or for an ex-Big Sab boarder to gain entrance using a key that he hadn't handed in. Now the police were questioning Rick, but he was a slick customer, and I watched him playing the offended innocent to the hilt. Another policeman was questioning Richard who was panting and out of breath. He was waving his arms in the air and not making much sense.

"Sir, all I want to know," the policeman said in a grim voice, "is did you attack this man with that axe?" The axe leaning against the wall was one Larry used for cutting trees in the bush, and it was usually stored in the basement, but with this event it had taken on a sinister, murderous quality.

"He showed up wearing my coat," Richard explained, trying to speak calmly. "I opened the door, officer, and he was there as plain as day wearing my coat. He's a rotten, dirty thief..."

"But you didn't know for sure it was your coat," sobbed Vicky, her breasts heaving under her purple V-necked sweater. "Shouldn't you have checked that out before you attacked him? You could have killed him!"

"I've never liked him!" Richard shouted. "I've always thought there was something sneaky about him..."

"Richard, slow down a moment," I said gently. "Remember the raincoat used to belong to your brother, and you showed me his name on the inside of the collar?"

Relief flooded Richard's face. The coat was produced and inked on the inside of the collar in tiny, neat letters was the name Gerald Westlake.

With a snarl of rage Richard leapt to his feet and rushed at Rick with outstretched arms. Good God, I thought, he's going to strangle him. Fortunately one of the police officers grabbed Richard, confining him to a chair. Rick, to my satisfaction, looked genuinely rattled.

I took the nearest police officer by the arm and led him into the living room. "Richard is usually a very gentle man," I explained, "but he was devastated when his only raincoat was stolen. I can't believe Rick was so stupid as to show up here wearing it. He's bad news. Other things have gone missing—we could never figure out who the thief was. Please don't be too hard on Richard. He's schizophrenic, but he always takes his meds and he really tries hard. I've never seen him lose his temper before. He really isn't a violent person."

The police finally took Rick away and Vicky went sobbing to her room. "He must have packed it with his things by mistake."

"Yeah. Like my radio and sweater," said Ron sarcastically under his breath.

There was a moment's silence after all the bedlam. That's when I noticed Richard sitting sprawled in a chair loosening his collar and fanning himself. He was as white as a sheet with rivulets of perspiration streaming down his brow. He looked ready for a heart attack.

"Are you all right, Richard?" I handed him a Kleenex.

He turned to me, his eyes wild and desperate. "What is the world coming to, Diane?" he wheezed, mopping his brow. "That asshole stole from me but the police were going to arrest me! They nearly locked *me* up." He threw his arms in the air with exaggerated disbelief.

"But Richard," I said, with a gently reprimanding note in my voice, "you were chasing Rick with an axe. An *axe,* Richard?"

"Diane," he replied, with a small sound of heartbreak catching in his throat, "I was only fighting for justice." With a majestic tilt to his head he retrieved the axe leaning against the wall. Then burdened with the apparent injustice of the world, he staggered punch drunk down the stairs to the sanctuary of his room, the axe clunking behind him.

I heard quiet laughter coming from the hall. "No wonder Richard is all knackered out," said Ron. "He was waving that bloody axe around in the air like he was the Last of the Mohicans. It's a wonder he didn't behead himself, never mind the rest of us. He was wild man."

Dave, Larry's newly arrived nephew, was standing, a silent statue by the kitchen window taking it all in.

"How you doing, Dave?" I smiled reassuringly at him. "Your first dramatic experience at Big Sab. Talk about breaking the ice on your first day."

"My mother wants me to come home—*now!*" he said solemnly, waving his cell phone. "She thinks it's too dangerous here."

"She does?" I guess hearing an axe story would make any mother nervous. "What did you tell her?"

"I told her, 'Not *now,* Mum! I'm having too much fun!'"

We all laughed. I knew right then that Dave and I were going to become good friends.

"Maybe your first assignment should be to retrieve that axe from Richard and store it out of harm's way in the tool shed over on Haliburton."

"We have to change his name," said Ken, looking Dave up and down. "We have too many Daves here. You're a big bugger, aren't you? What are you? 6 foot 4, around 240 pounds?"

Dave nodded, smiling. "It's our Norwegian genes."

"Let's see then. How about Mr. D? Like Mr. T. on *The A-Team*? Big Sab will have its own big guy—Mr. D."

There were smiles all around. It fit perfectly. Dave was grinning ear to ear. "My mum is going to love this! You're kidding? Mr. D?"

But from then on that's what we called him.

32
Gina's

I worried about the guys at Big Sab. They just didn't eat enough. When they came out of prison, they were given welfare, which was $535 a month. They paid Big Sab $350 for their rent, but they all smoked so that took a big chunk out of the $185 left, which didn't leave much for groceries.

They all tried desperately to get work. When the Island Highway project was advertised in the *Nanaimo Times,* every single man in the house applied. I helped type up resumes and there was a feeling of hope in the house. Everybody had their fingers crossed.

Not one man received a call.

It was pretty hard justifying a two-year working blank on a resume. It became obvious to me that businesses did not want to hire ex-cons. But these guys weren't lazy. They often worked happily for Larry for a package of cigarettes, which made me mad. It was cheap labour per-sonified, but as Larry said at least they were doing something instead of hanging around the house bored out of their trees.

I watched them cooking up wieners—Bavarian smokies were a big favourite. But Kraft dinner had to take the prize, and I wondered if Kraft knew how many hungry men ate their macaroni and cheese for dinner every night. And if Kraft knew, would they try and make their product more nutritious? Add soy extract or something. The guys also ate baloney sandwiches, fried eggs, and the ever-present Lipton's chicken noodle soup.

Nanaimo had some great food programs for welfare recipients at that time. One church ran a morning coffee and donut club, but it was on the wrong side of town for our guys. Like an hour's walk. The Salvation Army charged $2.50 for their nightly dinners, but the guys couldn't afford that every day. A local bakery donated loaves of bread to the Salvation Army, and you could pick up a free loaf on certain days of the week. But it wasn't enough to really help. The fact was that the guys came out of prison looking their normal weight and soon became thin.

I came up with an idea.

"Larry, let's treat the guys to Sunday dinner every week. A real home-cooked meal."

"We can't afford it."

"Don't be such a scrooge. Look, I can make up a good nourishing dinner for about $25. That's only $100 a month."

"How can you feed ten men for $25, Diane? Get real here, kid."

"Well, I can make spaghetti or lasagna, get pork chops on special, and go heavy on the mashed potatoes. Come on, these poor guys don't eat properly all week long. It will be such a treat for them. They're all so thin."

"Okay," said Larry, self-consciously looking down at his rounded belly. "But don't promise them every Sunday. Just see how it goes."

I had such fun cooking those dinners. The guys lined up every Sunday, plates and knives and forks ready for the go. I made sure the gravy was thick and rich and the mashed potatoes had extra whipped butter. When I bought the cheaper cuts of pork chops, I cooked them slowly in mushroom soup so I could make delicious sour cream gravy. Rice was cheap so I made up a huge pot and served it covered with Chinese stir fries and chow mein noodles. I made chili con carne with cornmeal muffins, and once in a while I scored a roast on special, and then it was roast potatoes and Yorkshire pudding. Rich, fattening, comfort food. I made potatoes every way known to man—scalloped was a big favourite.

Our guys lapped it up and would look forward all week to that home-cooked Sunday meal.

Then I tried some creative thinking. Until then the only item I had made sure the house didn't run out of was toilet paper. (Each man would grab rolls and hoard them in his room in order to take his own roll to the bathroom with him—a weird habit that I was afraid would result in toilet roll wars if anyone raided another man's supply.) But now with my creative thinking in gear I called local businesses and asked for food donations. My spiel was that we were trying to help the guys in our halfway house get back on their feet. These guys had nothing, I explained, but they were really trying. Could they help?

I was astonished at the outcome of some of my calls. A coffee company donated coffee that was approaching the end of its shelf life. Kentucky Fried Chicken donated a bucket of chicken each Tuesday, and I rounded out the meal with a dozen baked potatoes. A pizza parlour donated two large pizzas every Thursday as long as I picked them up, and a local video rental donated two movies a week. These little treats helped the morale in the house beyond measure. The value of the kindness of strangers. The guys appreciated everything I did for them, but Larry seemed to think I was spoiling them.

I had my chance to show him that they were grateful when one of his houses was trashed by its departing tenants. He was devastated. It was a beautiful character home higher up the hill in a respectable neighbourhood, and he had rented it to three preppy kids living away from home for the first time and attending Malaspina College. After two of the boys had returned home, the third became a wild party animal. Other wild kids had moved in and then street people. When we saw the damage, it was colossal. Filth everywhere. The bathroom looked like a disease-making lab. Broken doors and windows. Signs of drug abuse. Used needles and blood on the floor. When I opened the fridge, I almost threw up. Larry was going to call in a commercial clean-up crew but shrank at the prices he was quoted. I had a better idea.

"Let the guys at Big Sab help. Come on! They sit around bored to death most of the time. They'll help us, I know they will."

"Okay, but you call them... I won't blame them if they tell us to go to hell."

I made the call. *All* the guys came over to help.

"Larry," I said smugly, "they're *all* volunteering." Then remembering the used needles scattered around the place, I added, "But you better buy everybody rubber gloves."

The guys worked cheerfully beside us all day. Loads of broken furniture, boxes of garbage and broken glass were loaded into Larry's truck, and he took two full loads to the dump. Scott and the Little Professor organized the washing of floors and the nightmare in the kitchen. I took on the bathroom until I could stand it no longer, and Ron stepped in to finish it for me. We were both literally gagging. It was around 5 o'clock when I pulled Larry to one side.

"Let's do something special to thank these guys," I whispered in his ear. "This was the clean-up job from hell."

"Like what?" he said, eyeing me suspiciously.

"Let's take them to dinner at Gina's." Gina's was a colourful Mexican restaurant in the downtown region but not too far from the South End.

"Come on, Larry. It would have cost you a fortune to clean this mess up, and our guys have been here for six hours. Mexican food isn't expensive. Say everyone spends around $10 or $15 each. They never go out—it will be a real treat for them."

"Okay." He was looking at the shining clean house, the polished floors and the tired faces of the guys. They had worked like dogs and he knew it.

The guys couldn't believe it when we returned to Big Sab and I told them, "Okay, you have an hour to clean up and dress up. Larry and I are taking you out to dinner as a thank you for bailing us out today." Thank God, Big Sab had three bathrooms. All of them were immediately thrown into action.

Gina's was just the right place. Not too fancy to be intimidating but fancy enough to have tablecloths and candles on the tables.

We all crowded in. I had called ahead and reserved a table for eleven, but it wasn't until we were sitting around the table that I realized the guys were feeling self-conscious and shy. There was no banter, and some of them were sitting with their hands on their laps like they were kids in church and had been told to behave or else. Larry, who was very intuitive, gave me a wink and then asked the guys if they knew why I was labelled the girl who can't say no. They all shook their heads, looking at me and then back to Larry expectantly waiting for more. Faint grins on their faces.

Larry started singing softly that song from *Oklahoma*, "She's just a girl that can't say no."

I knew the routine and what was expected, so I threw him the customary indignant look. "I've improved over the years," I said. "I tell the Jehovah's Witnesses to go to hell now... which is something, seeing they are trying to get me into heaven."

"Oh yeah," said Larry. "Never mind the Jehovah's Witnesses! Go on, tell the guys the story about the Potato Men. That story says it all."

I couldn't help but smile. That story does tell a lot about me. What a pushover I used to be... or at times still am. I find it hard to say no to people. I wish I knew why... but I don't. Something about disappointing other people's expectations? Who knows? Anyway, I looked around the table at the guy's expectant faces and told the story.

I was married and young and had a load of kids to look after. Actually, more than look after because they were all living with me and my husband, and I was the surrogate mother for half of them. My niece and nephew because their parents' marriage had failed plus two little Indigenous children I was fostering. This on top of my own three children. Yes, seven children that were all under seven years of age. You could say I had my hands full. Old ladies used to come up to me when I was shopping and coo over the children. They were all adorable, sweet, chubby kids, and the old ladies would say in their cackling old voices, "You don't realize it now, but these are the best days of your life! Bide my words, dear." And I would look at their wrinkled, kind faces and think, "*Have you lost your minds?*" But looking back over the years with the perspective that the reality check of time brings, I realize those wise old ladies were right. Those happy, innocent and very busy days were some of the best in my life.

There was a fly in the ointment of my life at that time, however. It was the Potato Men. They came to our neighbourhood every month and sold 100-pound sacks of potatoes off the back of their truck. They were two huge, blond men weighing close to 300 pounds each. Go figure. *Three times the weight of a sack of potatoes.* They were brothers and they could have won the salesmen of the month award for the whole of the Lower Mainland if not the whole of BC on any day of any month of the year.

I was quite happy buying a sack of potatoes from them as their price was right, but when they started trying to sell me two sacks, I faltered.

"See how it goes. You must use up a lot of potatoes cooking for all of these kids," they said merrily as they carried the extra sack down the basement stairs to the cool dark place where I stored the potatoes. They slung those 100-pound sacks effortlessly over their broad shoulders, though on more than one occasion I couldn't help but notice the huge rosy cheeks of their buttocks peeking out of their sagging jeans as they laboured down the stairs. Very big, plump, rosy-cheeked, mounded buttocks. These guys were giants. Their bums used to make me grin.

When the second sack of potatoes started to sprout before we used them up, Reg, my husband in those days, protested. "Why in the hell would you get two 100-pound sacks? We only need one. Don't get two again. It's crazy."

But the blond potato men always seemed to step over my protests and the second sack would huff and puff down the basement stairs.

I tried everything.

"My husband says no more than one."

"My husband will be mad."

"The potatoes are going rotten."

It didn't matter. Their sales expertise always ended up overriding my arguments. What they said to justify their actions I can't remember. In a daze I would see the rosy buttocks disappearing down the basement stairs with my doom resting on their shoulders.

Reg and I were now fighting every month over this. He had gone from puzzled to raving mad. I started dreading the monthly Potato Men's visits.

I was having a tea break one day when Lance, my sweet four-year-old nephew, shouted, "The potato man's truck is here." I ran out of the room shouting, "Tell him I'm out, Lance," and ran into my bedroom and hid in the clothes closet. Lance followed me, running fast on his short little legs to keep up to my roadrunner pace, and as I slammed the closet door, he said, "Why are you going in there, Auntie?"

"Tell him I'm out," I yelled, muffled by the hanging clothes.

Now my bedroom had two doors. One came in off the back hall from the kitchen and the other into the foyer where Lance was now opening the front door to the Potato Men.

I heard one of the Potato Men say, "Is your mother here?" and Lance saying importantly in his four-year-old lisping voice, "Yes. She told me to tell you she's out."

I almost fell over in the darkness of the closet.

"Mrs. Foley," the Potato Man yelled down the hall. "Where are you? How many sacks do you want today?" Then he turned to Lance. "Where is she?" I closed my eyes and prayed. Me, the atheist! Coats and dresses dangling around my head in the pitch black.

"She's hiding in the closet—in there." Lance's voice piped. The little traitor. The sudden shock of his treason almost made me wet my knickers.

Heavy footsteps strode into the bedroom. Now the other children were running into the room, and Lance was saying excitedly to one and all, "She's in there."

I held the knob of the door with clenched fists, sweat streaming down my face. It felt like the Israeli Army was pulling on the other side. Now the children were shouting, "Mummy! Mummy, come out!"

The Potato Man's voice boomed out amused and loud and confident. "Mrs. Foley, come on out. What are you doing in there? Come on out, Mrs. Foley." Coaxing. The cheek of him standing in my bedroom in front of my marital bed, the very symbol of the sanctity of my marriage that he and his potatoes were threatening to destroy. The kids were still shouting and shrieking and laughing. This was great fun. "Mummy, why are you in there? Let me come in too, Mummy. I want to come in, too."

There was nothing left for me but to hang on to that doorknob as though my life depended on it, dignity and sanity long gone.

When I heard the sound of his retreating booming steps, I opened the door and weakly fell out. A damp steaming heap. The kids were all jumping up and down with glee.

"Mummy, why were you hiding?" I brushed them off and, weak-kneed, stumbled to the kitchen and poured myself a cup of tea. I really should have had a double Scotch, but in those days we were too broke to stock alcohol. Whatever was brought in on payday was immediately consumed. Had I really hidden in the closet from him? What kind of a moral coward was I?

The next month when the Potato Man knocked on the door, we exchanged pleasantries. No word of closets. He carried two sacks of potatoes one by one down the stairs. I had arranged to sell the extra sack to a friend in another neighbourhood. Reg was not to know of this arrangement. I had given up. Or shall we say, I had developed a new self-awareness. I knew I was the girl who couldn't say no.

"The funniest part of this story is this, guys," I told them. "Guess who those blond giants with the rosy-apple buttocks were? Larry's cousins, Syd and Jim. Two Norwegians with an unbeatable sales pitch. If I had known that when I had first met Larry, I would have known I didn't stand a chance. Are you kidding? I was a goner. Come on. With Larry having those Potato Men's salesman genes? Never mind the buttocks."

I surveyed my audience. The guys were howling with laughter. They loved it. The whole table was bent over. Ron seemed to have loved it the most, tears running down his face. It was good to see him belly-laugh like that.

Now the table was relaxed, Scott told the story of how his Scottish aunt was arrested for shoplifting in Toronto's Honest Ed's store. She had been so thrilled with all the bargains that she hadn't noticed the store had closed for the night. She was locked inside and had been shopping for a while not noticing there was not another soul around. She couldn't figure out what the security guard was on about when he arrested her. And her Scottish accent complicated her explanation. The guy didn't have a clue as to her predicament between the "nae then, wee laddie "and "the graaate bargaaains. "What the hell she was on about? She had only been on holiday in Canada for two days and here she was slammed into the Black Mariah.

Suddenly we were all having a wonderful time, laughing and swapping stories like carefree gypsies around a campfire. Larry winked at me across the table. True stories stranger than fiction always do the trick. The awkward moment had passed.

I had said beforehand the guys could order whatever they wanted as long as it wasn't over $15. Now they all stared at the menu in wonderment as though it was in Chinese or Arabic.

"What's an enchilada?" asked Craig, and worldly-wise Scott explained.

"If I order an entrée costing $8.95 can I order a dessert?" asked Little Larry, very seriously. "Like I'm thinking Mudslinger Pie?"

"Yep, you can order whatever. Go for it," Larry assured him as he scanned the menu. "Mudslinger pie... Little Larry, where did you see that?"

I looked around the table. Our guys were mostly wearing jeans and clean T-shirts. A few wore casual shirts. They had all shaved and showered and were looking their best, their faces glowing in the candlelight. I saw their eyes roaming around the room, checking out families and romantic couples flirting over glasses of wine, but they seemed ill at ease with our dark-eyed waitress who was young and pretty. She wore a mini skirt and a white, low-cut peasant blouse that accentuated her sensuous young body. Her Latino eyes flashed with fun as she gently flirted, taking the guy's hesitant orders.

The food came and the gang ate slowly, minding their manners. Would anyone have guessed we were a table of ex-cons? Except of course for Little Larry, our non-con abnormal normal. He was enjoying his food so much that later Larry said he would never forget the orgasmic look on Little Larry's face as he ate his Mudslinger Pie, slowly savouring each bite, literally making every mouthful count.

Months later Ron told me that night had been magical for him. "Not just for me, but I think for quite a few of the boys. We talked about it later," he said. "I hadn't been in a restaurant for years. I'd forgotten what it was like. Then sitting there with all those other classy people, dining in the same room as them, being part of the whole scene, I felt human again. I thought, I'm sitting here like a respectable human being, part of the human race. You know—not a bum."

That night Larry and I curled up in bed, bone weary but happy.

"Geez, I'm stiff," I said, sighing. "That was back-breaking work today."

"You did good, Di," said Larry, tucking his arm around me. "I guess I get down on the guys too much. I always think they want something for nothing, but you proved me wrong today. They really gave to us. I'm glad you came up with that idea about taking them to dinner."

"Why are you always so worried about money? Like are you in trouble here financially?" I had been trying to ask this question for a while, but Larry always seemed to change the subject when I broached it.

Silence. "I've screwed up here," he said at last. "Bought too many houses with high mortgage interest rates. Been a fool, I guess. I'm in *doo doo* so high now... up to my neck in it."

I felt alarmed. Turning to face him in the dark, I said, "Honestly? Why haven't you told me before?"

"I kept thinking I'd pull it off. Hoping a shot on the stock market would come through and save my bacon. I don't know, love. I guess I'm a lousy businessman. Or a fool. Big Sab sat empty for months while I was trying to sell it, and the mortgage rate is 18 percent on that house alone. Anyway, I'll fight my way out of it somehow, but that's why I'm always moaning about money. I'm not really a cheap bastard—you know that."

Eighteen percent interest rate. Ye Gods! I lay awake feeling disturbed. I should have realized sooner. Larry was one of the most generous people in the world. I'd seen him stuff $5 bills in street people's hands on rainy miserable nights and had seen him giving money to down and out prospectors in the bar on times too numerous to mention. I should have caught the clues when he started tightening up on the money.

I realized with a shock that Larry was out of his element here in this real estate world. The people he had arranged his financing with had always struck me as a bunch of weasels. One even looked like a weasel, so help me God. Beady eyes and a red twitching nose. The familiar mining world and the honour system of the bush, the men he had worked with for decades and the trust built up between them did not apply here. Larry had been fodder for the real estate cannon with his open personality and trusting nature. *Shit.* And here I had always been arguing with him about loosening up the purse strings. Tomorrow, I vowed, we would sit together in the office and I would get more details. Find out how bad it was. The bottom line. Try and figure out how to cut down expenses. Somehow.

33
High Noon

The Metis brothers were something else. Huge, physical Amazons with an overpowering, rugged presence that made you feel that even a bulldozer couldn't take them down. Put it this way—they made Larry look small!

Jean-Claude, the older brother, came to Big Sab first. He had been in jail and then Surfside Rehab. He had a badly pockmarked face, flinty grey eyes and a ponytail. Sort of brutish-looking, arms like tattooed tree trunks and a gruff husky voice. But he had a soft side to him, his eyes lighting up when he talked about his two children and his kid brother. Would we take his brother in at the appropriate time? He was still doing time and would be out in a month.

"No problem," I said. We had two empty rooms.

"If you're full up here when he comes out, I'll share my room with him. Would that be okay to share my room?"

Larry had often worked with Metis in his crew at La Ronge in northern Saskatchewan and could relate to what Jean-Claude was all about. They swapped stories about working in the bush, but I noticed Larry was restrained around him, not quite himself.

"What is it?" I asked.

"Well, these guys are the toughest sons of bitches you'll ever find. They are great workers. You won't find better. Never complain, take the cold and the worst conditions in the bush, but man, stay away from them when they're drunk. They'll kill you as soon as look at you. I have a deep respect for them, but..." Larry shook his head. "I would never want to get on the wrong side of them."

Jean-Claude was full of his new life now that he was clean, and he looked forward to reuniting with his children. He told us casually that his wife had become a prostitute while he was doing time and was long gone, and his children were living with their grandmother. He religiously attended all the NA meetings. He was a fevered new convert to the idea of going straight, and the endless opportunities of his attractive new life were now beckoning.

Gordie came often to Big Sab to talk with him, and I would watch them sitting out under the willow tree, Gordie not holding back on his punches—doing his magic with his words.

Once I heard Jean-Claude talking to Gordie about his brother and how much his kid brother looked up to him.

"Jean-Claude," Gordie said, "the most important thing you have to do here is be a good role model for your brother when he comes out. You have to hang on to him and keep him clean. You have his life in *your hands.*"

And Jean-Claude going on in his sing-song accent, "You don't have to worry, man. I'm gonna do it for my brother. I love that kid, and I haven't seen him in five years. I'm kinda like a dad to him, you know. Our old man passed on when Michel was just this high—so he's always looked up to me."

The long-awaited kid brother finally arrived. I was more than a little surprised. As much as Jean-Claude looked thug-like, this kid was movie star gorgeous. A sweet smooth face, the blue eyes of an angel, a shy, winning smile, soft brown curly hair. A Brad Pitt. The only thing the brothers had in common was that Michel was just as big an ox as his brother, maybe even bigger.

Jean-Claude was so delighted, so thrilled during those first few days, introducing Michel around proudly. "Hey you! Come on over here, meet my kid brother."

The brothers went everywhere together, joined at the hip. Then Gordie showed up one day to say he was afraid something was amiss. The younger brother had been to only one NA meeting, and now Jean-Claude was starting to miss meetings as well. Not a good sign. The brothers didn't spend much time at Big Sab, but that was usual with our guys when they had been in jail for two years. They wanted to be out and about, enjoying the freedom of the wide-open spaces.

Then it happened. I found a burned and blackened spoon, matches, a candle, a toilet paper roll carelessly left in the upstairs bathroom sink at Big Sab. The tools of a crack addict. I felt goosebumps on my arms.

What to do?

I went downstairs and looked around, taking my time but with a sick feeling in my stomach as I examined the peaceful scene, checking for dilated pupils. The guys watching TV in the living room, the kitchen with its coffee drinkers—trying my best to pick up on any different behaviour. Everyone seemed normal, but then not everybody was in. I was leaving Big Sab when Jean-Claude came unexpectedly out of the basement door. We almost crashed into each other, and his eyes briefly took me in. They shone... No, they glittered into mine. He gave a short wild laugh. "Eh... sorry there," and he staggered for a moment before he lumbered down the street. I watched him go with a heavy heart.

I was going to have to throw Jean-Claude out. Larry was in Vancouver. Should I phone him or try to handle this alone? I didn't think Jean-Claude would hurt me, so maybe it would be best to leave Larry out of this. A man intervening might cause a fight whereas a woman could get away with it. I tussled with the decision, but the more I thought of trying to handle it by myself the more I thought Jean-Claude would just laugh in my face and ignore me. What to do? Finally, I called Larry.

"You over there with your other life," I started sarcastically. "I have a problem over here. Jean Claude is on crack."

Silence. "Are you sure? Hell. I was afraid of this."

I told him about finding the items in the bathroom and Jean Claude's eyes. "Definitely sure—110 percent."

"Okay. I'll come over on the next ferry and throw him out in the morning. Sorry you're alone with this, Di. Don't go near him or aggravate him. Hang in there, kid. I'll be there as fast as I can."

When Larry and I woke the next day, a feeling of dread hung over us. I made coffee, but Larry wanted to get the job over and done with. He struggled into his jeans and pulled his sweater over his head. He was pale and anxious-looking.

"I feel like Grace Kelly in *High Noon*," I joked nervously, "watching her man confront the bad guys against impossible odds."

"You're not far from wrong."

"Are you scared?"

"I'd be crazy if I wasn't."

"Larry," I said, "let's be smart about this. Why don't we call the police for back-up?"

He wrestled with this.

"What do you say? I'll call them and give them a heads-up," I said. "Just warn them we might have trouble."

"No. I'm just going to do it. I think the less fuss the better. If I tell them quietly with no ruckus from anyone else around, they might be okay... but if I'm not back in ten minutes, dial 9-1-1."

"Do you want me to come with you?"

"No. Stay here—just call for help if I'm not back in ten."

It was 8 a.m. when I watched him walk across the road—a big, overweight, middle-aged guy with mussed-up hair who was scared to death. His arms swinging loosely by his side. *Almost* like a gun fighter, I thought. The street empty and silent on a Sunday morning. I felt proud of him, a swell of pride actually. He had guts, but the knots were tight in my stomach. Those Metis brothers were huge, and there were two of them. One wild on dope. *Maybe two.* The minutes ticked by. I should have gone with him, I thought. I felt such relief when I saw him emerge from the front door of Big Sab and start across the street. I felt like running to meet him.

"How did it go?'

"He accepted it. Both of them are going. I'm driving them to the bus depot in an hour."

"You're kidding. No fuss? No arguing?"

"Nope. I guess he's come down from last night's high. He was subdued, just said, 'Okay.' Cut and dried."

"What did you say when they opened the door?"

"Jean-Claude, I'm here to ask you to leave. You're on drugs. You know the rules."

"Wow—just like that."

Throwing guys out was the part of the job that both Larry and I dreaded the most. Some guys had begged and pleaded for one more chance. Others had broken down and cried. It made us feel inhumane, uncaring, but as Gordie had schooled us, if we didn't adhere to the rules, we were letting the rest of the guys down. They were with us to learn about life's consequences, lessons they had skipped during childhood.

Larry was usually the one to do the throwing out. One time a quiet, pleasant man, one of the guys called John, came home hopelessly drunk. This guy was an artist. He had an incredible talent and just the day before had shown us his pencil drawing of the Beatles. You could have taken it for a photograph it was so life-like. Larry had given him the usual "throw-out speech" then said he would drive him to wherever with his stuff.

That night in bed I told Larry that I had heard from the other guys that John had tied one on because he'd found out that very day his youngest daughter had cancer. All of the men at Big Sab had felt stricken for him.

"We shouldn't have thrown him out," I cried. "I feel so awful, that poor man. And now he's somewhere on the street in the cold."

Larry had pulled me over to his side of the bed and said, "I wasn't going to tell you this, kid, but I booked him into the Big Six Motel for a couple of nights until he could find a place. And I slipped him a few bucks. Don't worry. He should be all right."

"But you didn't even know his daughter had cancer, did you? Or did he tell you?"

"No, I always liked the guy. He was a decent man, Diane. He just screwed up. I felt sorry for the poor bastard."

I had smiled in the dark, feeling relief over John, but then thinking with a grimace how many other soft-hearted stories were there that Larry hadn't filled me in on? Throwing a user out and then putting him up in a motel? *Oh please.* Gordie Ryder would shit a brick.

But that morning's throwing-out ritual had been different. There was a deadliness about it. I made us more coffee. We were both still tense and unusually quiet. These Metis brothers still had time to cause trouble—big time—as they weren't gone yet.

My mind was thrashing around like a prairie combine harvester. "Are you going to be safe driving them to the bus depot? They could kill you and abscond with the truck." Larry threw me a look that could have withered an artificial plant.

Then came the knock on the door. We both jumped. There on the doorstep stood the massive, bleary-eyed Jean-Claude, wearing a faded red-checkered logger's shirt, the usual large haversack carried by transient men strapped on his back. He was smoking a cigarette. "We're ready," he said.

As Larry walked the brothers to the truck, the younger one, Michel, grinning like a Cheshire cat, Jean-Claude turned and nodded slightly in my direction. Tersely, he said one word. "Sorry." It surprised me. No anger. Instead, the dignity of a remorseful man.

Gord came around the next day and told me the whole story. "It's a little unbelievable," he said. "We were worried about Jean-Claude with his heavy drug record being a bad influence on his brother, you know, but it was the other way around. The younger brother turned the older brother back onto drugs. I knew as soon as Michel didn't turn up for NA meetings something was wrong. I could smell it... Jean-Claude had a chance until that asshole younger brother turned up."

"That Michel with his baby doll smile like butter wouldn't melt in his mouth! Puts a new twist on the Good, the Bad and the Ugly," I mused aloud. "Like Michel was the Bad and the Ugly in this case even though he looked so good. Though you have to admit Jean-Claude looked like the Ugly one. I guess I should phone Jean-Claude's probation officer and tell him he's back on drugs. They'll put him back in jail, right?"

"You can't do that, Diane." Gord was looking at me strangely.

"Why?"

"Well, they're them and we are us. Do you know what I mean?"

"No," I was staring at him, only faintly comprehending the message. "You mean you don't want Jean-Claude back in jail?"

"Right. You can't turn him in like that."

I stared at him in amazement. I wanted to say, "Je-es-us, Gordie! You still think like a con." But I was saved from saying that as Larry interrupted us by charging through the kitchen door.

"Guess what? I was just talking to a Mountie down at the station and found out those Metis brothers have a rap sheet as long as your arm, violent assaults being their most favourite occupation. And I was fool enough to single-handedly throw them out!" He stood framed in the doorway wearing an idiotic smile, obviously totally enraptured with himself.

"Sit down, Gary Cooper," I ordered, "and take off your guns. Enough of fighting bad guys for one day. I'm making you a hero's lunch. Gord, would you like to join us? Can I rustle you up some grub? Cheeseburgers? Home-made fries?"

"Oh look, Di. That's my cousin Patsy on that real estate commercial." Larry was pointing to the TV.

I turned in time to see a smiling, glamorous face on the screen. "Wow—that's *your cousin*? Bloody hell, she's gorgeous. Movie star gorgeous. She actually looks like Grace Kelly. The blue eyes and that blonde hair."

"Well, she's Norwegian. That's why she's blonde... Same reason I'm blond," Larry joked, making his eyebrows go rapidly up and down like Groucho Marx. "I haven't seen her in years. I guess since I was twelve. I keep thinking I should look her up. Her dad is my dad's brother so that makes us first cousins. Uncle Gord came over to Nanaimo in the forties, and I think Patsy was even born over here."

I served up lunch, but there was an unfamiliar cloud darkening my horizon just flitting over there in the far corner of my emotional eye. A worrisome nagging feeling of unease. Was I worrying the Metis brothers would come back? No... I don't think so, not that. So what then? Oh, what the hell. There had been enough drama for one day. I threw sliced Walla Walla onions and tomatoes on my cheeseburger and bit into my lunch.

34
Swapping Stories

Sitting on the back porch listening to the guys swapping stories was an education of sorts. They loved talking about different highs as if they were different love affairs. They would describe the ecstasy of heroin as a bigger thrill than an orgasm. Can you believe? And they all had stories about how crack was an instant addiction. So many times they had heard the line, "Maybe I'll try it once—just once—to see what it's like, but that's all." Then as soon as the drug was taken, the users with a bright new hunger shining in their eyes would say, "Wow! Do you have any more of this stuff?"

Steve, whom I never did grow to like, related a story about a crack house that he had lived in where most days everybody sat around getting high. One afternoon he realized the guy sitting beside him wasn't snoozing. He was dead. He had OD'd. Steve had waited for a suitable moment, and when he thought nobody was watching, he frisked the dead man for his wallet then got out of there. "My only regret was I couldn't lift his boots. They were fucking neat-looking boots."

I visibly winced.

Then Gordie started. "I have a story for you. This one is kinda brutal. This prominent business guy had screwed the Hell's Angels out of a drug debt. Kept promising to pay but didn't. They had hit men looking for him, waiting for the right moment. They were basically going to wipe him out, but the guy was smart, kept eluding them and only going to crowded places. So, the Hell's Angels devised a plan. They knew he had a quirk for young girls, so they promised two fifteen-year-old kids big money to call him up and invite him to an out-of-the-way lakeside cottage for a weekend of sex and fun. They were pretty explicit on the phone about the sex... and the guy fell for it. And so they finally got him. Wiped him out at the cottage... but you know what they had to do then?"

The guys were listening, nodding.

"What did they have to do?" I asked.

Gordie turned slowly and looked at me. He hadn't realized I was sitting back there listening.

"Well, then they had to get rid of the kids... because they'd witnessed it."

"Get rid of them?" I didn't get it. "You mean get them out of town?"

A silence, but not too long. The guys all were listening, a tension in the air.

"They had to kill them as well." Gordie's voice was flat and hard. Impersonal.

I stared at him horrified. *The two young girls?*

"Yes," he said. "Quite a day's work. I had a drink with the guys who did the job when they got back into town. They were pretty freaked out." Gordie's eyes were a hard, bottomless blue.

That night in bed I hugged up against Larry's back.

"Do you think Gordie Ryder killed people when he was in the Hell's Angels?" I asked.

"Who knows?" said Larry. He was reading one of my favourite books, Gabriel Garcia Márquez's *Love in the Time of Cholera*. His reading glasses were perched on his nose, making him look sweet and vulnerable, like a John Walton sort of a guy. I related the story of the two girls being murdered.

"Diane, these guys are from a different world. Don't try and understand this stuff. Don't open the door to it. Keep it out."

"Do you think Gordie was one of the hit men who killed those girls?"

"*Jesus Christ*, Diane..."

"Larry," I said. "*Larry...?*"

There was a silence as he closed his book and turned off the light. Then his arms were holding me close, and I relaxed against his familiar warmth and smell.

"Maybe we shouldn't be doing this... this Big Sab stuff," he said, kissing my face and hair. "I love you, kid. I don't want you to get screwed up."

35

Beach Bums

When I woke, a thin pink light was poking in through the window, and I leapt out of bed before the alarm went off. I hadn't been so excited about going to the beach since I was a kid in Wales. God, those days brought a wry smile to my lips. Wales has atrociously rainy summers, but as long as it hadn't started raining before we left home, our family undaunted still went on beach excursions. We huddled together wrapped in blankets, eating soggy cheese and tomato or egg salad sandwiches, inordinately happy to be spending our summer days shivering on windswept beaches.

Now here I was excited about going to another wild, windswept beach. Except I was an adult, and instead of my family, I was going with a motley bunch of bums. Scott had talked us all into it last night.

"Are you kidding? You haven't been to the west side of the Island yet? You haven't seen Long Beach or Tofino?"

I shook my head. "I've heard it's beautiful over there."

"It's glorious. The sea pounds in from Japan. The full fury of the ocean." He threw his arms up dramatically in the air. "The waves on Long Beach are spectacular. So... guess what, kiddo?" Scott was delivering his news like the Sermon on the Mount. "John says I can borrow his van, so how about us all taking off for Long Beach tomorrow?"

"I'll come," said Little Larry, beaming. "I'd like to do that trip. I've never been to Torfino."

"Me too," said Craig, inviting himself.

"How long will it take to get there?"

"Two and a half to three hours each way so we'll have to take off early."

"I don't know," I said hesitantly. "I shouldn't really leave the Old Codger for a whole day."

"Please," said Scott. "Where's your sense of adventure? Just pack John some sandwiches for lunch, and one of the guys can run up and get him McDonalds for dinner. It's not going to kill him for one day. You never get out. It will do you good to get away."

True. I had been down in the dumps lately, feeling tied to the house with the ailing old man. "Okay," I said. "Let me ask the Old Codger. If he's okay with it, it's a deal."

Old John was agreeable. "You fuss too much over me. I can manage. I'll cook myself a couple of eggs and bacon for dinner if need be. Go and enjoy yourself. But make sure Scott drives safely. I'm not sure of him sometimes."

I laughed. "Not sure of him, eh? Hello. That's because he's crazier than a shit house rat. You're a good judge of character, John." I loved making the Old Codger laugh. It was like squeezing blood out of a stone to make that old man guffaw, so I was gratified when a hoarse rumble surfaced from his chest.

So here we were climbing into the truck. It was a glorious day, the air drifting off the ocean clean and fresh, dawn's fingers of pink and scarlet streaking the sky. I had made up a ton of sandwiches, but Scott in his ingenious way had organized everything else, preparing a big thermos of coffee, filling a bag with plastic cups and napkins, and arranging blankets and pillows in the back seat of the truck.

It was 5:30 when we rattled down the street, Scott whistling, Craig and Little Larry hunched sleepily against the pillows in the back.

"I hope this van is good enough to get us there," I said, alarmed at the creaking and groaning.

"Of course! Don't worry, just enjoy," Scott said and began humming "On the Road Again." In spite of the early hour he was as bright and alert as a raven, his hair slicked back and shining black as coal and his dark eyes alight with delight. He was in thrall just to be driving, to be behind the wheel of that old van.

I sat back and relaxed. This was fun. Life at Big Sab could be so dreary. Cooking, cleaning, making endless cups of coffee and listening to sad, beaten men tell endless stories. Here we were on the road on our way to one of the most beautiful beaches in the world. Hip, hip, and yippee!

We stopped for gas in Parksville, had coffee and donuts at Tim Hortons and stretched our legs.

"Wait until we get to Cathedral Grove," said Scott through sugar-coated lips. You are going to be in awe."

"What is it?" I asked.

"It has some of the tallest, oldest trees on the Island. Hundreds and hundreds of years old. Maybe over a thousand. It really does feel like a cathedral there. A sort of mystic religious feeling that has nothing to do with the church."

When Scott stopped the truck, I realized I had dozed off, but we all trundled out of the vehicle and walked among the trees. And Scott was right. Cathedral Grove was magically spellbinding. The trees were so tall that even if you craned your head back, you still couldn't see the tops. I ran my hands over the bark of one of the giants. History imbedded in nature. The roots alone were so big and gnarled they were taller than an average-sized man.

Little Larry stood gazing around, a look of simple pleasure upon his face, but I watched Scott and Craig wandering off, Scott explaining the history as they walked together, and I marvelled at the strange bond that had developed between the two of them. Scott had so much patience with loony tunes Craig.

We had been travelling for at least an hour since leaving Cathedral Grove, and I was thinking we must be almost on the other side of the Island, but we kept climbing and climbing up a steep winding road between lakes and majestic, blue-tinged mountains with higher, snow-capped mountains in the distance. We had already discussed strange diseases with Ebola being rated our most fascinating, our favourite foods with Little Larry presenting a list as long as your arm, and strange phenomena. We all loved the story of spontaneous combustion, which Scott insisted was documented, of a man dancing with a girl when she went up in smoke, leaving her clothes in a steaming heap on the floor. What a way to go!

"How much farther, Scott?" I demanded at last. "And how much higher? My God, we'll be lucky if this old van makes it."

"Almost there, almost there. Just look at the view! When we come down the mountains on the other side, you are going to see the most beautiful lake you've ever seen. It's the most unusual shade of blue. Hard to describe."

But I was getting anxious about the gas. I had used up most of my cash gassing up on the way. This was a hell of a lot farther than I had figured. I stared suspiciously at Scott.

"Nearly there," he said, laughing.

Then an incredible blue-coloured lake came into view. It was huge, and as we drove along its shore, we were mesmerized into silence by its beauty. Eventually we left it behind, but where the hell was Long Beach? It seemed we had been driving forever, and I was half-asleep when I heard an unfamiliar sound.

"Long Beach," Scott shouted, pointing.

The water was screened from the road by trees, but now I recognized that unfamiliar sound as the mighty roar of the Pacific Ocean pounding onto the beach.

"Let's go into Tofino first. It's just down the road and then we can come back and spend the rest of the day being beach bums."

We were all too spaced-out to care. Let's find somewhere, anywhere to get out of the van and stretch our legs.

Tofino was delightful. Charming little restaurants and pubs dotted here and there. A little beach. Art galleries, including that of Roy Henry Vickers, the famous First Nations artist. We explored the pier and I was glad to sit for a moment and watch the guys talking to the local fishermen. Craig came dashing back to me. "That guy down there says he'll take us out on his boat up the coast. He has to deliver something and says we can go with him."

"How much would he charge?"

Craig yelled at the top of his voice, "How much?"

I cringed. Jesus... this kid.

Craig smiled. "It's for free. What do think? Can we go?"

"When would we get back? It's a long way back to Nanaimo, and we haven't seen Long Beach yet."

Craig yelled, "When would we get back?" Disappointed. "You're right. Not until 5 o'clock. Oh well, it was good idea."

I watched him running like a puppy dog back to the fisherman still talking to Scott on the beach. Craig always had people wanting to give him stuff. What was it about him?

When we finally arrived at Long Beach, I stood there, stricken with love at first sight. The waves thundered. They roared, they crashed. And there was a panoramic view that stretched as far as the eye could see.

Scott coming up beside me waved expansively at the giant waves. "See what I mean? All the way to Japan."

"I am so glad you made me come, Scott. I wouldn't have missed this for the world." We grinned happily at each other.

"I knew you'd love it. Come on, let's make camp."

We organized our blankets and pillows within the arc of some huge driftwood logs and I handed out tuna sandwiches and ham and cheese-stuffed Kaiser buns. I'd even made a chocolate cake. It was wet and sticky in the heat, but who cared? Everyone ate solidly enjoying every crumb. I noticed Craig eating very delicately, making sure his mouth was closed. He didn't grab for the food but waited until I offered another sandwich and said, "Thank you," in a small polite voice. Trying to get on my good side.

I stretched out in the warm sand as the guys took off for the ocean, which was still a fair distance away as the tide was out. I watched them go, Craig and Scott travelling at a fast clip, Little Larry huffing to keep up. Craig doing cartwheels in the sand like a carefree sand boy. I closed my eyes and dozed, enjoying the warmth of the sun on my bare legs and back. I woke to the sound of their laughter as they came back up the beach, Scott holding something. A crab? I shielded my eyes as they all looked soaking wet and they glistened in the sun. Plunking down at my feet, Craig showed me a sand dollar. "Here, this is for you. I know you collect stuff like this."

I had a collection of shells arranged on a bookcase in the living room at Haliburton, but I was surprised he had noticed. "Gee, Craig, thanks."

He looked bashful for a moment. "Any more cake?'

We spent the afternoon searching for shells and frolicking in the sea. Then sun- tired, we all stretched out in a row and snoozed on the blankets. When we awoke, we laughed at the beginnings of sunburns on our noses and shoulders.

"When do you think we should leave?" I asked Scott, looking at the sun in the sky. It must have been at least 5 o'clock. Not one of us was wearing a watch.

"I guess in about a half hour or so."

I hated to leave. It had been such a perfect day. A day without worries or concerns, a play day, a day I had felt just like a kid.

When we were in the van pulling onto the highway, Scott said casually, "Looks like we'll need more gas to get back. This old beater really sucks it up."

I was immediately concerned. "How much? I don't have much money left."

"At least $25–$30."

"Bloody hell!" Now what? "I'll have to talk the gas station into taking a cheque."

Scott laughed merrily. "Oh, I have faith in you. If anyone can do it, you can."

We ran out of gas just as we were coming down the hill leading into the tiny jewel that is Ucluelet. Scott was lustily singing "The Night They Drove Old Dixie Down," and I held my breath as we rolled magically all the way down the hill and right into the nearest gas station. Remembering the lonely mountain pass we had crossed, I shuddered. We could have run out of gas in the middle of nowhere, been forced to live in the wilds for the rest of our lives. For a moment I had thought I had been travelling with normal people. More fool me.

The Esso gas station owner was a friendly, middle-aged man with trusting eyes. "Would you accept a cheque?" I asked. "My friends own an Esso station in North Vancouver. Do you know the Lees?"

"Never heard of them," he said cheerfully.

"Um... I thought maybe with the Esso management courses you might have run into them. They could vouch that my cheque is good... I thought..." I trailed off, not knowing what else to say.

"Not to worry, you have an honest face. I'll take your cheque, dear. No big deal." Scott gave me the thumbs up from the corner of the store where he was browsing through a *Penthouse* magazine. I loaded up with chocolate bars, potato chips and cans of pop as Scott pumped the gas, and Little Larry and Craig hooted with delight as I tossed the goodies into the back seat. And we were off again.

We passed the incredible sapphire-blue lake, and the van creaked and groaned as it climbed slowly up through the rugged mountain pass, but we made it, and in relief we sang songs all the way down the other side. A darkened Port Alberni greeted us and then a sleepy little Parksville. Slowly squeaking and trundling we finally wended our way through the silent streets of Nanaimo's South End and pulled up in front of Big Sab.

We were all drowsy and sun-tired. Scott had driven the last half hour with all of us asleep. As we tumbled out of the van, Craig—a chocolate smudge on his cheek—said shyly, "This was one of the best days I have ever had. Honest, it was so much fun. Thanks, Diane." And he ambled away into the house. I stared after him for a moment, seeing a big overgrown kid in a man's body. A kid who had been probably deprived all of his life. No Dairy Queen ice cream cones on a hot summer's day, no tooth fairy, and a skinflint Santa Claus. Just a neglected little boy with a sunny disposition who was always hoping somebody would notice him. And I finally got it. I got what Craig was all about. Why people were always trying to be nice to him. Why everybody got a kick out of giving him stuff. Somehow the universe has this yin yang working, and the universe had clued in people around Craig. Except for me. I had resisted being clued in until now.

I've often looked back on that day and, remembering the simple pleasures of the beach, the sun, the camaraderie of the guys, all of us misfits in our own way, and I would think, "Hey, Craig, that was one of my favourite summer days too." I wish I had told him.

But timing is everything. We were literally almost robbed of that summer outing. A friendly, good-natured Indigenous boy named Jason with a bright winsome smile had moved into Big Sab, and he could often be found chatting in the Old Codger's room, swapping stories about favourite fishing spots. One night I found them together eating from a big plate stacked with grilled whitefish that Jason had caught and cooked up. How nice for John, I thought, and how kind of that kid. Then three weeks to the day after Jason moved in, both he and the Old Codger's van went missing. The old man had given him permission to use it for "a moving job."

A little later the police charged Jason with a break and enter that had taken place up-Island, but John's van was never recovered. I knew the Old Codger loved that van. It was the one he had driven back and forth to Mexico, and it held special memories for him. I think he realized he would never be well enough to drive it again, but that wasn't the point. "Bloody criminals" was all he said. I think he was taken aback at his own judgement and how easily some friendly conversation and a plate of cooked whitefish had bought his confidence.

36
The Gazelle

It was a busy day. I had to get rooms ready for two new clients and drive the Old Codger to his monthly doctor's visit and Larry was coming in on the 5 p.m. ferry.

Figuring I would set up the rooms first, I organized an armload of the necessary bedsheets and clean quilts, and humming "Lady in Red," kicked open the street basement door to Big Sab and stopped dead in my tracks. The young girl who was leaning against the hall wall gave me a startled, frightened look. She was wearing a black silk tank top and a black leather mini skirt, and there was a needle sticking out of the back of her bare, slender leg. And right at that very moment as I was staring at her, she slumped against the wall with a look of utter euphoria in her eyes.

I almost dropped the linens in my fright.

"What are you doing here?" I managed. "Who are you?"

"I'm a friend of Jim's." She smiled vacuously and pointed to the door of one of the bedrooms I was just about to clean.

What the hell! Jim wasn't supposed to move in until the next day.

I flung open the bedroom door. Jim was lying on the bed's bare mattress fully clothed. The zipper on his jeans was undone. A big battered travelling bag sat on the floor beside the bed. He was around forty and would have been good-looking except he was so thin and grubby. A sense of sleaze, a smell of human waste, like in soul rot was emanating from the room.

"What in the hell are you doing here?" I asked. "You aren't supposed to move in until tomorrow!"

"Well, I have the money now, so I came over." He smiled hazily and pulled a pile of creased bills out of his jacket pocket. "The door was open. I didn't think you'd mind." He didn't sit up but kept lying on the bed like it was too much effort to move.

"Who is that girl out there? She's on drugs, Jim. What the hell is going on? You know this a safehouse."

"Oh, that's Julie. She's a good kid. A friend..." His eyelids fluttered for a moment. He seemed almost asleep, a happy smile trickling over his face.

I walked to the bottom of the stairs and yelled up. "Little Larry, are you there?"

The door on the top of the basement stairs opened. Little Larry's round, good-natured face peered down.

"What's up?"

"Get a couple of guys down here right away. I've got trouble here."

Ron and Craig came thundering down the stairs.

"Throw the guy in there out." I pointed to the room. I looked around for the girl. She was gone. I ran to the door and looked out. She was staggering down the road like a wounded gazelle, almost falling over on her ridiculously high heels. She hailed a passing taxi, half-fell in and was gone. I bit my lip. Hell. She must have been all of seventeen years old.

As Jim was being hauled unceremoniously out onto the street along with his travelling bag, I called a cab. I had seen his stack of money, so I knew he could afford one. I wanted to get him out of here. Fast. Away from me. Away from Big Sab.

"Why the tears, Di?" Ron asked.

"There was a girl here, too. A kid with a needle sticking out of her. Big brown eyes." I swallowed. "Some mother's precious child."

"I've made some coffee, Diane," shouted Little Larry. We trooped up the stairs and grouped with comfortable familiarity around the kitchen table.

"I met Jim two days ago with his social worker and he seemed normal," I explained to the guys. "He said he wanted a safehouse, and his

social worker recommended him. Of course he gets money from welfare *only* because he's moving into a safehouse... and the first thing he
does is have sex and drugs in *our house*!" I banged the table with my
fist. "So help me God," I cried, standing up with clenched fists, "I will
never be conned by another worthless, drug-hungry piece of shit like
that ever again."

It reminded me a little of that scene in *Gone with the Wind* when
Scarlett scoops up a handful of dirt and shouts, "As God is my witness,
I'll never be hungry again!" But I think the guys were enjoying the
drama of it all. Good against evil. A table-thumping Welsh woman all
puffed up with saving the world.

Then Little Larry reminded us it was Pizza Night and brought us all
back down to the ground, and just like that our mood lightened.

37
Scott's Island

Larry was looking out the kitchen window gulping down his coffee. He and Ken were on a health kick. They set the alarm for 5:30 a.m. and went off jogging down the road to the oceanfront. Quite a sight so early in the morning. Two big white guys wearing shorts and sporting their huge, naked white thighs, and Ken wearing his yuppy sweatband. Good job it was so early in the morning, and nobody in the South End was up yet to notice him as he sure would have taken some ugly jeering. The two of them jogged around the harbour sea wall, a route that offered a spectacular view of picturesque Protection Island and Newcastle Island, and returned home up the road an hour later panting and dripping with sweat. The irony of this was that they were starving when they returned to Big Sab after their workout and had me cooking bacon and eggs and hash browns—in other words the works—for their breakfast.

Larry was now waving a piece of toast wrapped tightly around a thick rasher of bacon and saying, "Well, lookie who is coming down the road... this is the third time this week."

I looked out the window and there was Kathy marching towards us. She had the determined air of a woman on a mission. She was such a strange, odd little thing. If you were unkind, you might say sexless. Probably forty years old, give or take a year or two. A petite woman around 5 foot 2 inches, but very sturdily built. She had a very plain face, her nose dominating hawkishly and taking up most of the space. She wore thick glasses, and as she always pulled her hair severely back, the nose had nowhere to hide. She was the sister of our friend Mick and for the last six months had been living on Gabriola Island, a half-hour ferry ride from Nanaimo, and hadn't made many friends there. Mick had told me his sister's story, hoping I would befriend her now that I was living in Nanaimo.

According to Mick, Kathy had been abandoned by her husband in the middle of an Alberta winter when the temperature had hit 40 degrees below. They had been living on a bleak farm in the middle of nowhere outside Edmonton when without warning the husband had taken off with another woman, leaving Kathy with their two small daughters and no money. But the abandoned wife showed guts. She made it through the winter, then enrolled at the University of Victoria. She had taken her youngest daughter with her to start a new life. The older daughter had gone to live with her father.

On completion of her university courses, Kathy bought a small run-down cabin on Gabriola Island and single-handedly renovated the property, even building a bedroom extension. It was an amazing feat for anyone, never mind a pint-size woman like her with no carpentry or building experience. To give you an example, she had pulled up every board in the living room and sanded them by hand before nailing them down again. The result was a beautifully restored hardwood floor. She had taken how-to books out of the library, made mistakes along the way, but learned by her mistakes. She was a force to be reckoned with.

"She's coming here trolling," said Larry.

"Whatever do you mean?"

"She's after our guys. You'll see—she's going to try and scoop one of our guys."

"I hardly think so," I said, laughing as I buttered more toast. Kathy always struck me as a prim and proper type. She wouldn't be interested in our ex-cons. I knew she was lonely and that she appreciated having *me* to visit and *me* to chat with. I was sure she wasn't lonely for *a man*!

Still, three visits in one week when she had to take a ferry ride over to Nanaimo to do it seemed a bit much.

Later I watched her through Big Sab's kitchen window sitting at the picnic table laughing and talking to Scott. Kathy was a good debater, could really make her point, but I personally thought her extremely opinionated. Hardly the sophisticated intellectual that was Scott's type.

A week later Scott came to me with a funny look on his face. Was it sheepish? What was it? "I need to have a talk with you."

"Okay... what's up?"

"Well... you know I have a motorcycle in storage. They've given me until July 31 to pay for the overdue storage fees or they're going to sell it out from underneath me."

"Yes." I remembered the stories about the bike, Scott's pride and joy. He had been trying to figure out how to reclaim it, but he would have to figure out how to pay for the repair work that was needed as well.

"Kathy has come up with a proposition for me."

I stared at him intently. Larry's word *trolling* sprang emblazoned in red to the forefront of my thought process.

"Kathy?"

"Yes, well... Kathy has offered to give me free room and board if I work on her property over on Gabriola Island. She is stuck at the moment with her work. Needs a man's input, and of course she's on limited funds so can't afford to pay proper wages. This deal would mean I can pay for my bike and I can help her out as well. A two-way street."

Why was he looking slightly embarrassed? That flush under the tan of his darkly handsome face.

Hmm. "Scott, really, *darling*, are you ready for this?" It was our latest inside joke to call each other "darling" like we belonged to the Hollywood crowd. "You've been out of jail five months, and you'll be isolated over there. Kathy's place is really small, and you know how you like your privacy. You'll be right in each other's face—no room to swing a cat."

"Yeah. I know... it's small. I went over last week to have a look."

"*You went over there?*" I couldn't hide my surprise. Had Kathy been planning this without saying a word to Larry and me?

"I loved it over there. It's glorious, so peaceful, nature at its most beautiful. The beaches are totally unspoiled. It's paradise. And one of the projects Kathy wants me to do is create a Japanese garden behind the cottage, you know, where that steep cliff is at the back of the property. I have some really good ideas for it. It's going to be a challenge, but it will get me back in shape as well."

He really seemed revved up. Bubbling over with enthusiasm. I was taken aback, jealous in a strange way. Scott had opened up to me, confided in me as a friend. We had chatted daily about everything under the sun, but he had never mentioned going over to Gabriola for a visit last week. Still he was a grown man, not a kid. He was an intelligent human being who could make his own decisions, yet how would a free spirit like Scott deal with Kathy's straight and narrow ways? Let's face it. She was a total eccentric, and I'd been over there and seen how she lived like a zealous missionary.

I forced myself not to be negative.

"You're right. The island is beautiful. I'd love to live over there myself. But... oh Scott, I'm going to miss you. I can't believe you're going."

"I'm not *going.* I'll be back visiting. *Darling,* you're not saying goodbye to *me.*" He was smiling fondly now, his coal black eyes gentle. "I can't thank you enough for what you've done to help me here, Di. I hope you realize how much I appreciate everything. Taking me in straight from the can when you didn't know me from Adam." Saying the phrase *straight from the can* in a British accent, he was trying to be funny, but his voice was suddenly gruff, and he leaned over, surprising me by giving me a quick hug. Scott was never one for sentiment.

Larry was furious. "I told you she was here scouting for one of our guys. Now she's stolen one of our clients and we're out $350 a month. The devious little bitch."

"Maybe it will do him good over there. At least he'll be working on something. He was getting bored to death here."

Larry was grim. "You don't get it, kid, do you? Kathy just wants a good fuck."

"Jesus, Larry! I can't believe you said that! You've got to be kidding! Kathy is almost a *man-hater*. She's never gotten over her husband abandoning her in the middle of an Alberta winter. What was it? Minus 40? And she does need help over there on Gabriola. I can't believe what she's achieved already, a tiny woman like her... it's unbelievable. And I can see how she needs a man's muscle to get certain things completed. She is stuck at the moment, but what I don't get is that she never talked this idea over with us. Like, what we thought of Scott. Was he trustworthy, ectera? You would have thought she'd want a reference from us."

Larry snorted. "Well, you're right about her needing a man's muscle!" I hit him with the tea towel. "But as far as her asking us about him, I guess in the screwing department we're as much in the dark regarding his credentials as she is right now."

I hit him again with my towel. "Men! You all think that single women are just dying to get *it.* That's all that's missing from our lives, and that's what you men have to deliver so you can be our salvation. Larry, there's more important things in an intelligent single woman's life besides sex! Larry, stop it!" He was trying to pick me up and throw me onto the bed. But now that I thought of it, there were only two small bedrooms in Kathy's cottage. She slept in one and her daughter slept in the other, and there was only a small love seat in the living room. As I hit the bed and bounced, Larry breathing hard with the effort of hurling me there, I thought, where the hell *was* Scott going to sleep? On the living room floor?

I called Kathy on Gabriola. "Kathy, hi! Scott has just told me he's moving over to your place."

"That's right," she said. No tone in her voice.

"Well, I just felt it was sort of my responsibility—as you met through me—to tell you what he went to jail for... just so you know everything."

"He's told me already."

"Knifing someone? That he had to serve two years?"

"Yes."

"Has he also explained that he has a drinking problem?"

"Yes, he's been honest. He's told me everything I need to know." She sounded brisk and business-like. "He's agreed he won't drink here."

Scott was packed and gone that same day. So fast! Or had they been planning this for a while and he hadn't known how to tell me? One last duty call. I felt compelled to do this before I could feel fully discharged of my responsibilities. I phoned Kathy's brother in Vancouver. He was a very conservative man and worked in the Administration Department at UBC. I dreaded his reaction.

"Mick, it's Diane. I just feel a little concerned. Kathy has invited one of our guys from Big Sab to go over and live with her, to do work on the property in exchange for room and board."

"So, is the guy okay? Like, what are your concerns?"

Concerns? Hmm? I filled Mick in on the details. It did seem grim when I was explaining the two-year sentence for knifing. There was a heavy silence. As if I had just told him I'd introduced his sister to a serial killer when all he had asked of me was to befriend her. Have the odd coffee, cheer her up. Like Diane... hello!

"Mind you, he's been no trouble here at all," I finished lamely.

"Jesus. That sister of mine. That Kathy! I don't know, Di. What can I say? She's a big girl, supposedly intelligent, but I wonder sometimes... When she was going to university in Victoria, she was working part-time in a group home for psychiatric patients."

"Yes?"

"She ended up having an affair with one of the patients in spite of all her courses on psychology... and the guy ended up attacking her."

"Holy mother," I exclaimed. "She had sex with a mental patient! Is she a victim-type personality or what?"

"Who knows? We can't do anything but hope this all works out. Keep me posted, Di."

We didn't see Scott for three weeks. Then he turned up on our door-step looking tanned and healthy. Full of energy, wickedly handsome.

"Look at you! That island living is agreeing with you!"

"Well, it's hard work but wait until you see the Japanese rock gar-den. I've really created something. Not finished yet but you'll have to come over and see it. It's a work of art, I tell you."

We drank coffee and caught up on the news. I kept mulling over how to ask him. How do you ask a man if his relationship with a woman is business or sexual? And was it my business anyway?

"You do look happy, Scott... Everything is okay then? Between you and Kathy?"

He smiled at me, ruefully showing me his hands. No longer mani-cured, they were the hands of a true labourer, broken nails, calluses on top of calluses.

"Besides Kathy working me to death?" He laughed. "She's a hard task master. But in the evening I go down to the beach and relax. It really is lovely. The fishing is excellent, so we've been eating a fair bit of fish." His eyes were smiling. He still wasn't telling me what it was really like.

The next visit was two weeks later. Scott arrived with mini-bottles of rum.

"Look," he said pulling a package out of his knapsack "I love these little bottles. They're even smaller than a mickey. You can't get into trouble with these. They have just enough for three good drinks, and they're only $5.95."

I locked eyes with him. "Are you sure you're up to drinking *without* getting into trouble?" Now he wasn't living in a safehouse anymore, he could drink whatever he liked.

"Oh, I've been doing this off and on for a while. A drink here or there. I'm fine. Don't worry! I'm in the driver's seat with it." He flashed a smile of reassurance. "I'm going down to the beach on the Reserve for my Happy Hour today. Sit in the sun and relax. By the way, I've already paid off more than half my motorcycle debt."

"Good for you, Scott." I felt pleased for him. "Kathy doesn't come over and visit us anymore. Everything okay with her?"

"We've been so busy we're usually tired at the end of the day. We work from 8 a.m. to 6 p.m. I've never met anyone like her. What a go-getter, Di." He had a faraway look in his eyes. "She's up early in the morning, totally focused. Man, I tell you, she's hard to keep up with. You know, when she started this renovation, she cut down on everything. Half-starved herself to get the money for supplies, ate rice and vegetables, used the same tea bag all day, just totally concentrated on her goal. You have to admire that sort of spunk. And have you seen her book collection over there? It's pretty damn good, so I have a good reading supply for the evenings."

Used the same teabag all day? I've been broke, but I've never been reduced to that. Sort of like having to drink your own urine when you're stranded in the desert.

"Hmmm... Pretty strict regime if you ask me, Scott. All work and not much play."

He laughed. "Maybe it's agreeing with me."

"Really? I never took you for a monk!"

Waving him goodbye, watching him stride down the road, I felt myself relax. Maybe all this hard work and Kathy's strict regime was good for him. But who would have thought that rebellious Scott would be happy toeing such a straight line?

The next time Scott came to visit, he was drunk. He pulled a mickey from his knapsack. No more little bottles. He was in a wild party mood, his hair falling over his face, his shirttail hanging out of his pants. "Come on, you guys. Let's go to the Pat for a couple."

Larry was blunt. "Scott old boy, you can't drink here. Come back when you're sober." We watched him stagger down the street. Kathy phoned at 10 p.m. It was the first time I had talked to her in three months.

"Diane, have you seen Scott?"

"He was here earlier. What's up?"

"He was supposed to be on the 8 o'clock ferry, and he hasn't arrived. The 9:30 is the last ferry, so I'm worried about him."

"He must have missed it. If he shows up here, I'll get him to call you."

"Hmmm," I said to Larry. "Trouble is brewing in paradise." Then thinking out loud, I added, "She sure has a tight rope on him. It's not like they're married or something."

"Or something," said Larry.

When Scott showed up the following week, we sat under the backyard cherry tree and had a heart to heart. He was dressed immaculately as usual in white cotton slacks and an open-necked, black, Indian cotton shirt. Sometimes when his hair was slicked back, he looked like one of the romantic film heroes of yesteryear, and I often teased him that he looked like Rudolph Valentino. Dangerous yet so tantalizingly tempting.

"Oh yeah, sure," he would scoff. "Valentino." But I knew he liked it.

"Kathy is so hard line," he was explaining now. "That's the problem. There are strict rules, black and white, no grey areas. I agreed not to drink in her house, so no booze whatsoever in the house. But I'm not allowed to drink around her anywhere else either... not even a glass of wine if we go out for dinner. It's hard to take all the time. So when I catch the ferry and come over here, I think, 'Okay, make the most of it.' It's like a different world away from Gabriola. She's not around, so I think I'll have a couple of drinks, have some fun... as long as I'm sober and all back together again by the time I have to catch the ferry back. But sometimes it doesn't work out that way. I start having too much fun, so then I think what the hell and I don't stop. And I know if I get on the ferry drunk, and she's picking me up, all hell will let loose. So... this last time I was just too drunk to go home... so I didn't. Go home, that is. I crashed at a friend's house. But then she was mad at me for that."

"What are you going to do?" I asked. I was curious to hear his answer.

"I guess I'm not going to drink for a while." We stared at each other. Interesting. This mousy personality, this little pipsqueak of a woman had already so much power over him. Scott who was cunning and adventurous and who in my mind was a devious, modern-day version of Lawrence of Arabia had been reduced to what? Fighting to keep his camel? Or should I say his motor bike?

"Geez, Scott darling, you sure as hell must want that bike," I teased.

He avoided my eyes.

38
The Desperado

I was chopping up red banana peppers and onions when Lewis and Louise came through the kitchen door. Lewis was drinking a beer. He slammed a six-pack down on the kitchen counter, tore off a can of beer from its plastic ring and tossed the can to me. I was so startled I almost dropped it.

"Gee, it smells good in here. What you cooking?"

"Chicken cacciatore, one of my specialties." I flashed him a grin as I threw chopped garlic into the pan with the sautéing peppers and onions.

"Get the recipe, Louise. This lady here," he said, pointing to me, "is a good cook." He beckoned impatiently to her. "For Chrisake, woman, come on in, sit down and stay a while." Smiling, he pulled a chair out and sat down, all hale and hearty.

I glanced over at Louise standing by the door. She looked tense and stiff and something else. What?

"Louise... how's it going?" I smiled at her, enjoying the prettiness of her. She was wearing a white peasant blouse accentuating the darkness of her hair and tanned arms. An ankle-length, midnight blue skirt splashed with bright yellow roses flowed around her sandaled feet.

She came slowly into the room and sat on the edge of a chair. A bird ready for flight?

"What's new, you guys? I haven't seen you in ages."

"The big news is we've moved to Louise's mother's place—you know out on the Reserve. I love it out there, man. Just love it." Lewis ripped the tab of a fresh beer and gulped it down.

He was leaning back on his chair, his shirt unbuttoned to the waist, the light golden curly hair on his chest exposed. His skin was tanned a nutmeg brown.

"Her family have accepted me like their own. Her mum is a living doll, spoils me rotten. Right, Louise? Her brother and I go fishing nearly every day."

"Why would you leave that lovely apartment of yours?" I asked. "You lived there for a long time, Louise... I thought you guys were comfortable there." I was also thinking at a clickety-click pace that Louise had told me she deliberately stayed away from her family on the Reserve because of the out-of-control drinking that went on there. She had been sexually assaulted as a child and had dark memories of the place. Had, in fact, not talked to her father and brothers for a long time and only saw her mother when she came into town.

Lewis answered for her. "Well, I figured life's too short for family feuding. I talked Louise into re-uniting with her family. We started visiting and they invited us to live out there in the big house so we could start saving money."

"We were evicted from the apartment," Louise said quietly. "Too much partying."

"Bitch! Why'd you have to bring up that?" Lewis slammed his beer can down on the table. There was a dynamite silence.

I looked in embarrassment at Louise. What the hell was going on between these two? What was up with Lewis?

He sprang to his feet. "I saw Jack visiting your neighbour. I'll be back in a minute." He shouted back over his shoulder, "If he's there, I'll bring him over." He left without a backward glance.

I sat down next to Louise. "Okay, what's up? What's happening here?"

She was silent for a moment, fighting for composure, and then her face crumpled, and she cried, "Oh Diane, it's getting crazy. He's just drinking too much. Remember what Nairie told us and we wouldn't believe her? About him always abusing women and it would only be a matter of time before... before he hit me? Well, it's started."

I pulled back from her, shocked, scanning her face. Nairie had once casually said Lewis was capable of hitting women. We—meaning Louise and I—hadn't believed her.

"He's hit me already four or five times. Dragged me along the gravel one day, ruined my dress, grazed my legs raw. He's always sorry afterwards, cries and begs forgiveness... but I'm already scared of him. I feel like sometimes I don't know him, like he's a stranger. Like he's not the Lewis I fell in love with, the Lewis I married."

I stared at her silently, her hunched shoulders, her pinched white face, the tears. God help me! Lewis. My favourite, the one for God's sakes that I loved. We heard him outside yelling to someone across the road.

"Don't let him know I've told you. Please. He thinks the world of you. He couldn't bear for you to think badly of him. I'll go and fix my face." She walked hurriedly to the bathroom as he came into the room.

"Jack's going home," Lewis announced. He reached over and grabbed another beer from the counter.

I busied myself, hiding my concern by fussing over the pans on the stove. The chicken pieces were golden brown; I placed them in a large casserole dish and poured the tomatoes over them, adding the sautéed peppers, onions and garlic. I carefully sprinkled the chicken with oregano and basil flakes and searched for the parsley, avoiding looking at Lewis.

Finally I took a deep breath and looked up. Lewis was motionless, studying me, scanning my face. He could read me like a book. I knew he could feel the tension rolling off me. I forced a grin. "Can you guys stay for supper? I have loads of chicken here." Where was the Parmesan cheese? I sprinkled the cheese generously into the sauce and positioned a square of foil wrap atop the casserole dish. Now into the oven. Done. I thought I could look at him now with a normal face.

He relaxed, looking fondly at me. "Oh sure, we can stay—great! You know, I miss you, Di, I really do." He grinned his sweet boyish grin. "I've got a good story for you. Come and sit down." He patted the chair next to him. "You know what I did last week? Something a little crazy."

"Yeah, it was crazy all right," said Louise, coming into the room. "He almost killed himself. He dove off the Ladysmith Bridge into the Nanaimo River." She must have put makeup around her eyes as they didn't look red or swollen.

I had heard about this bridge. You could climb up forty feet and dive into the river from it, but it was considered an act of bravado that could kill you as the river was full of huge boulders, and just a few places were deep enough to take a dive from that height. Only the young Indigenous teenagers tried it, and one of them had died the previous year from a broken neck.

I stood looking at Lewis, speechless for a moment. "Are you crazy? Do you have a death wish or what?"

"Trying to be young, I guess." He leaned back in his chair, laughing, his hazel eyes lazy and content. "I almost chickened out, but when I was at the top, I realized it was almost as dangerous to try and climb down. I'd been drinking a bit too much and was starting to feel dizzy."

"Jesus, Lewis! God almighty, promise me you won't try that again." I stared at him, my hands on my hips.

He was laughing, enjoying my concern. The sunlight was shining through the window, spilling onto him, turning him into a golden boy, his eyes lazy and glinting gold, and his hair alight. He looked like a cat, a big sleek wild one. Relaxed, dangerous and ready to spring.

"You're lucky to have survived it," I said sitting down beside him.

"I think he was showing off for me—like in a weird way trying to impress me." Louise was straining to put a normal note in her voice. "I told him afterwards, 'What good are you to me dead?' I was scared to death watching him climb up, but you know Lewis. All the kids from the Reserve were egging him on and his pride was bigger than his fear. Or his common sense I might add." Louise laughed, but her eyes were sad, not smiling. "When he dove in, I closed my eyes. I was that terri-fied—so I didn't see his circus act anyway."

Lewis laughed and headed for the bathroom. He staggered slightly and caught the doorframe to steady himself.

I looked over at Louise helplessly. "You have to find a way to stop him drinking," I said in a low voice so he wouldn't hear. "He's back where he started before he came to Big Sab."

"I know," she said, leaning towards me, "but he's possessed, I swear. He won't listen. When he's sober, he wants to clean up, and after one beer he won't listen."

When Lewis came back into the kitchen, he went to the counter and pulled another beer free from the plastic ring. He was downing them like a kid with Kool Aid on a hot day. "I guess we better get more beer, sweetheart," he said to Louise. "Throw me the hooks." The hooks being his name for the car keys.

"Lewis, honey, I don't want you driving when you've been drinking. Anyway, we should get going in a minute. We don't need more beer."

"Diane has invited us for dinner. So throw me the hooks." He held up his hand. His eyes glittered with a terrible seriousness.

"No. You know I won't let you drink and drive in my car."

Lewis crossed the room and dived for the black leather purse lying on the kitchen table, but Louise, who had anticipated his move, leapt up and grabbed the bag first.

They tussled, both breathing heavily.

"Lewis, please. Don't do this." I was on my feet, horrified and beg-ging. "Please, Lewis. Let's sit down and talk this out."

His face was wild, his lips drawn back in a feral snarl. He pushed Louise so hard that she banged against the hot stove and loosened her grip on the purse. He rummaged for a moment, retrieved the keys, glanced at her with a satisfied gleam in his eye and was out the door.

"My God!" I said, sitting down. "My God! Louise, this is crazy. He's like a berserk animal."

"I'm not waiting for him to come back," she said. "Can I use your phone? I'll get someone to pick me up downtown. I can't be around him when he's like this. He's going to get uglier and uglier." She picked up the phone and called her friend Marie.

I hugged her and she left, fairly running down the road, her dark hair flying like a mane, her skirt billowing, the patterned yellow roses dancing like real roses in the wind. I shouted behind her, "Call the police, Louise! Let them know he's driving your car."

As I closed the kitchen door then locked it, I felt an unfamiliar spasm of fear. I sat down heavily on the chair Lewis had vacated and waited for what seemed like a long time before I realized he wasn't coming back. I felt a massive relief and finally rose and unlocked the door. It was only then that I realized my face was wet with tears.

The next day as I was washing dishes, I saw him through the kitchen window. He was standing under the big old cherry tree looking furtively about, and when he saw me watching him through the window, he beckoned for me to come out. Reluctantly I went outside and crossed the small stretch of lawn to meet him. The sun was blistering hot.

"What are you doing here?"

He was shirtless, and his jeans were torn. He had a dark bruise under his eye and a cut on his left cheek. His lower lip was swollen and split. He was looking down, kicking the dirt at his feet with his cherished brown cowboy boots, preferring not to meet my gaze. There was a silence and when at last he started speaking in a low voice, his swollen mouth interfered with his words.

"I've really screwed up this time, Di. I'm sorry, real sorry for yesterday. Can I come in and talk to you for a moment?"

"No, you can't come in. I'm sorry, Lewis, but no." I shocked myself by how harsh and clear my words sounded as they shot out. He looked hot and flushed, sick almost. He must have one hell of a hangover, I thought. "Can I get you some Aspirins and water?"

He nodded.

I fetched him iced water in a large glass, and he threw the Aspirin into his mouth, tilted his head back and drank the water down with one long thirsty swallow. He plonked down to sit on the grass under the tree. There was a stale smell of alcohol and tobacco coming off him. I pulled up a garden chair and we sat there for a moment silently taking each other in, he looking away and then back again, searching my face briefly, registering my lack of sympathy, a world of unspoken words exchanged in our glances. I was the first one to speak.

"What happened after you left? Did you get into a fight? Your face looks like you've taken a few punches..."

"I crashed Louise's car, hit a pole. No one was hurt but the car is beaten up. Then I hitchhiked to Louise's mother's house on the reserve, but Louise wouldn't talk to me. I got into a fight with her brother. We went at it pretty good. Someone called the cops, so I took off. Ended up drinking all night." He tapered off. "I'm sick as a dog, Diane. Can you do me a favour? Can I just crash here for a couple of hours?"

"I can't have you here. Not when you've been drinking like this. Don't ask me."

"I won't come into the house—just let me crash under the tree here. I've got nowhere else to go," he begged. "I just need to sleep for a few hours, get my head together."

I stared helplessly at him. I had never seen him look so beaten, so hang dog.

"Okay," I said expressionlessly. "You can sleep here for a few hours, but please don't come into the house. We'll talk when you wake up." And I returned to the house.

The prone figure under the tree held a magnetic pull, and all afternoon I kept watching him through the window. He never stirred for hours, the sun circling, dappling through the branches, playing on the bare skin of his back. I went out after a while and put a pillow gently under his head and stood back looking at the beaten face. He looked pained and weary even in his sleep. It was evening when he woke. I saw him stretching in the rosy darkness of the dusk, sitting up, wondering where he was. I took out two mugs of hot tea and a wet cloth filled with chipped ice and some more Aspirins.

"I've really done it this time... I think I've lost Louise. I don't deserve her anyway."

He was sitting up, leaning against the tree, pieces of grass in his hair, and tiny bits of debris, dead twigs, caught in the curly hair of his chest.

"What the hell happened, Lewis? I have to tell you, I couldn't believe it was you—acting like that—hurting Louise."

He gulped his tea. Silence. He held the cloth with the ice against his head. "I don't think I'm going to win this fight, Diane. So, help me God. I don't think I can lick it. It's got me."

"You mean your drinking? You don't really believe that."

"Yes, I do." He stood up and came over to me, quietly putting his arms around me. His bare skin radiated heat like hot coals. He smelt of everything stale in life, things that had been overlooked and wouldn't go away.

"I love her... you know that, but I can't seem to beat this booze and drug thing." He was crying quietly, hiding his face against my shoulder, ashamed of his tears but unable to stop. My tough, macho Lewis.

After a while I went into the house and found a T-shirt for him and heated up a can of French-Canadian pea soup, the best hangover cure

I have ever found. When I went back out, he told me he had started taking cocaine again.

I just sat there under the tree, listening in disbelief. "Why? Now that you have Louise and a chance at happiness—*why?*"

"I don't know, except I'm afraid of losing her so I seem to do all the things that would make me lose her. Sort of speed things up. Get it over with quickly. Doesn't make sense, does it?"

No, it didn't. I thought he had more confidence than that.

"And this violent stuff... what's this? I just can't believe it's you."

Lewis raised his head and looked at me with old sad eyes. We both knew he had no answers to my questions. For a moment we just sat still, relieved to be friends again. Probably feeling the same wave of relief that fighters in a ring must feel on hearing the bell signalling the end of the fifteenth round.

There was a pleasant evening breeze finally coming off the ocean, cooling the heat of the day, gently ruffling our hair. It seemed so peaceful sitting there in the dusk, under the rustling canopy of the big old cherry tree, listening to the summer sounds of buzzing insects, and the distant barking of a dog on the Reserve. But there was a sickness in the air, something insidious, an evil underneath the surface, squirming and slippery, making me feel sick and nauseous. Too close for me, this undercurrent of something bad. Had Lewis felt it, too?

I raised my face to listen to him.

"I'm afraid, Di," he was saying in a low voice. "I always thought my partying was just raising a little hell. I always thought I was in control but I'm not. I'm not in control. I'm afraid these goddamn drugs will end up killing me."

The next morning I was up early and on the phone to Gordie Ryder.

"Gordie, I need help here. I need to get Lewis into rehab right away. I know there's a waiting list but he's in serious trouble. He wants to get into Surfside as soon as possible. What do you think? Can you swing it?"

"Hmmm... I'll have to call you back, Di. I'll phone around and see what we can do, but he might have to go over to the Mainland. There's a good rehab in Abbotsford... but let me find out for you."

He called back later that afternoon. "Where is he? I've got him into Surfside here in Nanaimo, and I'll take him in myself tomorrow morning at nine sharp."

"Thanks, Gord. Big time thanks!"

"I just hope he's ready. There's a tough six weeks in front of him. He's got to really want it."

"He's ready. He's reached the bottom." I hung up the phone, thanking my lucky stars for dear old Gordie Ryder's pull.

I phoned Louise and told her Lewis was going into Surfside. There was a profound silence. Finally she said, "Well, I'll wait and see if he makes it through the six weeks. If he does, maybe there's some hope. Maybe I'll feel like trying again."

I looked over at Lewis sitting on the living room couch tensely listening to my every word. After I hung up the phone, I hesitated for a moment to tell him about Louise's reaction.

"Don't worry, Di, I know," he said softly. "She doesn't want anything to do with me. But thanks for phoning Gordie. I won't let you down, you watch me. I'm gonna do what I have to do. Jump through every hoop. Whatever they want me to do there. And after that I'm gonna get my girl back."

His bruised face managed a small smile. For a moment there was a flash of the old Lewis. The old bloody hell and great balls of fire. It was just the way it was. I couldn't help loving this guy.

39
Nobody Does It Better

A month later I was hanging towels out on the line, the weather being perfect for line drying. Sunny with a slight breeze.

I stopped to watch a shabbily dressed Indigenous couple pushing a broken-down pram full of kids past the house and found myself reflecting that their proud ancestors' feet had probably walked past this very spot for thousands of years, when there weren't any roads or concrete or any white man's buildings. And for a moment I could almost look back into the past and see them.

And I thought about what a lousy deal it had been for them. How we had taken over their land because this West Coast area was a paradise beyond. Taken it over completely and nonchalantly in less than a hundred years. And then again, also nonchalantly, thrown them onto cramped parcels of land called reserves, changing their ancient culture forever. And I was wondering why the land allotted to them had been called reserves when I saw Scott coming down the road.

There was something in the stoop of his shoulders that told me all was not well, and I went into the house and put the coffee on and waited.

"She's thrown me out," he said. He was wearing a loose white cotton shirt and khaki shorts, and he was so tanned that with his black eyes he looked like an Egyptian. But it was the first time I had ever seen him unshaved, scruffy.

"What happened?"

"I came over to Nanaimo and got drunk. Stinko might be the best description, and I was fool enough to catch the ferry back over to

Gabriola. Apparently I sang lewd songs in her car and kept insisting we'd run someone over. I can't remember. You know, country roads... It was a dark night and my alcohol-swollen imagination must have taken over. Anyway, she's freaked out."

"No second chance?"

"Nope. That's it. I've blown it."

"Did you make enough money to get your bike?"

"Yep, but not enough for the repairs. I've left it over there on the island for now."

"That's good, Scott. At least you achieved what you set out to do."

He sat looking at me, puzzled.

"The bike," I said. "You've almost paid for the bike."

He sat there frozen. Motionless. Then to my horror, a tear rolled down his face.

I stared at him mortified.

He bowed his head and raised his calloused hands to hide his face. And then, horrifying me even more, an anguished whisper escaped through his fingers. "Di, surely you must know... I'm in love with her."

That night I lay in bed trying to figure out life, men and relationships. Kathy had run roughshod over Scott, jumping him through the hoops, bringing him to his knees. And he had ended up loving her. Why did he love her? Out of loneliness? Or that old cliché of *after two years in jail she looked pretty good?*

No, that wasn't it. Scott was too smart, too deep for that.

Did he secretly like the control? Need that control? This man who had always lived on the edge? Had he finally been punished enough by society to want to quell that love of danger? Punished enough to yearn for a safety net?

She was a bossy woman. No nonsense, no softness, no empathy for him.

And a realization cut into my heart like a knife. *Larry's sergeant-major wife.* Here I was so in love with Larry, running his business interests in Nanaimo with no pay unless you called my room and board pay. Cooking and cleaning like a skivvy. At his beck and call. And whose fault was that? Always waiting endlessly for that damn ferry to deliver him to me, feeling lonely most of the time, with my own family way off in Vancouver. It was the bossy wife that he kowtowed to, was so afraid of making angry.

Not me.

What the hell was I doing? I didn't know anymore.

It seemed the more you loved a man and showed it, the less value you were to him. That little pipsqueak, that sexless, horse-faced Kathy had more know-how in her little finger than I had in my whole brain on how to handle a man. And I had been feeling sorry for her!

I cursed and tossed and turned all that night, dreaming of Lawrence of Arabia being chased through the sand dunes, cars running over shadowy people on country roads, and ferryboats sailing in empty, no one on board, like ghost ships in the Bermuda Triangle. And all the time Carly Simon was singing in the background, "Nobody does it better/ Makes me feel sad for the rest..." And Larry smiling. Every time I surfaced from a dream, lying there among my tangled sheets and hovering for a moment in a conscious state, I was aware of one thing besides the pain. Rage. I was a patsy, a fool, an idiot, a loser and a joke. Me!

I was waiting for Larry. Dave, alias Mr. D, had gone to pick him up from the ferry terminal. I had made hot chicken wings and guacamole dip for the nachos. A Friday night snacking feast. Cold beer was waiting in the fridge. And here he was, bigger than life, bounding up the path. Why did my heart lurch whenever I saw him?

"Larry," I began as I opened two beers. All the pent-up versions of rehearsed speeches tumbled forth. "We have to talk. I have to know what's going on in your head. I'm over here by myself a lot. You said you would leave Phyllis last September, and then you got talked out of it because she said it would interfere with Chris's first year at college, depress him, throw him off. But it's the end of June now, for God's sake. *When are you going to leave?* I have to know. Like have you fallen back in love with her or what?"

Larry, undeterred by this verbal attack, was munching on wings, gulping down his Molson's Canadian.

"Come on, kid," he said, "be serious. Fall in love with her again! I've told you her mother is sick. Seriously sick."

"Larry, please don't tell me I now have to wait for her mother to die?"

Phyllis's mother, a wreck of woman who apparently was so slothful she had lost the use of her legs, was in a senior's home.

"Well, what do you want me to do? Am I supposed to leave a twenty-five-year relationship when her mother is dying? You want me to be that cold-blooded? I mean, is this *really the right time* to do it? What's another few months? Be realistic, Diane."

"Then," I said sarcastically, "it will probably be the dog dying or Andrew getting married or Phyllis will fall down the basement stairs and you'll have to nurse her in a wheelchair for years." I cracked open another beer.

"Look, I just got off the ferry. I've had one hell of a week. I don't need this."

A long heavy silence. I felt full of resentment. Where was I on this man's priority list?

"Look, Diane, I spend most of my time with you over here. More time than with my family, my friends, anyone, anywhere. Doesn't that count for something? I do my best. I know my travelling takes me away, but prospecting is what I do... I know it gets tough for you here but..." He tapered off. He was wearing the blue shirt I had bought him for Valentine's Day. It had brightly coloured tropical fish swimming all over his chest, and spilt guacamole was adorning the head of one of the fish. He looked tired and worn out, sad even, his hair in its usual disarray was falling over his eyes. "I'm just doing the best I can without being a jerk. I don't know what else to do. I don't know what else to say!" He shrugged and spread his arms out in a pleading gesture, looking Italian when he was Norwegian.

"Scott fell in love with Kathy, and she's thrown him out."

"Why? Because he fell in love with her?"

"No, because he got drunk!" But he'd made me grin with his *because he fell in love with her* comeback. "I guess I get insecure about how you really feel. Geez, I have friends who have been divorced and married twice while I'm waiting for you to throw in the towel with *her*. Maybe you need her more than you realize, Larry. Maybe you're hanging onto her because I'm just fun but not marriage material."

At least he let me lock into his eyes when I was giving him heck. No eye avoidance here.

"Can you believe it?" I blurted. "Scott of all people falling in love with Kathy?"

"Come here," he said, rising to feet. "Come here, you old sad sack." He hauled me up off my chair and pulled me into a hug. "Di, you are the best thing that ever happened to me. I'm nothing without you. You're the brightest spot in my life. If you hadn't come along when you did, I wouldn't have made it through. I mean it. I love you, kid."

So we went to bed, and I could hear Carly Simon singing somewhere out there—or was it the music of the leaves rustling on the cherry tree outside the bedroom window? I wasn't sure. Maybe I was hearing the cosmic music of the universe humming and harmonizing, buzzing around the world, around galaxies, reaching out everywhere the way it was supposed to and always had, connecting us all to those stars studding the Milky Way light years away. It felt peaceful. Good. Like I belonged to a unique but secret scheme of things that was unfolding exactly the way it should. Who knows? "Nobody Does It Better" drifted

on the night air with Carly, and I guess the phrase "living for the moment"—or as I was fond of saying, "getting laid by lightning"—had taken
on a new meaning.

40
The Plague

I had never seen Scott so enthusiastic. He was on a roll. It seems that every seven years bugs breed themselves silly, and a plague of them emerge, and this year cockroaches were going to win the breeding prize. That's why he had applied for the Pest Control Officer's position he had seen advertised in *The Nanaimo Times*.

"But what about your health—breathing in all that pesticide?" I ventured to ask.

"No problem, *darling*. I will be issued masks, and anyway I won't be doing this all my life. I just need to make Big Money now while the plague lasts."

How in the hell had he known this plague thing was about to erupt? Scott had done his homework. We shook our heads in wonderment at his timing because we knew from past experience that Scott was always right. He was a genius waiting for his time to come, and if a bug explosion was going to help him along the way, so be it.

The owner of the business, which was headquartered in Vancouver, interviewed Scott over the phone, and from what Scott related to us afterwards about their conversation, the man was blown away by his knowledge of bug statistics. I could believe that. From the number of eggs each lady cockroach was capable of producing in a lifetime to the fact that twelve cockroaches could survive for one year on the glue of a postage stamp, our Scott had the facts down pat. In my mind's eye I could see the owner frantically scribbling down notes as Scott pontificated. Species 400 million years old, man's oldest enemy, the spreader of dreaded pathogenic organisms and allergens. No wonder Scott cinched the job,

For Scott the biggest perk to the job of Pest Control Officer was access to a smart company van that he was allowed to use in his leisure hours. He drove the gleaming maroon vehicle over for us to inspect, and it was a beauty. Larry good-naturedly gave him his first three spraying jobs to get him started. He was on his way to a big bank account. I was thrilled to bits for Scott. He had been so depressed and lost after Kathy had dumped him. This was just what he needed.

We often saw Scott driving around town. He seemed to be all over the place, and we would honk merrily at each other as we crossed on the town's intersections. He looked pretty good sitting behind the wheel in his uniform. At last, one of our Big Sab guys had a decent job!

Then one afternoon about three weeks after he got the job as I was chopping up chili peppers and onions for the pot of chili con carne I was cooking for dinner, Larry spotted Scott through the kitchen window, his shoulders slumped, walking down the hill and coming straight towards our house.

"Where's the van?" Larry asked.

"Disaster struck," Scott said. "I was on my way to Port Alberni the other nght. I had six houses and two businesses booked to spray there when this speeding car came from the opposite direction into my lane. The jerk was trying to overtake a car on a two-lane highway! Anyway, I swerved too hard, the van spun out of control and I rolled over and down into a ditch. I had a hell of a time getting out through the window. It was in the middle of nowhere and there was no one around. Pitch black."

"No one stopped to help?"

"I don't think anybody saw me go over the edge. Anyway, I walked for a while and eventually hitched a ride into Port Alberni and headed for a pub."

"A pub? Why didn't you get a tow truck?"

"I thought I'd wait until the light of day. Anyway, it gets worse. I got pretty loaded. Don't look so surprised! I was shaken up and pretty rattled. The next morning I went back to the scene and all hell had broken loose. All the pesticide containers had been damaged and the pesticides had leaked into the water in the ditch. There was everyone and their uncle out there. The cops. The fire department. Environmental Control people in uniform, lights flashing everywhere. The van looked totalled. It was a major disaster. I flipped. I just snuck away. *Panicked* is not a strong enough word."

The silence was shattering. Larry and I sat with our jaws dropped around our ankles, staring at him.

"My boss might be phoning here looking for me. For God's sake, don't tell him a thing. Say you haven't seen me in weeks... or something."

"You sure did it good this time, Scott," I said, stirring my chili. "They'll probably catch up with you through your driver's licence."

"What driver's licence?" he said. "I was going to take my test next week. My licence expired while I was in jail."

"You've been driving without your licence?" I exclaimed, rooted in shock. "But you drove us all the way to Tofino in the Old Codger's van!"

"I know... well, I'm a good driver. I didn't want to tell you my licence had expired. You wouldn't have come on the trip. Would you?"

We were speechless. What could we say? Our bug fighter was totally incorrigible.

"What would you have done?" Scott asked plaintively as he registered his major drop in credibility. "I mean, would you have gone up to the Disaster Crowd—and believe you me, they were an impressive lot—and like a Boy Scout say, 'Hi there. Here I am. I created this entire mess all by myself. Single-handedly last night. I alone am responsible for poisoning the entire Port Alberni district water supply'—and let them rip you to shreds—while on top of everything else you're struggling with the hangover from hell?"

"I'd say your bug-fighting career is in the ditch with the van, Scott," Larry said cheerfully.

"Oh look," said Scott, pointing to the TV. "*The Simpsons* are coming on. Hey guys, do you mind if I stay and watch the show?"

"You are the bloody show around here, Scott," I said. "And now that I think about it, you'd fit right in with *The Simpsons*. Like Homer move over!"

But nobody was listening to me. They were already in the living room piling onto the two chesterfields in front of the TV.

As I ladled hot chili into bowls, I reflected that it's a wicked wind that does no one any good. I could picture all the cockroaches in the South End standing up on their creepy little legs, waving their spindly antennas in relief and cheering their buggy little heads off.

41
Click Go the Wheels

Larry's voice, muffled under the sheets, said, "Come over here, you big, warm, wonderful thing."

I stiffened. I had been putting on weight, so his remark hit a sensitive nerve with the subtlety of a pickaxe.

"Where do you get off on the *big*?" I asked coldly. "You, of all people, should talk. And I am a *thing* now?"

"I'm sorry... Okay, come over here you warm, wonderful woman."

I rolled over towards him. He put his arms around me. "I've been waiting to tell you this all day," he said, "but I figured I'd wait until we were in bed. You know privacy—just you and me."

"Well, you have that right." I smiled in the dark. "Don't ever try and get anyone else into this bed with us or you're dead. This is our last bastion of privacy. I thought moving to Haliburton we'd have it. Privacy. Now this house has become a drop-in coffee centre for all the guys at Big Sab and Harmony House. Then with Mr. D and the Old Codger and Ken always watching TV or videos with us, I'm never alone with you anymore."

"Hush, I don't want to talk about everyday crap. I want to tell you I am leaving my marriage—totally, completely—and I am going to live full-time over here. With you."

I was blown away. "You're sure?"

"I should have done it years ago. It's hard for a man. I honestly think women handle walking away a million times better. A man always agonizes that he has promised to look after his wife 'till death us do part.' I know you don't get it... but I always felt that I was abandoning my family. Leaving them in the lurch. Unprotected. it's a big thing for a man to feel dishonourable. You feel like you're such a fucking cad. I know you're going to say, 'Well, isn't the act of adultery being dishonorable? Isn't that being a cad?' And it is, but leaving your family is somehow worse. Ask any guy, believe me. But now the kids are grown up, and there's no money left to fight over. Though it was never about money anyway. Phyllis can have the damned house and the furniture and all the rest of it. I'm fine with starting over from scratch. What the hell, eh? Well, what do you say? You're kinda quiet."

"I'm in shock," I said into the soft curly hair on his chest. "Though actually I feel scared. I've waited for this for so long. I can't believe it. When will you do it? Leave?"

"I have a three-week job up north at Babine Lake outside of Smithers coming up next week. When I come back from there."

"Phyllis won't be able to talk you out of it?"

"No." He gave a short laugh. "I don't think Phyllis could think up one more reason. She's used up her bag of tricks. I think she'll be as glad as I am it's over. Nothing will stop me, I promise you, love. This is it. All you get with the deal is me though. I'm broke."

"I was never in love with your money, Larry."

"I know, honey bun. Was it the way... you know, the reason why you love me... because of the way I make love?"

He could always make me laugh, and my laughter rumbled against his chest deep down in the bed. "You mean like the story of the big society snoot who, after witnessing a big ugly fight between Ava Gardner and Frank Sinatra, asked Gardner, 'My dear, how do you stand being with that horrible man?' and Ava replied dryly, 'Darling, he's hung like a horse!' Yeah... I guess that must be it... Larry, sweetie pie." We both shook with laughter in the dark.

But we didn't make love. We just held each other, then I rolled away from him as I always did just before I drifted off, and we fell asleep holding hands.

It was 5:30 by the bedside clock when I woke the next morning, and a soft greyish-pink light was filtering through the curtains.

The start of another day.

A cool breeze was skittering across the ocean and whispering through the open window so that it rippled the curtain into graceful curves. It was so peaceful. I should wake up early every morning for this. *Yeah sure...* but I was enjoying it.

I snuggled up, smiling behind the warmth of Larry's back and put my arm around the curve of his belly. Crunching my face against his back, tasting the salt of his bare skin with the tip of my tongue. The soft hissing of his breathing, the only sound in the room. Somewhere, the house creaked comfortably.

The dawn creeping in the window became gradually pinker, less grey, suffusing the room with an unreal pink light. The walls, the ceilings glowing pink. A surreal feeling. Larry's eyelashes were pink, the curve of his cheek a rosy hue. Oh, how I loved this man. This sleeping great huggy-bear hulk under the sheets. Why I loved him I didn't know. Other men were more intelligent, more distinguished and had more charm. Funny, isn't it, trying to figure out why you love someone? There were men I had met that were more idealistic, genteel gentlemen, scholarly types that I admired and had treasured friendships with, but never in a million years would I have wanted to have sex with them.

For some reason, it was Larry, a guy who was more comfortable in the bush, who had something so simple as the ability to make me laugh, that made my heart go boom. I had waited for so long for his chaotic marriage to end, waited so impatiently in the wings, and now he was finally mine. A peaceful contentedness crept up from my toes flooding over me to the roots of my hair. I hadn't felt so good in years, so happy, so brimming over with simple uncomplicated happiness. My mother used to say men never get what makes a woman happy. It's not diamonds or pearls or anything like that. It's making her feel loved. That's all she really wants.

Like in that song: *Little things mean a lot... touch my hair as you pass my chair.* I lay there remembering the song, humming it gently. *Try a little tenderness...* No, no, that was another great song... the one that kid with the big voice sang in that great funny movie *The Commitments.* I lay feeling so complete with the rightness of life. One of those rare perfect moments. I thought idly wouldn't it be great if you could crystallize moments and then years from now take them out and hold them and feel them again. Like this moment. It was frightening the power of another person's ability to create so much happiness in you. I felt momentarily scared at being so happy.

Larry stirred. His hand moved under the sheet and gently stroked my leg. I shivered for a moment waiting for his next move and pressed myself against him, letting him know I was awake.

The phone rang. "This is the Chevron Station on Needham. Do you own a husky cross?"

No way—not *this* morning!

"Dear God, so help me. Do you have him there?"

"Yes, we do, ma'am. He's been running around on the road with a little black dog in front of the station. I just managed to get him inside and saw the phone number on his collar."

"I'll be there in five minutes. Thanks."

I left my lovely peaceful room with its surreal pink glow and threw a coat over my cotton nightie. Shiner, as usual, was pleased to see me as if this was a consensual game of hide-and-seek. *How much fun it was when Mum is clever enough to find me.* A little black dog, a bitch, tried to jump into the car with us. She had blue eyes—how extraordinary—

and a little bell around her neck that tinkled musically. She was so tiny she seemed to have no legs.

"I think your dog has fallen in love," shouted the gas attendant as we drove off. Shiner acted like it, barking frantic goodbyes out the window.

The world seemed to be in love this morning, I thought. The gas station's windows glinted a pretty pink as did the gas attendant's glasses. Like it was a magic pink hour for the whole of the South End.

42
Ol' Blue Eyes

The little blue-eyed dog kept coming to visit. As soon as Shiner heard her bell tinkling, he would go insane. Running up and down the fence barking and leaping like Romeo trying to climb the balcony to reach Juliet. He couldn't get out, but she was so little she could find a way to get in, and then they would romp and play like two teenaged lovers. I found out that her name was Sally. She was from the Reserve where blue-eyed dogs abounded, a dominant gene having been handed down over the years.

Shiner loved to sleep outside on warm nights. Larry and I would grin, watching him lying in the dark, his tail wrapped around his face making him look like a furry pretzel. Then one night I started up in bed at the sound of savage howling. What in the name of Jesus was causing this? I ran down the hall and opened the door. Shiner and Sally were caught, or should I say stuck, in the act of copulation. Both were howling in pain. I stood frozen, not knowing what to do. Their cries were piteous. I rushed back to Larry asleep in bed.

"Larry, wake up. Sally and Shiner are having sex."

Larry murmured and rolled over. I leapt on the bed and shook him. "Larry, wake up. I don't know what to do."

"It's just nature, Diane. Leave them be."

"But it's hurting them. They're crying."

"Well, what do you want me to do about it?"

"Help them. Should I throw a bucket of water on them?"

"For God's sakes, no. Why in the hell would you do that?"

"I heard it somewhere. It separates them."

"They'll come apart by themselves, Diane. Water is not going to do it."

The crying seemed even worse. I ran outside again. Poor little Sally had been lifted off her feet into the air, and she and Shiner were now back to back. This was a horror story. This tiny little dog should not be mating with a husky wolf dog. This was not a natural act of nature. Suddenly they came apart and Sally fell to the ground. She whimpered, rolled over once, then hightailed it through the fence and down the road home. Gone in a wanton woman flash. I looked over at Shiner and almost fainted in horror. His penis was so large it almost touched the ground. It was like a huge, monstrous aberration. I ran yelling back into the house.

"Larry, come quickly and see Shiner's penis. I can't believe it. It's like he's deformed."

Larry finally half-sat up in bed. "Can't a guy get any sleep around here? Huskies have big penises, Diane. Get into bed and go to sleep."

I reluctantly climbed into bed and snuggled down. "You should have a look. It's too big! It's not normal! He can hardly move it's so big."

"You mean he's hung like Frank Sinatra?" Larry was chuckling.

"Frank Sinatra should have been so lucky! On second thought, he was Ol' Blue Eyes, too, wasn't he? There's some weird cosmic connection here." The last thing I remember before I went to sleep was both of us chuckling in the dark.

The next day Larry came home with a little bell and an evil look on his face. He went to the open window and tinkled the bell. There was an ominous silence and then a huge rushing noise, paws on wood swooshing down the hall. Shiner, bright-eyed and bushy-tailed, shot into the room like a catapult. He looked expectantly around. Larry smiled maliciously at me. "Pavlov's dog," he said. "Now I've got control."

There was something about the way he said it I didn't like. I couldn't help it, and I asked, "What kind of bell do you use for me?"

He turned slowly. There was a certain look in his eye. What was it? I wasn't sure.

"Don't get weird on me, Diane," was all he said.

The cutest part of the story, though, was a few months later when Davey's son Jesse excitedly told me that a girl in his class had brought a puppy for Show and Tell. She had proudly held the puppy up and said his mummy's name was Sally and his daddy's name was Shiner.

Jesse, his nine-year-old eyes sparkling, said, "You know what, Diane? She was telling the truth because that puppy looked like a wolf! Just like you, Shiner." He kissed Shiner on the head. "You're a dad! She said they wanted to have Shiner for a dad because they figured he was the best-looking dog in the whole neighbourhood. That's why they let Sally come here when she was in heat."

"Procreation South End–style. No stud fees," Larry said, grinning.

"One last important question, Jesse," I asked. "Did the puppy have blue eyes?"

All eyes had riveted on his young face waiting for his answer.

"As blue as the summer sky." He smiled.

43
Hell's Bells

The phone rang at 4:30 a.m. I answered sleepily on automatic. It had to be a wrong number.

"Diane?"

"Yes."

"This is Marilyn. Larry's sister in Vancouver. Do you know how to get in touch with Larry? Where is he right now?"

"*Marilyn?* Yes, he's at Babine Lake, up north."

"Sorry to say, it's bad news. Christopher, Larry's son, has had a terrible accident. He's in Vancouver General. It looks like he's going to lose an eye." And she told me the horrifying story.

I was immediately wide-awake. "I'll call him right away. No, hold on—I'll have to wait until 6 o'clock... That's when the camp's radio operator starts his shift."

"Oh Diane," she said, "of all the times to finally get to talk to you. Dave, my son—your Mr. D—has told me so much about you. He loves you to bits. How sad I am to be finally talking to you in the midst of this mess."

"I'm sure we'll meet one day in happier times, Marilyn. I'll get Larry to phone you..."

You can say I'm psychic—well, I know I am—but I knew then and there that my destiny, my karma, my fate, my future—all that I wanted in love and life—had been dealt a deadly blow.

Because now Phyllis had another excuse?

No.

Because Larry couldn't handle it?

Probably.

Larry loved his sons with all his heart and soul. That fact made me love him more. But this was going to take him down. Spiral him. Because it was happening now when he was already in the dirt, broke without a cent and emotionally bereft on leaving his marriage. But when is it ever good timing to hear your child is hurt, is about to lose an eye?

Was I ready for the ride? I thought of Bette Davis's famous line in *All about Eve*: "Fasten your seat belts. It's going to be a bumpy night." And I thought, bitterly, Bette, you *femme fatale* from hell, you ain't seen nothing yet! Have a good look at this one.

I waited for dawn then made my call. I started to retell Marilyn's story.

Larry was curt, a note in his voice I didn't recognize. "Just give me the facts. Don't gloss it up."

"The worst scenario is that Chris could lose his left eye. Capilano College's social club arranged a Halloween party at a local hotel. Some drunken kid out of control threw a full bottle of beer at somebody who'd made him mad. Instead, he hit Chris who was an innocent bystander. A freak accident. He's in Vancouver General."

"Okay, I'll call Marilyn."

The phone clicked and went dead. I felt an instant internal click and recoiled from it, feeling irrationally afraid. Somewhere within, my heart and lungs kept on working tirelessly, my blood flowed automatically but deep inside me where the Welsh kid who had grown to be a woman lived—where who I really was hung out and hoped and laughed and dreamed—responded to that click, and everything emotionally in me immediately felt frozen and in limbo. Like I was waiting for a jury to come back with a life or death decision.

When Larry came back from Babine Lake, it was as if he'd had a lobotomy. He was a walking robot. No laughs, smiles or wickedness left. It was frightening. When I tried to talk to him, he cut me off.

Bringing up Chris and the accident was waving a red flag, but instead of the bull charging, the bull just left the arena.

When he did finally talk about it, his anger was shocking. He wanted to find the boy that threw the bottle and kill him. Or pay someone to kill him.

"Have you lost your senses completely? How would killing some-one help Chris?"

"Oh, you'd rather just an eye for an eye?" A nasty bitter laugh.

"I think you need counselling. This is really making you crazy, Larry. I know it's tough—someone you love being so badly hurt. It's a tragedy. But life does go on."

"Leave it alone, for God's sake! Chris is only twenty—his life is all ahead of him. He had such beautiful brown eyes." Larry looked like he might burst into tears. "He didn't deserve this. He's one of the nicest kids you'd ever want to meet."

"Plastic surgery does miracles these days. I remember when my son David had his face smashed in that motorcycle accident..."

"Diane, everybody wants to tell me how fine everything will be. How this and that happened to a relative or a friend and everything worked out fine. It's not what I want to hear. It's not going to be all right. Chris is missing an eye for Chrisake. Nothing is going to make that right." And he stormed out of the room.

I was stumped. His grief was inconsolable, his anger frightening. I thought of all the tragedies I had experienced in my life. There had been too many over the years, and I had always been thankful for every lull in the storm though still aware a sniper's bullet could be lurking in every tree. But Larry had never confronted real tragedy before. He had enjoyed a peaceful life. He had pulled a drowned friend out of a lake when he was twenty, a pretty traumatic experience. His dad had died in his late seventies—a pretty normal age. He'd had a bad marriage, but who hasn't? (Okay—I'm trying to be funny here.)

But this was all new to him—this pain of seeing someone he loved so much hurt and experiencing this feeling of complete helplessness.

But it was making him one big asshole.

Chris had the operation for an artificial eye, and I thought that as soon as Larry saw the result of the operation he would settle down. But when Chris came over to the Island, I was horrified. Apparently, the attacker had not only thrown a bottle at Chris but had also picked up a chair and smashed him in the face, shattering the bone around the eye socket. And the artificial eye looked so artificial. More plastic surgery was needed.

Then the court case unfolded. Because it had been Halloween night, and everybody had been dressed up, they couldn't identify the attacker properly. He had been dressed as a woman, and though a policeman outside the club had seen him running from the club and driving like a maniac out of the parking lot and had taken down the licence plate number, he hadn't seen him hit Chris. And Chris's friends had conflicting descriptions of the kid's outfit—black hat, big white hat. In the end the charges against the kid were dropped.

I thought Larry was going to end up in a strait jacket. He was angry at the world, but mainly he was angry at me. Our arguments started when he suggested he should go back home to live temporarily.

I hit the roof. "You only left home five weeks ago. If you go back now, you'll never leave again. Larry, this is really important that we handle this from here. I don't care if you stay over in Vancouver as much as you need to, but you can't go and live in that house again *with her*. It would mean the end of us."

He said I was being insensitive and heartless. I said I was fighting for everything that represented our future. He said that of all the times Phyllis and the kids needed him, they needed him now because they were going through hell. I thought of all the times I had gone through hell alone. "Larry, go there every night. Have dinner there every night, but don't *live* there. Please."

He started spending most of his time in Vancouver and slept at his mother's house... or let's say I think that's where he slept. I kept waiting for the storm clouds to pass, for a sunny break to appear in the sky. I kept busy with the boys from Big Sab and Harmony House, and I waited. I felt discouraged and tired, lonely and abandoned. I had always thought bad times brought people together, gave them a chance to show their true grit. This was the time to stand by your man, but my man was nowhere to be seen.

Critical friends had always questioned whether Larry really loved me, had voiced their concerns that he was being careless with my heart. They said that a man with good intentions would have left his marriage long ago and would have not kept me hanging in limbo all these years. But I had always listened to Larry's anguished reasoning for not leaving his sons and had understood that, but now I was thinking maybe all this time my friends had been right.

If Larry really loved me, wouldn't he want to share his anguish with me? I reflected on how grateful I had been for the loving support of my family and friends when tragedy had struck in my life, but Larry seemed to resent the sympathy I offered. I couldn't believe that, after all these years together, after everything we had shared, I could feel so at arm's length with him now. I pined for him and yet when he arrived off the ferry to stay for a brief day or two, this stranger—this new, cold Larry—made me shrink away, and I grew weary of trying to appease him. Where had the real Larry gone? How could someone change so much?

I stood on the sidelines and waited. From my vantage point inside our tumbling relationship it looked like it was going to be quite a wait. But I was curious. I had waited six years for my man. Now I was curious what the ending of my love story was going to be. I had read Lawrence

Durrell's *Alexandria Quartet,* and the fascinating message that had poured from its pages struck me with full force—that we can never figure out what our lives are all about because we don't have all the information. Now I was wretchedly conscious that my life was like the first book of the *Quartet—Justine.* I was in the dark, oblivious to what was really going on, and it was going to be one hell of a shock when I finally realized what the contents of the fourth book of my life would reveal.

As Durrell suggests in this brilliant masterpiece, we can seldom contemplate the whole truth in all its shocking clarity, never mind see it because we are grounded in familiar perceptions and naively misread unfamiliar clues. And perhaps earthbound humans are not emotionally designed to examine aerial views. Perhaps the savagery of truth is too cruel for us to comprehend.

44

The Christmas Grinch

After much discussion, we made plans to go to Vancouver for Christmas Day and Boxing Day. I hadn't seen my children for three months and I missed them desperately. So it was decided that I would cook the traditional turkey dinner for the guys at Big Sab on Christmas Eve, and after dinner Larry, Guy and I would catch the late ferry over to the Mainland. The Old Codger's friend Doug was picking him up on Christmas Day and hosting him until December 27 to help us out with our plan. Some of the guys, like Richard and Little Larry, were visiting relatives. I had bought all the guys presents of cigarettes and lighters except for Ron who badly needed a wallet, his old one being in tatters, and I sent Larry out with a shopping list of last-minute items including the wallet.

The South End was cloaked in a light covering of snow. Everyone on the street was filled with good cheer. People scurried home with packages and secrets while kids threw snowballs at passersby from secret hideouts behind bushes. Christmas music belted out of the Pat Pub on the night air, and Christmas lights were strung up on even the poorest of houses. People kept knocking on our door asking if they could cut some holly from our trees.

By Christmas Eve there was an air of festivity around Big Sab. The guys had decorated it with red and gold paper trimmings and encased the light in the entrance hall in a big gold bell. Holly twigs heavy with red berries perched on picture frames, and we installed a lovely little Christmas tree in the living room window with coloured lights that blinked on and off.

Christmas music wafted from the radios in the guys' rooms, but Christmas was the hardest time of the year for discarded people like the guys at Big Sab, and I wondered what they were really thinking. Were their thoughts on Christmas celebrations of the past, on happier times with families and friends? Were they full of regrets for past mistakes, making them feel empty and sad?

I busied myself cooking sausage rolls, cherry almond bars and a multi-layered trifle bursting with fruit, custard and whipped cream. And, of course, I made the famous Nanaimo bars. (I guess you have to believe by their name that they really originated from here, and I reminded myself to ask Scott about that one day.) The turkey was slow roasting in the oven, so the pungent smell of sage stuffing was permeating Big Sab's every nook and cranny when Larry arrived back from shopping. I was peeling potatoes and carrots in the kitchen, and I put the peeler down when he showed me the wallet he'd bought for Ron. "Larry, that isn't the right kind. He needs a slim wallet that will fit in his back pocket. This one is too big."

"It was on sale," Larry said curtly, unpacking the crackers, cheese, potato chips and dip. "For Christ's sake, Diane, these guys are lucky to be getting anything from us. This all costs money." He waved his hands airily around the kitchen, ending by jabbing a finger toward the turkey in the oven.

"Stop being a Scrooge. Loosen up. This is the only celebration these guys will have." I glared at him. There was fresh tension between us because he not only intended to spend Christmas Day with Phyllis and his sons but also was planning to sleep there on Christmas Eve so he could share Christmas morning with them.

I was taking the last of the sausage rolls out of the oven when there was a knock on the back door. Scott stood there in the half-light cast by the porch lamp, a suitcase at his feet. I could smell the stale booze on his breath.

"*Scott!* What's up?"

"I need a big favour... I know it's out of line, but can I stay here just one night? They're full up at the Sally Ann... and I don't have anywhere to go. Just one night?"

I stepped out onto the top step and closed the kitchen door behind me. My breath spun out of my mouth like ribbons into the cold night air as I tried to figure out what to do. "Have you been drinking?"

"Not today. I've been on a binge but I'm sober now. I'm feeling sick and I'm just gawd-awful tired. Di, I just need a place to lay my head for the night." He stood there hatless, his black hair dusted with snow.

A dog shouldn't be out in this weather, I thought. It was Christmas. What the hell—I couldn't send him away. "Go up the back stairs. I'll unlock the door... but Scott, be very quiet!"

The Willow Room was empty. I could make up the bed in there for him. I went up to the second floor and opened the locked back door, and together we tiptoed quietly down the hall. I led him into the room and closed the door before I turned on the light.

He sat on the edge of the bed blinking in the sudden bright light like a rabbit caught in the headlights. I was astonished by his appearance. He was a mess. His clothes were dirty, and he was wearing a thin summer bomber jacket, no protection at all against this winter weather, and it had a tear in the sleeve. So un-Scott-like. His face was flushed like he had a fever, and he had bruises on his cheek. His hands were visibly trembling.

"What the hell have you been doing, Scott?"

Always ready with the caustic comeback, he laughed and said, "Destroying myself—I guess you could call it that."

I viewed him silently. He turned away embarrassed at the pity he saw in my eyes. I decided against grilling him. I would find out later why he was in such a mess.

"I don't want the guys to see you like this," I told him. "I shouldn't really let you stay, but I can't bear to think of you out in such a cold night. I'm making Christmas dinner for the guys tonight because Larry and I won't be here Christmas Day, so I'll bring you up a plate when it's ready. Okay? Jesus, Scott, you look frozen." He was literally blue with the cold. "Why don't you jump in the shower and warm up? I'll get you one of Larry's warm sweatshirts and I'll bring you a hot drink."

Christmas dinner went off without a hitch. I served it buffet-style and the guys lined up in the kitchen with their plates, and we all pulled crackers and wore paper hats. Some of the guys took their meals to their room as there weren't enough seats around the kitchen table, and I could hear them laughing and calling out to each other through their open bedroom doors. Gordie called in and stayed about an hour talking and laughing with the guys.

They ate like they were going to the chair, some coming back for seconds and thirds, but I loved seeing them all enjoy their food. The desserts were a huge hit, and as the guys were eating and sipping on coffees, I brought in the gifts and handed them around, giving each man a hug and a Merry Christmas. The look in their eyes as I made the rounds wasn't gratitude. No, I think for that moment they loved me like a surrogate mum, and it was there in their eyes, warm and soft. Ron, who had been quiet all evening, opened his present and went immediately downstairs to his room.

Later I knocked on Scott's door and took in his dinner, the plate piled high. I had already taken him up a hot chocolate earlier. The room was dark, but when I fumbled for the light switch, I saw he was lying under the quilt on his bed. He sat up looking dwarfed in Larry's huge sweatshirt. His eyes were swollen and his face still abnormally flushed. He ran his fingers through his hair, now clean and damp from the shower.

"Here you go, love," I said. "Merry Christmas." I reached over to give him three packages of cigarettes wrapped in cheap Christmas paper.

"Would you have any Aspirins, Di?" he asked. "Sorry to bother you but I have one hell of a headache."

I fetched him a glass of water and two pills and sat on the edge of the bed. "How are you doing, kid? Did the hot shower help you feel any better?"

He astonished me by bowing his head and crying. I patted his back awkwardly and went for toilet paper from the bathroom next door. I took my time and when I returned and handed him the wad of tissue, he had recovered. We stared quietly at each other, awkward and embarrassed, both of us at a loss for words.

"Larry and I are catching the 9 o'clock ferry tonight. Promise you won't go downstairs."

"Don't worry. I feel so sick I'll probably just sleep through. I'll be gone in the morning. I'll get up early and go down to the bus depot. I figure I'll go to Victoria. I've lived there before..."

"What about your bike?"

"It's over at Kathy's. It's been in her garage there since we broke up. I don't want to see her. Kathy. Just yet. Maybe I'll get my bike next month."

"Oh Scott!" I hugged him impulsively. "Please keep in touch. I'll be worrying about you. What a lousy Christmas for you."

"I'm a pagan," he said. "So Christmas, so what! Now a good summer solstice celebration and I'm in!" He was trying to recover control, his usual banter hiding how low he really felt.

"Yeah, you're a pagan, all right! Now eat your Christmas dinner or I'll give it to Little Larry." I blew him a kiss and left. Later I was to remember how the ready smile on his lips hadn't reached the dark sadness of his eyes.

When I went downstairs, some of the guys were washing and drying the dishes, while others sat around the table playing cards and smoking. A peaceful scene. Larry and I said our goodbyes, then I remembered Ron. I knocked on his door, and he responded gruffly, "Come on in." He was lying on his bed, his arms under his head.

"Just wanted to say goodbye. Catch you in a couple of days, Ron. Have a good Christmas."

He didn't smile.

"What's up?" I asked.

He got up, went to his closet and handed me a flat box wrapped in Christmas paper. "This is a little something for you. Open it on Christmas Day." Still no smile.

"Ron, what's wrong?"

He threw the wallet we had bought him across the room. "If you're going to buy someone a present at least give it some thought. This is a bloody woman's wallet, for Chrisake."

I stared at him stunned. He was white with rage. Had he been drinking?

"No, I haven't been drinking," he sneered. "I can see that's what you're thinking, but I haven't. Would you please shut the door on your way out."

Larry was shouting down the stairs, "Diane, get a move on! Guy's already in the truck! We're going to miss the ferry."

I closed Ron's door without another word. I wasn't angry, just tired and bewildered and hurt.

The ferry was decked with Christmas decorations and Christmas music was playing. While Larry read the newspaper, I watched the waves rolling up the Strait and was filled with a wave of foreboding. "Larry, something is very wrong. I almost feel I should go back." And I told him about Ron.

"Come on, kid," he said. "You take things too personally. He'll apologize to you when you get back."

Now I said again, "How could you have bought him a woman's wallet?"

"Will you cut it out! I didn't do it deliberately. Jesus, I'll buy him a guy's wallet in Vancouver. Will that make you happy?" He disappeared behind his newspaper.

"He bought me a present," I said, pulling the package out of my carry-on bag.

"Really? Open it," he said, lowering the newspaper.

I pulled the wrapping paper off and gasped. It was a small, exquisitely framed picture of the old Nanaimo waterfront, a picture I had admired one day when Ron and I had been browsing in a downtown antique store. Tears came to my eyes.

"Poor devil," said Larry with a soft understanding look in his eyes. "He's got a crush on you, Di. This must have cost every penny he had."

Christmas passed uneventfully. It was wonderful seeing my family again, but they all asked the same questions.

"Are you safe over there with all those criminals?"

"Why don't you come back to Vancouver and live a normal life?"

"Aren't you afraid of being raped? These men have just come out of jail... if you know what I mean."

Larry spent the entire holiday with Phyllis and his sons, returning to my daughter Kelly's house at nine on Christmas night, just two minutes after my son David and his family had left. I tried to hide my disappointment and heartache from my children, but it's hard to hide your desire to strangle someone when you're a Celt.

As well, my foreboding and uneasiness that there was something wrong at Big Sab persisted, and when we returned to Nanaimo three days later, I literally ran up the stairs of Big Sab and burst through the front door.

The place seemed unusually quiet, but I found Little Larry drinking coffee in the kitchen. "Hey Diane! Did you have a good Christmas?" he smiled his good-natured grin. "I'll pour you a coffee."

"Is everything okay?"

His smile faded. "Oh, you haven't heard yet?"

"What?" My heart lurched.

"Ron's gone. He and Scott ended up in a fist fight here on Christmas Day."

"A fist fight?" I sat down on the nearest kitchen chair with a plunk.

"Scott came downstairs looking for a coffee and..." Little Larry looked at me apologetically. "I think Ron had been drinking... he just wasn't himself. Anyway, Ron asked Scott what the hell he was doing here and tried to throw him out. Scott tried to keep his cool, but man, it was really ugly. They ended up punching the hell out of each other. Somebody called the police and Ron took off. Scott left—he said he was going to Victoria..."

I went down to Ron's room. It was spotless, the bed made, everything in its place. The closet and dresser drawers were empty. I sat down on his bed remembering what he had promised: "If I start drinking again, I promise you I'll leave." Sitting there, I wondered if he was gone for good. He was.

Then the really bad news came like a north wind skidding over the icy water. The phone rang. It was the RCMP. *Scott was dead.* He had fallen off a cliff on Gabriola Island and broken his neck. I could hardly comprehend the words. *Scott was dead?* Apparently he had been drinking with a group of guys. They had been partying and had built a small fire on top of the cliff. Without them realizing it, Scott had wandered off into the night. He hadn't cried out when he fell, so they hadn't even known about the accident until the next day.

Why hadn't he gone to Victoria? What was he doing on Gabriola? Had he changed his mind about getting his bike? We sat around stunned, trying to piece the puzzle together. Then Kathy phoned. Scott had called her on the night he died and said he was coming over for his bike, and she had told him she was charging him for two months of storage fees. They had argued. That was the last she had heard from him.

I was devastated. I kept remembering his roguish smile, the deep black eyes surveying the world and his brilliant, cynical humour. His loneliness and his desperate effort to belong. I couldn't help wondering whether he had deliberately jumped. One night I dreamt he leapt off the cliff laughing into the wind, soaring like a falcon with his arms out-stretched gracefully, diving in slow motion to his death, like he was en-joying himself on the way down. In the daytime I heard his voice saying, "You're such a romantic, Di!" I felt in some way I had let him down, and I wondered if Kathy felt the same way, but I doubted it. Kathy felt responsibility only to herself. But maybe that was the way it was sup-posed to be.

And where the hell was Ron? I couldn't face another casualty.

45
Electricity

Karen phoned. I had never heard her sound so strung out. I had never heard her get even emotional. She was always in complete control, regardless of the swirling chaos her regular workday created around her.

"Diane, I can't tell you how upset I am. We went to pick up Guy tonight as I'd warned you we would... with Car 87. I was the attendant nurse." She started crying and couldn't continue. I knew Car 87 was only called upon when mental patients had stopped taking their medication and become violent or dangerously unpredictable.

I waited motionless. Perturbed. "What happened?"

"Well, for starters, Guy resisted the police and they pepper sprayed him."

"Oh my God! Where?"

"In his apartment lobby. In front of a bunch of people that live there. Guy was so out of it... they handcuffed him and dragged him off... It was awful. Poor Guy... but then when we took him to Nanaimo General, the admitting doctor refused to take him in."

"Where is Guy now?"

"I hate to tell you, but he just ran off into the night... refused to let me give him a ride home. He was so freaked out... but he doesn't have a coat. He just had jeans and a light shirt on, and it's so cold out tonight."

"It's freezing. On the BCTV News tonight they said it's minus 15 right here in Nanaimo. Karen, do you have any idea which direction he ran?"

"No. I jumped in my car and circled around trying to find him... he's so out of it. Like a wounded animal." She started crying again, soft muffled sobs.

"They mace him, handcuff him, and then they don't admit him. Why in the hell wouldn't the doctor take him?"

"Sometimes, like tonight, I wonder what I'm doing in this business. Do me a favour, Diane. Would you phone the psych-admitting doctor on tonight at Emergency and demand as Guy's mother that you would like an answer on why he didn't think Guy was sick enough to admit? I'd like to know his answer. I just wanted to let you know firsthand about the whole mess. I'm so sorry." I heard the phone click off.

Karen had been monitoring Guy's behaviour for the last three weeks. I had wanted to get him into hospital two months earlier, but Karen had warned me I was jumping the gun. "He's not quite sick enough." She was referring to the Canadian Bill of Rights ruling that unless mentally ill people were a danger to themselves or to others, they could not be hospitalized against their will or forced to take medicine. "Just hold off," she cautioned. "There's nothing worse than trying to get him in and going through all that hell of getting him picked up by Car 87 and then the doctor refusing to admit."

So we had waited and then Guy's landlord had phoned. Guy had punched a hole in the lobby wall, shouting that the electrical currents weren't working in the elevator. Karen had immediately commandeered Car 87 for the pickup.

I phoned the psych-admitting doctor at the hospital and was surprised when he answered his extension right away.

"I'm Guy Foley's mother, Doctor. Would you please explain why you didn't admit Guy tonight? We all think he is more than sick enough. His mental health nurse, Karen, thought it appropriate to bring him in."

"Mrs. Foley," said this tight, clipped voice, "we have had Guy in a few times now. What is the use of bringing him in and cleaning him up when all he does is refuse to take his meds when he leaves the hospital? The whole cycle only starts up again. It is a waste of time admitting him, Mrs. Foley. We have a lack of beds here and many people responding to treatment needing them."

"You're giving up on him? Is that what you're saying? How will he ever get better if we don't keep trying?"

"I'm sorry, Mrs. Foley, I am a busy man. That is my answer to your question. Good night."

I sat there stunned, almost physically sick with anger. How could he call himself a doctor? I would report him. But for what? How could I make a case about his indifference? How could a sick person like Guy get the message he was a schizophrenic and needed meds when there were doctors like this in the healthcare system not wanting to try? Only that morning Rafe Mair, on his radio talk show at JACK-FM, had been saying that if physically ill patients in Canada were treated the same way as mentally sick patients, there would be blood spilled on the streets.

I paced up and down looking at the clock. If Guy had run home, and in this freezing weather I figured he would run, it would take him about forty minutes to get home from the hospital. I phoned Guy's landlord. I was so glad he was Welsh like me. It was like we had a bond and I knew he would be helpful and understanding. "Mr. Lewis, could you possibly check and see if Guy is home?"

"He came in a few minutes ago. I know because I was changing a light bulb in the lobby when he came through the front door. I saw that whole fiasco tonight, Diane, when they came to pick him up. The cops buzzed me to let them in. It was terrible. They did it in front of everyone. Handcuffs, the whole thing. So embarrassing. Shocking really. Then the macing... inhumane. You have my sympathy, girl."

"Thanks so much, Mr. Lewis. Can you believe? And after all that they refused him admittance at the hospital?"

"That's a damn disgrace, that is. That poor son of yours is sick and needs help. I don't know what to say, dear."

"The problem is there's always a huge backlog of people waiting for beds, and so there's no help for even seriously sick people like Guy."

"I saw a show the other night that said one percent of the population has schizophrenia, and yet they still have no idea what causes it."

"That's maybe because mental health gets almost zero funding. Nothing compared to the monies received for cancer research. There is still a stigma attached to mental illness, so help me. People don't talk about it the way they would if their loved ones had diabetes or cerebral palsy. I get so frustrated."

"You take care of yourself dear," Mr. Lewis clucked sympathetically. "You're sounding pretty rough. Call me if there's anything I can do."

The next day I went over to the apartment and knocked on Guy's door.

"Who is it?"

"It's Mum, Guy."

I heard the door being unlocked and then it slowly opened an inch with the chain still on. One eye peered through the crack.

"It's me, Guy. Open up."

The door swung open, and Guy stood there in a stained white shirt and soiled jeans. Matted hair, ragged beard. Barefoot.

"Hold on just a moment." He was staring at me suspiciously.

"I've brought you some beef stew and crusty rolls."

"Oh. Okay, Mum, come on in." He gave an apologetic smile. "I had to make sure it was you in your body." To my questioning look, he added, "Well, sometimes people call by but it's someone else in their body. You can't be too careful."

The place was a mess. The sink full of dirty dishes. Pots crusted with rotten food on top of the stove. I had been there a week earlier to clean up, but it was unbelievable that such a mess had taken only days to create. The place smelled rank. I opened the balcony door to let the fresh winter air rush in, rolled up my sleeves and started cleaning. I scoured out a saucepan and started heating the stew. I tried to check out Guy's eyes to see if they were swollen from the mace. How much damage could mace inflict? I didn't know. I stared through the window at the beautiful view. The seagulls swirling. The waves choppy and cheeky rushing at the beach across the road. Like normal life was a given. Deceiving, wasn't it, when I was in the middle of such madness?

Guy sat back contentedly in his easy chair munching on a roll. Crumbs clung to his beard. His feet stuck up on the coffee table were filthy. Like he'd just been marching for months on the Napoleonic retreat from Russia. "Any chance of a cup of coffee, Mum?" he asked casually as if he was lord of the manor. Actually, he looked like Rasputin.

On Friday, just four days later, Mr. Lewis phoned. "You better get over here, Diane. Just come. Is Larry there? Bring him too."

We jumped in the truck. What now? I felt a huge sense of foreboding. Doom.

Mr. Lewis was waiting in the foyer. He took us up in the elevator to Guy's suite. The door was ajar, and we filed in. The saying "double-take" doesn't even describe it. I stood in shock and Larry was speechless, all of us just staring in stunned amazement. Every electrical wire had been cut. The lovely living room chandelier taken down, the wire stumps, ugly and frayed, sticking out naked from the ceiling. The TV and VCR smashed. The stove pulled away from the wall, the cable slashed. All the coverings for the electrical appliances were unscrewed and thrown on the floor.

"He could have set the whole building on fire," said Mr. Lewis, looking grimly at the mess. "We wouldn't have stood a chance. I mean he cut the bloody stove cable, didn't he? 220 volts that one. Thank God, he had the smarts and sense to turn the electricity off at the fuse box. Otherwise the whole apartment would be gone. And he'd be gone with it."

"What in the hell can be going on in Guy's mind?" Larry wandered around the room, scratching his head. "What do you make of this, Diane?"

"He's been going on about electricity for years. Electrical this and that. The devil uses electricity. Electrical currents control the world. I don't know. What the hell do I know? This is one big unholy mess. I almost feel like suing that damn doctor that refused to take him into the hospital. Look at this and they don't think he's crazy enough?"

"But where's Guy?" said Larry, looking around. "We'd better find him in a hurry or the whole of Nanaimo is heading for a power blackout."

For a quick flash moment I imagined Guy running stealthily in and out of businesses and cabarets and the mayor's office with a big pair of wire cutters. Snip, more lights out. On to another building. Snip, snip. And, of course, that made me laugh. Hysterically, perhaps. So much for my twisted humour. Mr. Lewis looked disappointed in me.

We went back home, and I made us a cup of tea. Then I phoned Karen at the Nanaimo mental health team, and she put the office on a red alert to pick up Guy. I called everybody I knew to be on the lookout for him. I called the Sally Ann on the off chance he'd gone there for a meal as he'd gone there before with Richard, and he knew their policy that, if you were down and out, they would give you a free meal. And we asked the guys at Big Sab and Harmony House to keep their eyes peeled.

Two days went by. No Guy. It was like looking for a needle in a haystack. Then I had an alarming thought. What if he had boarded a ferry and gone back to Vancouver? Oh my God, I would lose him then for sure. Forever. Larry and I rushed down to the ferry terminal and talked to the office. They put out a bulletin to all the ticket booth employees to be on the lookout for a scruffy, dirty man in his thirties with matted hair and a beard. They were to phone the office immediately and not sell this person a ticket. What else could I do? I had run out of everything but worry.

By the end of a week I was at my wit's end. I couldn't sleep. I was distraught, inconsolable. In my worst moments I feared Guy was dead. The weather had turned wet. Rain pouring down, cold windy nights. Where could he be sleeping at night? He must be getting soaked through. Was he eating? Was he still on the Island? I remembered the schizophrenics I'd seen living in Stanley Park when I lived in Vancouver's West End. They would stagger out of the park early in the morning, laughing and talking incoherently to themselves. Filthy, covered in sores. Sunburned in the summer. Freezing and shivering in the winter. Too sick to figure out how to get a welfare cheque. Too sick to know who they were. A mother's nightmare.

There were days I would cave in on hope and think he's probably dead. *If he's dead, it's for the best, poor tormented soul.* Poor darling Guy, who had been the sweetest, most lovable, chubby, adorable little boy in the whole world. A bright, funny and sensitive teenager. To have your life ripped from you at seventeen, the classic age when schizophrenia strikes. To grow up only to be inflicted with horror and pain. He didn't deserve it. Then I would jolt back to crying and begging the Chess Board Kings of Life to please bring him back. There must be better times ahead. We must get him better. We will get him better. There has to be a way to make him realize he's sick and has to take his meds. Give me one more chance to get him a better life. *Are you listening up there?*

Almost three weeks passed. Then the phone rang. It was the Sally Ann. A raggedly dressed man had been coming into the Sally Ann for dinner the last few nights. He was in bad shape. The staff had tried to talk to him, but he just ran out if anyone approached his table.

I didn't dare hope. I had received other false leads. I'd had a call only the previous week from the Reserve office saying there was a hobo living on the beach there, and it had turned out to be an old wino who was sleeping off a binge. And then a chilling scare. The police had shot a psychotic man on Commercial Drive in Vancouver when he had waved a knife and run towards them. It hadn't been Guy.

Larry and I drove down to the Sally Ann. We parked the truck so it was hidden around the corner behind the Sally Ann's kitchen building where it was obscured by thick bushes. Karen and the Nanaimo mental health team waved from a car parked across the street. The chaplain signalled us from the Sally Ann door that Guy was not there yet.

We waited huddled in the shadows, the rain and wind cutting into the warmth of my coat. A trickle of rain beaded off my hair, hit my neck and started down my back. I shivered, straining my eyes in the dark. A few men, laughing and talking, walked across the lot and entered the building. A shaft of light hit the blacktop before the door slammed shut again. Silence. The wind was making dancing shadows of the trees and bushes bordering the small parking lot. A sudden flurry of stones skidding down a small cliff at the end of the lot made us jump. A small animal maybe?

Or was it?

Then out of the mist and rain, a muddy, ragged man emerged, sliding down the last few feet of the cliff and then limping as he made his way to the door of the kitchen. Dear God. Could that shambling figure be Guy?

"Guy," I shouted to the wind. He hadn't heard. I started to run towards him. "Guy?"

The bundle of rags stopped in the light of the door and peered through the rain. I kept running. "Guy?" The figure hesitated then bolted, started running for the trail up the cliff like an animal running for its life. Larry passed me. Through the rain I saw the figures stumbling up the cliff, the mud making them slither and slide. The ragged bundle sliding down as Larry hurled himself upward. The sounds, animal-like, desperate, protesting, howling into the night.

Karen was beside me, her hair plastered against her face, rivulets of rain making her eyes blink. "Is it him?" Cell phone in hand. Ready.

"It's Guy," shouted Larry, holding the struggling twisting figure helpless in his bear grip.

"Car 87," I heard Karen shout against the wind. "We've got him. Please get here *now*."

I was trembling like a leaf as Larry half-carried and half-dragged the spent, thin bundle of rags under the shelter of the kitchen veranda. Car 87 came swooping from around the corner where it had been parked out of view. Blue and red lights flashing. The static crackle of the police radio. Larry's mud-splattered face shining eerily under the overhead streetlamp. Driving rain glittering beneath the light.

"Guy, it's Mum," I said. "It's okay. Don't be afraid."

Frightened animal eyes peered out at me from a tangled mess of hair and beard festooned with twigs and leaves. He was mumbling incoherently. Giggling. Whimpering as he was placed in the back seat between two policemen. I thought I heard him say "Mum?" I wasn't sure though, with the wind blowing and my tears stinging and blurring my vision.

Karen was giving me the thumbs up sign. She went running to her car to follow Car 87 to the Nanaimo General Hospital.

"How did you know for sure it was him?" I asked Larry as we settled in the truck. "I could hardly recognize him myself and I'm his mother."

"It was easy," said Larry, smiling at me mysteriously. His big mud-caked hands rested loosely on the steering wheel. "It was something he yelled as I grabbed him and threw him down. I knew it had to be Guy."

"What?" I said.

Larry started the truck.

"Don't fool around with me, Larry."

"Electricity," he said softly. Taking his time. Being dramatic. "He said *electricity* and then the fight went out of him. He went limp in my arms... as though..." He struggled for the right words.

We stared at each other. I finished his sentence.

"As though he was finally grounded," I said.

46

Elvis Was a Hound Dog

Elvis was unhappy. I tried cheering him up.

"Want to come grocery shopping with me?"

He shook a "no" with his ragged thatch of hair, his face looking as mournful as a caged hound dog during hunting season.

"Elvis, what is it? What's wrong?" I asked, although I knew already.

"Elvis misses Mummy and Daddy. Elvis loves them and he misses them." He sat in the big stuffed armchair by the fireplace, his legs dangling, not quite reaching the floor, looking like a five-year-old. The brown eyes behind the Coke-bottle glasses brimmed with grief. His hands were still, placed in his lap.

I had phoned Elvis's former foster parents in Williams Lake to give them an update on how he was doing. He had been thrilled to talk to them, but since that conversation he had been depressed. He refused to understand the definition of the word parole, brooding that he wanted to go home *now*. That was his one and only thought. He wanted to go home.

His foster mother, though a remarkable woman, was also unsophisticated in understanding the parole system, and she refused to understand how black and white the rules were. "After taking Elvis away from us for almost two years already. He's done his time and that was a blasphemy, God knows, locking the poor kid up... but now they're keeping him away from us even longer."

She had a point. Why couldn't Elvis finish his parole back in Williams Lake?

I called Gordie Ryder and asked him if there was anything we could do. No, he said. Elvis was going to have to stick it out. The powers-that-be thought he would keep out of trouble if he stayed away from Williams Lake, and he needed to keep out of trouble of any kind while he was on parole.

"Any infraction and he will be sent back to jail. I don't want to see the kid back inside."

"But Williams Lake is his home, Gord," I argued.

"Diane, it's out of our hands. We're stuck with this."

"Elvis homesick." I could hear him saying in his sing-song voice to Larry in the living room.

And Larry was saying, "Let's go to the Dairy Queen." Larry's solution to all depressions.

I phoned Greyhound and asked the price of a one-way ticket to Williams Lake. Elvis's welfare cheque was coming in a few days. I wrestled with what to do, but in the end it was Elvis who called the shots.

I found him struggling down the stairs with his suitcase packed, clothing sticking out. The suitcase looked as big as him. He was dressed in a thick layer of T- shirts and sweaters, his coat over top making him look fatter and smaller. In response to my incredulous, inquiring stare he announced stubbornly that he was going to hitchhike to Williams Lake.

"No way, Elvis," I said in a determined no-nonsense voice. "It's 800 miles to Williams Lake. I am going to call Gordie Ryder right now."

Elvis started to cry.

Gordie listened quietly to me. "Gord, I can't watch him twenty-four hours a day, and I'm afraid he'll try and take off at any time. And I'll worry myself sick if he takes off. I'll be thinking of him sleeping along the highway... or even worse, getting hurt."

Gord was silent for a moment. "Okay, let's get him on a bus," he said, adding, "but you never heard me say that."

The next morning Larry and I drove Elvis to the Greyhound bus depot. He was wearing his favourite Williams Lake Rodeo sweatshirt, and he held my hand tightly, looking distraught and anxious until I bought the ticket and handed it over to him. Then he relaxed. I think he'd thought there was a small chance we might be taking him back to jail for being *bad*, that we were mad at him for trying to run away. I had packed him his favourite ham and cheese sandwiches for the trip along with some cookies and juice. Larry chatted with the bus driver, asking him to look out for Elvis. "He's really just a kid."

Finally, there was Elvis hanging out of the bus window and waving his chubby hands. He was already munching on a cookie. "Elvis going home." His round face beaming joyfully reminded me for a moment of ET. *Home.* We waved him off, a little choked as we watched the bus round the bend. It was then that Gordie joined us. He had been watching from his parked car.

"Elvis has left the building!" said Larry to nobody in particular.

The three of us stared down the empty road as though hypnotized then turned and walked back to the parking lot in companionable silence. Gord stopped by his car and punched Larry in the arm. Why do guys do that when they get emotional?

"Well, there you have it," Gord said. "I can't believe he's gone! I'm missing that little short-sighted runt already."

"I can't believe he didn't say, 'Thank you, thank you, thank you very much'," Larry said, glancing over at me. Rummaging through his pockets, he handed me a Kleenex then reached over and tousled my hair, messing it up.

"Stop it, Larry. You know I hate you doing that." I blew my nose.

"You're an old sad sack. What do you say, Gord? Shall we take old sad sack to the Dairy Queen and cheer her up?"

So that's what the three of us did. We all ordered Peanut Buster Parfaits and sat there chatting as we spooned the ice cream down knowing full well that Peanut Buster Parfaits wouldn't replace Elvis for a second.

47
Running the Roads

Lewis had been in the Surfside Rehab for three weeks and had been doing so well he was allowed an evening pass and had come over for a visit. I was thrilled at the difference in him. The healthy shine in his eyes, his skin glowing. Everything. Even the way he talked. We were sitting around the kitchen table having coffee when he brought up the subject of Louise.

"She still won't talk to me. She wants me to complete the whole course at Surfside before we even talk about resuming the relationship."

"Probably a good idea. You know six weeks isn't that long and you'll be on solid ground by then. Look at you now—already you look like a million dollars. Like our old Lewis."

"I know. It makes sense. I just miss her." He grinned ruefully. "At least I have some hope she might give me another chance."

I was pouring more coffee when Larry came in. "Where's Shiner? He's not in the yard."

"Not again! That bloody wanderlust dog!" I jumped up and ran outside. Shiner was always going AWOL. He would dig under the garden fence to get out or if someone forgot to close the gate he was off like a shot. He was the biggest freaking escape artist since Houdini. As a result he had become an accepted character in the South End, and we were often astonished at the kindness of people taking time out from their busy schedules to bring him home from his AWOL excursions. One day the postman had opened his van's rear doors and tossed him back over the fence, and on another occasion a whisky-voiced lady had phoned to say she had Shiner locked in her garage. She had noticed our telephone number written on his collar—Larry's idea—when Shiner had entered her yard to play with her dog. When I went to pick Shiner up, I said, "I guess I'd better get him fixed. You know, neutered. Maybe that will keep him at home."

She had gazed steadily at me while dragging on a cigarette then said in her whisky voice, "Honey, I wouldn't do that if I were you. I had Tracker's nuts cut off six months ago and that damn dog hasn't spoken to me since."

I glanced over at Tracker, a dignified black and white sheepdog. He stared steadily straight ahead.

"They know you know," the whisky voice continued. "If you want a relationship with your pup, leave his nuts alone."

Then a sweet blind lady, who used to call Shiner to our garden gate so she could lean over and pat his head, brought him home. Shiner had been cruising up and down the main street in town and had run up to her outside the Scottish Bakery. She had grabbed his collar and resolutely walked him home. For God's sakes—a blind lady—tap tapping with a white cane bringing him home!

Then listen to this: we had a call from a cargo ship anchored in the harbour that was leaving for China the next day. Shiner had been running on the docks, and the crew had invited him on board to spend the night. They had loved spoiling him but had noticed our telephone number on his collar, otherwise our wolfdog would still be sailing the Seven Seas. He had almost walked onto an early morning ferryboat to Vancouver, but an alert ferry official realized just in time he was not attached to the family he was walking beside.

The dog pound had caught him twice and charged almost enough for a down payment on a BMW for his release. The clerk at the SPCA explained cheerfully that huskies were the worst AWOL offenders and were always trying to go on walkabout. Call of the wild stuff. On top of all this, I was always afraid that someone would steal him. He really was the most handsome, gorgeous-looking, wolf-like dog on the whole of Vancouver Island. Whenever I walked with him, people would stop to pat him and comment on his looks, and it seemed like everyone in the South End wanted to buy him from me, so I was paranoid whenever he went missing. But Shiner had become my dearest pal. He went everywhere with me, even slept under our bed every night which I think he regarded it as his cave.

And now here he was gone again. Lewis was already out on the street whistling and calling, "Shiner!" at the top of his lungs. Larry went out and circled the neighbourhood in his truck to no avail. Finally, Lewis hugged me goodbye. He had to honour his 8 p.m. curfew at Surfside.

This time nobody brought Shiner home. He was gone.

Larry and I went to bed with the front door wide open just in case Shiner came back in the night. (Need I say leaving the door open was an unusual occurrence in the South End?) I had a fitful sleep and then woke up at 5:30 a.m. and crept out of the house. I drove the truck through the sleeping streets, around and down the gravelled roads of the Reserve calling his name, my voice travelling on the quiet, cool morning air. Then downtown and around the harbour. Out as far as the ferry terminal. Not one stray dog was to be seen.

The day commenced. I called the SPCA and the dog pound. No Shiner. Larry spent hours in the truck driving around looking. He kept saying, "No one's to blame." That afternoon he called Big Sab to ask the guys if they could help us search. They all signed up, and Larry started organizing them. Two of them would go toward town. A new Indigenous tenant from the isolated fishing village of Bamfield, with the unlikely Scottish name of Angus McNabb—those randy Scottish explorers again—would go with Jack onto the Reserve. The Little Professor and Little Larry would go north towards the busy Island Highway. Larry and his nephew would head towards Cedar. I would stay at home in case the phone rang.

As darkness approached, I was distraught. And when the guys all wandered back an hour later with no good news, my heart was in my boots. Little Larry tried to cheer me up by saying they would make up posters and spread them around the neighbourhood first thing in the morning.

Larry kept saying, "Remember he's not your regular dog. It's the wolf in him that makes him take off." And he told the guys, "He's not really a dog... he has a hide." Forgetting to add that wolves have hides. I mean what the bloody hell? But I knew he was as upset as I was. He adored Shiner and quite often when I picked him up from the ferry, he made more fuss of Shiner waiting in the truck than of me. If I was neurotic, I could have suspected a love triangle.

The guys from Big Sab walked the neighbourhood tirelessly putting up posters. Many caring people, Indigenous and white alike, promised to keep an eye open for our runaway. Someone put a big poster up in the Sally Ann to spread the word around town. It was a true South End effort. Even one dear old lady who lived on our street —she must have been at least eighty years old—followed a path overgrown with thick bramble bushes that meandered along beside the railway tracks, using her cane to prod the bushes, "Just in case no one has thought to look down there." With so many people looking for him, how the hell could he have vanished so completely into thin air?

Three days passed. Shiner had never been lost for this long. Had he been run over? Stolen? Was he dead or alive? I cried until my eyes could weep no more. I had lost my dear heart, my buddy. The guys at Big Sab were wonderful, trying to comfort me, self-consciously giving me little hugs and telling me animal survival stories. The weirdest one was about a cat that came back to his owner after being lost on a moving day four years earlier.

I blamed myself for not being more careful. I blamed Larry for not being more helpful in securing the battered fence around the yard. I blamed the guys from Big Sab for not being more conscientious about securing the gate when they visited, but mostly I had a leaden painful feeling of absolute loss in my heart. I missed Shiner's breathing under our bed at night. I missed the way he skidded like a maniac down the hall to greet people he loved. I missed his quiet presence when he lay on the rug as we watched TV. I missed his steady eye contact just before he barked a big, deliberate "Woof," his way of asking to go out, and the way he tilted his head back and howled like a wolf when he heard a police siren or an ambulance.

It is amazing how a pet can evoke so much love. Then maybe it isn't. Who else gives the total unconditional love of a pet? Even John, the Old Codger, tottered to the door in his pajamas and peered bleary-eyed down the street a dozen times a day. This man who had scoffed at the notion of pets living inside a house and insisted dogs should work for their keep was also missing Shiner.

Shiner had a favourite trick. When the front door and the back-kitchen door were both open, he would skid down the hall and out the front door, race around the yard to the kitchen back door and enter, streaking with the blurred speed of a greyhound to skid down the hall and repeat the whole procedure again. We would all jump up and do "the wave," roaring, "Yeah! Go, Shiner, go!" as he flew by, which would of course make him streak all the faster. My own favourite cry was "Go Shiner, Dog of the North!" We would all be reduced to hysterical tears and laughter, Elvis had especially loved it, and would be shouting, "Here he comes again!" jumping in the air, waving his stubby arms more frantically than the rest of us.

That night, remembering all this and thinking maybe I'd never see the Grey Streak again, I pushed my head into my pillow and let the tears fall, trying my best to cry quietly, hiding the sound of my heartbreak in the pillow. I felt Larry's hand searching for my mine under the quilt. His hands were so huge my smaller hand felt comforted, disappearing into the engulfing warmth of his. He gave my hand a small squeeze. In the silence of the room, with just the ticking of the clock, I strained my ears. In spite of my tears I had to smile a tiny smile that I wasn't the only one feeling heartache. Larry was crying in the dark as well. I gently squeezed his hand back and holding hands like that, we two bereft, grieving parents finally slid into sleep.

Then the phone call came. It was 10 o'clock the following night.

Larry took the call. He hung up the phone and said grimly, "You won't believe this."

"What? What?" Did I dare to hope?

"This guy... the one that just called... is asking for a ransom for Shiner. He's got him."

"A ransom? How much?"

"Fifty bucks."

I plunked down on my chair, aghast. "I don't believe this."

"I'm going to meet him now. He's waiting by the phone box outside the Terminal Hotel." Larry pulled on his boots.

"You're not going to pay? This is crazy, Larry. It sounds too weird... asking for money for somebody's lost pet. What kind of a person would do this? This guy must be the biggest asshole known to man."

"I know, but what else can we do? He's probably a drug addict wanting money for a fix. I'll go and meet him and find out." And out the door he went. I stood watching the truck disappear down the street, thinking how glad I was that Larry happened to be a big, strong, no-nonsense man. The Terminal Hotel was a rough bar with an unsavoury clientele. I was still waiting at the open front door shivering, not with the cool night air but with nervous anticipation, when fifteen minutes later the truck reappeared over the hill. Larry climbed out. I held my breath. But lo and behold and *Holy smokes!* climbing out of the truck behind him on the end of a frayed rope was Shiner. I rushed forward, a cry of joy escaping my lips as my dog leapt towards me.

Later Larry and I sat in front of the dying embers of the fire. Shiner had been starving, and he had eaten a huge bowl of food and dog biscuits galore. He was bone tired now and already asleep in his favourite spot under our bed. Fortunately he seemed none the worse for wear. A little thinner perhaps. His coat a little dirty but nothing a bath and a good brush tomorrow wouldn't fix.

I curled up on the couch in front of the fire, my legs tangled comfortably in Larry's as he described his meeting with the kidnapper, a thin, unkempt man in his thirties. Nervous and gruff. Larry had offered him $25, saying that's all the money he had and had held out the bills. The man had hesitated for a moment then grabbed the cash and told Larry that Shiner was tied to a lamp post a half-block away. Larry had insisted that the guy accompany him down the street in case he was lying, but there was our dear old Shiner tied up with the frayed rope. The guy had taken off like a nervous jackrabbit. Larry had tears in his eyes when he described Shiner's dazed expression. "He couldn't believe his luck when he saw me. He just sat looking at me as though he was dreaming. Like he was Oliver Twist being rescued from Fagan. It wasn't until we were in the truck that he leapt all over me licking me like a berserk fiend. Like he only then believed he was going home."

"Another Shiner missing story," I said. "It's like that old movie *Lassie Come Home*. I think he'll make the *Guinness Book of Records*. No other dog in North America can have gone through all these harebrained adventures."

Larry liked that. "Right on! And we'll do a TV series called *Shiner Come Home*. Maybe we'll make some money."

"Did the guy tell you where or when he found him?"

"No."

"And you didn't ask?"

"I just wanted Shiner back."

"You shouldn't have paid the jerk the money."

"Actually, I would have loved to have bopped the guy smack in the head, but a deal's a deal. Shit, Diane! What's twenty-five bucks in the big scheme of things? We got old Shiner Boy back."

That night we were all sleeping together in the same room again. I could hear Larry's even breathing beside me and Shiner's soft muffled breathing under the bed. I was content and happy. I wondered whether Larry and Shiner woke up in the night and heard these same familiar sounds? Would they also smile sentimentally in the dark? Would they feel the same way as I was feeling now? *Together again. Home. Content.*

Well, that is, until a certain freaky-deaky, goddamn, Houdini-type escape wolfdog artist decided to run the roads again. I rolled over and went to sleep. I wasn't even going there.

48
Cigarette Break

Two months after that Christmas Day that Ron had disappeared, I got the call. It was the Salvation Army Detox Centre out on the Island Highway. Ron had been admitted. Would I come and see him? Also, could I bring cigarettes?

I didn't know what to expect when I arrived at the Detox Centre, but there was Ron looking thin and pale. He had lost weight but there was a genuine, happy smile on his face when I walked into the room. He seemed a little embarrassed as he hugged me.

"Did you bring the cigarettes? Oh thanks, Di, you're a real brick." He lit a cigarette right away and inhaled deeply. "Thanks so much for bringing these."

"Is that the only reason you wanted to see me? Cigarettes?" I laughed to break the tension.

"Hell no! You know that! I owe you one hell of an apology. I don't know why that Christmas caved me in. I felt so damn lonely and out of it. I guess I was feeling sorry for myself... that stupid incident about the wallet."

"The woman's wallet?" We raised our heads and looked at each other and started laughing.

"So help me God, I never took you for a cross-dresser, Ron. It was that damn Larry who picked it out. You know how he is. In another world half the time. It's his why-am-I-out-here-in-the-middle-of-Christmas-shopping-hell mentality. So... come on... please tell me what happened Christmas Eve after we left for the ferry?"

"I went to the Pat. Started drinking. Bought off-sales there and took it to my room and really tied one on. I promised you if I did that—started drinking—I would leave, so I was kinda burning my bridges behind me and I knew it. I was in the frame of mind that I didn't give a damn about nothing and nobody. Then came the fight with Scott."

"You know he's dead?" I interrupted him quickly.

"Dead? You're kidding me..."

"He fell off a cliff and broke his neck." I felt my stomach lurch as I blurted it out.

"No, I didn't know. Jesus, Diane," he ran his hands through his hair. "When did this happen... not right after the fight?"

"No, it was nothing to do with the fight or with you, Ron. So don't even think that. It happened over on Gabriola. He had argued with Kathy. A drinking accident, you might say. He was so unhappy. I don't know... he just couldn't handle booze and yet he couldn't keep away from it."

"I know all about that." Ron gave a brittle laugh. "Not staying away from the booze. Not handling it. I don't know why I was so mad at him that night. I'd never really gotten along with him. He was an arrogant bastard in some ways. Rubbed me the wrong way. It was like he'd been drinking but he'd been allowed to stay. One rule for him and another rule for the rest of us. It was irrational and stupid. I just wanted a reason to fight, I guess. I was pissed off at the world and poor Scott arrived conveniently for me to vent."

"I just couldn't send him away on Christmas Eve. I just couldn't do it. He was hung over from the night before. Well, to be honest, I guess he was still a little drunk from the night before, but if I had sent him away on a cold night like that, I would never have forgiven myself. But I still can't believe he's really dead, that I'll never see him again."

"Well, you almost had two corpses," Ron said. "I went on a god-awful binge. Tried everything. Cocaine even. I drank myself unconscious, collapsed on the street and woke up in hospital. They told me I almost died. My friend who got me the job in the Sally Ann kitchen got me in here. I reckon this is my last chance. This is it."

I looked at his sad eyes and tired face. At the inner beauty of the man.

"I don't get it," I said. "You have so much to live for. You're intelligent, talented. Your writing is something else. Your English teacher at Malaspina has been calling, worrying about you. She's thinks you're the next bloody Hemingway." That got a smile. "You're a lovely, lovely, attractive man. There's a life waiting for you out there." I waved expansively around at the waiting world.

Ron looked away self-consciously to where the garden sloped down to the ocean. "If I could find a good woman like you to stand by my side, it would be a hell of a lot easier, Di. Larry's a lucky man. I get so darn lonely. All my friends are drinkers so I have to steer clear of them. It's like starting all over from scratch. Like living on another planet."

"Dear Ron," I said, "I know there's a woman waiting for you out there. A woman who is getting bloody impatient. Clean up your act. Get yourself out there and get cracking." I stood and cupped his face in my hands. "Don't let your dad keep on blind-siding you, Ron. He's gone. He can't hurt you anymore."

He was visibly startled by my words. I gave him a kiss on the cheek and left him there. He phoned me a week later to tell me he was being discharged and that he had a job as a taxi driver. The same friend at the Salvation Army was helping to set that up. He called periodically after that to let me know he was "still clean and sober." But he didn't call around to visit.

49
The Devil's Disguise

Richard was knocking on the front door frantically, a soiled and blood-stained handkerchief held to his mouth. "I had a tooth pulled this morning, and it won't stop bleeding." He was in an obvious state of panic.

"Okay, Richard. Let's get you home. I'll call the dentist. Why didn't you tell me you were going? I would have given you a ride."

Dear old Richard was so independent. I often saw him walking miles away from home. He would never think to ask for a ride.

"Aw... I'm in pain, Diane. This hurts like hell." He was a really good groaner though.

I walked him over to his bedroom in Harmony House and made him lie down on his bed, bolstering up his pillows. Then I phoned the dentist who seemed totally unconcerned.

"It could be a dry socket. Give him Tylenol, and if it doesn't stop bleeding, bring him back. I might have to put in a stitch."

I gave Richard the pills and covered him with a blanket, but when I checked on him later, his mouth was still bleeding profusely.

"Come on, love," I said. "I'm taking you back to that dentist. You need a stitch in there."

On the drive downtown Richard started telling me how he hadn't been able to sleep the night before. His toothache had been excruciating, and he had been sitting in the living room near the window when he had seen the devil standing outside on the street.

"The devil?" I exclaimed.

"Yes, he was waiting for me out there. Calling for me to go outside. It was foggy but I could see him. He was standing close to the porch. I was scared, Diane. I don't mind telling you that."

Richard's type of schizophrenia did not respond well to the medicines available. I felt so sorry for him. He tried so hard but was often victimized by terrible fears and hallucinations. The previous week I had heard him tell Ken that Nazi planes had been dropping bombs on the neighbourhood, keeping him awake all night. He had been terrified hearing the *ack-ack* bursting overhead. Ken had sweetly dispelled his fears by putting his hand to his mouth to imitate a radio phone. "Yellow Dog over to Scaredy Cat. Don't worry. The enemy are only dropping pamphlets in Nanaimo. It's a propaganda operation. My dad is top brass in the RCAF, and he's told me not to worry."

"Thanks, Ken, for that info," Richard said, heaving a big sigh of relief and giving us a toothy grin.

But now this devil story.

"It was probably just someone prowling around the neighbourhood late at night, Richard. Probably a drunk from the Pat stopping to pee in the bushes."

"No, he was beckoning to me to come out. He shouted for Louis to come out, too."

Louis had only been at Harmony House for a couple of months. He was around thirty-three, extremely intelligent and he played a wicked game of chess, but he was a true eccentric. He always looked serious and sad, and when I heard his story, I understood why. He was the son of a rich, successful couple, and as a teenager had enjoyed all the advantages of a privileged upbringing, had travelled around the world with his parents—St. Moritz, Venice, Tahiti—you name it, he'd been there. His schizophrenia had hit twelve years earlier right after his parents were killed in a car crash, and his older brother, a professor at McGill University, had been at a loss on how to cope with him.

But as a generous trust fund had been set up, Louis had wandered aimlessly around Canada ending up out west. Unfortunately, his problem was that he desperately needed supervision because, when he was on his own, he forgot to take his meds and invariably that landed him in trouble. He had just served time in jail for throwing chairs and life jackets overboard while travelling on a Nanaimo to Horseshoe Bay ferry. He had then fought violently with the ferry crew when they tried to restrain him. So rich spoiled kid to jailbird, just like that.

Now that he was living at Harmony House with a supervised medication program, he was a pussycat—calm and placid and, as the old Eagles' song goes, full of "that peaceful easy feelin'." He kept his room spotlessly clean and full of the trophies he collected from Mother Nature. He loved taking the ferry over to the peace of Newcastle Island and roaming the beaches, collecting shells and driftwood and picking wildflowers to adorn his bedside table. The ferry crew soon knew him well, understood that he was a bit odd, but as he seemed like a lonely soul, they very kindly let him ride the ferry for free.

He was a loner except for one friend, a man of forty with mental problems caused by a brain injury. They had met in a group home, and when I saw them together, they reminded me of Tom Sawyer and Huckleberry Finn, always laughing and planning how one day they were going to buy a boat and sail around the world. It was sad because this friend's name actually *was* Tom, and in his old life before his brain injury, he had been a successful businessman and had owned a beautiful yacht named *Moon River*.

Tom was an extremely handsome man with laughing blue eyes, dimples and a shock of wavy dark hair. He must have been quite the ladykiller in his day, and it filled me with pity to see him reduced to the behaviour of a thirteen-year-old, his lack of short-term memory confusing the simplest of his everyday decisions. He and Louis would drink beer at the Pat on Welfare Day and then sing loudly as they came down the road, all cocky and flushed with happiness, arms around each other, almost staggering into the hedges. Louis had been thrown out of his last group home because of this, but I turned a blind eye. A couple of beers once a month seemed like small compensation to these two who had been robbed of everything else in life.

I had just returned from the dentist with Richard when the phone rang. It was Nanaimo Hospital Emergency. "We have a Louis Beau-champ here with a head injury. Says he lives with you. He's had quite a few stitches. Can you pick him up?" For a moment the words didn't quite register. Louis? Head injury? How the hell had that happened? What kind of day was unfolding here anyway? A blood, guts and gore day by the look of it.

"I'll be there right away." Leaving a note on the kitchen table to ex-plain where I had gone, I rushed back over to Harmony House to make Richard comfortable. I made him lie on his bed, tucked him un-der a blanket and gave him two Tylenol. Warning him over my shoul-der, "Now don't try to eat or drink till I get back," I hurried out.

When I saw Louis, I felt my knees buckling. I couldn't quite believe my eyes. His head had been split open. He had a jagged wound that ran from his eyebrow and disappeared into his hairline that they had pulled together with large railroad track stitches. His shirt and pants were drenched in blood. And while Louis had looked eccentric at the best of times with his unruly mop of hair and pale serious face, now he looked like something out of *Frankenstein*. Why had they stitched him like that? It looked brutal. I hoped it wasn't because they thought he was some kind of bum and wouldn't complain about a hasty stitching job.

"Louis, what the hell happened?"

"I was on the dock waiting for the Newcastle ferry. This guy hit me with a piece of wood."

"Why? What did you do?"

"Nothing. He said I had to pay. I told him I don't pay. He said no way, 'You pay up or I'm going to hurt you.' When I pushed him away, he started fighting with me. Then he hit me with this big piece of wood."

"My God, Louis! He could have killed you." I stared in horror at the ugly wound. I knew he would be scarred for life. "Did anyone call the police?"

"Someone did. Somebody called an ambulance as well. The cops came and asked me questions here in the hospital. But I didn't know the guy, the one that hit me. Can we go home? I've been here a long time."

Louis didn't want to go back to Harmony House. He wanted to stay with me. He was more rattled than he was letting on. I ran over to Harmony House and picked up some clean clothes out of his chest of drawers. His blood-stained clothes were so gross I felt I should throw them out. I settled him on the couch, put some pillows under his head and tucked a blanket around him. "Take these Tylenol... Louis, did you lose your temper with this guy? Like you know... did you start a fight with him? Just tell me. It won't matter if you did."

"No." His intense grey eyes locked onto mine. I knew he was telling the truth. He could never be bothered to lie about anything.

"Okay, you poor old thing. Try and sleep. I bet you have one hell of a headache." His eyes registered mute gratitude. He was asleep within minutes.

I went back over the road to check on Richard. He had already heard the gory details about the attack on Louis.

"I told you the devil was here. Remember I told you he was out there last night? I hope he doesn't come looking for me again." He looked stricken with fear.

"I won't let any devil near this house, Richard. I've already phoned the police, and they'll be in the bushes watching the house for us." He looked at me so gratefully that I felt a momentary pang of guilt for my lie.

I walked back home thinking, what a day! It was a windy dark night with the moon disappearing behind racing clouds and causing moving shadows and weird light patterns. I nearly jumped out of my skin as some dry leaves rustled across my path and tangled against a bush. Why would a complete stranger attack Louis like that? Tomorrow I would go down to the Newcastle ferry and ask the crew if they could shed any light on what had happened. I turned the corner and hurried toward the welcoming light of my living room lamp beckoning from across the street.

The next afternoon the ferry crew were sympathetic but could shed no light on the attack. They had seen a skirmish in the ferry lineup and had seen the ambulance arrive, but from their viewpoint on board they hadn't even realized that Louis had been the victim. It was obvious they were shocked because he had never been any trouble.

I was puzzled and a little alarmed, even more so when John, the Old Codger, informed me over a cup of tea that someone had phoned a few days earlier looking for Louis, and he had given him the Harmony House address. Who could that have been? Louis had no friends that I knew of except Tom. Was the call connected to this savage beating?

50

A Day in the Life

"Okay," said Larry as I entered the house. His voice came from behind his newspaper. "What was the video like? Was it funny?"

Bobby, our neighbour, had called me over to see a video he had taken of a nightclub act he and his wife had gone to see the previous night.

"It was certainly different. Maybe I'm a prude, but I found it offensive... it was a hypnotist act."

"Why would a hypnotist's act be offensive?"

"The hypnotist was amazing really. I can't believe how people can be so easily controlled like that. It's scary. The first part was funny... he got all these volunteers from the crowd to pretend to be Elvis impersonators, so they were jumping all over the stage gyrating their hips. That really was funny. But then the hypnotist brought up more volunteers, all women, and one by one told them they were having an orgasm."

"An orgasm?" Larry put the newspaper down.

"Yeah. I felt like I was a voyeur watching them. Quite honestly, it was too much for me. I quit watching after four orgasms."

"You mean the women *had* orgasms?"

"Yes. It was unbelievable... how can a hypnotist do that? I mean it begs the question if some of these women had never had an orgasm how they would know how to have one..."

"Beats me," said Larry a little too thoughtfully. "So it wasn't your cup of tea, love?"

"No. It wasn't. Some of the women came quietly with just a few grunts and moans, but you know that heavy-set lady that works at the 7-Eleven? I think her name is Barb. Well, she was number three in the lineup. She became drenched in sweat and shouted, 'Dear God! Oh God!' and then started yelling, 'Jeeesus,' and almost levitated off her chair. It was embarrassing. I won't be able to look her in the face when I go into the 7-Eleven now."

"Wow," said Larry. "Where was this show? Which club?"

"I don't know. Somewhere downtown... Larry, do you get my point? These women didn't know when they volunteered for the act that they were going to expose something as intimate as *that* about themselves. Of course, Bobby and that crowd next door think it's hilarious, but I think the hypnotist is an asshole. He went too far. I think if he had set me up like that, I would sue him. These women have to go to work and face everybody in their everyday lives, and Nanaimo is a small town. I mean, would you like to have everybody watch you have an orgasm? It isn't right. I mean, the audience had just seen people doing Elvis and those women thought they would be hypnotized to sing or dance or something innocent like that. Larry! I hope you're not laughing behind that newspaper."

The phone started ringing. "I'll get it," Ken shouted from the kitchen. "I'd hate to interrupt your fascinating story of public orgasms and 7-Eleven clerks."

"You weren't supposed to be listening. Ken, it's not funny. You better not be laughing." I looked over suspiciously at Larry. The newspaper hiding him was shaking like a willow tree in a hurricane.

"Hold on one minute," Ken was saying into the receiver. He came into the living room. "Is Shiner here? This lady on the phone says she has a dog with this telephone number on his collar."

Not again. I looked frantically outside. No Shiner. That runaway sod of a dog.

"He was here ten minutes ago. So help me, that dog is going to be the death of me. Ask her if we can meet her and pick him up."

Ken hung up the phone, smiling. "I'll go and get him. This girl sounds interesting. She works in a club. She says Shiner walked right in and caused quite the commotion around the bar."

Ken came home fifteen minutes later with Shiner and a blonde who was almost as tall as him. She had cascading blonde hair and too much makeup, and she was wearing a flimsy harem outfit. Her exposed belly button glittered with jewelry. She looked like she was right off the set of *Aladdin.*

Ken was smiling like a Cheshire cat. "Meet Cher," he said introducing his newly found trophy.

Shiner was panting over her the same as Ken. With his tongue lolling out.

I thought they both looked ridiculous.

Now Mr. D. and Larry joined them in the kitchen, doing double-takes and panting. *Men!*

And now here was the Old Codger in his tattered bathrobe, limping out of his room on his cane, his eyes spinning like roulette wheels. He looked like he had just said the magic word, "Abracadabra," and been allowed into Ali Baba's cave.

Cher, however, was not a bit unnerved by being half-naked in my kitchen surrounded by a circle of admiring men. She laughed and pouted and sashayed around, tossing her hair and winking at me cheekily behind their backs. Like she and I were sharing the age-old Eve secret. *I wish.*

"Yes, I'm an exotic dancer at the Cat's Meow. You'll have to come and see the show sometime. I do the poles. Have to keep in shape for that."

I must say Shiner had done it again. Another "Unusual Dog Finder" to add to his list. Chalk another one up for the *Guinness Book of Records*.

The next thing I knew Mr. D was serving beers, and Ken had hauled his guitar out and was singing. Cher was saying, "Oh Ken and Mr. D. you are a wonderful find. Tall guys like you are hard to find." And just like that Ken's life suddenly perked right up.

Cher told me later that when she had heard Ken sing, "I fell for him like a ton of bricks." Later that night as Larry was sitting on the side of the bed pulling his socks off, I clicked on the evening news on our bedroom TV. Larry was just saying, "Well, that was quite a night," when he halted, and we both sat mesmerized, our eyes glued to the TV. The story unfolding on the news also made a big splash the next morning on the front page of the *Nanaimo Times*.

A man living on Protection Island had heard noises carrying across the water on the evening air, and peering through his telescope, he had seen a man and woman struggling together on a yacht. He had called the Coast Guard and they had dispatched a boat. By the time they reached the vessel the woman had to be pulled from the water. She was barely alive, and an ambulance had sped her to hospital. She had multiple broken bones and fractures, and her face was smashed beyond recognition. It was Nairie. Her husband, Jerry, was charged with attempted murder.

I wondered later that night, lying in bed listening to the muffled foghorns warning ships of the hidden dangers in the bay, whether the prosecution would be more lenient with Jerry if they knew that in some ways he was the victim. Could they understand that Nairie was a Siren, desirable and irresistible, and that she lured men as surely as the Sirens of old had? Would they understand that men like Ken and Jerry, driven by passion and desire were blinded, just like the doomed sailors in the legends were fooled by the beautiful sirens calling from the peaceful waves that were hiding those jagged, treacherous rocks?

51
Fallen Angels

It was a happy day. Louise and I were going to pick up Lewis from Surfside. He had completed his six-week rehab, and Louise was giving him a second chance. She was nervous but also excited while we sped towards the Rehab Centre.

"For Christ's sake, Louise. Slow down. Let's get there in one piece."

She giggled. "Sorry. Sorry. I feel like I'm sixteen all over again. Crazy about my man." She glanced over at me. "Keep your fingers crossed and remember me in your prayers. Oh, look, there he is." He was waiting for us on the sidewalk smiling and waving. His white V-neck sweater and blue jeans immaculate. His dark blond hair combed back, cowboy boots shined up, gleaming.

"You have to come in and meet all the guys." He pulled Louise against him and kissed her gently on the cheek. Taking it nice and slow. "I've been bragging to everyone about my beautiful girl. Come on in, you lovely ladies."

We followed him into a large, bright lounge. His classmates and some of his teachers gave us an enthusiastic welcome. Lewis was obviously well liked by everyone. The Pied Piper, I thought, watching him laughing and talking to everybody. He was the one making all the jokes, drawing people around him. He had such a natural way of making people feel at ease and eager to have fun with him. So much charisma. All the while, he held Louise's hand, introducing her as his beautiful wife.

Dear God in Heaven—I, the atheist chanted—please help him make it.

We drove back to the cute apartment Louise had rented on Chapel Street in downtown Nanaimo. It was modest, but the view overlooking the harbour was breathtaking. Lewis was in such high spirits hanging over the balcony yahooing at the seagulls, telling me how the rehab courses had made him think differently about life. How his instructors had made him fill out questionnaires about his past life, making him dig deep. How he had finally confronted being abandoned by his mother when he was three. Stuff like that.

He was a new man. Vibrant and healthy with an energy explosion. Singing and pirouetting around the apartment. Hugging me quietly in the kitchen, kissing my forehead.

"Di, Look at me. No... really look at me! I'm brand new."

I shared a cup of coffee then left them there with their harbour view. Holding hands, stars in their eyes.

The months unfolded. Lewis and Louise visited at least once a week. We had family dinners, barbecues and movie nights. We had a lot of laughs, a lot of fun. Gordie Ryder told me they both attended the NA meetings faithfully every week. But they were having money problems. Lewis couldn't get a job. I would often see him busking on the sea wall, singing his heart out, stomping his foot to the music, his cowboy hat in front of him for donations. We would buy coffees and sit on the sea wall benches and call out requests to him. Larry would put some bills in his hat and we would clap our hands and stomp our feet, encouraging him to put on a show, doing our best to get other sea wall walkers interested in listening to him and throwing more change into his hat. It was a game.

Then one day after Lewis had been clean and sober for five months, Louise phoned in great excitement. "Lewis has a found a job in Lanceville selling cars at a Ford dealership."

The trouble started immediately. Lewis was making good money now and began hanging out after work with the boys at the dealership.

"He says it's part of the territory," Louise confided when she dropped in for coffee. "But he's drinking again, Diane. I'm so sick at heart. It's not bad at the moment, but I know it could get bad pretty fast."

Ken called to tell me the news. "Louise is in hospital with a broken arm and cracked ribs. Get this, Diane. You won't believe it! Lewis kicked her out of a moving car."

I went up to the hospital and wept. Dear sweet Louise. Her pretty face black and blue.

"This is the end," she whispered. "I swear I will never have anything to do with him again. He's lost the job at the dealership already. He's drinking... and on drugs. What's the use? Once he got his hands on money, he went berserk again."

"Did he really kick you out of the car?"

"I was trying to get out at a traffic light, and he started the car real fast and pushed me at the same time. My face hit the gravel." She broke down and cried. "What hurt more than that was... when he pushed me out, he called me a squaw..."

I phoned Gordie Ryder. He was brief and to the point. "Diane, be tough. He has to learn that nobody wants him near them when he's on drugs. The only way to help him is to turn your back. He has to hit rock bottom. He has to lose everything."

The next time I saw Lewis busking on the sea wall, I walked right by. He had seen me coming or I would have turned and walked the other way, and for a moment our eyes met. He had started to smile, but I averted my eyes and stared straight ahead as I walked past him.

He didn't look well. He was pale. He had a bruise on his face and his shirt was grubby. I felt his eyes boring into my back as I walked away. That first time, I fought tears that stung, but many times after that I steeled myself to walk past him as though I never saw him standing there.

Lewis, the one I had loved the most. But I'll be honest. I did more than walk past him that day. I did more than cry. It broke my heart. It was the first time addiction made me look it squarely in the eyes. And I knew now that it stole people's souls. It stole their lives and who they were. It stole from my safekeeping the people that I loved.

52
Ed Wood

We were sitting around eating Sunday breakfast and watching a rented video of *Ed Wood*, the funniest movie I had seen in ages. We had watched it twice the night before, back to back no less, the first time I had ever done that. And even now on the third go-round we were unbelievably in stitches again, laughing hysterically over little things we hadn't picked up before.

"Oh no, here comes the buffalo herd stampeding again!" Larry had tears running down his cheeks. Ed Wood had to be the most delightfully insane man to ever come out of Hollywood. We were all in love with him. How could you not be when he mixed up buffalo stampedes, Bela Lugosi and cross-dressing in his movies. The possessor of a simply marvelous crazed imagination that made you realize we all take life too seriously.

Larry reached over and answered the ringing phone. I could hear him saying, "Hi, you mean you're here? Oh... great stuff! Sure, I would love to come on down."

He looked over a little apologetically as he hung up the phone. "Russ and Jean are here from Deep Cove. They've sailed over on their boat, and they want to take me out for a trip around the harbour."

"They're your old next-door neighbours, right?"

"Yep, they're good people. A little stiff but well-meaning. Oh well... goodbye, Ed." He waved at the TV screen and lumbered off to the bathroom to spruce up.

After he left, I resigned myself to watching the rest of the movie by myself, but without Larry's explosions of laughter it wasn't so much fun.

I was contemplating turning the movie off and attacking the dirty break-fast dishes when I heard the door open and recognized Larry's foot-steps coming down the hall. Funny how the sounds of someone's foot-steps can be easily identifiable, isn't it?

He stood in the doorway beaming. "Get your coat, honey bun. They want you to come on board as well."

"Really. Are you serious?" These people were Phyllis's close friends.

"Yes, seriously! Get a move on. They think we just work together, so don't start getting familiar with me. Like hugging or grabbing my ass..."

"No grabbing your ass? Yeah, yeah." I threw on makeup and a change of clothes. I had luckily just bought a really pretty yellow blouse with a scoop neck and matching shorts. But I felt nervous driving down to the harbour. This was the first time I had met any of Larry's marriage friends, those who had hung out with Phyllis and Larry as a married couple. I knew they would be giving me a keen once-over. I had done the same thing when my divorced or separated friends turned up with a friend of the opposite gender. You know, the old *Hmmm... I wonder.*

Russ had a nautical-looking beard and was wearing a captain's white cap complete with gold braid. Within a half an hour I had him figured for a stuffed shirt and a snob and, more sadly still, a complete bore. Jean was one of those middle-aged, compactly built women with a take-charge air. She had a well-paying, secure government job and felt she knew everything about all other areas of life in an elevated way. In other words, they both had dill pickles stuck up their bums.

She and Russ argued obliviously and comfortably in front of us about everything. This was obviously a familiar marriage game that they played with finesse after twenty-five years of living together. What time should lunch be served? Should we eat anchored at the dock or out at sea? Should we open the wine now and, more interestingly for me, what direction should the boat take? Russ was positioned at the helm and

Jean pored over the harbour maps as they snarled and bared their teeth.

Larry and I sat back and enjoyed the bickering, struggling to suppress grins. It was really comical to see how much they got on each other's nerves. Mind you, it wasn't up to the *Ed Wood* level of entertainment. Not even close.

Russ was the bombastic type of debater who threw out colourful expletives like *God damn!* and told his wife that she was "bloody ridiculous!" and "You talk such bloody rot, woman," and once threw in a mean "You're a fucking idiot," while dear old Jean polished and sharpened her saber and her more articulate tongue and went directly for his throat.

Anyway, we ended up having lunch at the dock with the wine opened and then sailed pleasantly around the harbour. By that time my nervousness at being scrutinized by our hosts had passed, and I began gabbing to Jean about life in Nanaimo and I guess about life in general. It seemed I had a load of stories to unload, and it felt great for once having a woman to talk and relate to. I realized with a pang how starved I was for female companionship. Larry seemed strangely silent. I kept glancing over at him. This was a different Larry. Guarded in speech and sort of stiff, like someone had starched his shorts. Was he giving me warning looks? And if he was, why?

It really was a fabulous day. Hot and sunny with just enough of a cooling breeze skipping daintily across the ocean to ruffle our hair. The sea was a brilliant blue with gently frothy white waves. It was so peaceful out there on the water removed from the hubbub of land noise, the only sound the lamenting cries of distant, swooping seagulls. The sun was warm on my bare arms and legs, sensuously soothing on my skin, like a lover's massage. I started to relax to my core, and in my head I could hear John Denver singing, "Sunshine on My Shoulders." This was certainly the life.

I was thoroughly enjoying myself when the sweetly peaceful scene was disrupted with angry discordant notes as Jean and Russ began a heated discussion regarding the shallow areas of this particular area of the bay. Jean was having a fit because Russ was grandly overriding her concerns that we were heading for a sandbar. He shouted a loud and dismissive "Bollocks!" and stubbornly forged ahead.

Larry and I sat back helplessly and listened. Jean angrily and sloppily poured overflowing helpings of wine into our glasses. Her chest was heaving. "Asshole," she hissed under her breath.

I looked at Russ gripping the steering wheel in a delirium of triumph. It was *The Caine Mutiny* all over again. *Who ate the strawberries?* His eyes were shining with power. The guy was a definite megalomaniac, but his little wifey was a professional nagger. What a star-crossed pair. Why were they still together? It was obvious they hated each other's guts.

Finally the situation became a little too wearing, and I sat up and looked over at the distant shore. Could I swim that far? Probably. But maybe the endless glasses of wine had given me a false sense of courage, never mind a hazy judgement of distance. But Larry was a good swimmer. Maybe he could pull or float me back to land. I was lazily and tipsily reflecting on all of this when the boat suddenly lurched and threw us all onto the deck. Russ's nautical beard tickled my face and Jean's bottom sprawled across Larry's lap. It looked like we had suddenly made lewd moves for each other.

"God damn you, Russ!" Jean was spluttering. "You never listen!"

We staggered to our feet and assessed the situation. Right in front of us was a pole designating a shallow water area. Clear as day, it stood tall and upright, its bottom end sturdily planted in the floor of the bay. Even a blind man could have seen it.

Russ scratched his head in bewilderment.

"Does your radio phone work?" Larry asked hopefully.

"Unfortunately not," said Russ. "I have to take it in. A small repair. It broke down coming over here actually."

"Don't even go there," snarled Jean. "This man is the world's most incompetent ass. You have no idea what my life is like, never mind sailing on a boat with him. He's a total..." She hesitated, spluttering for the right word to arrive on her tongue. "Hazard," she spat out at last triumphantly.

She looked like she might hurl Russ overboard, and for a moment he had real fear in his eyes as he stood contemplating her wrath.

I looked around. There wasn't a boat in sight. We were stuck far from the busy traffic of the harbour.

"Someone has to come by fairly soon," said Larry, voicing my thoughts. "Let's relax. It's not too bad, Russ. At least we're in close proximity to help here."

I sat back and drank more wine. We had run out of ice cold white and were now drinking full-bodied warm red. The men tried pushing off the sandbar with oars, but we were truly grounded. Nothing budged an inch. Up to now it had been close to being a perfect afternoon, sitting in the sun and drinking wine while out on the water. Too bad we had to share it with two fighting cocks. Well, it was more like a fighting cock and a pit bull.

Eventually a boat sailed by. We waved our hands furiously and the holidaymakers waved back cheerily... and kept on going. Did they think we were waving at them for fun? An hour passed and then most of another. For the first time I started feeling uncomfortable about our plight.

"When does the tide come in?" I asked. "Maybe the tide will float us off the sandbar. Does your map have tide information, Jean?"

"I think it turns and comes in around seven o'clock... but surely someone will come by before then."

Just at that moment a broken-down rowboat badly in need of a paint job came into view. It was loaded down and I shouted, "Help!" at the top of my lungs. The men waved back and started rowing over, and I recognized some faces from the Reserve. The guys looked like they had been fishing, and they were all half-drunk, but then in fairness so were we. It was apparent they thought it was highly amusing that we were stuck on the sandbar.

"How come you didn't see the pole?" They snickered at the foolish white men.

Russ was very curt with them. "Can you pull us off? Do you have a rope?"

They looked at him as though he was crazier than a shit house rat and laughed some more, taking their time to answer, chugging down contentedly on their bottles of beer.

"No way, man. You need some power to get you off that sandbar. This boat here won't do the job. Diane and Larry, would you like a ride back to the dock? You can get some help from the Harbour Office there." Their soft voices sounded so civilized compared with the afternoon's shouting match.

"That's a good idea," said Larry. "Thanks, boys. Come on, Di. We'll take the lift."

We threw our shoes over into the rowboat and then gingerly dropped into the shallow water and half-swam the few yards to the boat and tumbled in headfirst, everybody laughing and jolly. One of the guys handed me a cold beer out of a battered cooler, and we all squeezed together like sardines in a can. To say the boat was overloaded was the understatement of the year. Someone started a worn-out 5HP motor and we put-putted slowly to the distant dock.

"That guy couldn't have known much about sailing," observed one of our rescuers, a wild-looking guy with waist-long black hair and nicotine-stained teeth. "Shit, the pole indicating shallow water was right there, man. Is the guy a bit of a fool, Larry?"

"You could say that," said Larry.

"How about a pompous asshole on top of that," I added.

We could see the stranded couple really going to town on one another now they were alone. Now that we rats had deserted the ship. I was happy to be a rat.

We called the Coast Guard when we hit the dock, and Larry gave our new friends a few bucks for the gas they had used in the rescue. When we finally arrived home, we walked straight into the bedroom and peeled off our wet clothes. We were both so bedraggled we looked like we'd been in a triathlon. Sunburnt red noses and legs. Wet hedgehog hair sticking up. Larry even had some gleaming seaweed strands twined in his pubic hair.

"Want to share the shower with me?" I called from the bathroom. We giggled, soaping each other down in the lukewarm refreshing spray.

"What an afternoon and what a pair, Larry. It's a wonder they haven't killed each other by now. And what was wrong with you? You hardly spoke a word all day."

"I know. I was always quiet around Phyllis and the Deep Cove gang. Phyllis was the talker in our family—I never seemed to find anything to say."

"You? Having nothing to say?"

"You are the one who makes me chatty. Honestly. Now I think of it, I do really talk *a lot* around you, I guess because I feel relaxed—but hell, I couldn't have got a word in this afternoon anyway. You never shut up. You talked and talked, never ending, like someone had wound you up. I think it's an understatement to say you took them by surprise. Actually, I think they thought you were right off Mars... like some kind of alien," Larry finished.

"*Right off Mars?*" I asked, astonished.

"You told some pretty amazing stories. Like that one how you invited that Dutch family travelling on the CPR from Toronto to stay with you because they were brand-new immigrants in Canada and didn't have accommodations booked, and they ended up staying with you for five months. And you didn't know how to get rid of them? And how you called the husband Mr. Hollandia because he sold Dutch cookies. And how you always lose your bra when you're out because you pull it off under your sweater and throw it somewhere...and have to go back to bars and restaurants the next day to pick them up in brown paper bags. And I have to tell you, you knocked the wine back faster than Dean Martin at a wine tasting."

"It was hot out there and I was thirsty. So?" I felt disgruntled at his interpretation of the afternoon's events.

"And as you waved goodbye to them, to Russ and Jean, you jumped into a boat with a bunch of drunken guys as though you felt completely at home and promptly started drinking beer with them. I wouldn't call it a grand or gracious exit."

"Good God, are you saying they see me like a degenerate Sally from Somerset Maughan's *Rain*?" I laughed. And shit, here I had been trying to make his friends like me. I towelled myself off. Seriously, did I give a rat's ass? "Okay. I guess I was nervous, but you should have kicked me or something. Got me to put the brakes on."

"Well, Phyllis will be delighted. I am sure Jean only wanted to meet you to report back anything of interest to her. Phyllis will gloat at the possibility that I have hooked up with a raunchy, uncivilized, disorderly drunk."

"Well, you can just add to that by telling her I'm Welsh. The favourite pastime of the English is trashing the Celts..." I was laughing until I saw his face. He could be surprisingly Old School sometimes. There were times I felt I only knew part of him. The reckless, careless part.

"You never take anything seriously, do you?" he said.

"For God's sakes, Larry... am I supposed to say I'm sorry? Maybe I don't know how to be normal anymore. You know, socially interactive, politically correct. I'm surrounded by the abnormal all the time here. I don't really have *normal* conversations anymore." For a moment I felt depressed. I hate criticism even when it is irrationally presented... but then, oh joy! I remembered *Ed Wood.*

"Larry, we still have *Ed Wood!* I have the greatest idea. Let's order in Chinese food and watch the rest of the movie. What do you say?"

We pulled on our comfy cotton sweats and raced for the living room. I ordered the food and Larry threw on the video. And so help me, it seemed even funnier than before. Mr. D. and Ken arrived in time for the Chinese takeout, and we all sat around and ate plates of heaped chow mein, garlic honey ribs and crunchy almond chicken. Vampira made the guys howl. That Ed Wood, he was definitely our kind of a guy. Sweet and loveable and so totally out in left field, so deliciously and lawlessly abnormal. So "un-Deep Cove-ish." We all loved him to bits.

53
Changes

One night the Old Codger and I were playing crib at the kitchen table, and he was making mincemeat of me.

"I keep forgetting to tell you," he said, shuffling the cards. "There was a guy looking for Lewis here yesterday. When you went out. A big rough-looking guy."

"Did he leave a name or phone number?"

"No. I told him Lewis was out of town for a few weeks over at that rehab in Abbotsford... or is it Mission? That one you told me about. I told him if he called back you could tell him more... I couldn't remember the name of the damn place. I told him it was King something."

"It's called Kinghaven. But why would someone come here asking for Lewis? He hasn't been around here in months."

Louise had phoned me the previous week to say she had just learned Lewis had gone to a rehab centre on the Mainland. She was perplexed because he hadn't told a soul, not even his parents, that he was going. She had only found out because a guy who had just finished treatment at Kinghaven was her neighbour's brother, and he had recognized Lewis when he arrived.

"He's too proud to let us know he is trying to clean up again in case he fails," I had said. "He wants to make sure he's totally well and then he'll surprise us." And I had made a mark on the calendar to note when his rehab had started.

"I'll believe it when I see it," Louise had said, and we had left it at that, both too afraid to put into words the hope that Lewis might come back from the Land of the Half-Dead.

"Diane," the Old Codger asked, suddenly changing the subject. "What financial interests do you have in Larry's houses over here?"

"Well, none," I answered, surprised. "They belong to Larry and his wife. He's separated, but everything's still jointly owned."

"That's what I thought, my dear, and that's not good news. You work too hard over here, my dear. He's not around much... and what do you get out of it all. Eh?"

"Room and board, I guess. I'm in love, John. It can be a dangerous business—love."

"You should think about yourself, what's best for you. Don't get me wrong. Larry is a nice enough bloke, but you're not getting any younger. You should have a good think, dear. I worry about you."

The Old Codger worried about me? That made me smile. When had he ever worried about anyone but himself? But a week later he told me he had been accepted into a senior's home and felt well enough to live on his own. He could get a lovely little bachelor suite especially built for people on disability for $203 per month. It really was a great deal.

Still, his decision surprised me as I didn't think he was well enough to look after himself. And I thought living alone would seem lonesome for him now, the hermit having been re-socialized as he loved playing cards with the guys, and one of them would always come over from Big Sab to have a game of crib with him in the evenings. The Old Codger had never been a favourite of mine. I hated cleaning up his sick room and being at his beck and call, but still I had done my best to make him comfortable, cooking special dishes and running to the Scottish Bakery downtown to buy him the apple turnovers or steak and kidney pies he loved.

I helped him move. Went to the Goodwill and the Salvation Army and found him a great buy in a La-Z-Boy chair and a bed. Bedside table, lamps. Helped him set up his kitchen and went grocery shopping and stacked his cupboards. He finally used the electric wheelchair they had given him at the hospital. I don't think he had been out to use it since he had moved in with us almost a year and a half earlier. Had it really been that long?

I felt relieved when he moved out but guilty as he self-consciously wiped tears from his eyes as I turned and waved goodbye from the door of his new apartment. "I'll be over to visit, John. This isn't goodbye." Did I mean that? I really wouldn't enjoy visiting the old fart. Well, *he* had been the one who had wanted to leave. I hadn't pushed him out.

I took him to a doctor's appointment a week later, and when I went to leave after helping him ease into his chair in front of the TV, he said, "Go over there to that cupboard near the stove. There's something for you."

I opened the cupboard door and there stood a big bottle of Kahlua.

"That's for you, for everything you've done. I've appreciated it, and I wanted you to know that."

I stood there, flummoxed. Confused. The Old Codger giving me a present.

"This is lovely. Thank you so much." I reached over and kissed him on the cheek. A gnarled knotty hand came over mine and squeezed my fingers.

"Off you go. Take care of yourself, girl."

A week later Doug called. "John passed away last night."

"John?" What John did he mean?

"Yes, in his sleep. Well, the doctors had told him. He knew it was coming."

"You mean our John? Are you for real? He's just moved into that lovely little apartment. He didn't have a chance to enjoy it. He's only been there two weeks."

A quiet silence. "I guess it's all right to tell you now. He moved to spare you finding him, you know, when he passed away. He felt it would upset you too much, especially if you were by yourself."

"He moved because he didn't want me to find him *dead?*"

"The doc had told him he only had a month, two months max. He knew it was pretty close."

"I can't believe it. I'm so shocked at this, Doug. He never said a word."

"Well, he was very fond of you, my dear... He told me to make sure I gave you any money he had left in his wallet. I have $300 for you here. I'll bring it over later this afternoon. Of course, now he's *dead* his wife and daughters want him back over there in Vancouver. Doesn't make sense, does it? I guess, though, if you're throwing a fancy funeral, you need a corpse."

I went out to sit in the garden. Like the Tin Man, the Old Codger had finally found a heart, worrying over me even as he was dying. Life does keep you guessing.

Larry arrived later that evening. He was unusually quiet, subdued. I think he was taken aback by John's death. Death has a habit of doing that, making you examine the value of your own existence.

Larry picked up on my troubled feelings. "Come on, Di. You gave that old man another year of life. Remember how sick he was when he first arrived? Don't feel guilty that you never grew fond of him. He was lucky he ran into us."

I had made lasagna for dinner and was putting the salad on the table when I saw the TV screen in the living room light up with a real estate ad. "Quick! Look, Larry. There's your cousin Pat again on TV."

He swivelled around in his chair to see the screen. Then, his back to me, he said, "I finally met her a few months ago."

"You did?"

"Mum had a little family gathering at Christmas. Pat and her parents were in town, so she invited them over."

"That was nice. What did you think of her? Is she as pretty as her picture?"

Larry slid a square of lasagna carefully onto his plate. "Well, she looks older than that picture, but yes, you could say she's pretty."

I looked over his shoulder at the blonde hair and smiling face. The blue eyes on the screen seemed to be trying to tell me something.

The next day Larry was whistling the theme song from *Beauty and the Beast* in the bathroom as he shaved.

"What's on the venue today, kiddo?" I asked to the open bathroom door as I scrambled eggs for him.

"I'm listing the Rosedale house and the Irwin Street place with my cousin Pat. I talked it over with her at that family gathering at my mum's. Why not give her the business? I'm meeting with her this morning."

"Oh, that's a good plan. Giving the business to a family member."

"Yeah, I thought so. She's been in real estate here for years. Knows the local scene inside and out. I'll probably have lunch with her today."

I turned to look at him. What was that smell? I couldn't help but grin. He was standing in the doorframe reeking of Paco Raban, his hair combed to one side as neatly as a choirboy's.

"Bloody hell, Larry. You look like you're auditioning for a part in *American Gigolo.*"

"I look that good, eh?"

"On top of all that you smell like a whorehouse."

"You sure know how to cut a man off at the knees." But he laughed as he sat down for his breakfast. "And how, pray, does a sweet Welsh girl like you know how a whorehouse smells?"

I laughed with him. It felt good to see him in a happy mood.

That night in bed I snuggled up against Larry's back and plunged into the uncharted waters. "Larry, we haven't made love for at least four... maybe five weeks."

"Is it that long? I'm slipping, am I?"

He rolled over and pulled himself on top of me. It was all over in five minutes.

I lay there for a moment, misery flooding over me. He had immediately rolled over to his side of the bed and seemed already asleep.

I slid out of bed and crept down the hall to the bathroom. I stared long and hard at myself in the mirror. The woman staring back wore a black lace nightgown and had boyish, cropped black hair. Her eyes were a deep spice brown and right now they were full of hurt and spilling tiny rivulets of tears down her face.

The question begged to be asked. How can a man do that? Get an instant hard on and fuck you on demand when he no longer loves you? Are they really that cold-blooded? The answer, of course, came back like a worn-out message that had been travelling for a thousand light years. You didn't have to read *Men Are from Mars, Women Are from Venus* to get it.

54

Back Seats

I was sitting on the porch rugged up in my thick fleecy jogging suit, drinking my morning coffee, when Gordie Ryder came roaring down the road on his Harley. I went out to the road to talk to him as he pulled up outside the house.

"Where the hell are you going?" I asked, looking at the loaded-up motorcycle.

"I'm driving across Canada, all the way to Montreal."

"You're kidding me?"

"Nope. Want to come with me?"

I shielded my eyes against the winter sun and looked at him. There'd been a rumour that he and Joan had broken up. The sapphire blue eyes looked intently into mine. Like an Indian scout on a fact-finding mission, looking for tell-tale smoke signals "in them thar hills."

"Best offer I've had all week," I said.

"I mean it, Di. It's a one-time offer. I'm not really sure if I'll be back."

I stood back a bit to stare at him more fully. What was he saying?

He patted the empty seat behind him.

"You wouldn't leave for good!"

"Maybe I've had enough. Maybe the addicts around here deserve someone with a little more pep in him than a burnt-out, middle-aged biker."

"What are you talking about? You've got more energy in your little finger than most people have in their whole body! Don't talk like that."

"Well, I can see you're not coming with me. But come and give me a goodbye hug."

I went into his arms and he held me. He put his face against my hair and I felt his lips kissing my cheek. There was a surge of energy coming from him like a hum, a vibration, an emotional Molotov cocktail of sorts. I was suddenly holding him too tightly, gripping his coat hard to pull him tighter against me. Too many people I cared about were checking out on me. I said into his ear, squished against my cheek, "What will I do without you?" And I meant it.

When we pulled apart, I had to fight with the tears in my eyes. Gord was obviously upset and started up the bike right away. He roared away and didn't look back. For over and year and a half he had been a constant solid rock for me to lean on. I had been so naïve when I first came to the South End... and so judgmental, and of all the things Gord had taught me, it was the true meaning of walking a mile in another man's moccasins that had made the most difference in my life.

He never came back to Nanaimo so maybe he was finally burnt totally out. The drug community lashed out viciously at his abandonment. It was crazy—as if he had left them all personally. Rumours abounded that he had gone back to the Hell's Angels in Montreal and back to a life of drugs. I didn't believe that... or maybe it was a story I didn't have the heart or the stomach to believe. I wanted to remember him the way he deserved to be remembered... as someone with an everextended helping hand, an optimistic smile and that devilment dancing in his eyes. My definition of a hero.

But sometimes I just wonder... what did I miss by not hopping on the back seat of that bike? Okay, Bette Davis, I know. It would have been one hell of a bumpy ride.

55
Premonitions

I awoke from a semi-dream-like state, knowing there was a message that I had just been given, but it was disappearing on me before I could pull it out of the dream and into my waking state. It was a troubling feeling, one that persisted all morning. What the hell was causing this feeling of "a wicked wind cometh"? This feeling of fear riding before an advancing wind?

All morning I waited apprehensively to see what the bad news would be and who would be the messenger. It was Ken.

He was white-faced and shaken when he came down the hall and stood in the middle of the kitchen.

"What's up? You look like you've seen a ghost." On closer inspection, he also looked like he'd been crying.

"It's bad news, Di. I don't know where to start."

"Just say it." I felt the inner dread, the tensing, the automatic bracing of my heart. The premonition had been the warning. Now here *it* comes.

"Lewis is dead. He was murdered."

I felt the blood drain from my face. My legs felt weak. There was a terrible silence. I held onto the kitchen table and sat down.

"You mean our Lewis? Louise's Lewis?"

"Yes. He was in that rehab in Abbotsford. You knew that, right? He had a weekend pass and apparently was coming over to the Island, but these guys got to him over there."

"What guys? Why? Why would anyone want to kill him?"

"They figure it was because of a bad drug deal. Lewis owed them big money. They'd been after him for a while."

"A drug deal? Lewis in a drug deal? It doesn't make sense."

"Yeah, it does, Di. He was in pretty deep. Even before he came to Big Sab. I think they were after him then."

I had an immediate flashback to the ransacked room when we had gone to pick up Lewis's belongings. It seemed so long ago—a million light years ago.

"What did they do to him? Did they shoot him?"

"No. Are you sure you want to know?"

"I have to know." I stared at him, suddenly afraid of the stricken look in his eyes.

He was silent for a moment, mulling over what to say. "I'll tell you because it's better you hear it from me than someone on the street. It's pretty rough, Di. They took him to an empty farmhouse in Abbotsford, and for some reason they partially skinned him. They think it was while he was still alive." Ken covered his face, half-crying, half-talking into his hands. "I don't know if they were taking off his tattoos to hide his iden-tification. They... the police don't know, or maybe they did it to torture him. Then they set fire to the farmhouse, but somebody called the fire department, and they got there pretty fast."

I stumbled into the bathroom and almost fell and hit my face as I crouched over the toilet bowl and threw up. All I could see was Lewis's smiling face. His tanned golden skin. *Oh my God.* I was conscious of Ken behind me running the tapwater, helping me up, wiping my face gently with a warm face cloth. We held onto each other. My legs were trembling.

"He would have gone down fighting. He wouldn't have gone down easy," Ken said through his tears.

I nodded, remembering one day, it seemed so long ago, Lewis and Ken had had a fight. Lewis's devil-may-care laugh as he put his fists up.

It had been over something stupid but they had punched the hell out of one another. *Oh God, dear God. Think of something, anything to hold onto.* "He would have finished it like Butch Cassidy and the Sundance Kid," I said incoherently. Everybody loved the ending of that movie because you never saw the heroes go down, and just remembering how Butch and Sundance went out fighting in a blaze of glory, I vowed that was the way I would remember Lewis—dukes up and laughing in the face of fate.

We sobbed and sobbed against each other for what seemed forever. After the tears subsided, I put on the coffee and we talked things out.

"Do you think he originally came to Big Sab to hide out because he knew these guys were after him?"

"Maybe to hide out," Ken said, "but he desperately wanted to clean up. Get drugs out of his life. But I always knew there was something else. Something he wasn't telling me. Remember that time Louis was attacked at the Newcastle Ferry? I think it was these same guys after Lewis, and they got the names mixed up. You know Lewis, Louis. They sent somebody to rough Lewis up and got poor old Louis instead."

Jesus Murphy. That made sense. Now I thought of it, there had been these strange shadowy characters calling around, asking for Lewis, trying to find out where he was. I could never figure out who they were. Then it hit me. "Ken, do you know what? A man came here just before the Old Codger moved out, and he told him that Lewis was in a rehab in Abbotsford. Dear God, that's probably how they knew where to find him. And I wonder now about Richard's devil waiting in the shadows outside of Harmony House. I bet that was one of these thugs thinking Louis was Lewis, waiting for him."

It was coming together, all the clues that had been under our noses.

Louise phoned later that day, so did Little Larry and Davey. Everybody in the South End was buzzing with the story. Louise was heartbroken. Even though she hadn't voiced it, I knew she had been harbouring the hope that this time Lewis would make it and permanently leave the drugs behind.

You can philosophize as much as you want about the effect that meeting certain people have on your life. How some people just seem to circle you and never once touch your soul and how others become part of your life, become entwined in it. Lewis was one of the latter. He will never really leave me because I have all the memories. I'll always remember that first day opening up Big Sab's front door to find him standing on the doorstep. The silly pink flamingo shirt. It was a door I wouldn't have missed opening for all the world. The Sundance Kid with the million-dollar smile that should have carried him into the movies instead of to a violent end on an abandoned farm.

I loved him in the way you do when a person walks through your door and your heart gladdens, and you hope they will stay awhile because so much sunshine comes pouring in with them. But I was just one of many people who on crossing his path found out that to know him was to love him. And I will always remember how hard he tried. I believe he could have done anything and become anybody. An astronaut, a politician, a movie star. He had that know-how about people and life, the capacity, the intelligence and the fuelled energy of a soaring rocket destined to reach unexplored territory. But maybe it's a little overwhelming for someone to recognize they have that power and everybody is sitting back expecting great things of them. He was just thirty-four years old when he died.

Drugs are the corruption of North America, will be the downfall of North America, and until we treat addiction as the sickness it is—and not a crime—we are in a losing battle. Who knows why some people need to take drugs and why others are never tempted? How people we love and intimately know get tangled in a web that we can't even see. Addiction is not selective. It takes its victims across the board of life wherever it can find them. Rich or poor, poet or pauper, the beautiful or the ugly. It really isn't fussy. Just roll up your sleeve.

56

Real Estate Hottie

Patsy was a real estate hottie. I hadn't met her yet, partly because she was a workaholic machine, selling houses like hot cakes evenings and weekends. She had been married to a wealthy man twenty years her senior who had babied her, so she had always lived a protected life. Now she was a divorcee, seduced by the ability to make her own money out there in the *real* world. She had one child, a nineteen-year-old son who was in college, and a boyfriend whose name was... guess what? Larry. I didn't ask if he had a lazy eye. She and the boyfriend often fought because she was too busy to see him. (It was Larry who relayed all these gossipy tidbits to me.)

Patsy had both the Rosedale house and the Irwin house sold within a month. Then Larry listed three more and she sold two of them. He lost money on each sale, though not a lot, so that the burden of financial strife began slowly loosening its stranglehold. But Larry didn't seem to cheer up. He just became more introspective and moodier and always seemed irritated with me.

Now he stood in the kitchen holding up a bottle of spiced Captain Morgan rum. "What's this?" he asked me. "Are you stashing booze away now? I found this behind the bag of sugar in the cupboard."

"It's mine and it's not stashed." I glared at him. "I enjoy a drink while I'm cooking or after dinner. So what?"

"I thought you had stopped drinking in front of the guys. You agreed on that long ago."

"Larry," I said, exasperated, "I drink around the schitzos, not the guys at Big Sab. *Hello?* Remember we don't live there anymore? Anyway, the schitzos wouldn't have a clue. They think I'm drinking coke."

"They pretend they think you're drinking coke. You're not getting away with anything."

I stared at him, the blood rushing to my face. "What difference does it make? Maybe they're into pretending. Maybe they're just like you—hanging around here pretending that you still love me."

Larry slammed the bottle of rum down on the counter and left the house.

There. I had said it. I had put the unmentionable into words, words I had been skirting for weeks. I poured myself a generous glass of rum—what I thought of as a two-finger drink.

I had hardly downed the glass when I heard the front door open and the sound of Larry's footsteps coming down the hall. He stood in the kitchen doorway looking miserable, his face set with a wretched, determined look.

"Okay, kid," he said. "I know I've been rough on you lately. Do you feel like going for a walk? Let's go and talk it out."

I felt my heart hit my boots. Here it comes.

"How about Piper's Lagoon?" I asked, getting my sweater and Shiner's leash.

We walked along the beach. It was a breathtaking day. The waves were rollicking. The sun was warm on my face, but my hands and my heart were like ice.

We sat on a big, comfortable driftwood log, watching Shiner run in and out of the waves. And I waited.

"We've been through a lot—you and I," Larry started. "I don't know what I would have done without you, Di. It's been a rough year. But times change." He paused. "I don't know how to tell you this so I'm just going to say it. The money problem has become an out-of-control monster. I have to sell Big Sab and Harmony House. There's no way out."

I had been staring at his face ready to read every word. Ready to listen to every nuance in between every line. But I wasn't ready for this. I was hit with such a slam of shock I almost lost my balance on the log.

"When did you figure this out?" I said at last. "My God, Larry, you should have talked it out with me, not kept all this worry to yourself." But part of me felt an enormous relief. This was the dilemma that had been causing his withdrawal, his mood swings. *It wasn't me! Oh, thank God, it wasn't me!*

We walked up and down on the sand talking it out, the rhythmic sound of the waves drumming on the beach and Shiner running back and forth as though joined to us by an invisible string.

"Maybe the NA in Nanaimo would take over Big Sab," I suggested. "Then the guys wouldn't lose their home. The drug community here can't afford to lose a safehouse."

Harmony House? I would have to find new accommodation for Robert and Richard and Louis. That was going to be a difficult, almost impossible task. I cringed at the prospect of telling my poor lost, un-loved schitzos this awful news. Who would look after them now? I could not bear to think about it.

"I want you to go back to Vancouver," Larry was saying. "Get a nor-mal job again. Get back on track with a normal life. Let's face it, Di, this has been a burn-out situation here for some time. There's more to life besides addicts and schizophrenia."

And death, I thought.

Staring out at the waves and the Five Finger Islands saucily dancing on the water, I suddenly agreed with him. Since the deaths of Scott and Lewis I had been inconsolable. I had come to the terrible realization, the painful conclusion after a year and a half of working with the guys at Big Sab that I did not have anything in my heart and mind and soul that was powerful enough to save addicts. Anything to offer that was more powerful than drugs. I could not make a difference. But then I always would hear Gordie Ryder's voice when I thought that: *We still can save 11 percent, Diane. Someone has to always be there for that 11 percent.*

I thought about my children in Vancouver. I thought of candlelight dinners with friends who would ask red or white as they poured the wine in a civilized Old World gesture. Suddenly I was more than ready. I wanted to go home. Larry seemed enormously relieved that he had finally got everything off his chest, and we linked arms in a familiar, companionable way that we hadn't shared in months and plodded across the sand, plotting our course for the next few weeks.

Back at the house Mr. D made plans to return to the Mainland, and Ken said he would probably move in with his new girlfriend. Larry approached NA about taking on Big Sab, and after several meetings they forged a deal. It was so easy we couldn't believe our luck. But telling the Harmony House guys was just plain awful. They were tearful and afraid. I committed myself to finding accommodations for Richard and Robert, but the mental health team was responsible for finding a new boarding home for Louis.

Unfortunately he had the worst reaction to our news, locking himself in his room and refusing to come out. Then he went completely haywire and painted his bedroom windows with black paint to shut out the world. God knows where he had found the paint. I called his social worker and they sent a team over to deal with him, finally coaxing him out of his room and taking him to his new boarding home. Disgruntled, Larry replaced the windows, and I thought, thank God, that crisis is over.

But then three days later there was a knock on the door. There stood Louis. He pushed past me like a zombie and walked in. I didn't like the look of him. His body language was intense, and his face had a flushed, unnatural look. My antenna went up, way up. I made him some tea, making idle chit chat. Louis never said a word. He took one sip of his tea then abruptly stood up. "I'm leaving," he said. He started choking back strange guttural noises as he bolted for the front door.

Alarmed, I followed him down the hall. He was almost running now, his face a terrifying mass of purple and red blotches, like he was holding his breath. I followed, making sure I was two steps behind him. As he reached the door, I could see an awful internal struggle was taking place. Suddenly he half-turned in the open doorway, one foot in the house and one foot out on the doorstep, and paused as if he was coming back into the house. The snarl on his face made him look only half-human. I managed in that split half-second of his indecision to push him out and lock the door just as an awful yell left his throat. He crashed against the door, hammering and kicking it in fury. I stood against the door, my hands pressed against my mouth, trembling. I was terrified. Silence.

Then suddenly a huge crash. A brick came hurtling through the living room window and landed on the carpet. Fragments of glass sparkled everywhere. Then the kitchen window. Crash! The glass shattering into the sink. I staggered, weak-kneed, to the phone and called 9-1-1, crouching down and peering cautiously through the broken living room window. Louis was running down the road with a stumbling gait, waving his arms and omitting wild jungle animal cries. It was unbelievable but heartbreaking. He was losing his home and the people he had grown to care for and depend on. He was unhinged with despair. I figured he had come to say goodbye, but his emotions had overcome him, and when he felt the fury building up, he had valiantly tried to get away and out of the house as fast as he could. I didn't want to contemplate what would have happened if he hadn't. With just a week left of my time in the South End I had experienced yet another close shave with death.

Larry's truck arrived outside one minute later. He had seen the final act of the drama from half a block away, and as he walked down the hall, he shouted, "Bloody hell! What is it with that Louis and fucking windows?"

That did it. I started to laugh in uncontrolled hysteria. I had never needed to laugh so badly in my life.

57

Broken Hearts

I had just come back from taking the final load of Richard's possessions to his new apartment, and as I came down the hall it was so quiet that I thought everyone must be out. Then I saw Ken at the kitchen table drinking a beer. As soon as I saw his face, I knew something was wrong. He stood up, went to the fridge and opened a beer for me.

"What?" was all I said.

"Sit down, Di," he said. "This is going to be rough."

I really didn't want to hear. I didn't need to hear any more *rough* news. But I sat down, downed a big gulp of beer and prepared to listen. I often wonder if I had an inkling before he told me. I don't think so. I honestly don't think I would have bullshit myself that deviously.

"I was in the Hyatt Hotel lounge this afternoon with my mum and dad," he said. "I saw Larry and Patsy in there."

That made sense. They were there to meet someone interested in buying Haliburton.

"They were holding hands," said Ken.

"Holding hands?" I repeated like a parrot. "Holding hands?"

"And kissing."

The room swam. I tilted the bottle of beer and drank it down the hatch. I raised my head, and Ken and I looked straight at each other. His Irish blue eyes were troubled, but they never faltered.

Suddenly it all made sense. Like when fog lifts and you find yourself on the edge of a perilous cliff. The danger you sensed is finally revealed. Now you understand the meaning of the sound of those little pebbles ricocheting.

I thought I said, "The fucking bastard." And I thought I said, "Let's go to the Pat." But no words left my lips. The caves inside my heart were being stormed by tremendous icy waves. Like a tsunami, the tempest roared in and collapsed the surrounding landscape. My heart imploded and all I felt was pain.

I heard the key turn in the front door. Ken and I exchanged looks. Larry's footsteps were coming down the hall.

"I'm outta here," Ken said over his shoulder, already halfway across the kitchen as he made for the back door.

Larry plonked down on a chair. "What's wrong with you?" he asked cheerily.

"Someone saw you holding hands with Patsy at the hotel."

"So... what if I was?" His head whipped up sharply to look at me.

"And kissing."

"What are you getting at? She's my cousin, Diane."

"Larry... don't bullshit with me. Just say it."

"Say what?" His face had gone pale, making his eyes look even bluer. A strange tense shade of blue.

"Larry, for God's sakes... do you have a crush on Patsy?" I stared right at him, daring him to look away. It was longer than a New York minute. More like a BC normal minute.

"I do... yeah," he said. There was wretchedness in his eyes that spoke of guilt entwined with agony.

"Larry!" The cry was wrenched from my throat. "When did this happen? When did it start?"

He was staring intently at the car keys twisting in his hands. "The first time I saw her. At that family reunion. You know, Christmas time at Mum's. I never thought anything would come of it. You know. Us being cousins. But then she broke up with her boyfriend... and we became close."

"The boyfriend called Larry?"

"Yes. She opened up to me, and I sort of started to realize she was interested in me, too."

"Why didn't you tell me? My God, Larry." I started to cry. I simply couldn't help it.

"I couldn't... I tried. We've been through so much together, you and I... You're my best friend, Di. The best friend I could hope for in the whole world."

"Yeah, but I don't have the blonde hair and the beguiling smile."

"I didn't want it to come to this, Di. I didn't want to hurt you."

"Hurt me?" I screamed, jumping to my feet. "You've just torn my heart out and ripped it to shreds. I waited for you all these years. All these wasted years. For what? For you to fall in love with some pretty face?"

Larry put his head down and covered his face with his hands. It looked like he was crying. "It's been hell. I am so messed up. It's like I'm obsessed with her. Like I've been hit with lightning. I've tried to fight it, so help me."

Hit with lightning. He used those words, those special words. I stared aghast at him. "How far has this gone?"

"What do you mean?"

"Have you slept with her?

He kept staring at the floor.

"Have you? It will hurt me more if you lie to me, Larry. You at least owe me the truth." Goading him for an answer. Terrified of the answer.

"Yes. On her birthday last week." The words were guttural, like he was choking them up, as if they were pieces of wood stuck in his throat.

The impact of the words sliced cleanly through the air like a spear and I actually shook with the impact of the pain. "What have you done? Dear God, Larry, what have you done?" I jumped to my feet, staring wildly at him. "Don't you see? I will never be able to be with you again. Never. Not in this life or the next." Dramatic, foolish, crazy words. I stumbled blindly from the room, grabbing my coat and calling for Shiner.

I drove the truck out to Piper's Lagoon. The wind skipping across the water was winter cold, and the islets called the Five Fingers loomed out there, barely discernable in the mist, eerily poking their heads up in the grey choppy sea. My eyes teared up in the wind as I walked along the beach, Shiner running ahead, skittering in and out of the shallow icy waves. Seeking warmth, I shoved my hands into my pockets. I was in so much pain, in chaos with it, consumed by it, and I talked incoherently as I walked, telling myself, "You know your happiness should never depend on anybody else. You know that. All the psychology books teach you that. You have to find happiness within yourself. Independently of other people. Of men, of lovers. Only then will you be strong enough to be happy." Then turning on myself viciously, "Why don't you just shut up, you trusting, stupid bitch." I choked on my anger.

I was suddenly conscious of how dark and treacherous the beach seemed under the dark, lashing rain, conscious of how late it was and of being wet and cold to the bone.

"Shiner! Let's go home!" I called out. But the distant animal streaking along the sand was not hearing me. Standing there, shrieking full tilt into the sniping wind, shouting for the dog, I found myself suddenly laughing. Can you believe laughing? Why, I don't know. Crazy, I guess. Laughing at the helplessness and hopelessness of a trapped heart, crying out, "I tried, so help me I did. I gave it my best try. For love, I mean. I gave it my best try for love."

I was glad the beach was deserted. I was glad the wind was cruel and bit into my cheeks. I was glad no one was there to hear and see my wildness, see me on my knees in the sand, keening in the wind, Shiner standing over me trying to gently lick my face. "Just as everything was going to be perfect, *you* had to screw things up." Who the *you* was I was accusing and yelling at wasn't at all clear to me. With the dog following, I trudged through the wet sand to the solitary truck pooled in the lamplight of the deserted parking lot and went home to a man who didn't love me anymore. I couldn't think of anything else to do.

A day came when the arrangements were finally complete. Jack and Yvonne, of all people, were buying the Haliburton house. That was a happy part. I had settled all the Harmony House guys into their new digs. I had split up the furniture between them and made sure they all had a set of dishes and linens, pots and pans, the usual everyday necessities.

I had gone through all the motions as if in a dream. Part of me couldn't believe Larry and I were over. Another part of me, wiser and older, knew he was gone. He was staying at Patsy's house until I left for Vancouver, and though he tried to help in every way, I kept him at an Ice Age distance. He wanted to stay friends with me, he said, but his betrayal of my trust and love was so complete that I couldn't even bear to be in the same room as him.

It is funny how physical heartache is. My chest ached like I had pneumonia. I did dumb things like call Patsy's phone number in the middle of the night to see if he answered. Called his old business line in Vancouver numerous times just to hear his voice on the recorded message. *Hi, this is Larry Sostad. Please leave a message and I'll get back to you shortly.*

Wistfully, I remembered years earlier picking up a nephew at the Vancouver Airport. He had decided to come out west from Toronto and I remembered how I had been feeling apprehensive as I drove to the airport. What would we talk about? I hadn't seen him since he was eight, and now he was twenty-five. But it was astounding—that old "blood is thicker than water" stuff. From the moment he climbed into my Toyota Corolla until he left town a year and a half later, we never could catch a breath talking about everything. Art, literature, our Welsh heritage, lovers, wine, holidays. It never stopped. We were made from the same material, the same fabric of life. We had a thousand common denominators. I wanted to call Patsy and tell her, "It's just because you're cousins that you feel so close, so familiar. Not because Larry is your long-lost love. Because he's mine. My love. My dear beloved love."

I couldn't eat and lost the weight that I had dreamed of losing for years. I couldn't sleep. I felt disoriented like I didn't know where I belonged anymore. I would throw Shiner in the truck at weird times of the night and race the old Ford to God knows where. Stopping at out-of-the-way little pubs. Walking on deserted beaches. Drinking too much. Trying to outrun and out-drink the pain.

The Stevie Nicks song "I've been afraid of changin' 'cause I built my life around you" kept ringing in my head. Lewis. Scott. Gordie Ryder and now Larry. I was definitely going to have to build a new life. My old one had been powdered.

You can fall in love and sometimes it is a casual fun-time thing. You can fall in love and it can be like an explosion of passion. Fantastic but short-lived. But I had really loved Larry. Loved him in spite of himself. Loved him for all the right reasons. And when he said I was his best friend, then he was certainly mine. He had been there for me with Guy and had been there to cheer me up and make me laugh on many a cloudy day. He wasn't being mean or malicious. He had just been struck by lightning... like I had been with him. And now when everybody was shocked and angry with Larry, I tried to explain lightning to them, and people who hadn't been hit with it didn't understand. They went by the rules of loyalty and common sense.

And then with mixed feelings I had to face that I was going to leave the Island. The Rock, as Davey called it. In almost two years of living in the South End, living on the wrong side of the tracks, I had learned a lot and more importantly unlearned some lessons, if you know what I mean. I had learned that heroes come in different packages, and we all have to reach out and help each other more. I learned that you have to give people a break. Don't be black and white or uppity moralistic. Life isn't like that. It's like the weather on the West Coast—a comfortable grey most of the time. I'd learned most people are trying damn hard to make it with the little they've been given. That life isn't easy. That sooner or later all of us face a curveball. That all most people want is to be loved for themselves. And that shouldn't be too much to ask for, should it?

58
Taxi!

I was coming off the ferry from Vancouver feeling pretty jubilant. I had gone for a final interview at a computer manufacturing company, and it looked like I had scored the job of Dispatch Manager. I almost didn't see him at first and then he yelled my name. Lo and behold, there outside the ferry terminal was Ron, standing beside a cab.

He drove me to Haliburton and we talked non-stop, desperately trying to cram in all the latest news. He was in the process of buying his own cab. He had worked double shifts to get the money together to put the down payment on it, and his brother was helping him with the financing. He had met a lady, and she was, in his words "a good woman." They were living together. Life was looking up. He looked fit and well. Not fat, but for the first time since I had met him he boasted some healthy weight on his bones. His eyes were bright and clear. He had been clean for over seven months.

His news was all so happy and positive that I almost didn't tell him Larry and I had broken up. That I was leaving the Island. But I did. He was stunned. Shocked. But being Ron, he was intuitive enough not to use clumsy words of sympathy. Just before we reached Haliburton Street, he said, "Let's go and have a last look at Big Sab."

We pulled up outside the big old house. The wind was stirring the willow tree into restless murmurs, and someone was sitting all bundled up on the white veranda engrossed in a newspaper, drinking coffee, smoking a cigarette.

"It seems like it was a thousand years ago in another time when I lived here," he said, his eyes sentimentally scanning the scene. "Like in another life. I was so desperate... so damn lonely back then."

We held hands for a moment, absorbed with our memories. "It was another life, Ron," I said, giving his hand a squeeze. "But ain't it just grand when sometimes you have the luck to find a new one?"

He drove me down the road and around the corner to the house on Haliburton, to the last-minute packing still left to do, and where Shiner and Guy were waiting for me. When I stepped out of the cab, we didn't say goodbye, but I stayed on the curb waving until the cab was out of sight.

59

Back on Track

Davey drove Guy and Shiner and me to the ferry, and he laughed and joked a lot along the way. "Well, Di, I can't believe you're really leaving the Rock. Going back to the Big Smoke. My bet is you'll be back here in a New York minute." He laughed self-consciously, having stolen the term from me and never quite being able to say it smoothly in front of me. Like he *knew* he'd stolen it.

He unloaded my two suitcases and carried them into the terminal to place them on the luggage rack where they'd be picked up by the shuttle bus because it is a long hike down to the ferry dock. He looked strained as the moment to say goodbye arrived. "You'll be back, so no goodbyes here. I'm going to miss you big time, girl." He gave me a hug, and suddenly I was holding onto him for dear life.

"There, there. It's all going to be okay. Larry is a big fucking jerk. We all think so. He didn't deserve you, Di. I used to love the Big Guy... I really loved him... but now..." He shook his head and looked down at his worn-out runners. Then he pulled away and eyed me seriously, his grey eyes kind and troubled. "It's time for you to turn the page, Di. There are other blokes out there, you know." He laughed to break the tension. "If I were single, I'd marry you myself."

Now it was my turn to laugh. "And if you *were* single, I'd have left Larry long ago." We were both relieved to laugh at our little jokes.

Then a horn beeped. A yellow cab had pulled up, and there was Ron bounding out of the driver's door. Ken jumped out the front passenger seat and Little Larry was struggling out of the back.

I stood there watching them, my hand to my mouth. "I don't believe this! What a lovely surprise, you guys!"

Ken grabbed me and hauled me into the air. "Had to do this one more time!"

"Put me down, Ken! I mean it." He always knocked the wind out of me.

"We were worried we were going to miss the ferry. Then Ron came along up there on the Island Highway and gave us a lift."

"I didn't know you were leaving today, Di." Ron looked upset. "Thanks for letting a guy know."

"It's all happened so fast," I explained. "Packing up, getting the boys at Harmony House settled. It's just been crazy."

Davey flashed Ron a warning look.

Ron got the message. "I can imagine," he said. "Well, Di, come here." He gave me a hug. Actually, he squeezed me tight. (He still needed to put on more weight.) I pulled away and could see by his eyes that he couldn't say anything more.

Little Larry hugged me awkwardly. "Write to me. You have my address."

I nodded numbly.

The loudspeaker announced last call to buy tickets just as Ron said, "Look over there... I think it's old Richard. See? Walking over there by the parking lot." Richard was loping at a fast pace, his Netherlander walk covering the ground at an amazing speed.

"Give me your money. I'll stand in line for your ticket," Davey said. "Give you a chance to say goodbye to Richard."

Richard had almost made it. He saw me from halfway across the parking lot and smiled and gave a half-wave. "Thought I had missed you," he said as he huffed and puffed his way up to me. "Good." He was out of breath.

"You almost did! I have to get going, like *now*, Richard. Thanks so much for coming to say goodbye." I leaned over and kissed his cheek. He smelled as usual like a wet dog.

"Ron, can you give Richard a ride back?"

I walked through the door and turned for one last wave. They were all standing there still like they were frozen in time. Richard smiled one last toothy grin, and Davey blew a kiss. I cried as I walked down the walkway. Guy was in front with Shiner trotting by his side.

The ferry left on time—a small miracle. Guy took Shiner to the pet level while I went up to the passenger level and leaned over the rail to watch the Nanaimo Harbour skyline recede. The ferry parking lot, the people and cars, the buildings becoming smaller and smaller. I couldn't see Ron's cab now or Davey's car. They were probably already driving back home along the Island Highway. The world I had grown to love over the past two years was disappearing in front of my eyes, slowly becoming lost in clouds and mist.

I was leaving so much behind. I gripped the rail and gave in to the tears. A sympathetic English gentleman, leaning further down the rail, commented, "Always rough saying goodbye to those you love. Your family?"

"Yes," I said.

www.ingramcontent.com/pod-product-compliance
Lightning Source LLC
Chambersburg PA
CBHW061511020726
47502CB00006B/2023